DAWN AMONG THE STARS

THE STARLESS SERIES BOOK ONE

SAMANTHA HEUWAGEN

Published in the United States of America First Printing: 2018

Print

ISBN-13: 978-1-943407-41-5

E-Book

ISBN-13: 978-1-943407-42-2

Trifecta Publishing House

1120 East 6th Street

Port Angeles, Washington

98362

T

TRIFECTA PUBLISHING HOUSE

Contact Information: Info@TrifectaPublishingHouse.com

Editor: Elizabeth Jewell

Cover Art by Designed by Diana

Formatted by Monica Corwin

For Hannah, my real-life embodiment of Leslie Knope and the one who started it all.

JUNE 19TH, 2012

My family sat in silence—equally mesmerized and horrified—as we watched our dawning reality play out on the screen. Cramped in my grandparents' small farmhouse, no one spoke or dared to breathe. Keeping me tethered to the ground were the voices of panicked newscasters while images showed hysterical crowds as they ran screaming through the streets.

Aliens are real.

Our sense of security diminished, blown away into oblivion.

Aliens are *real*.

[PART 1]

Kayin Aves
Detroit, Michigan
Earth

[1]
APRIL 27TH, 2013

My roommate, Maria, liked to sleep with the TV on during the night, claiming it calmed her nerves.

"The US Government is urging all able-bodied citizens to enlist in any branch of the armed forces," the newscaster said, blasting through my room, echoing against my bare walls. "All positions are currently being filled, from solider to medic—even childcare. Make sure to stop by your nearest Shelter for more information."

The noise pulled me away from my dreams, back into a reality I didn't want to be a part of. Rest hadn't come easy since the arrival of the Shielders; sleep was one of the first things to go in my new world.

A shiver ran down my spine as I stared at the ceiling.

"Just once I'd like to hear my damn alarm instead of that TV!" I grumbled, reaching toward the nightstand to switch off the alarm before it could pierce the morning stillness, aside from the TV. I rolled back over, covering my face with a blanket, hoping to block out the rays of light tugging at my eyelids. I may have blocked out the light, but I couldn't block out the sound.

A flush of rage propelled me out of bed toward the living room, where the TV blasted another news segment about extraterrestrials. I didn't listen—it was always the same thing: prepare, stay calm, and avoid them like the plague. I mashed the buttons, turning off the TV before heading into the bathroom for my shower.

After I turned on the water, more thoughts of Shielders—the aliens from another part of the galaxy—flooded my consciousness. The familiar wave of sickness, making me dizzy from losing control, pulsed through my veins. The third panic attack I'd had in two days threatened to overtake me. I grabbed at my favorite rose-scented soap as it slipped through my fingers, falling in the tub with a clang.

Ripping off my pajamas, I stepped into the stream of water. "Don't think, just breathe. Don't think about them—they can't hurt you!" I pleaded.

I focused on the cool water as it weaved itself down my body in zigzag forms. The scent of rose filled my nostrils, sending the signals of relaxation and sleep to my brain. Yet it wasn't enough to keep the wave of crippling grief from washing over me. I reached out to the stone wall—enough to keep myself upright—steadying my weak knees as memories of fear and confusion clouded my senses.

I slid down the wall, landing on the cold tile of the shower. "Those fucking Shielders," I gasped, holding myself as tightly as I could, allowing the stream of water to crash against my back. "Fuck!"

Bracing my back against the wall, I tried to think of anything but the staggering death toll—the losses on both sides—and the ragged sounds of civilians screaming for help during the chaos. The video footage of the clashes between Humans and Shielders burned inside my mind's eye.

"Breathe," I gasped, my shoulders aching. "Just let it pass. It's all right; you're safe. Everyone you know is safe. *Breathe*. They aren't here to hurt you. They aren't here to hurt *you*."

While I still battled the initial shock, it was getting better. My panic attacks grew less frequent, allowing me to go about my day without getting sucked into the news reports. Just like the rest of the world, my life was falling back into place, but the erupting moments of dread were still painful. When I let myself fall into the pit of despair, the razor sharp fear plunged into my soul.

"You have to snap out of it," I breathed, staying under the water for a few more minutes. "What would Layla say if she saw you like this?" My sister's spirited smile normally irritated me, but this time it brought me back from the brink. Most days I could control my fear, but days like today made me want to jump into a black hole and never climb out.

"You're being a baby," she'd told me once, shortly after Earth had calmed down. "They aren't *that* bad. They're going to help us—look at what they've done so far. Bringing new technology to the masses, and who knew all that cool stuff about Space?" A twisted smile had crawled across her face. "Besides, look how cute they are! They can't be that terrible if they come in such nicely wrapped packages."

I'd laughed then as I did now—she had that effect. The laughter melted my hesitation, pushing the panic into the pit of my stomach as the cool water washed the rest of it away.

"But we don't know why they're here," I'd added after the initial wave of relief subsided. "We can't possibly understand their motives—"

"You worry too much," she'd sassed, waving her hand.

"I'm not! Are we supposed to accept their presence and hope they're telling the truth about the Universe and everything?"

"Yes, Kay, we are—it's called faith. And you know what? I have faith they'll do what they've come here to do. Maybe they'll leave—or something—after. I don't know; I don't need to know. You, on the other hand, worry too much. *Cálmate.*"

We would never see eye to eye on Shielders. After the shocked shouts of *they're real* gave way to panic-fueled horror, society crumbled on itself—that killed my faith in humanity. Layla believed the pushback of the riots and political upheaval showed gumption.

Every night, Humans watched program after program explaining everything known—or imagined—about our new neighbors. New laws sprang up all around the world, allowing these newcomers to enter our society as valuable, contributing members. It became illegal for anyone to harm them.

That caused a whole new set of problems.

Some accepted this new reality without question. Others fought for their rights as natural-born Earth citizens to attack and kill our visitors, creating all-out war in some places.

After months of debate and turmoil, Humans settled and relaxed, accepting the fact they weren't the only ones in the Universe. Soon, the world fell in love with our new neighbors, welcoming them to Earth. When the media started worshipping them, the fever spread like wildfire. Even my friends and family couldn't get enough of them. *At least I don't have a poster on my wall, like Layla. Now that is just wrong.*

Tilting my head back to allow the water to pelt my face, I sighed. There was nothing I could do to stop their integration into our society. I unraveled my arms and legs to stand.

When I was done putting myself back together, I stepped out of the shower, slowly drying my body. I trudged across the bathroom and wiped off the foggy mirror. My light brown skin shone with left-over water droplets; my green eyes narrowed on the curves of my body, my vision going in and out of focus as I tried to regain control over my thoughts.

I combed my hair back, staring a hole into the wall as I thought about how much I regretted, having let go of the one good thing I had in this world before it all fell to hell. It was getting harder to avoid thinking about the past with a current reality I wasn't interested in.

Don't you dare, I told myself. *You both made the decision to break up. You knew what you were letting go. He's happy where he is now, and you have your work. It's important, especially now ...*

I put on some makeup, avoiding looking into my own eyes, the truth patiently waiting behind my irises. I've never been one for pageantry, but a little makeup helped me avoid looking sleep deprived.

I slicked my hair back into a thick bun, glancing at the clock.

"Damn, *damn*, damn! I'm going to be late!" I shrugged on a T-shirt, my favorite skinny jeans, and a slouchy black blazer.

"Hey," I heard Maria yell, "are you almost done? I need to pee."

"Yeah, give me a second!" I hollered, charging out the door, stopping just soon enough to avoid colliding with her petite body.

"Late again?" she asked, eyeing me. "For someone who never sleeps, you run late all the time. You look like shit, *amiga*."

"Thanks," I grumbled. "What are your plans today?"

"*Dale*, it's time you knew. I'm leaving for good—I mean it! I can't take any more of this, and I refuse to deal with one more Michigan winter. I'm sorry I couldn't give you more notice, but my *tio* managed to get me a plane ticket out of this horrible place. You know how hard it is to get airfare, so ... I'm going."

Since the news had broken about the Shielders, Maria had been a nervous wreck. She'd focused more on complaining than actually trying to make it home to Miami during her bouts of depression. She'd pace around the apartment, going in and out of Spanish, talking about how she was sick of the cold winters of Michigan, adding an afterthought about the truth. "Those aliens don't make it any better. Flying overhead every day, telling us what to do. They all around scare the shit out of me—*Dios me bendiga!*"

"Oh ... " I managed to mumble, stepping aside to look her in the eyes. Honestly, I was relieved she was leaving. Going home to Miami would do her frazzled nerves some good and no more TV! "I'm sorry to see you go, but I understand," I said awkwardly, the corners of my mouth trying to hide my immense pleasure as they bounced up and down. I set down my bag to reach for a hug. "Take care of yourself, *chica*. Tell your family I said hi."

"*Cuídate, amiga*," she whispered in my ear. "*Espero que nos veamos pronto.*"

She enjoyed speaking Spanish a lot more than I did, but I added, "*Te extrañaré. Cuídate también, chica. Nos vemos pronto.*"

And I really hoped we would see each other again one day—complaints and all.

The drive to my office was quick, even if that was out of the ordinary for Detroit traffic. I passed several protestors holding signs that read, "Give Our Planet Back" and "Human Rights Over Alien Rights," just like any other day. As much as I believed the same, I avoided their glares and shouts. I didn't have time to get sucked into the mania.

I thought about the long day ahead, making a mental note of all the things to do: PR statements about our stance on shelters and a list of items we needed for the office, on top of handling the ever-growing pile of complaints from US citizens about their rights. I sighed as the realization of today's press conference with the La'Mursians—the god-awful alien name in their own language—bombarded me. They were hosting it live to discuss plans about technology promised to ensure Earth's victory in an upcoming battle with some other alien race.

I pulled into the parking lot for Freedom of Voice, or FOV, an activist group in the States that fought to protect Human Rights. We'd been around since the 2008 election but had been much smaller back then, focusing on democracy and equality.

FOV leadership had promised me that I'd be sent to Washington to start lobbying for our cause, but those plans had to be put on hold. When I'd signed up with FOV, I wanted to work against the bans on abortion, but since the Shielder arrival, my focus had shifted to getting Human voices heard by Congress. Humanity deserved to be informed of intergalactic negotiations and have some say in what happened to our planet. Some of our DC staff had met with the Shielders, never getting much feedback. The incessant chatter about what they could and couldn't do for us drove me nuts.

The office looked small on the outside, but contained enough space for our various needs. The rest of the space was wide-open, filled with computers and desks. The bleak walls were a painful reminder we needed funds to support our organization, though the dreary atmosphere didn't stop us from doing our best to make lasting change in the world.

Entering the office, I found everyone huddled around the small TV in the conference room; the volume was on full blast with a few murmurs from the expanding crowd.

"The Shielders always do this," I overheard my manager say to another coworker as I walked to my desk. "They give their stupid little speeches about safety and how they're here to help—same thing week in and week out—nothing new. What could it be this time?"

"Kayin!" I heard from behind me. "Kayin Aves!"

Melissa Pebbles ran up, her thick curly hair bouncing behind her. She slowed her pace enough for me to see the worried look on her face. The rest of my coworkers hushed her as she thudded into me.

"What's up, *chica*? Why the long face?" I asked awkwardly, pushing her upright again.

"Sorry, but Prince Naluba is on TV right now," she squawked.

"Fuck," I grumbled, following her into the conference room.

"I know! The representatives have always said the High Chancellor would send his eldest son to Earth if and when there was news from the Galactic Royal Court."

"How do we know this is *the* son?"

She frowned and pulled me close, our arms locked together for support. "You can tell. He doesn't look exactly like the rest of them. He carries himself differently. They showed him among the rest, and they won't get too close to him—it's really weird."

"You sound interested. Is he *the one*, Melissa?" I teased, focusing back on the television.

"Oh, hush! They're cute and you know it—even if you won't admit it," she whispered as she nudged me in the ribs. "No, this one is, like ... I don't know—the hunk of all hunks! Just take a look at him." She pushed me toward an empty chair to stand on so I could get a better look.

I stopped dead in my tracks. Melissa was right. I couldn't look away. I couldn't pay attention to what he was saying; I could only look at his big, gorgeous lavender eyes.

He was an albino Hercules with flowing white hair, all muscle and the tallest of the Shielders on screen. A face with chiseled cheeks and a strong jawline, yet his eyes were kind, almost glowing. The length of his hair, falling just below his chest, said he was in his mid-thirties. Shielders with a high military rank had tribal markings—almost like tattoos— all over their bodies. While intimidating, they suited the Shielder appearance. His body was littered with the markings of his military rank, leaving almost no blank space. For a Shielder with power and status, he was young.

Turning away from the TV, my stomach let go of the knots it had been holding.

The last time I felt such a powerful connection to another person was when I'd first laid eyes on Luke Skywalker—I'd been eight years old. He's not real, so it was more of a connection to Mark Hamill, but still. I'd fallen hard for that future Jedi. I'd never experienced that reaction to someone in real life, not even my ex.

I shook off the longing, disgusted by my reaction. It was a fantasy, nothing more.

"So, what's he talking about?" I asked, still trying to shake off the feeling. "Hello?" I called out, looking to my coworkers, who ignored me.

I turned back to the TV, looking at the screen, not the Shielder's face.

"I have been sent by my father to command my troops in battle with the Temorshians, foes we have faced before," Prince Naluba said, looking over the crowd. "Our reports indicate they will be here within the week. Their ultimate goal is not known, but we believe they want the resources of Earth. Rest assured, we have come to Earth, vowing to stop at nothing to ensure your safety before and after the looming war. We can and will stop them—with your help ... " Everyone gasped. There had been whispers, just wild theories, that other aliens were headed toward Earth. No one took them seriously.

With albino Hercules looking stern, we had to take it seriously. Earth was in trouble.

Coworkers I'd known for years packed up their various belongings in silence. I watched them hurry out of the room with tear-stained cheeks. Their departure left Melissa and me in the empty conference room with Derrick, the office prick.

"So, you ladies want to have a threesome real quick before we die?" he asked.

Melissa and I glared at him in response.

"Okay, okay! I just thought I'd put it out there. So ... what do we do now? Call someone in Washington?"

"That seems like a perfectly good idea," I told him, keeping my distance.

"Do you think Susan Michaels would answer her cell?" Melissa asked, turning down the volume on the TV. The screen went back to Anderson Cooper, looking surprised with no words.

"I don't see why not," I answered. "This is big. I bet she'd want us to start working on a statement."

Don't fall apart; don't let them see you're scared. They need you— focus! I forced my stomach to settle. Panic had become a constant hum in the background of my life. It was easier to ignore it when there were things as big as this that needed my attention.

Melissa gaped at me. "How can you be so chill about this? In a matter of days we could all be dead! I don't want to work! I want to spend time with my family and boyfriend!" Her eyes glistened with tears.

"Melly, dear, just go. No one will blame you. Derrick and I can handle whatever it is the higher-ups would want us to do." I reached out to her, but she pulled away. "I can stay to finish alone."

"*No.* Just call her—she'll have an idea of what's going on. I'm going to live through this, Kayin. I'm going to survive this—with all of my family, too!" she stated with such fierce determination I didn't question her.

"I just tried—the line's busy," Derrick interrupted, filling the awkwardness growing between us. "What do you think that means?"

"She's probably just doing her job," I replied. "Don't make things worse—she's a busy woman." I sat down on a nearby chair, my mind busy weighing our options.

My cell phone rang: it was my mother. I let out a small sigh of relief as I answered the phone.

"*Donde estas*? Are you okay? Did you hear what that prince said? When are you coming home?" Her voice was quiet, but the panic was obvious.

My family lived on the other side of Michigan in a small town a few hours away. Things were moving so quickly I hadn't thought that far ahead.

"Mom, I'm fine, and yes, I heard," I reassured her, my mind spinning in circles. "I can't say if I can make it home or not." I wanted to stay at work and help with whatever I could, but I also had a deep desire to go home. "I'm going to try my hardest to make it back. I have time. We should have a day or two at least. So, if I don't leave now, I can leave tomorrow."

"Traffic will be a mess!" she screamed into the phone. "You can't possibly wait until the last minute! *Necesitas tu familia, mija!*"

"*Mira, Mamá*, this is what you have to do: you need to make sure that you have enough provisions for the rest of the family ... " I knew she'd take responsibility for my grandparents on top of caring for my sister, Layla, and our father. If anyone could live through this, she could. I took comfort in that. My grandparents had invested in a safe house big enough for my entire family before all this mess, too, which was prudent.

"Now, *please, Mamá*, call the rest of the family and get them together. Tell everyone what I told you, and please stay calm. Make sure Papá gets enough weapons and ammo—I know he was against it for so long, but now is not the time to have such values!"

"I will, but I'm worried for you," she said. "I know these Shielders will protect us ... They have to ... "

"You're putting a lot of faith in them. Who knows if we are even fighting the right *things?*" I countered.

Silence lingered on the line.

Finally she said, "We can only hope we are fighting the right beings, Kayin. Have faith and good things will happen. *Te quiero, amorcita.*"

"*Te amo, también Mamá.* I'll see you soon, I promise."

[2]

"I've emailed some documents if you want to look those over and pass them out—honestly, though, go home. There's no need for you to stick around that miserable place," Susan Michaels told us once she finally called back. "Who's even left?"

"Just me and Melissa. Everyone else just vanished after that prince spoke. Derrick was here, but he left a few minutes ago," I told her. "Probably to find someone else to have sex with," I added under my breath.

"Please, Ms. Michaels," Melissa interrupted, "is there anything I can do to help my family?"

The silence on the speakerphone filled the room as my curiosity grew.

Susan let out a long sigh. "Look, there's a way to get off this planet—God, if it comes to *that.*"

Melissa and I locked eyes, questioning if we'd just heard her correctly.

Leave Earth?

My mind blurred. "It would be impossible—outrageous—to leave!"

"Selucia is millions of light years away!" squeaked Melissa.

"Their planet is similar to ours, at least in the sense that we can breathe the air," Susan added. "That's what we think, anyway. They can breathe our air, and we supposedly can breathe what they call *Meluva*. It can be done, it's just not what any of us want."

"What are you talking about?" I caught Melissa's gaze: those beautiful eyes were begging me to make sense of all this for her.

"Oh, God. Okay, if it *really* does get bad—I mean, we don't even know what'll happen, if anything happens at all." Susan inhaled and exhaled loudly. "Those stupid Shield-fuckers won't explain anything. It's like they want to keep us unaware! I just can't—"

"Whoa! Wait! You aren't making any sense. You're going to have to spell everything out—every detail." I paused, trying to catch my breath through all of the crazy. "What aren't they telling the general public?"

We could hear Susan's strained breathing through the phone. She could easily hang up now and be done with our whole conversation.

"Please," Melissa begged, "I think we've proven ourselves over the years. Tell us what you know to help our families."

"It's not personal, it's just … just so shocking." Susan cleared her throat. "That meeting we recently had, the one that showed up on everyone's calendar as a breakfast meeting before management deleted it? Well, it wasn't about getting our say in what happens to our planet, like we'd been told," she explained. "It was about how to live through what is about to happen."

Melissa and I avoided each other's line of vision as sweat formed on my brow.

"Those aliens came because they felt we'd be able to do the most good with the knowledge we were about to be given," she continued. "For the past fifty years, the Shielders have been in contact with this planet. You know Area 51? Well, that's where they would meet. To discuss what? I don't really know—*things*.

"Over time—I'm talking decades—some branch of the CIA learned our galaxy is the smallest in a chain of about 500,000.

Shielders watch over planets that need protection, aid those in need, and are amazing charity workers. Saints, really ... "

"They've been here for fifty years?" Melissa whispered. "We didn't know ... "

"This is useless information that's not going to save my life," I snapped. "How is this relevant?"

Susan's breathing elevated like she was running a marathon. "I'm trying, Kay, I really am. This stuff is relevant, just calm down."

"I can't calm down, Susan. Our lives are at stake! If you know anything that's useful, you better tell us and stop wasting our time!"

The walls of my heart pressed against my ribcage. They fought each other for space as I sucked in my breath, trying to inhale. Beads of sweat trickled down my neck. I fought to hide my nerves, staring daggers into the phone. I was holding on as the panic that had plagued me since they'd arrived took over my senses.

"Kayin, this isn't helping," Melissa mumbled, trying to reach for me.

I pulled away. "Melly, this shit is stuff we know—"

"Please," she pleaded, "pushing her away won't make her tell us any faster. Just take a breath."

"Anyway," Susan huffed, "for the past fifty years, everyone got along just fine. The Shielders were letting the rest of space know about Earth, taking a few Humans with them to teach the rest of the galaxy about us. It was a time of education and peace.

"Until recently, maybe five or ten years ago, the Galactic Royal Court—a group similar to our United Nations—started experiencing problems with the Temorshians. As Prince Naluba said, this group of aliens is the most territorial and malicious of all the kinds out there." Another cold shiver ran up my spine as Susan continued, "I'm guessing it's because they lost their planet not too long ago and are tired of being nomads."

She stopped to take a breath as we listened to her close her door, shutting out the background noise I hadn't realized was so loud.

When she returned to the call, her voice became more serious and quieter. "So, for the past handful of years, our planet and the Shielders have been coming together to work out a plan of action. The Shielders are capable of protecting us with their technology but the Temorshians have gotten other groups to aid them in their quest for domination. They want to control our planet because our resources are extremely valuable. What they'll do with us is beyond me. What's clear is they want our resources."

We heard more movement from her end before she continued in a hushed voice, "Sorry, I'm not really allowed to explain any of this. Shame, isn't it? This is what we were fighting against and trying to avoid, and now I'm on their team, keeping secrets from my friends ... "

Words came tumbling out of her mouth as she tried to fit in the last few bits of information. "The Shielders are a hundred times more advanced than we are, and if they can't stop the Temorshians, they'll ship whoever they can back to their planet until we can regroup. In that case, they hope the Royal Court would give us, and anyone else willing to help, permission to blast the Temorshians to hell."

Fear pushed its way to the surface as the news settled within me. I tried to choke it back, and my head flooded with questions. The whole plan sounded flawed, and the information we'd been given seemed misleading. I'd been afraid something like this would happen, and now it was too late to do anything about it.

"Why was this Galactic Royal Court not helping us to begin with?" I asked bitterly.

"I know, it seems like the most logical thing to do, but they can't. They have laws just like we do, and because Earth isn't part of those laws, the Shielders can't help until the Temorshians have attacked."

I glanced up to find my friend pale faced and green around the eyes. It made my stomach sink further as a wave of dread washed over my body; the cool sickness covering my insides threatened to spill out.

Melissa took a deep breath and asked, "Who gets to go with them? Is there a system in place?"

"Yes, there's a system," Susan whispered. "It's stupid, in my opinion. All the people who've been working with the Shielders, along with their families, leave Earth right off the bat. I think they're getting shipped out tomorrow ... All the leaders of the world will be gone by 6 p.m. tomorrow evening. Whoever they leave in charge will then determine who gets to go when the time comes. I believe I heard they'll go in a few days, as well as their families and whoever else is hanging around when it happens." Susan hesitated but pushed through her reluctance. "After the last ship leaves ... the rest ... *the rest* will have to fend for themselves."

The silence was deafening.

The room began to spin as I used the conference table to steady myself, no longer able to control my panic. The uncertainty of my future weighed heavily on my shoulders.

"You've got to be kidding me!" I exploded in a high-pitched squeal I barely recognized. "That's how our species will survive? Whoever helped those ... *those* ... assholes?" Hives began to dot my neck and chest. "Where do we have to be to get picked up? Who do I have to talk to? What Shielder ass do I have to kick?"

"Or kiss," Melissa whispered, staring off into space. A few tears escaped her eyes, rolling down her cheeks.

"Kayin, please calm down. I know it's hard, I'm so sorry you had to hear this from me," Susan paused to let out a long sigh. "They'll be going to all the big cities: New York, LA, Chicago, Houston, Atlanta, DC, Miami, and Philadelphia, I believe. Those are the ones I know about in the US. I'm sure any place with a highly concentrated population would be an immediate target."

"You're abandoning us!" I shrieked. "The whole fucking government is abandoning us just to try to save themselves! *Puta Madre!*"

Staying in that office was a waste of time—work be damned!

"Thank you, Susan, for letting us know everything," I said as calmly as I could, swallowing the bitter panic, pushing it deeper inside. "Good luck to you and yours."

"Yes, thank you, Susan," Melissa added. "We'll use what you've told us. Thank you, God bless."

Susan hung up the phone after a few seconds of lingering silence, the ties of friendship broken between the three of us.

After a few moments, Melissa walked over to where I sat and embraced me like it was the last time. I began to tear up, hugging her back just as tightly. We clung to each other, crying and praying something would change and we would live through the horrors that awaited all of us.

Making it back to my apartment in one piece proved to be quite a challenge. Traffic had exploded into a chaotic mess. It took me three hours to drive what normally took only fifteen minutes. As I drove, all the radio stations talked about where to get the best weapons, who was passing out the most food—not to mention the quickest way out of Detroit. But every lane, highway, and side road had cars lined up for miles. All roads to the nearest army shelter were blocked, and many people were walking on foot to get to safety. It couldn't be out of the question to think they'd have a ship headed to Detroit. It was a major city, after all, but no one mentioned it.

After hours of confusion and pushing away my panic, I entered my apartment. Stopping to survey my space, I realized I'd no idea what to do. I was already exhausted. My brain felt heavy, and my body couldn't take the steps it needed to get home to my family.

With a sigh, I did the only thing I could think of: pack. I tried packing meaningful things into a bag, but I just couldn't make myself do it after several sad attempts. Looking through kitchen cupboards for food upset my stomach—it looked disgusting. Clothes didn't pan out either. I didn't know what to take at a time like this. One of the pamphlets said, "Take what you need." That was no help; it's not like I'd ever been in a situation where humanity might be destroyed. Would you need more underwear than socks or more undershirts than pants? In the movies I'd seen and the books I'd read, most of the characters wore only the clothes on their backs.

I wanted to call my mother but I knew that'd mean more worry for her, and I didn't want to accidentally reveal what I'd just learned. Though it was complicated, I decided that the safest person to call was my ex-boyfriend—who was still my best friend. Even if we weren't together anymore, he was the first person I went to when things became too difficult.

"Hey, you, I'm glad you called." His voice was like honey. Henry had a way of making everything sound like it was going to work out. He'd never worried about anything, but that was before the press conference with the Shielders. His shaky voice gave away how scared he was.

Henry Rickner was the great love of my life and one of the few people I could trust. "I kept trying to call but with the cell phone signals jammed I couldn't get through. Are you all right? Where are you?" he asked.

Though he was tall, dark, and handsome, he had a quiet strength about him hidden deep inside. It wasn't how he looked that drew me to him, but his respect for others and how he radiated intelligence and joy.

"Hi, Henry, I'm fine—still in Detroit. Worried about you, too. Have you planned on coming back or ... " I knew he'd never be able to get a flight back to Michigan. Last I'd heard all air travel was suspended until further notice.

"You know I can't, darling," he said, his voice hitching. "I'm so sorry, but I'll talk with you as long as I can. I miss you terribly. How are you holding up? Are you going to *try* to make it back to your parents' house?"

"I miss you so much," I stammered as a few tears ran down my cheeks. I sat on the couch, curling my legs under me. "I'm going to leave tomorrow, I think, and try to get there. I know things will be a mess, but I'd rather be with my family than here."

Suddenly, remembering my reason for calling, I blurted, "I need to tell you something very important. Please, don't tell anyone, but ... " I told him everything Susan had said. Henry listened with interest, mumbling the occasional unintelligible sound.

As though he couldn't keep his thoughts to himself any longer, he blurted out, "I don't believe this ... are you *sure?* There has to be a way to get on those ships!" he yelled. "It's our responsibility to tell people and to get the word out—"

I stopped him, "We can't. You think there's panic now? Just tell them they're—*we're*—all about to be enslaved or I think, for the most part, *killed*. I doubt many people are going to live through this ... " I pushed my fear aside, my throat closing, tightening around the few words I managed to get out.

We sat in silence for a moment, unsure where our conversation should go.

"I know they gave us a week at the most until the Temorshians attacked, but if the leaders were leaving so soon, do we really have that much time?" I asked. "I thought the Shielders could defeat these jerks, but it's not looking good. If they could, they wouldn't be taking Humans back with them. They wouldn't be running away."

"I have to go, Kay," Henry said unexpectedly, breaking my train of thought. "There's got to be something I can do to help or at least save some people—anything is better than nothing." Henry paused. "I'm going to fight."

"You can't!" I screamed into the phone. "You'll be killed or enslaved or ... or ... I don't know! Why can't you just hide or try to get on one of the ships—you're close to DC, Philly, and New York even. You could make it!" Tears flowed freely as my body began to shake. I was supposed to protect him, not let him march to his death.

"You know that chance is slim to none, Kay. I need to know I helped protect you in some small way." I could hear the tremor in his voice; he was crying too. "I need to be at peace with the fact that I'm not physically with you. I can only do that by helping our army defeat those fuckers. Go to your grandparents' house and stay there—maybe we can meet up after ... "

"No! Don't protect me. Just stay safe," I begged him. "That'll make me feel better and help me out more than you trying to get yourself killed. I don't want you to do this—you don't *need* to do this!"

Henry was many things, stubborn being one of them.

"If you want to do anything, come home. *Come to me,*" I pleaded. "I need you here!"

"Does your family have a safe place to go?"

"You know I told you about the safe house weeks ago. They're prepared. We have space for you—they'd love to have you!"

"You need to make it there, Kayin," he whispered. "You need to stay safe and stay out of the way."

There was a long silence before he spoke again. "Babe, I love you more than life itself. You're the love of my life. I need you to live through this—do whatever you can to make that happen. Take care of your family. I love you so, so much, and I promise we'll find a way to be together one day. I love you."

And just like that, he hung up.

I couldn't move. I couldn't breathe. I gasped for air but nothing met my lungs. The room began to spin, pulling my limbs down to the floor with a clash, my mind thick with worry. I started crying again, tears falling hard on the floor. My heart burst into a million pieces.

Little by little, everything I'd been pushing away for so long came snapping back. In my despair, I began to list everyone and everything I'd ever cared about. The friends I'd never see again, the music I loved so much, the books and movies filled with stories that got me through hard times; the wind brushing against my cheek, the grass between my toes, the ocean splashing against my legs, the smell of fallen leaves. Simply looking up at the sky to watch the shades of blue change with the sun seemed like a distant memory.

My tears refused to stop. I let my grief wash over me and fill every part that was once filled with hope. The hope I'd carried with me my whole life flickered out. Like a cloud of smoke, I felt it leave my body.

Everything was gone and it was never coming back.

[3]

The morning light flicked through the blinds as the leaves outside danced in the breeze. Pushing myself up from the spot I'd occupied for the last twelve hours, I stopped myself from reaching out to Henry. Instead, thinking of my family, I grabbed my cell and dialed my mother's number.

The call went straight to voicemail.

She probably forgot her charger during all the chaos, I thought as dread tickled the back of my throat, my breathing becoming strained.

I tried my father. The line crackled with static but eventually connected to his voicemail as well. *My sister, Layla, would have her phone charged like any good millennial.* I clicked her profile photo, waiting for the familiar hum of the phone, but still nothing.

The tickle turned into a fiery blaze in my throat, scratching my tonsils, my heart cracking under the pressure. My breath hitched, causing me to gasp, only to feel the same choking sensation I'd become accustomed to dealing with.

Not now, focus! They're fine. We just don't have service. I paced my breathing—a sad attempt to relax my racing heart—but my instincts screamed.

After rummaging around the living room, frantically trying to find the damn remote, I spotted it on the side table, hidden under an outdated *Vogue* México. I pressed the power button to find my TV devoid of cable service. I raced around the apartment, trying anything needing power: my computer, iPad, and even my radio—worked but didn't have Internet or service.

I flipped my lights on and off. *Mierda!*

I sat on the couch and picked up my useless phone. Farewell text messages from friends greeted me. *You're my best friend and we've been through worse—See you on the flip side* from Melissa, along with missed calls from my parents. It stopped at 8 p.m. last night.

A lot can happen in twelve hours, I thought bitterly. *How could I be so stupid?*

A large gust of wind smacked a branch into the window. I jumped. I padded toward the sound, parting the blinds at a snail's pace. Everything looked fine except the pond outside my apartment, usually teeming with wildlife, was empty.

I'd watched enough horror and science fiction movies to know that you never go anywhere alone, and you always follow the animals. Now there weren't any animals to follow.

My heart raced. I tasted the horror bubbling inside me, yet I didn't have time to worry. I threw underwear and clothing into a backpack, and grabbed enough food to last me until I reached my parents.

I mentally kicked myself as I realized I needed protection. I didn't have any weapons—I didn't believe in owning pepper spray or guns. I raced around my apartment searching for something—*anything*—that'd give me the illusion of safety. The dull kitchen knives were of no use. I searched my room frantically until I found my old softball bat.

Having something would be better than nothing, right? I thought, picking it up to examine it. *Yeah, it'll do.*

I grabbed all my identification documents—driver's license, birth certificate, and passport—and counted the cash I'd stashed away for emergencies. I didn't know what I'd need to survive after it was all said and done, but it was too late to second guess. I had to leave.

A pang of nostalgia flowed through me as I took a final look at my apartment. The family portrait hanging in the entryway had slipped yet again in the night. My ritual before leaving always consisted of making sure it was centered. Sighing, I locked the door behind me, leaving the family portrait askew, with one final creak from the old wooden floor.

The air stilled as I peered out of the large window in the open hallway overlooking the parking lot. The familiar dread was tickling the back of my throat once more. I swallowed it, focusing on my plan instead.

I stood at the top of the stairs, immobilized by the panic seeping into my mind. I willed my feet to move. My left foot crept forward, landing softly on the first step. The right followed. Crouching down in fear that I'd be seen, I made my way down the staircase.

I stuck my head up enough to peer out the window, clutching my bat; I began to reach for the door handle. Sweat trickled down the side of my face, frozen by the realization that I wasn't prepared for any of this.

The memory of the prince rushed to the forefront of my mind. If he was out there fighting for me, I sure as hell could fight to go home. My family was worth more.

I took a small step forward to get a better look of the blue sky above. I didn't see anything except fluffy, white clouds. I smiled in spite of myself, opening the door as a rush of cool air hit my face. The smile vanished.

I ran to my car—the only one left in the lot—and struggled with my keys to unlock the damn thing. Throwing my stuff into the back seat, I threw myself in after, hastily locking the doors. Sparing a moment, I checked to make sure I had everything.

I started the car and pulled out of the complex. The roads were empty—no soul in sight, all the businesses seemingly closed and deserted. There were no policemen or rescue workers—a staple on every corner for the last few months—in their usual spots.

I reached Highway 75 in record time, stopping before pulling onto the interstate. A few cars were parked on the side of the road, but still no one. I hit the gas and sped in the direction of home.

Driving the fastest I'd ever driven, I passed mile after deserted mile. The roads were clear except for the occasional abandoned car on the side of the road. The usually bustling buildings looked like ghost towns. Some had boards bolted to glass windows and doors, while others hadn't faired so well. Shattered glass sparkled, catching the rays of light from the morning sun like diamonds. Forgotten trash twirled in the wind as I passed. Once free of the urban areas, the scene changed to peaceful farms and tree lines in perfectly straight formations, their leaves swaying in the breeze.

The drive normally took me three hours, with Lansing being the halfway point. At this speed, I made it to Lansing within forty-five minutes. The muscles in my neck relaxed as I pictured my grandparents' farmhouse. I loosened my grip on the wheel, watching as color crept back into my fingertips.

I'd made it outside of Portland in just over an hour when a loud bang filled my ears.

Shocked, I swerved, barely missing the parked car to my right. I slammed on my brakes, their screeches piercing the air. Trying to regain control of the car, I landed in the ditch.

My anxiety made its mighty comeback as the dust and debris settled.

Shit, I thought as a loud pop rang out even louder overhead.

I ducked out of instinct, the sound vibrating through my bones. It felt closer than before; the echo was ringing in my chest.

I sat up straight to see where the noise originated. I was

surrounded by wide-open farmland for miles, and nothing seemed out of place.

The hairs on my arm rose as the sick feeling of dread took hold.

Tilting my head slightly to rest on the cold glass of my driver's side window, I lifted my eyes to the sky. Filled with bright lights and smoke, it was no longer the beautiful blue Michigan sky painted with white fluffy clouds, but a horrible mixture of darkness and explosions.

The Shielders had said the fighting wouldn't take place on Earth if they could help it, but there was darkness in Earth's atmosphere, making me think they'd obviously failed. Looking closer, I realized it wasn't a black hole at all, but a huge, ebony spaceship. Neon beams shot out from the ship, colliding with different targets. The giant black hole in the sky was created to destroy—exactly what the Temorshians wanted.

Dozens of tiny blue ships dotted the horizon. I could barely see the other little ships—the Shielders, I supposed—flying around the big ebony ship. Their ships left me with little confidence they could beat the monstrosity in the sky.

Little balls of burning smoke made their way up toward the action. I'd watched enough History Channel specials to realize they were nuclear warheads being sent to help. How much good they would do, I didn't know, but I wasn't going to stay around to find out. I put the car back into drive and took off again like a bat out of hell.

Give 'em hell, motherfuckers!

Far off, over the horizon, bits and pieces of alien ships fell to the ground. I knew that things would get worse before they'd get better. This was a fight for our planet—this was war, but my heart sank as the alien threat crept closer.

I pushed the gas pedal down harder and focused on my driving, ignoring the shock threatening to consume my whole body as it waited at the back of my throat.

Another loud, whistling noise enveloped my ears.

Forced back to reality, I immediately slammed on the brakes. A huge, mangled piece of ship—a crushed wing—sped toward me.

Trying to gauge where it would fall, I put the car in park and scrambled out. My eyes never left the burned metal as I forced my body into motion—the ship falling closer and closer.

The roaring of the ship descended toward me, making me cover my ears. I struggled to move away from my car fast enough to avoid the inevitable impact. Parts of the ship began to litter the ground—one piece heading in my direction.

I ran to the other side of the road, rolling into the median as the debris landed on my car with a bang. Fire and scrap metal shot everywhere.

I raised my head slightly, still covering the vulnerable parts of my neck as I watched in horror. The rest of the ship landed with a crash in a deserted field about a mile away. It exploded upon impact, turning into a pile of ash and twisted metal. Its final resting place was a giant hole.

I stayed low, frozen in place. My body started to go into shock, but I fought against the instinct and pushed myself to stay present, although my body was screaming to run away.

I shivered against the dampness of the grass, but pushed myself onto my hands and knees. Barely able to move my legs, I forced them to do what I wanted. I stood up and brushed myself off, looking around to make sure nothing was coming toward me.

Burning flames caught my eye. My car was totaled, a smoldering pile of metal now. My heart skipped a beat as I tried not to be sick.

My mind quickly turned to the ship.

What remained of the ship burned brightly. I could feel the heat coming off of it, the smoke intensifying. The markings on the side were intact. Some of it was recognizable—definitely a Shielder ship!

I let out a sigh of relief, erasing the taste of bile from my mouth. *Gracias a Dios!*

Unsure of what I'd find in the wreckage, I went against my better judgment, deciding to walk toward the burning pile of junk.

It couldn't hurt to check for survivors—they might need my help, I reasoned, inching toward the burning ship.

I quickened my pace into a run to where the damage was most prominent. The remains of one burning body caught my eye. My stomach turned in on itself as I fought the urge to puke, waiting for my breathing to slow and the feeling of vertigo to pass before I continued onward. I coughed, trying to release the taste of burning flesh, my lungs already full of the smell.

I found another twisted body still breathing, but I was too late to help. The creature's back had folded in on itself, its limbs flattened to the ground; black blood poured from a wide cut along its stomach. It took its last breath as I knelt down beside it.

Silent tears fell down my cheeks, the grotesque scene flooding my vision. I pushed myself to keep looking for more survivors. Further away, I saw another one. The hump of the body appeared to be in better shape than the others.

I ran over to see if it was still alive.

The lump of limbs and bloodied fabric distorted my view. It was dressed differently, yet somehow I could manage to make out the rise and fall of its chest. Its tangled hair was matted into the burn on its cheek. Although it was bleeding heavily from its left shoulder, with more burns on the side of its body, the Shielder's injuries didn't appear life-threatening.

I looked around for something to stop the bleeding. I needed to find the source of the blood, but it was hard to see without moving the Shielder. I was beginning to lose confidence in myself as a makeshift nurse. Reaching out slowly to the nearest limb, I placed my hand on the body. I allowed my other hand to hover over the mess, trying to find a spot where I could move the creature without further harm.

Running out of time, I pushed with all the strength I could muster to attempt to turn it on its side. The Shielder growled, making my heart stop. I jumped backward, lifting my hands away, raising them high enough to show I meant no harm.

"I'm so sorry," I told it, hoping it spoke English. "I know you're hurt, but I need to try to get you somewhere safe. This really isn't a good place to stop. Let me help you—we've got to get out of here!"

I tried again. It seemed to help me this time. When I finally got it on its back, it relaxed a little more.

"My name is Kayin Aves. I'm a friend. I'm going to try to help you—"

A low humming sound cut off my train of thought.

Two ships were coming toward us, not too far off the horizon. They were small and long, flying fast and low. The cockpits seemed to be the only recognizable things on them. The rest of the bodies were just thin wings. They were buzzing around the various tree lines, searching for something.

The Shielder shot up like a rocket, knocking me over in its wake. It raced over to the wreckage and pulled out guns. It turned toward me, staring with dark purple eyes. It looked back to the ships, disregarding its pain and my presence.

One ship turned the other way, while the other flew straight toward us.

Without missing a beat, the Shielder yelled out in slurred English, "Get on the other side of the ship and hide!"

It fired one of the guns as I ran to my designated place. Surprised by the noise, I tripped and fell, landing on my right side. I scrambled to get up but stopped, paralyzed by the sensory overload. The humming of the Temorshian ship grew louder as it picked up speed.

I witnessed the Shielder take down the ship in three shots.

"Watch out!" I yelled. "The other one is coming back!" I pointed to the second ship on the Shielder's right.

It turned to look at me, wordlessly moving its mouth. The second ship came around too quickly, firing upon the wreckage. The leftover metal exploded. A searing pain clouded my vision. My world went dark.

[4]

"Red or white roses, *hija?*" My mother's voice called in the distance. "They'd look beautiful in the garden."

"What are you talking about? We've never owned a garden." I reached for her through the fog of my mind, screaming, "Mom, the world is ending! Stop this! We have to get out of here!" She ignored my pleas, her voice drifting deeper into the blackness.

As suddenly as the scene began, a soothing voice penetrated the darkness in a language I couldn't understand. A wave of tranquility washed over me. I tried to call out, but my tongue was thick, unable to formulate words. A cold hand caressed my cheek, placing a damp cloth over my eyes.

My head pounded and my left arm ached; no matter how hard I tried, I couldn't move. It felt better to lose myself in the darkness, exhausted by the effort to open my eyes and rejoin the world, even if that darkness threatened to never relinquish its hold over me.

Intuitively, I knew I was dreaming—*not dead*—because I could feel sensations with the various passes of a hand, soft voices in the distance, and lights that threatened to tear open my eyes. My consciousness still inhabited the curvy frame I called home.

Though I knew I was alive, the terrors of the day's events pinched and prodded their way through my subconscious nevertheless. The darkness enclosed tight around my body as the sensation of floating relaxed my muscles; my limbs were weightless, my body comfortable, but my mind was restless no matter how hard I fought to stay present.

Falling into one dream right after the other was like binge-watching your favorite TV show, only none of the episodes made sense as they blurred together. When the subjects switched abruptly, it became hard to remember what had come before.

The darkness accompanied me as something familiar and safe. It was broken by a stiff pinch on my right side, accompanied by strange piercing noises and bright lights that floated above me. Through heavy lids, my blurred vision wouldn't focus enough to make out the moving shapes around me. The strain made me unsteady, my thoughts fighting for attention, pulling me back into obscurity.

A loud, pained scream reached my ears. I could feel the presence of another next to me as the screaming continued, filled with heart-break that penetrated my soul. I wanted to reach out to the noise to make it stop crying, but I couldn't will myself out of my deep sleep. My heavy limbs stayed where they were, feeling the sad energy around me all at once.

Something hit the right side of my arm, and someone was yelling something I couldn't understand. Voices slurred and shouted around me. The pain in my brow throbbed as I tried to take it all in through my limited senses.

In the midst of the shouting, I fell back into the darkness. Safely hidden away from reality, my new world was vibrant. The air sizzled with a sweet energy that made me feel drunk with happiness—the eruption of warmth from the pit of my stomach emanated to the tips of my fingers.

Turning away from the bright colors swirling around me, I caught a glimpse of familiar faces. Now that I was finally reunited with my family, the troubles of the world melted away. I saw my grandparents' farmhouse off in the distance, though the entire large field out front had been turned into an enormous dance floor.

Aliens weren't real after all, I thought, smiling. *The Shielders never came to Earth! Gracias a Dios!*

I found myself pulled closer to the dance floor. My sister, Layla, was laughing and trying to tell me something over the joyfulness of the ever-growing crowd, but her voice floated away. After months of stress, I was able to finally relax and be with the people who loved me most in the world.

No one was worried about the end of the world or the Temorshians. It seemed the whole world was relieved—it'd all been a mistake. We returned to our ignorant state of mind before it'd been ripped away. People sang, laughed, and danced, filling the farm with overwhelming joy. It ebbed and flowed within me.

I found myself dancing until my feet were sore. Out of breath, I watched as my sister Layla fell down laughing with a handsome stranger who quickly lifted her back up. Shaking my head and leaving her to her folly, I ran into Melissa and her boyfriend, Joel.

"We're getting married!" Melissa yelled over the noise from the festivities. "We're going to do it today! Why wait?" She squeezed Joel's hand, turning her attention away from me and back to him. She radiated bliss with a wide toothy grin, elation filling her eyes.

I smiled at the two, who looked more madly in love than I'd ever seen them, their fingers interlocked as they stared into each other's eyes. For once Joel wasn't telling Melissa to cut the sappy love stuff. Normally, I would've voiced my concerns about rushing into something, but the pair glowed with love, evaporating my doubts.

"You have to come!" she squealed with excitement, peeling way from Joel and bouncing into my arms. "Come on, everyone's waiting!" She pulled us both toward the ceremony.

Melissa wasn't kidding. It seemed everyone in the world was in attendance, ready for the ceremony to begin. Beautiful white flowers dotted the aisle as soft music was played by a string quartet. The attendees were dressed in beautiful, delicate gowns and tuxedos. The whole area seemed to be set on a white, luxurious cloud. The land vibrated with anticipation.

A shimmer of light caught my eye, tearing my focus away from the ceremony. My clothes transformed into a soft pink gown, which clung to my hips, leaving little to the imagination. Rosebud sleeves graced my shoulders, and the neckline plunged low to showcase my cleavage. The layers of flowing fabric swished as I walked down the aisle to my place next to the happy groom.

Once I stood to Joel's far left, I turned, a gasp escaping my lips. Melissa wore a long white dress with lace sleeves and a jeweled bodice; she appeared to be the epitome of a fallen angel. The glow of romance whipped through her tamed curly hair, fluttering the lace veil placed on her head, the train flowing for miles behind her.

As the couple sealed the ceremony with a kiss, the crowd cheered, celebrating the newly formed union.

My joy plunged into excitement, rippling through my entire being as I watched. I, too, wanted to share a special kiss with someone. I looked out into the sea of people trying to find familiar eyes. The same eyes that filled my heart with such love, I could burst from happiness.

I walked slowly around couples—love radiating from them. Then I felt the familiar taste of panic in my throat, like spoiled milk. *Would I be alone even now?*

Still searching, I stopped, air escaping my lungs. My vision locked on the deep lavender eyes staring back at me.

Our gaze never parted as I walked around the other couples to get to him.

Apparently flustered but relieved he'd chosen to stay, Prince Naluba smiled, motioning me to follow him into a meadow filled with a million little fires burning a bright shade of amber. They dotted the ever-expanding field. The tall trees weren't green; instead, they were turquoise with huge flowers that dwarfed anything on Earth. Blue and yellow bushes scattered the area. Flowers like massive dandelions, but bright orange, dotted the field.

Why's he still on Earth? I thought as a wind gust carried some of the seedlings around us.

My sister shouted as we walked, "Don't take too long, you two. There's cake!"

Naluba gave her a sharp look, triggering Layla's laughter. She joked to one of my cousins, but I couldn't hear. The cousin snickered. I waved back, embarrassed. They ignored me, disappearing into the crowd.

Prince Naluba turned around unexpectedly, looking amused by my confusion. He reached out, grasping my small hand. His hand, double the size of my own, held mine delicately. He emitted an energy that made me feel loved and cherished. We walked, hand in hand, further into the meadow. The music from the wedding party faded into the background. We walked far enough to be out of sight of the others, something I secretly relished. I enjoyed being in his presence and having him to myself.

The prince towered over me, but leaned in slowly, his delicate lips caressing my temple; the kiss, soft and warm, sent shivers down my spine, igniting a fire within. Even after his lips left my skin, I could feel their warmth. My heart raced, with eagerness burning a deep red blush on my cheeks from sheer exhilaration.

Naluba's eyes took me in, his purple gaze filled with happiness. "You know ... " he began, his voice a whisper. He looked concerned yet nervous, tucking a fallen piece of chestnut hair behind my ear. "You might not understand. There is so much you don't know ... "

I stepped closer. His body overshadowed me in every way, but I was safe. As I reached back for him, the well-known darkness tugged at the corner of my mind.

I fought hard to stay with him. "No! Wait!" I shouted, grasping for him. "What do you mean? Of course, I could understand—if it's important to you, it's important to me. Tell me ... "

It was too late—the darkness was here to stay.

In the back of my mind, snapshots of a dream replayed over and over. I could barely make out the details, but the emotions still lingered. The warmth of anticipation swelled into every part of my being from my toes to the top of my head. It vibrated until it extinguished itself, providing me with the courage to finally re-enter the world. I readied myself to open my eyes, and strength returned to my limbs. I was tired but mentally restless.

Violent tremors shook my body, causing my eyes to spring open; I was nearly blinded by the shock of light. It took a moment to see anything clearly, but slowly blurred shapes focused abruptly.

Lying on a large bed in a dark room, I awoke. It was too dark to see the details of paintings on the other walls. A small desk sat in the corner of the room, shelves lining the other wall. The air in the room was cold, but I was warm under the thick quilts that covered my body. I trembled as my senses worked overtime to register if I was safe.

My arms buckled from my weight when my attempt to sit up stalled. The bed rocked again, causing more things to fall with a clatter off the shelves.

I clung to the quilts, my heart beating wildly. I could hear muffled shouting as alarms rang outside the room. I pulled the sheets tighter.

It took effort to sit up, but I could lift myself just enough to steady the rest of my body against the bed frame. The bed stopped shaking, though my nerves were raw and my heart beat out of my chest.

"Help?" I muttered, my throat raw.

The room began shaking viciously again.

I braced myself against the bed as the rest of the hanging art crashed to the floor, shelves collapsing to the ground in a heap. As soon as it had begun, it stopped, leaving me breathless. The bitter taste of bile raced to the back of my throat.

Tearing my eyes away from the mess on the ground, I looked down at the rest of my body to survey the damage. Scratches and bruises curled up my arms in red, angry batches but a new layer of skin was forming. Nothing felt broken, luckily, just stiff and sore.

I pulled off the heavy blankets, and the chill from the room met my bare legs. They were fine, beat up like the rest of me, but I wore some type of lace dress. It was a silky, pale blue floor-length gown. It clung to my breasts and my waist but flared out at my hips. The fitted sleeves ended at my elbows. The dress had many heavy and warm layers underneath. I pulled the layers down over my legs to stay warm. I reached up to touch my head. My hair was tied back into a low plaited bun.

I'd seen this style before on a female Shielder.

I pulled at the gown, looking around at the mess on the floor. A feeling of dread surfaced, more bitter than before, but was immediately snuffed out as the entire room shook harder. Voices outside the door shrieked, dragging my attention away from the dress. I pulled myself out of bed, throwing my legs over the side with all my might.

As my bare feet reached the ground, a sharp shiver went up my spine, piercing my whole body; I shuddered from the cold. I spied my old clothes on a nearby chair, my shoes underneath it. I pushed through the pain, straightening my back, standing for the first time. With each uneasy step toward the chair, I felt my strength return.

I reached my shoes, pulling them on one by one. I shivered again from the cool air. The blazer offered little relief against the cold, but I threw it over my shoulders. I noticed my other clothes, covered in blood, with some other type of liquid—like black ink—smeared down the side of my pants.

"I'm lucky to be alive," I exhaled, trembling at the thought.

The room stopped moving. By this time, everything in the room was on the floor. Books, knickknacks, and documents were thrown in disarray. I watched my step as I tried to maneuver around the mess. I made my way to the door to follow the shouting. I walked slowly, trying to avoid stepping on broken glass.

The room tilted to the right, flinging the broken rubble and my tiny body toward the opposite wall. I allowed myself to be knocked around, while books, junk, and bits of glass pelted me from behind. In the mists of all the chaos, I instinctually covered my face.

Still tilting from the vibration, the room leveled out abruptly. I landed on all fours in a pile of books. One of the titles caught my eye: *Wuthering Heights.*

A strange choice, I thought, picking up the only volume in English. I remembered the plot points with blurry recollection. I stared at it in disbelief. *Wuthering Heights* isn't a novel about sunshine and rainbows. The main characters were abusive, and even though they both craved love, they never fully appreciated they had it.

More shouting met my ears, forcing me to focus on the task at hand. Tearing my eyes away from the oddity, I tossed the book, moving junk out of the way to the doorway.

I steadied myself, pushing the door open. A long hallway with multiple doors on either side met my eyes. Bright lights lined the ceiling, with an occasional flashing yellow light and accompanying alarm. Pipes lined the walls and part of the ceiling, making the gray walls look solid and secure. It seamlessly came together, but still it left the familiar metallic taste of panic on my tongue.

A large body passed in a hurry, causing me to sink back.

Now it was painfully obvious that I was on a Shielder ship. I gathered my resolve, staying as close to the wall as possible, and decided to follow it.

Another passed, giving me a fierce look—its eyes wild with agitation. The male Shielder didn't stop. Instead, he turned abruptly, running off in the opposite direction. My eyes followed him as panic rose inside me. I tried to remain calm, pushing him from my mind. Being so close to something so big and powerful freaked me out.

I took a deep breath and continued on.

I approached a giant, open intersection. The railings formed a circle on the outside of the structure, overlooking lower levels. Bright lights flashed in the distance as sirens roared.

I crept closer to the edge, resting my bony hands on the railing, looking down. The tower of layered levels showcased Shielders running throughout the ship, apparently barking orders at each other in their language.

As I tried to find my voice to break the madness, the ship tilted to the left, flinging everyone to the ground. I slid down the hall, catching myself on the lower railing before falling over the edge. I shifted my weight to grasp hold of the metal and push myself up as the ship shifted, straightening itself out and flinging us in the opposite direction. I slid again but managed to stop when the ship settled.

Shouts came from all over, angrier than before.

Worst drivers in the entire galaxy! I thought bitterly, pushing down the dress.

I pulled myself up by the railing and looked down, eyeing the first level. "I definitely wouldn't have walked away from that drop." I swallowed, the familiar metallic taste forming in the back of my throat.

"Kayin? Kayin Aves?" yelled a female Shielder over the confusion of the others.

I spun toward the direction of the voice.

The most beautiful female Shielder I'd ever seen ran toward me, pushing her kind out of the way. Her hair was wrapped halfway up her head in an intricate braid like a halo, with pieces flying from the momentum she created, and her eyes were the deepest purple. She smiled, showcasing the most striking full lips. She was tall for a female, but it added to her graceful presence. She wore a long floor-length gown with a red bodice and blush-colored skirt; her armored plate covered her breasts and back. Strapped tightly to her waist was a weapon.

"I am so glad I found you," she said in heavily accented English, a mixture of the sounds of Russian and Latin. "What are you doing out here? You must come with me, this is not a safe place for you!" she said, grabbing my arm with a light touch.

"No, I don't think so," I responded, pulling out of her grasp. "What the hell? Where am I, *and* who are you?"

"You are on Ship Vt9 en route to Orrendad," she said as she spun around to look at me, shocked by my outburst. "You are in what your planet calls *Space*, 30 light years from Earth. I am Norgiana. It was my task to look after you the past few days. Now, can we please go?" she asked, annoyed.

Air escaped me, as I became overwhelmed with the heavy feeling of shock. My head spun and my knees quaked beneath me, my stomach flipping in on itself.

I've left Earth? Blurred visions flashed across my mind's eye.

"What do you mean I'm in Space? I was just ... I was just on Earth!"

I massaged my right temple, trying to recall details of the last twenty-four hours. I looked up into Norgiana's beautiful face. Even with all the chaos around us, she was as cool as a cucumber.

She smiled and said, "I know this is hard for you, but we need to meet with the generals. So much has changed over the last day or so. They will be able to tell you more about what happened." She sighed. "He should not have brought you with us, but my brother didn't have a choice. It was not as though we could just leave you—not with ... " She placed her hand on my shoulder as she continued, "You will be safe now. Well, safer than ... It will be all right."

Nodding in agreement, I followed her down another long hallway. My head throbbed with the new information. Nothing was making sense. My body felt heavier than before. I followed Norgiana in silence, trying to keep up with her long strides.

[5]

Though Norgiana walked faster than I could keep up with, it was easy to follow her through the intricate hallways. People moved out of her way immediately. As we passed, Shielders rested their fingertips over their foreheads and bent at the knees, lowering their impressive bodies slowly, almost reaching the ground to avoid any unnecessary eye contact. When they bowed, their hands fell delicately to their side in a sweeping motion.

We dashed by the bowing Shielders, no one noticing me. Two guards followed close behind, wearing head-to-toe armor and sandwiching me between them and Norgiana. I glanced over my shoulder several times, trying not to stare too closely at the intricate markings etched into their skin.

Deep within the Vt9, every hallway looked similar to the one outside my room. Even with decorative staircases leading to different levels of the ship there was no way to tell what was above or below me.

"Stay where you are and watch me," Norgiana advised, nearing a moving staircase. The stairs resembled Earth's escalators but moved faster. "You place your feet here and once you get on, don't move," she told me, stepping onto the tiny platform and demonstrating how to stand: holding her arms to her side and looking ahead.

I listened to her without argument. She disappeared, allowing me to step onto my own platform. I kept my body still, trying not to lose my balance. In a flash I was moving higher and higher into the ship. I relaxed into the ride, but the stairs slowed, bringing me to where Norgiana waited. I stepped off in time to avoid being trampled by the guards.

We walked for nearly half an hour before Norgiana stopped, causing my petite body to slam into her. She turned to face me, giving a little nod to the males behind us. Without a word, the guards stepped aside, standing next to the other Shielders waiting under the large archway we'd come upon.

"We are here," she stated. "To warn you, there are a lot of powerful La'Mursians in that room—it is the main control center for the entire ship, you see."

I nodded, feeling a rosy flush gracing my cheeks as my heart raced. I rubbed my palms against my dress, wiping off the pooling sweat.

"The room itself is a little overwhelming, too. It is made of strong material similar to what you would call glass. You will see your *Space* for the first time, which of course is always a beautiful sight," she murmured, a smile tugging at the corners of her mouth. "We will be docking at Orrendad within the next twelve hours," she continued. "We will not stay long—it is only a port planet. We are heading for my home, Selucia. Have you heard of it?"

I nodded again.

"You will love it there!" she squealed, giving my shoulder a squeeze. Her excitement was more than I thought necessary. "We will be there in a matter of days.

"My brother is in command of this fleet. He has expressed great interest in you and wanted to talk with you personally, but unfortunately he is very busy and unable to answer your questions. I am sure you have many, too. So many things to discuss. Luckily, that responsibility has fallen to me, so before we go in, do you have any questions?"

"Do I have any questions?" I sassed back, eyeing her through thick lashes. I looked into Norgiana's eyes, trying to read the Shielder. Warmth and kindness radiated off of her, yet the nagging feeling of distrust followed like a cloud.

"I have a lot of questions, Norgiana," I finally said, looking straight into her face. "I'm sorry ... I'm still very confused. Why am I here? Why did you bring me with you?"

She fidgeted, her long gown swaying as she rocked back and forth, trying to avoid my glare.

"Well," she started nervously, "you helped my brother—the one from the wreckage? Do you remember that at all?"

"Vaguely."

"Either way, he felt as though he owed it to you to take you to safety. La'Mursians return favors when we can, you see," she purred. "There are no debts in our culture. Besides, it is the right thing to do."

"The right thing was to take someone away from their home?" I asked.

"Um, well, no, of course not, but when—that is, it all happened at once. You were injured when you came aboard. We nursed you back to health—as we would have done for anyone. And, because you helped my brother, we wanted to show our gratitude, feeling that we needed to see you survive your injuries."

"Were they *that* bad?" I interrupted.

"You were not going to die," she said flatly. "You did have a severe head injury."

"I see ... Wait, what?"

"You hit your head."

"On what?"

"Um ... I am not sure."

"Well, shit, I hope it wasn't too much trouble to take care of me," I replied, appalled by her lack of worry.

"It was not." Her fidgeting stopped. "We were unable to send you back down to Earth—which we thought, originally, we would do when you came on board, but you were still injured, so you stayed with us."

"And the fighting?" I asked skeptically.

"You understand, it would have put everyone in danger if we tried to take you home," she added, studying my face.

I looked back at her while emotion faded from my features.

Her sharp lavender eyes left my face, assessing my injuries else-where as she continued, "I am happy to see you are healing well. It is—*complicated*. At the end of the day, my brother decided to bring you with us ... and here you are," she finished, making a hand gesture of presentation in my direction. "We are happy to have you!"

"You mean ... " I asked her, my voice quivering. "It got so bad on Earth that you had to leave *and* ultimately left my planet to get destroyed by those—those Temor-fucks?" A tremor rippled through my body as fury erupted inside me.

"Well, it sounds worse than it really is ... " Norgiana trailed off, avoiding my eyes. "We will get the Galactic Royal Court to give permission to counterattack soon enough. You will see." Norgiana placed her large hand on my shoulder and gave it another reassuring squeeze.

"My brother is a ferocious fighter," Norgiana told me, placing both of her hands on my shoulders. "He will defeat the Temorshians and give you and your kind back your planet. Then we will all live in peace again." She smiled, her eyes sparkling with hope.

"If you say so ... " I stated, shrugging off her hands. I wanted to believe her, but I was not buying a word of any of it. "I'd like to go home soon. How much longer will I have to stay with you *and* this brother of yours? Have you heard what it's like for the rest of my people? Will they be all right?"

My heart sank as tears threatened to run down my cheeks. I looked away from Norgiana's smiling face.

She put her arm around me. "Come," she murmured, turning my body to face the archway, "we can see what the Elders are planning.

We will not forsake you or your people. Trust us." She opened the door and led me through.

I entered but then stopped.

The room was a sight I'd only imagined in my wildest dreams. The ceiling was the first to catch my eye, with one giant window overlooking Space and all its wonder. Various stars and planets whizzed by. I tried to follow Norgiana, but the beautiful sight held my attention.

"What is all this?" I asked no one in particular. I chuckled, thinking of NASA and all the time they wasted getting to the moon. The moon was nothing in this vast sea of amazement. Humans knew nothing beyond what they could see—we missed all this, being so shortsighted!

A teal planet filled the view from the cockpit. It seemed very small in comparison to the others I'd witnessed, but just as quickly the planet passed by. "*Dios mio,*" slipped from my lips as I craned my neck to see the orb float by. Most of the images flashed before my eyes, forming a blur whizzing around in spectacular color. The effect took my breath away.

The room itself was filled with gadgets I couldn't begin to understand. Various controls and buttons lined the walls and stations. Lights flashed here and there, alarms sounding every so often. The screens showed maps and GPS instruments. Others showed the ship itself with various camera angles from all over. Other screens seemed to show video conferencing with other Shielders. All of the machines were at least double my size.

A dozen or so Shielders appeared to control the actual ship from various machines around the room. Not one of the workers seemed to have noticed our entrance, which was fine by me. The more inconspicuous I could stay, the better.

The hairs on the back of my neck stood on end as I felt purple eyes follow my every move.

The richly decorated Elders stood silently watching. The ripples of sickening emotion I constantly fought to push aside threatened to spill over. I felt insignificant, causing the trembling of my limbs to worsen.

"What the fuck am I doing here?" I whispered. I could taste panic bubbling up in my throat. All of my worries settled in the muscles on the back of my neck, while the stimulation of the room threatened to snap my nerves.

My train of thought evaporated as the tallest of them looked at Norgiana and me, smiling.

I knew that smile. I knew those eyes, and I most definitely knew that face.

It was albino Hercules: Prince Naluba.

My breath hitched. *Was this really happening?*

He walked over to us in several strides as the room fell silent—all eyes falling upon the three of us.

I tried not to pick at the corner of my blazer's front pocket as his gaze burned into me. My fingers itched to hold something for reassurance, while my body swayed side-to-side as I tried to hold myself upright.

Naluba stopped in front of Norgiana, reaching for her hand. They embraced forearms—a traditional custom of the Shielders. They exchanged a few words in their language as he playfully patted her arm. Prince Naluba turned his full attention to me, his enormous lavender eyes taking me in. I tried not to sink back in intimidation. My cheeks flamed red. I couldn't make myself look up to his face. If I did, I would never be able to look away.

"I am glad to see you have finally awoken," Prince Naluba said in a soothing tone. "It has been many days since our first meeting on Earth. Do you recall?"

A rush of blood left my head, escaping through my numb limbs as a million inappropriate thoughts ran through my mind. I glanced in his general direction with a slight smile.

"My name is Naluba Ransardian Pelomena Turshkin," he continued, ignoring my awkward behavior. "I am the heir to the High Chancellor of Selucia, and this is my sister, Princess Norgiana. We met briefly, but I was not sure how much of the meeting you would remember. How are you feeling?"

Well, *damn*. The bowing, the fancy clothes, all that captain of the fleet nonsense, of course that meant they were both important royalty. And, of course, I'd saved the prince of one of the most powerful planets in Space.

Fuck me, I thought, slightly amused.

I gathered up all my courage to look Prince Naluba in the eye, reminding myself one last time to push aside my panic. "Hello, um, I'm feeling just fine, thank you. I'm afraid I don't remember much," I said all at once. "I'm sorry, this whole thing is new to me, and I'm still really confused, especially by this, but what exactly did I do to, um, get your help? I'm sure it wasn't much—not that it was a problem. I'm sure it wasn't a problem!"

I looked down at my feet, flushed cheeks and all. *This is not you, chica. Get it together.*

He smiled—no sharp teeth, which was optional for fighters—and explained, "You tried to help me when my ship crashed on Earth. You did not have to come and help, but you did. You put yourself in danger. If you had not gotten me to come back to consciousness, those Temorshians would have made sure I was dead." His voice was grave, but his eyes were kind.

"I guess that sounds like something I'd do … "

Prince Naluba continued, "I was told that you probably would not remember much, but one day when we have more time, we will sit and discuss more. How are you feeling now?"

"I'm fine, like I said. My head still hurts, but I'll live." *I'm starving, no big deal.*

"I am glad to hear it!" he exclaimed suddenly, unnerving me slightly. "You will let either of us know if you need anything—*anything* at all. You are our guest here. It would be better under different circumstances, but—"

"You should meet the Elders now," Norgiana interrupted gently.

"Yes, excellent point. They are curious about your kind and have not had many encounters with the females," he said, putting his arm around me to guide me closer to the table.

These Shielders are so touchy-feely. I tried not make things more awkward, allowing my body to follow his motion.

For the next hour I was paraded around the room, meeting many of the most important Shielders from their planet. Their names were so long and difficult to pronounce I started giving them numbers instead.

One reached for a piece of my hair that had escaped its bind, curling her long bony fingers around the strand and caressing it gently. I moved, pulling the strand from her grasp. We locked eyes wordlessly as she acknowledged that I didn't like to be touched. Many of them attempted to touch and play with my hair; I assumed it was because it's so dark—maybe they were not used to seeing such a color, but I was not here to satisfy their curiosity.

"I'm sorry," I mustered, between two such ordeals. "It's not common on my planet—in my country—to freely touch someone else without permission." My cheeks flushed.

Most of them didn't speak a lot of English, so Prince Naluba translated. "*Mezda* Raquiel is sorry for your loss and hopes you will find peace on Selucia. She is also sorry for touching you, but is impressed by your coloring."

"Thank you," I responded, taking her hand and awkwardly shaking it, making sure she didn't have another chance to grab me.

"Remind me to show you how to properly greet in La'Mursian," he whispered as we finished our rounds.

"Yes, please do, this is so awkward," I breathed, smiling at the next General—*Mezda*.

After being around Prince Naluba, I started to feel more comfortable. It wasn't just him, but the rest of the bunch. They might be large, but their hearts were pure and as kind as could be. They were sympathetic to my situation and seemed to care about Earth to a degree I had not anticipated. I was beginning to let my guard down, but my walls were in place. I still could not lift the cloud of mistrust.

Naluba was kind about helping and very patient. If he was such a ferocious fighter, as his sister said, I had to assume that he ruled with an iron fist or a guarded heart. I hadn't expected him to be so caring.

"I think it is time to get some dinner," Norgiana interrupted, politely.

Exhausted and in desperate need of food, I was done being handled by the Shielders and agreed with her.

She explained to the others while Naluba pulled me aside. "I will see you again, Kayin, after we leave Orrendad. We have much to discuss. Get some rest," he whispered, looking more serious than before.

He turned to Norgiana. "Take care of her."

His sister nodded and moved me out of the room without a chance for me to say good-bye.

"See, that was not so bad, was it?" she asked after we returned to the hallway. The guards resumed their position behind us. "What do you think of my brother?"

"I liked him just fine. Why?" I rushed, trying to keep my breathing steady.

She eyed me. "Most Humans see him and fall madly in love—they claim their undying love *only* for him. Are you really so different?"

No, but I'm not going to tell you that.

I made a disgusted face. Norgiana laughed and threw her arm around me.

"I'm joking, Kayin! *Ja ja ja!* You should have seen your face! Even if he is my twin, I can honestly say he is an attractive La'Mursian. I know you agree."

I nodded.

"All right, now," Norgiana stated, "let's find you something to eat and then get you back into bed. You will want to be well rested after the next couple of days."

"Why? What's happening in a few days?" I asked as we walked, her arm still draping itself around my shoulders.

"You will have to meet the High Chancellor and get yourself ready to meet with the Galactic Royal Court!" she exclaimed, a large smile spreading over her face.

"I'll have to meet your father? Why? I just want to go home and make sure my family is safe."

Norgiana stopped walking, letting me go, and looked at me hard. "You need to meet with my father if you plan on going back to Earth. Without his help, you will never get your planet back. As for the Galactic Royal Court, you will need to speak with them and explain everything."

"But ... I don't know everything!" I shrieked. "I thought you had a ship of all the leaders of the world? Why can't you take them with you? I don't want to help—I just want to get back home!" I fought to keep my body from shaking. "I may be well versed in the politics of my country, but in Space? Not a chance."

Norgiana sighed, looking pained. "You will understand soon enough what role you are about to play. We *need* your help, and your people *need* your help. Leave it at that for now. You will have to speak with Naluba about the rest. It will be all right."

She continued walking while I stayed back, staring at her. She motioned for me to follow, but I stayed where I was.

I didn't want to trust her or her brother or this High Chancellor. They could all rot for all I cared. If they thought I would be played like a puppet, they had another thing coming.

6

"Please," I begged between talks of clothes and vacation destinations, "has anyone heard anything about Earth?"

One of Norgiana's friends, Ossa, sent to cheer me up, shook her head no, continuing to talk about where to eat when we landed on Selucia. Throughout the day, Norgiana or one of her many friends onboard would come by to check on me, partaking in idle gossip about the latest trends on Selucia.

I felt like a burden, staying in my room worrying—half listening—pacing the floor through it.

"Trust me," Ossa said in rough English, her thick accent hard to understand. "Selucia will be a new home to you. You will love it, and I will show you all the best places to eat and shop. Do you like to dress up?"

"When the time calls for it, I guess; if not, I'd rather wear leggings," I replied, sipping *Canu*—La'Mursian tea everyone drank morning, noon, and night. The taste of the *canu* reminded me vaguely of green tea mixed with rosemary and sugar. The batch she'd made was thick and tasteless, the balls of leaves and herbs sticking to the back of my throat.

"What are *leg ins*?" she asked, eyeing me. She was beautiful, like every Shielder, with her long hair neatly wrapped around her head in intricate braids and curls, while her flowing purple gown clung to her breastplate and slender hips.

"*Leggings*," I corrected her. "Tight, extremely comfortable pants. Come on, all that time on Earth and you didn't see a pair walking around?"

"I was a little busy," she murmured, taking a sip. "Well, anyway, let me tell you about all the fashion in Henzon!"

I barely attempted to hide my rolling eyes.

Once we landed on Orrendad, though, I was able to leave my room and move to Norgiana's chambers.

Her room looked similar to the one I'd stayed in, but with more color and light. It was cozy with its intimate feel, beautiful trinkets lining the walls. There was a large desk on one side and a lavish bed on the other, with a small setup of chairs opposite the desk—a little sitting room for guests. I was sure the rest of the rooms on the ship weren't painted and didn't have such nice things, but it was part of Norgiana's charm—she knew how to use her royalty to the fullest.

"Take a look outside," she suggested as she rested her lanky body on a sofa. "It is one of the best ports in the area."

I looked out of Norgiana's window, quickly realizing it wasn't much. Compared to what I'd seen through the cockpit, Orrendad was lame. As a planet it was similar to Mars: sandy, windy, and rust colored, with a few ochre dunes dotting the horizon.

"The air is thick," Norgiana explained, "and not many creatures can breathe without some kind of help. That's why we won't be leaving the ship. While the port can hold numerous ships, not many wish to live in a place where the air is toxic and nothing grows. That is why the planet works perfectly for a port, because the less traffic, the better.

"The port itself is pretty small for a shipping yard," she continued, watching me, amused by my attempts to get a better look out the small window. "We have docked at bigger ones before. This one does just fine, especially on the way to Earth."

Peering out of one of the tiny windows that dotted her wall, I rested my forehead on the cold glass to try to see, though it was too small to get a decent look. The light radiating off the deep orange of the landscape burned my eyes.

"Ouch," I whined, drawing myself away from the window.

"You should not try to stare at it, you might hurt your sight. The light from the sun is five times hotter than yours. Be careful."

I blinked several times and went back to my post, trying to avoid overexposure. Through the dust and the light, there were about ten areas for smaller ships and about six larger ones for a ship like ours.

"Is our ship about the normal size for a vessel with more than just war machines?"

"No. The Vt9 is a traveling vessel that carries anything we need: people, weapons, food, you name it. It traveled all around the galaxy many times," she explained as she played with one of the wisps of hair that had fallen out of her halo of braids. "Naluba normally doesn't command a ship like this."

I moved away from the window to another, listening to her talk.

"He prefers fighter crafts, like the one you found him in. Those are in short supply, unfortunately." She paused, choking on her last few words.

Her pause made me turn around to look at her.

Norgiana wasn't looking at me anymore, but off into the distance. Her face contorted as though she might cry, her lip quavering from the corner of her beautiful mouth. One golden tear escaped her eye, but she hastily wiped it away, removing all evidence she was upset.

Norgiana let out a long sigh, realizing she'd stopped talking. She continued, "We suffered a great loss. They destroyed most of our fighter ships. Most of the La'Mursians you see on board are fighters who lost their crafts or Galianias who are misplaced."

"Galia—what? What is *that*? What does it do?" I asked.

She laughed, wiping her eyes with the back of her hand.

I'd learned a lot from Norgiana over the past few days, but throwing out words thinking I was already trilingual was her specialty. I was starting to learn bits and pieces of their language, but found it hard to master. I could form small sentences since the sounds reminded me of my mother tongue, Spanish. It was helpful to communicate, but I was nowhere near fluent. In the end, however, everyone seemed to appreciate my efforts.

"*Jajaja!* It is not a what, it is a who!" she giggled. "I am a Galiania: a peacekeeper. We do not fight like our military. We try to resolve issues with words and peaceful action by traveling all around the galaxy helping others."

"I see," I muttered, turning my attention back to the window. "You must not be good at it, since you couldn't stop what's happening to Earth." The edge to my voice outweighed the teasing.

When I didn't hear her normal retort I turned around. She was looking down at her long navy gown, picking at the soft material—her breastplate, along with the rest of her armor, had been thrown in the corner of the room.

"I know ... " she finally said in a low voice. "I am so sorry—truly I am. We did everything we could, but they would not relent. We underestimated them ... *badly*. Putting your species in a predicament they could never withstand." Her shoulders tensed with guilt. "How could we know it would play out the way it did?"

"So, now what? Are we leaving soon?" I asked, trying to change the subject.

She looked up, ignoring my question for a moment, and walked to her desk, lowering her body gracefully onto the seat. "We will be leaving within the hour," she stated, not bothering to turn around.

I sighed. "Shielders don't like giving exact times or days, do they? It's always *within this* or *in about that*."

"What is your point?" she asked.

"It took us more than twelve hours to reach Orrendad—"

"Because of a heavy meteor shower—"

"—It probably will take us another four days to get to Selucia!"

"And? We cannot make this ship go any faster," she said coolly.

Another sigh escaped my pursed lips. My hands, constantly searching for something to do, rubbed themselves raw. I paced around the room, sitting for only a moment before I moved to another corner of the room and back again.

In my rare moments alone, I'd push my anxiety away, yet it always came back worse than before; waves of panic washed over my heart, spreading through my veins and causing me to keel over in agony. I struggled to stay positive, but as the hours turned to days it became harder and harder. The more I stayed on a ship, with beings I barely knew, the more my experience was becoming too much to bear. My heart beat itself out of my chest as beads of sweat began to stream down my temples.

We left Orrendad shortly after our discussion. It was then that Norgiana noticed my misery. My panic attacks were getting worse and harder to hide from my new friend. She sent more friends to visit and had every meal with me. I was grateful for her time, but I still couldn't shake my melancholy.

"What is your brother doing?" I interrupted her lengthy explanation of the *logressta*, some random animal on Selucia.

"What?" Norgiana stammered, "Oh, Naluba? He is busy getting everything together for our arrival, making plans and the like. I know he told you he would speak to you after we left Orrendad, but I am afraid that is not possible."

"Why don't I believe you?" I asked pointedly.

With a look of desperation, she sighed. "Because you have been through an adjustment and are having a hard time dealing with all of this?"

"Perhaps," I snapped back, throwing a fit to rival any Shielder temper.

"He told me—in front of you—that if I ever needed anything I'd get it. I need him. *Now.*"

The Shielder and I stared each other down for some time before she continued, "Trust me. If he could talk with you, he would ... I would not lie about that. He is important, you understand. He does not have time for games." Her stare intensified. It lessened as she added, "For some reason he is quite fond of you."

The change of subject took me by surprise.

"Stop! I don't care how he feels about me. It's off topic!" I didn't want her to know about my confusing feelings toward him. "This doesn't feel right to you, does it? I should know what's happening because I could help. Helping more than being taken to some Galactic Royal Court to plead my case. I want him in here—*now*. You and I both know I'm being forced to stay, going against everything you stand for. Where is Naluba?"

Norgiana looked at me like I was talking gibberish, but soon a light shown brightly behind her eyes. "Of course," she murmured. "Why didn't he think of that? You would be a better source of information than anything else. I will send for him at once!"

She hastened to her bedroom door, opened it, and beckoned to a guard, saying something in her native tongue. He dashed off to follow her orders.

Closing the door, she turned back to me and smiled, saying, "It will only be a moment."

"Whatever you say, Norgiana. I don't understand why it's so hard to get him in the first place? I can help. Just because I'm Human doesn't mean I'm stupid. I could know something you people haven't read in a book!"

"Well, of course," she answered, "but no one is trying to keep you ignorant on purpose, Kayin. There is a lot going on, and we get new information all the time. It is hard even for me to follow."

"So you admit it. You know what's happening but you refuse to tell me. Why?"

"I do not refuse," Norgiana stated, all the while avoiding my eyes. "I have told you, too many times now, that Naluba wants to talk to you personally. He feels responsible for your welfare and wants to have a complete conversation with you." She went back to her work at the desk.

The feeling I was being tricked hovered in my stomach and tensed my muscles. I had no choice but to go along with her game. When Norgiana spoke quickly in La'Mursian, she did it for a reason. She knew I would be completely lost. This time she'd spoken to the guard faster than I'd ever heard before.

We sat in silence, avoiding each other's line of vision. After we'd waited another fifteen minutes, someone knocked on the door.

My heart skipped a beat.

I could admit that being in Naluba's presence made me feel safe. I'd only spent a few moments with him, and he was already making me feel powerful emotions most people only dreamt about. Either I was still in a state of shock, or I was letting the stress of this Space adventure dictate my emotional state. In the end, it wasn't real.

As my inner monologue raged on, a male walked in, carrying a tray with an assortment of goodies with *canu*. I liked the tea and just like Norgiana, it was starting to grow on me.

Norgiana got up and went to the tea. "Would you like some *canu?*" she offered in La'Mursian.

"Yes, please," I answered in La'Mursian. "Do you need any help?" I asked in English.

Almost dropping the cup she was holding, she caught herself, saying, "No, I can get it." Norgiana turned, crossed the room in a few short strides, and handed me my cup.

"Oh, thank you," I said, looking down into the cup. It wasn't chunky like with Ossa, which had almost stopped me from drinking the stuff altogether.

The sweet aroma filled my nostrils as the flavor washed over my tongue, filling my belly with its warmth.

"This is great, Norgiana," I said in La'Mursian. "Thank you again." I took another sip as I observed her watching me, her face hard to read. In English I continued, "This isn't going to make me forget your brother. He'd better be on his way. I don't like games either."

"He will be here," she whispered flatly. "He would not put you out."

"I'm so sick of all these *games*."

"I know."

"I can't imagine he's *too* busy. You people left Earth to die on its own. What else would there be to do? I don't suppose ... " A slow yawn crept across my features. "Sorry. I suppose he'd be concerned about getting his ass kicked by me?" I yawned again, my eyes growing heavier by the second. "If he's such a great ... " My vision blurred as my eyelids attempted to seal themselves. "He's so ... "

Norgiana walked closer to me, watching as I swayed back and forth from the drowsiness. She picked me up in one motion, taking me over to the bed.

I tried to fight her but my limbs were numb. "No! No, stop," I screamed, as tears slid down my face. "What did you—what did you do!"

"I am so sorry. It is for your own good. When you wake, we can explain everything to you ... " she whispered, softly stroking my hair. "I am so sorry about everything ... "

Her words were meaningless.

I dove into a deep, dreamless sleep.

"We owe her more than this, brother," Norgiana stated plainly.

I could barely focus on the Galiania's voice, but I willed myself to listen, pushing past the haze that enveloped my mind. Thankfully, she decided English was a good idea—perhaps to practice or to not be overheard by other La'Mursians. Either way it was similar to how I communicated with my sister, going in and out of both English and Spanish seamlessly.

"We owe all of them more," Naluba retorted back.

"You cannot bear the blame on your shoulders, Naluba. Father knew what would happen if we did not get the support of the Court. We did what we felt was right. We lost just as much as they have ... ”

“You have suffered a great tragedy, sister, and for that I am even more sorry. I should not have let her stay behind. She knew what she was getting herself into when she volunteered to stay behind.”

Norgiana moaned, but he continued, “Beenishia would not want you to feel the way you do. She would have wanted you to mourn and then do your duty.”

“Stop it,” Norgiana cried. “We cannot all be as heartless as you. I loved her, and we were partners. One cannot simply get over such a loss. You would know if you—”

“You are right, sister. I am being rude. I feel her loss too, but I cannot comprehend the loss of a beloved partner. I am sorry. Please, come here ... ” Naluba began to softly speak in La’Mursian as Norgiana wept.

“We owe her more, brother,” Norgiana said in perfect English. “We owe them all more. In Beenishia’s name, I will make sure there is justice for Kayin’s people. I am willing to fight to secure peace. Are you?”

“You know that I am,” Naluba uttered flatly.

“Then show her. She deserves an explanation. I am tired of lying and watching her break down. Humans are strong, but when their emotions are tested, they can break.”

Naluba sighed. “I understand. That is why I am afraid to tell her.”

“You? Afraid? Brother, you shock me!” Norgiana teased as she sniffed her last tears away.

“Do not laugh. I am ... ”

7

The familiar humming of the ship's engine wasn't present as a light warmed the left side of my face. I stretched my arms over my head, life returning to my body. A yawn escaped my lips. My mind felt heavy, like the rest of my limbs, while my insides felt thick with confusion. Shifting on the soft bed, dull pains crept through my veins. It took too much effort to move, so I waited to regain feeling as the fog in my mind started to slowly dissipate.

The memories of my previous adventures came flooding back like a smack to the head. No more tea from Norgiana. This whole being-dead-to-the-world thing was getting old.

I forced my eyes to open with a cold fury. An intricate ceiling with different colored panels hovered before me. Beautiful and detailed, it told a story of Shielder history, their long lean bodies bending to give food to others while off in the distance armies fought one another. I scrutinized the mural, trying to understand the story. Death and peace seemed to be the major themes, which I found oddly comforting. I knew death. Peace, on the other hand, was a distant memory.

Everything in the room, decorated in jewel tones, was unlike anything I'd seen before with its twisted metals, oversized seating area, and drapes covering walls, which made the mural on the ceiling stand out even more. The maroon-colored blankets and silver detailed sheets I had been sleeping in were made out of the softest silk-like material I'd ever felt. The room was dark except for a small stream of light coming from an opening in the curtains—the same light that had awoken me. I initially assumed it was a large window, but as I focused harder I realized it was a doorway.

Propping myself up on my elbows, I looked around to the opposite side of the room. The space was big, complete with a fireplace and a small sitting area. The furniture was detailed with different metals intertwined together. Though the items were old and weathered, they appeared to be comfortable—oversized for my small frame—but luxurious.

Sandwiched between two large, dark openings lived a fireplace. The first black hole opened to a room I could barely see into. The other one, closer to what I assumed to be an exit, was smaller, yet the same bright light flooded the glistening floor.

As I examined the room, it dawned on me that I'd made it to Selucia. My pulse quickened. It was thrilling, but I didn't belong here. Being the first Human so far out in Space terrified me.

Despite the stiffness in my limbs, I pulled myself out of bed. The air, as the blankets fell away, felt like a warm hug in comparison to the cold, stiff air on the Vt9.

I inhaled the air, which reminded me of Earth, yet it stung when it hit my sinuses, pricking my lungs on the way down. After the sensation faded, the scratchiness became less noticeable—yet still a strange reminder that I was far from home.

Velvety material slinked across my legs, catching my attention. A light pink nightgown flowed past my knees; the sleeves were short, barely covering my shoulders. My tan skin, still covered with bruises and scratches, was on its way to recovery, a welcome surprise.

My stomach gurgled its annoyance as I stepped out of the warm covers and off the bed to stretch out my stiffness. With every step I took, I felt the pinch of my nerves. I walked around to get feeling back into my legs. As my fingers lightly grazed the curtains on the large window, there came a knock at the door.

Turning my attention to the sound, I hobbled over, freezing when the door opened.

Two big lavender eyes peered out of the crack. "You're finally awake!" a voice said in La'Mursian. A large female Shielder burst open the door and stepped inside, causing me to sink back from her size. In accented English, she said, "Oh, I am sorry!"

She wore a gown similar to one I'd seen on the Vt9, but it was dark brown with a long apron. Her hair, pulled back into a low pony-tail with many small braids, hung down her back. Her face was rounder than the others I'd seen, with small lips, and she did not have any of the common markings; her gray-white skin was clear and bright. In her arms she held small packages. In one swift step, she walked over to the door closest to her, which opened into another large room.

"We will have this place filled in no time, Sorg Aves," she called from the room. I gawked at her while she opened each package, placing each garment into its proper place.

"Please don't call me that," I muttered.

Sorg was similar to Lady or Sir on Earth. They used the same word for both genders and sexes, no matter what. It was a sign of respect; not everyone was addressed by the term.

She ignored me, continuing, "They have only given me a few arti-cles of clothing for now, but I am sure I can get you some more if you have need. I have one dress for the meeting with His Majesty and another for the Royal Court—that one is my favorite! There are a couple for everyday wear and a traveling uniform. They are working on your armor as we speak."

What the heck will I need armor for? I thought, taken aback by the idea.

The female Shielder turned to look at me. She had a beautiful smile, without pointed teeth, that lit up her entire face.

The Shielder bowed like the other Shielders on the ship: fingers to the head with a bend at the knees. I rolled my eyes, made uncomfortable by all this nonsense.

"My name is Luvinga. I am to assist you in any way possible. Let me know if I can be of service." She smiled again, waiting for a command.

"This isn't nineteenth-century England. I'm all right for right now, thanks," I told her. "Please don't do that thing you just did—it's not necessary. I don't need much help, honestly. But, um, is there any way I can get a meal? I'm really hungry." She looked skeptical at my first request but Luvinga didn't argue. I quickly added, "Oh, and by chance do you know where I could find Norgiana?"

She nodded and walked back to the door to a guard outside. He quickly walked off, leaving her to close the door and turn her attention back to me.

"Your lunch will be here in a few minutes," she told me. "As for the Princess Norgiana, I do not know where she is. While we wait for your meal, would you mind if I helped you get ready for today's meeting?" She gestured to the closet.

I nodded, following her into the giant walk-in closet with shelving and storage spaces for clothing.

"I was told Humans usually wash standing up, but here we do it sitting down. We like to take our time with it, since it's the best part of the day—well, in my opinion, anyway," she informed me with a smile, walking toward the right of the room into a little bathing station. "How do you like your bath drawn?" she asked, looking up from her position near the tub.

"Um, warm is fine—no bubbles, though."

Her brow sank as she turned her head to face me but she said nothing, continuing her work over a basin that looked like one of our old style bathtubs, but bigger, much bigger. "Just take off your slip and get in. The bath is ready."

I hesitated, waiting for her to leave the room. "Will you be staying?" I asked.

"I am here to help," she said, giving me another stern look. "Do you need help getting undressed?"

"No, no, not at all—I just ... never mind," I said, slipping out of the nightgown, thankful she averted her eyes.

Once nude, I got in. The tub was the size of a small swimming pool, luxurious and warm.

"May I please have some soap?"

She handed me a small container with lime-colored goo in it. I scowled at the pile of vomit-colored gunk.

She laughed, saying, "I am sorry, I keep forgetting. We use it to wash ourselves. Hair included." She moved closer to me, settling herself near the end of the tub. Luvinga took some out and started to wash my hair.

The goo smelled great, faintly reminding me of hard candy—fruity but not overpowering.

"Thank you, Luvinga, for your help—you didn't have to," I told her after she finished helping me, my checks ablaze from such an intimate act. "I think I'm all set now."

She passed me a long sheet to dry off. I did so quickly, not wanting to take up more of her time. She handed me a ruby-red robe with orange beading all around the hem, neckline, and arms. It was a little big but the huge train was to die for, so I didn't mind. At least the sleeves were short.

Luvinga quickly combed my thick hair. It didn't take long, surprisingly—that concoction being a miracle worker. She threw it up into a bun. The heaviness from my neck disappeared in one quick motion of her long, bony fingers.

The sound of the door caught my ear, causing my stomach to gurgle with anticipation of the meal to come.

"Come," she said, smiling, "I am sure you will want to eat after everything you have been through."

We walked back into my bedroom, the train of the dressing gown swaying with every step. I sat down on one of the chairs closest to the fireplace, eyeing the meal on the table. Luvinga placed the tray of food in front of me. I was too hungry to care what was laid before me—I began tasting everything.

Luvinga sat across from me. She poured herself a cup of *canu*, sipping it slowly, watching the scene unfold before her. She didn't comment on my manners. Turning her lavender eyes on me, she explained, "You have a meeting with the High Chancellor this afternoon. His Majesty, Prince Naluba, will be with you and so will all of the Elders. I am told this is a very important meeting, though I do not know what it concerns. Probably your home planet."

I stared at her. "Why does everyone need to be there?" A nervous sweat began to trickle down my back, leaving a searing path in its wake. I could taste the panic as it bubbled up into my throat. I swallowed hard.

Luvinga looked alarmed. "I am sorry. I am confused. They did not tell you—"

The doors of my bedroom slammed open; Norgiana stormed in, looking frightened yet ready for battle, her yellow dress flowing behind her body, her armor on and a weapon at her side. She looked every bit like a warrior princess.

"That is enough, Luvinga. You are excused," she commanded in a stern voice.

I jumped inside. Luvinga dropped her cup and bowed swiftly. She was out of the room in no time, closing the doors behind her.

Left in the room with the crazed Shielder, I stood and readied myself. We stared at each other, neither willing to make the first move.

She walked to me in three steps, blurting, "How did you sleep? I am so sorry I had to do that to you, but I was worried for your sanity. Do not look at me like that—yes, I drugged you. I knew I could never get Naluba to speak with you, and I thought it would be for the best if you rested." Norgiana dropped her eyes for a moment.

"How could you?" I asked. "How would putting me to sleep help?"

"If our roles were reversed—like you said—do you think you could have watched as I broke in front of you?"

"I'm not a toy! I wasn't breaking in front of you!" I yelled through gritted teeth.

"And, please, tell me, what would you have done?"

The tension I held in my shoulders lessened. "If I were put in a similar situation, I would've talked to you or something less offensive!"

"Mmhhmm," she whispered through pursed lips, taking a seat.

I balled my fists, my temper raising. "No, you don't go around drugging people because it's easy—you fucking help them!" I sat back down, trying to get comfortable in my robe. "If you can't handle my emotional state, then leave the room. There doesn't have to be so many secrets between us!"

"I will not do it again," Norgiana promised as she poured herself a cup of *canu*. "I am sorry. My family may be many things but we are not good at lying or keeping secrets. That is why I have been forced to go to such lengths not to tell you what has been going on. I take full responsibility for my actions. I hope you can forgive me."

"It was unnecessary, Norgiana," I told her. "Just treat me with more respect. I may be Human, but I am stronger than you or anyone here gives me credit for. I can handle it."

She flinched.

"Humans may be less than Shielders in many ways but we still deserve just treatment. Keeping me in the dark isn't doing any good for anyone," I paused, not really waiting for a rebuttal. "I heard I have to meet with your father today. I can't say I'm looking forward to it. Care to explain why I am meeting with him?"

Norgiana let out a hiss. "There are many things you do not know—I am pretty sure you caught that rather quickly, but I am forbidden to tell you."

"What do you expect me to say to news like that?" We sat in silence for a while as I finished eating, my blood boiling again. "More secrets, I see. Tell me, when does it end?"

"I cannot say I am sorry enough, Kayin," she told me with a certain sadness in her voice. "Trust me; you will want to hear this from my father, not from me, Naluba, or anyone else. Things have changed on Earth. Things we *never* saw coming. Mistakes were made." She paused, looking down at her cup. I could've sworn I saw tears at the corners of her eyes, but she turned away quickly.

"You seem to feel as bad as I do about Earth. *Why?* It's just one planet in a long line of ones you've already helped. Why is it so important to you?"

"It is not just your planet, Kayin. It's more—" she paused, looking up. There were tears forming. "I lost someone in the battle. Someone extremely important to me," she confessed in a hushed voice. "For me it is personal."

"I am so sorry to hear that," I said, shocked. I reached out to touch her arm. I rested my tan fingers softly on her pale skin. She did not flinch or push me away.

"Thank you," she murmured with such sorrow. "It hurts but I know she went down doing what she loved: protecting the innocent. Is that not the most important thing to remember? That she was doing what she loved."

"That's true. She's one of the lucky ones to find her calling, but it still hurts—no matter how we try to justify the loss," I told her as gently as I could. "The pain will always stay with us in one form or another."

"Yes, my heart is broken. Beenishia was my life partner—a soul mate, as your kind calls it. We were lucky to love each other, but ... "

"I understand. I loved someone back on Earth," I admitted. "It didn't work out between us, but I know I've lost him as well. It doesn't make the pain of losing him any easier knowing he did what he thought was right."

"You were found alone. Naluba looked for kin, but no Humans were in the area. Where was he?" she asked me, wiping tears away.

Even if she did not mean it, her words stung. I pulled my hand away as if to protect myself from the truth. I licked my lips, gathering my thoughts. "He wasn't with me. Henry—that was his name—was elsewhere, joining the army. He wanted to save me, he said. He figured he made a mistake not being with me, so his way of an apology was volunteering to fight."

"You should be proud. Honor him by doing what you can for your people now. Here and at the Galactic Royal Court."

"That's easy for you to say, Norgiana. I don't know what I'm doing here——"

A knock came from the door, ending our heart-to-heart.

I was glad she felt comfortable opening up to me and that I was finally able to do the same. I watched her cross the room, smiling to myself. I hadn't realized how alone I'd been feeling until this moment.

My smile faded, and the sick feeling of betrayal bubbled over.

I got up to look outside. The view waiting behind the heavy linen turned out to be a doorway to a small balcony overlooking part of the palace. The archway decorated in a similar fashion as the ceiling depicted a time in La'Mursian history. The only difference was no depictions of battles hung above the door—only peaceful times were etched into the metal.

Peering out, I stepped into the light. I gasped as I finally took in Selucia.

The palace was large and off-white. It seemed to stretch on for miles, wrapping around the coastline, with turquoise water shining in the light. Towers dotted the coast and the winding walls, with large windows scattered throughout—unlike anything on Earth. The bulk of the palace connected with the city in such a way that it resembled a giant fortress with tan walls. Round huts were laid out between large brown and off-white buildings as far as the eye could see. The gardens of the palace were massive and contained bright-colored foliage. Some plants had large flowers and others had giant leaves. There were stretches of forest with various trees. Throughout the layout, various green areas containing wildlife dotted the landscape.

I watched as small figures went about their daily business doing various chores on the palace grounds. Some were mending broken areas, while others cleaned up the gardens. Most were running around in and out of archways into buildings and the surrounding areas. It was a peaceful place, with a few shouts from workers here and there, but no busy streets or humming from engines met my ears.

Norgiana joined me on the balcony. "Henzon, our capital, is the largest city on the planet. The palace takes up most of the space, but the port limits go on."

"It's beautiful," I told her. "The photos I've seen don't do it justice."

She smiled. "Yes, we are very lucky."

Just past the farthest city wall spread a large body of what looked like water.

Norgiana caught my eye, following my gaze. "Selucia doesn't have water, but we do have something that is very similar and made out of some of the similar components," she explained. "It's not blue, but more of a dark teal color—only because of the light. It is said to be denser than the oceans and lakes on Earth, but you will have to see for yourself. One day we will have to go for a swim in the *Golfth* bay. We are lucky it is always warm enough for a swim."

"I'd like that, especially if it's always warm. It beats—" I swallowed hard. "It beats the weather in Michigan." My heart contracted at my disloyalty.

"Selucia has only one sun-like source, like Earth, but it is ten times bigger—not nearly as hot," she added. "It's called *Colinga*. You can see it now, but do not try to look at it head on."

It was a breathtaking sight with shades of gold emanating from the orb. Its light bounced over the waves in the bay outside the city.

"Come, we've wasted enough time gawking. My father does not like tardiness," Norgiana finally said as she went back inside.

Layla loved to swim, I thought. How many times had we gone to Lake Michigan as children? The family gatherings we held near the fresh water—the BBQs, graduation parties, weddings—I'd lost count of how many times we'd rip off our fancy dresses only to dive deep into the sandy lake, the adults watching from the shore and drinking Oberon.

The more I looked out from my perch, the more the longing enveloped my senses—the cloud of mistrust darkening. The emptiness of being alone tickled the back of my mind, while the regret of not being with my loved ones proved to be stronger than I could handle.

There could be worse places for me to be, but at that moment, I was overtaken by grief, my body collapsing to the ground in a pile of limbs, my vision hazy from the tears. I felt my mind slip from my new reality into the dark void I fought hard to elude. I choked on the new air I needed to breathe.

"I can't!" I screamed. "It's not fair! Why am I here—why!"

Norgiana rushed back outside and knelt by my side, holding me close. "I know. You must stay strong. This will all be over soon, I promise. I vow to return to Earth with you and rescue your family and the rest. We will destroy the Temorshians together."

Her words did not comfort me. I cried harder, clinging to her for support.

The High Chancellor and the Elders would have to wait. I needed my time to grieve.

8

No one rushed me to get ready, but after the third or fourth messenger knocked politely on the door, Norgiana called for Luvinga.

"It is time," she muttered gently to me. "All you have to do is get through this. Then you can come back here for as long as you need."

"I can't," I moaned, my voice hoarse from crying. "I couldn't possibly ... "

She hushed me, pushing back a fallen strand of hair. "You can and you will. Just be the strong woman I know you are, you will see. It will be over soon. Come, we are both here to help you get ready." The Shielder helped me off the bed, and we slowly made our way into the washroom.

Both women went through my new closet as I watched, painfully aware I was being a baby. After some deliberation, they both agreed on one garment. The winner was a long navy blue gown fit for a queen. The sleeves were long, opening just past my elbows, the fabric stopping at my waist. Along the neckline lay intricate white bead-work, and underneath the skirt were about three different kinds of petticoats. The fabric was heavier than the others I'd worn before, but with the chill caused by my despair, I needed every ounce of help to stop shaking.

I let the Shielders fiddle as I stood, trying to regain my composure. Pushing my grief aside proved difficult. I stood in a daze of exhaustion and emptiness.

Luvinga played around with my hair, but because of the difference in texture she didn't know exactly what to do. Norgiana tried not to laugh while she watched.

"I really don't care what I look like—they can deal with a blotchy face and frizzy hair," I mumbled, trying not to wince in pain.

"Like we would let you go out looking like a fool," Norgiana snapped, stepping in to create a large, thick braid that fell down my back.

"I look ridiculous," I said. "This isn't what I'd normally wear. We don't wear this kind of thing in Michigan."

"No, absolutely not— you look like the strong and respectable woman you are," Luvinga protested. "Even if this is not the normal Human garb."

"We do not have what you wear on Earth with us. I can see if I can have some made, but try to get used to the way we dress," Norgiana added with a side-glance at Luvinga.

"I can work on that. It might take some time—"

"Whatever you say," I interrupted.

By the time we left my room I was already many hours late. Norgiana dragged me along. Luvinga and two guards I wasn't familiar with tried their best to keep up.

"No one will hold our tardiness against you, Kayin," she said as we dashed in and out of various hallways, avoiding the same bows I'd seen on the Vt9. "I believe we are all impressed that you are holding it together this well. Why, I have seen others fall apart in far less traumatic situations."

"That doesn't really make me feel any better," I snarled. "I did fall apart. It would be better to wallow in my grief alone and undisturbed—"

"Well, just try to keep up!" she said hotly.

"Fuck off," I spat.

She ignored me as we zipped through the palace. The rest of it was styled in the same type of decorative manner as my room, but with taller ceilings and more plants in large vases around the halls. Five windows overlooked various parts of the palace. Through one I saw a large garden. As we walked we passed various rooms and other hallways, I wondered where they all led.

We emerged from a dark passage to a large entryway overlooking the rest of the palace below. The steel of the infrastructure reminded me of the Vt9 with its round architecture and its various levels, but there was beautifully crafted ornamentation that pulled their history into the new millennium. The sight was oddly comforting: the past mixed with the present hinting at an unfolding future. The stories were filled with hope, with an eye on the positive things they'd done throughout history, like helping people, instead of focusing on the negatives, like destroying planets. I wondered where Earth would be placed in their history ...

As we descended a grand staircase, I grabbed my skirt, hiking it over my knees so I could watch my feet as I walked down slowly. I didn't need any more injuries.

Glancing up from my steps, I noticed more Shielders in this part of the palace—their purple eyes watching our every move as we descended. I couldn't blame them for staring. I was tiny compared to anything on their planet. I remembered when I first saw a Shielder on TV—I couldn't tear my eyes away from the screen. Besides, this might be as close as any of them would ever come to someone like me. My cheeks flushed at the thought.

Once we reached the bottom, we made a sharp turn to the right. A tall, massive doorway decorated with more intricate stories rose in front of us. This scene on the doors depicted another Shielder history that was different than the others. My stomached dropped as I realized it was a brief family history of the royal family.

I was fascinated; my jaw dropped. *I wonder where their mother is,* I thought, *they never mention her.* I was curious, but it was a private family matter. Still, next time I was alone with Luvinga, I would ask. Finding out that Norgiana and Naluba were twins was shocking enough because it was extremely rare in Shielder biology, but to not mention a mother? That was an entirely different matter. Parents were the prized members of a family—they were the glue that kept the whole unit together. To have one missing left a large hole in the system.

Prince Naluba appeared in front of us, blocking my view.

He was just as gorgeous as I remembered, wearing a long black cape connected to this brass-colored plated armor covering his whole body; the effect was intimidating. His hair was halfway pulled up into a braided ponytail. However, his eyes were not as happy as I'd seen before; his jaw was clenched tight as he avoided my eyes.

"Do not worry, brother," Norgiana teased him with a slight smile. "No one has told her, and you will not be held responsible for her lack of knowledge. It will work out, I promise."

The two of them stared at each other, wasting even more time.

"But," I cut in, "if they don't punish you enough, you'll then have to deal with me, because I'm sick of this shit," I sassed. "You should've kept me in the loop."

Prince Naluba looked down at me, mortified. Norgiana snorted, trying to cover her mouth.

"What I have done can never be mended," he stated, looking deeply into my eyes, shame and sadness shining out.

Becoming just as uncomfortable as the twins, I picked at the sides of my gown. The three of us stood in silence. The other Shielders held their breaths, trying to act like they weren't curious about what was happening.

"Is it really as bad as all that?" I whispered.

The two shared a look, ignoring my question all together.

Naluba shifted where he stood, stating, "My father will be kind to you, and the Elder generals you have already met respect you greatly. Go in and do not be afraid." He stepped aside, the doors opening without command.

"Wait," I stopped him, "what should I do? What should I say? I don't know why I am here."

The twins locked eyes. Neither spoke.

"Oh, never mind. *More* secrets, I suppose. Let's get this over with." I walked by the two, pushing them out of my way.

The room was large and looked like an American court of law, with seating on the sides and a giant throne in the front. The throne was decorated with precious metals and jewels of all sizes and colors. It was a sight to behold, taking my breath away. I struggled to take in the majesty that the room represented but managed to keep walking in the direction of the throne. After all, I wasn't sure what I was doing, but I wanted to do it with conviction.

Many Shielders sat around the room and whispered in hushed voices. Most of them looked old and wise with wrinkles cracking their pale skin, but a few others looked young with barely a blemish. They murmured to each other in La'Mursian, staring at the three of us, barely concealing their curiosity. They never let their eyes wander from my small form.

Walking on eggshells, I thought about turning around and running out of the room screaming, but I continued with both royals at my sides. I felt better knowing they were there with me, but I still struggled to trust them. One had drugged me into unconsciousness, and the other had done something I supposedly could never forgive; there were too many secrets and too few answers.

With a deep breath, I resisted my panic as my eyes fell upon the giant throne, the bile in the back of my throat disappearing.

Though he was much older with longer hair, the male sitting there looked like the older version of Naluba. He wore a gold-colored robe with a silver belt, rings on his fingers, and a large sword at his side. Even in his old age, I was pretty sure he could fight with the best of them. I didn't see much of him in Norgiana, but you could tell they were related; she must have gotten her beauty from her mother.

The High Chancellor watched us walk toward him with a slight smile tugging at the corners of his mouth. He showed all his emotions through his eyes, like his son, but Norgiana definitely had his smile. The royal looked pleased to see his children, but sad, his face darkened by worry. The curves of his mouth were tight as if he were trying to keep his innermost thoughts to himself—I'd seen this look many times on the faces of the twins.

The twins' father rose to greet the assembly, causing the rest of the room to follow. Surprised by his quick movement, I stopped suddenly, both twins running into me. Naluba grabbed my arm to stop me from falling over. A giggle or two rang out through the crowd, but with one fierce look from the High Chancellor, everyone quieted.

"Thanks," I whispered to my savior.

He smiled, giving my arm a light pat.

"Greetings, Sorg Aves, and welcome to our humble planet," the High Chancellor said in perfect English, extending his arms in welcome. "I am High Chancellor Nurginlo, ruler of Selucia and its surrounding planets. I trust my children have been taking good care of you." He looked at each of them. They bowed in response.

"Of course, your majesty," I said, trying to bow as I had seen the Shielders do so many times. "They are, um, very nice and hospitable." I itched to say more, but I held my tongue. I smiled faintly back to the High Chancellor, trying to convey true gratitude.

"Good! I am glad to hear it. I hear we owe you many thanks for helping my son. I daresay you have saved his life. I am grateful— Selucia is forever grateful," he said, and beamed as the room erupted in whispers of appreciation.

"Oh, it was nothing," I glanced in Naluba's direction. "Anyone would've helped."

"I doubt that," Naluba said quietly in my ear.

I gave him a long side-glance, annoyed that he underestimated Human nature.

Chancellor Nurginlo raised his hands to silence the room as he continued, "Either way, thank you. We are grateful," he said, sitting back down, the rest of the room following his lead. "We have much to discuss, my dear one. Where would you like to begin?"

"Well, you see, your Majesty," I began, caught off guard. "I'm not really sure myself. I'd like to know everything—at least everything that you know—about Earth. You see, I'd like to get back home as soon as possible. So, whatever you have to say, I'll listen, but mind you, sir, I'll be leaving Selucia. No matter what."

His face contorted, the corners of his mouth falling even lower. Naluba seemed to want to step forward, but thought better of it. Norgiana swayed back and forth. The crowd began whispering again.

The High Chancellor broke through the murmurs, "*Sorg* Aves, you have been very patient with us and for that we respect your wishes, but I am afraid we have done you a great disservice by keeping you ill informed.

"As you can imagine, with any kind of war there will be immense losses. On our side we have lost powerful soldiers and trusted allies. For you and your people, I am afraid it is much worse. I am not sure how to phrase this, so I will be blunt. Earth has been captured and, from what we can gather, destroyed. It appears you have lost the only home you have ever known."

A chill ran down my spine as the hair on the back of my neck stood on end. Tears escaped my eyes. My shaking intensified as adrenaline took over, keeping me in place.

He continued, "We may have asked too much of your kind by coming to your planet to make a treaty, but we thought it would be for the best. After all, as La'Mursians we value all forms of life in our galaxy—we did not foresee a problem. Since your kind wanted to use our technology and we wanted to gain new allies, it was a peaceful and powerful bond—even if most of the Humans were unaware of our existence. Throughout our connection over the last several decades, the entire galaxy lived in harmony and peace while Earth gained new knowledge.

"Just recently the Galactic Royal Court, a group of all the leaders of the galaxy, came together to include your small planet into its protection. It is a long process, but Earth was close to joining as a contributing member of the Court. If we had been successful, the Court would have been able to intervene long ago, yet before the move forward, the Temorshians decided that they would control and own Earth."

"Why?" I interrupted. "What did we ever do to them? As far as I understand, Earth is small compared to planets like this one. We do not have anything you can't find here or on similar planets."

"They lost their planet to death and disease; they did not honor and protect what they were given. Therefore, they have been hovering around in space for many decades," Chancellor Nurginlo answered unequivocally. "Because they are a greedy and malicious group of beings, they believed they could overpower your planet and take it into their command." The Chancellor paused, shifting in his seat. "Your planet, powerless to stop them, could have avoided all of this if the Court had granted them entrance, but a part of that agreement is for the entire population to be aware of and agree upon the alliance.

"The Temorshians searched for your planet for many years," he said, moving on. "Luckily, we were the only creatures who knew of Earth's exact location, and we kept its whereabouts hidden. Norgiana and other Galianias raced to your planet to explain to your leaders what was about to happen, but it was too late. A spy craft from the Temorshian fleet followed close behind, finally leading the rest to Earth."

A ripple of an intense anger flowed freely over my skin. I clenched my fists, my nails grazing my skin, causing pain enough so I could focus. Neither Naluba nor Norgiana stepped beside me to comfort me.

The High Chancellor continued, aware that I was growing restless, "That is where our plan for evacuation came in. Unfortunately, your leaders did not think it was necessary to tell all of the population in time. Therefore, we were unable to send ships to evacuate the whole planet before the arrival and in the end, your leaders thought it would be better to fight these creatures than to flee. After all, who wants to leave their home? It took the Temorshians a long time to reach your galaxy, which bought us time to plan and prepare for the war—"

Without thinking I interrupted him, "I'm sorry, Your Majesty, I know all this … What is happening now?"

He looked at me sharply. The murmurs of the Elders increased during the silence that followed. Norgiana shifted, reaching out to put a hand on my shoulder. I could tell she wanted to comfort me, but I shrugged away from her touch.

"I don't need your pity," I hissed.

High Chancellor Nurginlo cleared his throat, "Well, then. I heard that you had obtained a bad head injury, and therefore you were unconscious, unable to witness what happened after you met my son?" He looked to Naluba, who nodded.

He looked even sadder but carried on in a lower voice, "Are you aware that we evacuated your leaders out of the Earth's atmosphere the day before the Temorshians arrived?"

"Yes, I was made aware of it, but like you said, the planet was kept in the dark. Where are they now? Can I speak with them?"

The room fell silent. The twins stiffened at my side. The chill in the air was thick, causing my heart to skip a beat.

"That ship," he paused, "was supposed to meet with the rest of our fleet on the port planet, Orrendad." The Chancellor moved in his seat again. He seemed to be picking his words with more care than before. "It never made it."

"What happened to it?" I looked back at his Majesty's face, unable to comprehend what he was trying to tell me. Losing my balance in my confusion, I faltered. Naluba grabbed my waist, his hands resting on my hips. They stayed there while Norgiana patted my shoulder again.

"From what we gather," their father said, "the Temorshians tracked down the vessel and destroyed it, leaving Earth with no prime ministers or presidents or anyone capable of running what you call countries."

I couldn't breathe. I tried my hardest to fight back another wave of tears, but it was no use; they fell silently down my cheeks. Norgiana wrapped her arm around me, and Naluba came closer as well, his hands still firmly on my waist.

Nurginlo stood up, taking only a few steps to reach us, his face distorted by pain. "There is more, my young one," he responded in a low voice, laying a hand on my shoulder.

I choked back tears and readied myself by looking up into his dark purple eyes. I allowed myself to lean against the twins.

"We sent many ships down to Earth to collect your people—to save as many as we could before the attack. I am so sorry, my dear. They, too, were supposed to meet on Orrendad ... "

The whispers from the Elders grew louder.

Gasping for breath, I willed myself to look up into Nunginlo's beautiful face; he was fighting back tears as well. I turned toward Norgiana, who fought back her own. I felt Naluba tighten his grip.

"We were able to gather almost half of Earth's population. But ... but I am afraid that the Temorshians have destroyed those ships as well," whispered the High Chancellor.

Pulling away from the Turshkin twins, I emptied the contents of my stomach. I heaved until there was nothing left. Still bent over from the pain in my stomach, I heard Naluba call for *nanuna*—water—and a chair. Hot, angry tears fell freely as I held myself, shaking violently. Another round of vomit escaped my lips.

My mind picked up fragments of the rest of his news, "A handful of ships escaped but were missing—we can presume they are gone," the High Chancellor told the council. "Earth is a hostage. Most of the landmasses are destroyed or heavily damaged. Earth is now a shadow of itself—the beauty of it lost.

"We are not sure how many survivors there are left," the High Chancellor Nurginlo finished. "Now we must work together to help your planet, Kayin Aves. Even if the laws of the Court do not apply to Earth, they have attacked La'Mursians!" he yelled to the crowd, raising his fists in the air.

Cries erupted, as Elders spoke in their language.

Norgiana moved me to the seat they brought in. I sat down feeling empty, the effects of shock apparent to everyone. She placed a glass of *nanuna* in my hands. "Drink this, it will help."

"More sedatives?" I asked.

She snorted, while the chamber bust into open dialogue about what could be done to counterattack the Temorshians—in and out of English. "I will meet you in your room later. I have work to do; I am sorry I cannot stay. You understand?"

"I'll be fine ... "

She rushed out of the room, her skirts flowing behind her.

Naluba sat down next to me, reaching for my empty hand. I allowed him to take hold, but it looked silly. His hands were more than double the size of my own. I felt nothing as he stroked my small fingers with care.

Naluba pushed back a fallen strand of hair, placing it gently behind my ear.

I couldn't look him in the eyes; I knew if I tried, I would begin to cry harder. I turned my head in the other direction; I wouldn't let more tears fall.

He tilted his head, leaning closer to the side of my face. He whispered, "I will make this right. I will do everything in my power to win back your planet."

"How?" I asked, barely recognizing the sound of my voice.

"The Royal Court will send aid, and I will go back. I will fight as I should have before."

I snorted. "I don't understand how any of this happened. How you and your kind lost everything for my people. You brought this upon us. Now, you think you can change things? You have lost, can't you see that?" I turned to look him in the eye. "Earth is destroyed, and for all I know I could be the only Human left! We should never have trusted any of you in the first place. You did this and now Earth is gone."

"I am so sorry," he exhaled.

"I need action, not sympathy. Earth needs help *now!* Not after some Court decides they can help. Do you understand me?"

"I do—we all do. You need to let us do what we do best. You have to trust our process," he said, gently squeezing my hand. "If you cannot do that, then at least trust me. I will make this right. I will take you back to Earth when it is safe."

"I think trusting you and your kind got me into this mess in the first place, sir," I snapped back into his face, pulling my hand away. "I don't want to wait until the planet is under La'Mursian control or some Court that means nothing to me decides I can fight for a planet that is already mine. I want to go back *now.* My planet needs me and waiting isn't doing shit!"

"I can have someone teach you to fight."

I thought for a moment, taken off guard. "I do want to help, Prince Naluba. I want to be useful. I want my planet back. When do we start?"

"Please, you do not need to use my title when addressing me. I will send someone to you. Norgiana will help you learn the ways of the galaxy and anything else you will need to know. I will do my best to assist as well ... We will make this right."

"Stop. I understand I helped you in whatever small way, but you don't owe me anything. Just give me the tools to do the most good—that's all I ask. Help me help my planet."

Naluba stared back at me. His eyes narrowed, all emotion voided by his intense stare.

I'd wounded him—I could see it clearly on his face.

He got up silently and walked out of the room. My eyes followed him as my heart broke into another million pieces.

The air hung heavily against my body. Nothing felt right; my lungs tried to keep pace with the beat of my heart, but I couldn't breathe, I couldn't think.

How could I go home when I didn't have a home to go back to?

[PART 2]

Henry Ricker
Baltimore, Maryland
Earth

I slammed the phone down on the kitchen table with absolute confidence. *I'm doing the right thing.*

The beep from the end of the phone call still hummed in my ears, drowning out the silence of the room.

"God, Henry, what an ass," I scoffed. My mother would be mortified, but it was the only thing I could do to stay solid in my resolve.

I knew I was being selfish, but I couldn't bear the thought of Kayin's life ending without trying to protect her. I had to do what I could to make it up to her, to make up for everything I had done that had put us both in this situation.

Tears stung my eyes as the pain of heartbreak washed over me. A large lump formed in the back of my throat. *You love her—you've always loved her. We should have never broken up.* With a heavy heart, I wiped my tears away with the back of my hand.

I grabbed my old workout bag, throwing items into it: shirts, underwear, and pants. I had no idea what the Army would require, but they could deal with my ignorance. After all, I was offering to fight for the planet. Nobody would care what I was wearing.

The fight against the Temorshians would be a defense of tremendous proportions and, frankly, the military could use anyone willing to take up arms. In the beginning the government had tried to reinstate the draft. It never happened—there were too many protests—but it scared plenty of young men and women into enlisting anyway. Some brave souls enlisted right away, but others, like myself, waited or ignored the military completely. Back then, I didn't feel like I needed to serve in that way. Instead, I gave money and donated food to the various shelters. We were all hoping that the Shielders would figure out a way to stop the invaders before we had to get involved in an interstellar war.

No one is taking my planet! I thought with an air of confidence only a Human could have.

I took one last look around my house. I hoped this whole thing would be done and over with soon. The country, no, *the world*, wanted to go back into our cocoon of ignorance.

I thought back to all my regrets in life, especially things with Kayin all those months ago. Neither of us had been willing to give up our careers, and while we respected each other's decisions, leaving her was the hardest thing I'd ever done.

I should have stayed. I could have protected her and made sure we lived through this together.

I looked over my shoulder one last time before leaving the house with a renewed sense of purpose. Already hearing the traffic a mile away, I climbed into my beat-up car and looked toward the future.

While stuck in traffic, I took my last few hours of free time to make many calls to family and friends. Some said their goodbyes and shared their love, while some told me of their plans to fight back. Either way, it was difficult to swallow.

"Nick?" I asked, the line already crackling from static. "Can you hear me?"

"Yeah, man, I'm here," he said. "Just got a minute to talk, though."

"That's fine. How—how are you?" It'd been months since we'd properly spoken. My brother had been deployed for almost a year, serving in the Air Force over in the Middle East. Even before *their* arrival he'd always wanted to be a military man.

"As well as I can be," he answered. "You know how it is … "

I didn't, but I continued, "I'm glad I caught you. There was something I wanted to tell you. I know you're busy, but—"

"Henry, don't act like this is the end. We both know we're ready for whatever comes our way," he said flatly. "What are your plans?"

"I know, but I can't help but worry. You might be ready for war, but the rest of us aren't. No one knows what's coming except for those assholes."

"They aren't that bad, man. I like the tech they brought, and even if they are humorless, they're smart. Give them a chance. Look, I have to go, I don't have much time, and I still need to call Mom—you know how she worries."

"She mentioned she hadn't heard from you. Be careful, her nerves are shot, and she's beside herself." We snickered; she was always beside herself, but now she wouldn't be with her two boys—it broke her heart beyond measure. "When the fighting starts, take care of yourself—don't do anything heroic."

He snorted. "Henry, it won't get that bad, man!"

"Nick, don't do that. I love you—you're my brother. Stay safe, will you?" I pleaded with him.

"I'll do my best, bro. I—I love you, too. Get to a shelter or something. Talk after, okay?"

"Stay safe, man. I love you." Tears pricked my eyes. I wiped them away.

"I always do."

I pushed all unpleasant thoughts from my mind. I was strong, but dealing with feelings wasn't my greatest ability—burying them was. I was able to wipe the first batch of tears away, but the second was harder to ignore.

"Come on, asshole, merge!" I yelled, frustrated behind the wheel. "I see your signal light, I'm literally letting you in!"

The jeep stalling traffic looked as though it was second-guessing its decision to exit the highway—half in the lane, half out, making its sad attempt at figuring out its life. At the last minute, it pulled out of the exit lane altogether, speeding away in defeat.

"Are you fucking kidding me?" I squawked. "All that time wasted for a change of heart? Fuck me."

Deciding I was in a good place to walk the rest of the way, I got off too. I wasn't the only person with the idea; many families and other lone pedestrians walked in the direction of the military base.

It troubled me to see families. People needed to go to shelters, not here.

There were shelters everywhere around the country. A law had been passed last month requiring shelters every 15 to 20 miles. They were big, ugly buildings made of some material brought by the Shielders to protect and support life.

I parked my car on the side of the road with the others—a sign of the sheer number of citizens making their way to the military base. I followed the crowd for a few miles until I could see the outline of a military post.

The base didn't impress me by its size; it looked like the many sheltered areas that had popped up around the country: cold, big, and square. It had been set up in haste with a few buildings here and there, along with a large hanger for the rest of the military's equipment. I glimpsed the shape of the Shielder ships in the distance.

I could hardly see over the ocean of people waiting in line.

As I made my way closer to the entrance, I could see lines for various needs. One for veterans who were willing to reenlist, another for families and civilians, and one for people like me—lost and late to the party.

Once in line, I looked around, trying to avoid the anxious faces around me.

A few Shielders stood inside the fence. They were hard to miss: tall, slender, pale-skinned. They were gigantic creatures, but visually appealing to some. I never thought they were beautiful—too sickly and ungodly thin. It was hard for me not to stare. Graceful and elegant, even if they *did* look sick, and menacing with their big bodies.

As I watched, they spoke in their language, not paying any attention to the Human panic surrounding them. I would love to learn La'Mursian, but it would take time I didn't have.

When one caught me staring, I spun away and tried to focus my attention on the line.

The armed forces must be planning on leaving some Shielder fighters with us on the ground, I thought bitterly. *Those fucks better not fuck this up for us.*

I waited for over an hour, watching people come and go. *Mostly go.* It seemed they were turning more people away than anything. Granted, the line for families and veterans moved quickly, but the line for volunteers crawled, and few individuals were let into the compound.

As I got closer, I tried to eavesdrop to get as much information as I could before it was my turn. The disorder made it difficult to listen to an entire conversation happening barely five feet away.

"I heard they're already here," someone whispered. "They're just waiting up there."

"Hush, there's no way," his partner responded.

"New reports say it's all a hoax," another yelled to his wife. "We're wasting our time here."

As my eyes surveyed the chaos, they fell upon people being escorted away by Shielders. They were nonviolent, thankfully, but the tense movements hid the hatred and fear lurking underneath. I recalled the panic riots months before; one false move by a Shielder and things would turn sour.

Had I made a mistake yet again?

"Next!" a soldier yelled, breaking my concentration. The solider taking my driver's license was young—too young. He couldn't be more than nineteen years old; he still had his baby face.

"Do you have any experience firing a weapon, laser or traditional?" he asked, avoiding my eyes.

They upgraded to lasers now? I thought, startled. *Wow, I am way behind the times.*

The young man looked up at me. "Sir?"

"No, I'm sorry. I haven't ever had the opportunity. I just—"

"Do you have any computer training or experience working with advanced technology?" he snapped. Annoyed or tired, I couldn't tell, but either way he looked exhausted underneath the rough exterior he was trying to portray.

"I can work a computer—I know how to do some programming but as for the *advanced technology*—no, again, I'm sorry. I just play around with—"

"Spare me the story," he said. "I'm sorry to do this, but we won't be needing your services. If you need redirection to a—"

"Wait, what the fuck? Are you *kidding* me?" I interrupted him in turn. "That's *it*? Why? Because I don't fit into some mold, you won't allow me to join the fight?" I asked with a rage I hadn't anticipated. "Where's your superior? Who can I talk to—this is fucking ridiculous!"

"I'm sorry, sir. There's been a huge influx of civilians willing to help. Unfortunately, if they're not prepared for what is about to happen, we can't use them. You, sir, are one of those people. Your country thanks you anyway," he deadpanned. "Now, please sir, make your way to one of our various shelters. *Next!*"

Just like that, I was dismissed.

I stood with my mouth gaping open, pulled away by two other soldiers.

I burned with rage. *What am I going to do now?*

Being pushed aside by another soldier, I fought to stay, barely hearing what he was saying over the cries of the growing crowd.

"What?" I asked. "How does this help Earth if its people can't even be part of the fight?"

"Trust me, sir," the soldier said. "We have everything under control. You can put your faith in us, sir."

I raised my eyebrows, jerking my arm away from his reach. "You trust *them*?" I probed. "Do you trust the Shielders?"

His smile faltered a little, but he regained his sense of decorum, his eyes wrinkled with little sleep. "Yes, sir, I do. They're knowledge-able on strategy and their equipment is, well, out of this world!" He laughed at his own joke, stopping when he noticed I wasn't laughing. "What about you?"

"I ... I don't know ... "

"I've spent enough time with them. They're nice—stiff and humorless—but respectful. Give them a chance, okay? Give *Humanity* a chance. We can save our planet—it's the only one we have, and we won't let them take it. Good luck to you, sir. Get some-place safe." He patted me on the back and walked off.

The noise mixed with the bodies moving around created pande-monium. I was left standing in the middle of it all: families running around, people shouting, and others looking lost and calling to people in the crowd. Time had slowed to a crawl, and there I was, lost in the middle of it.

The thought of being useless once again tore at me, like an uncontrollable itch I couldn't scratch.

My Plan B was the only option: I was going back to Michigan.

The crowds were getting thicker as I made my way back to my parked car, pushing past everyone, making them get out of the way. I wanted to stop and tell them the truth of what awaited them; instead, I kept my mouth shut.

I glanced to my side, feeling menacing purple eyes watching me, as if the Shielder knew what I was planning but didn't believe in my mission. A chill ran down my spine. I stared back, my growing hatred for them fueled by my desire to get back home. They did this to us. If they'd left us alone, Earth wouldn't be facing a war it'd never be ready for or worse.

I was annoyed I had wasted all my time on this foolish mission, yet relief grew within me. I was glad I didn't have to fight. I planned on making it back to Kayin before the Shielders started the war. I was going to make things right between her and me. Once I was at her side, I would never leave it again.

My new goal made my heart race, causing me to pick up speed. I was in such a hurry I knocked down an older gentleman who had walked into my path.

"Watch where you're going, son!" yelled the old man, stumbling into his wife.

"I'm sorry!" I yelled back, not turning around to help them.

It took me thirty minutes to make it back to where I thought I had left my parked car. I looked around for anything familiar, positive I'd made it far enough, but saw nothing.

I kept walking back and forth for another fifteen minutes.

Pieces of shattered glass lay on the ground, sparkling in the setting sun, in place of my car. People were getting desperate; the scariest thing on Earth is a Human in a state of desperation. No one had anything to lose any more—it was beginning to show.

I yelled, furiously dropping my bag. "Why? Why is this happening to me!"

"Do you need a ride?" a kind and compassionate voice asked, scaring me out of my skin.

I turned. It was the same man I'd run into earlier. I looked over to his wife; she appeared hesitant, her eyebrows knotted in a grim scowl.

"I'm so sorry about earlier," I tried to explain, "I didn't mean to, I was just in—"

He waved his hand. "No need to worry about that nonsense, Roxanne and I are fine. I figured whatever it was you were so concerned about couldn't wait," he said with a slight smile. "My name is James Glen and this is my wife, Roxanne. Just Jim and Roxy for short." He winked.

"No, he certainly may not," interrupted Roxanne Glen, "Mrs. Glen will do, young man." She turned to her husband. "Oh, please, James, do we have to take him with us?"

"Come now, Roxy, you know we can't just let him stay here. The boy has nothing, and we can offer him a ride. We have the room. Besides, what's with all the Jesus gospel you're always telling me about? What would Jesus *do, Roxy?*" he reminded her gently.

I tried not to laugh, but it felt good to have a release from the obvious mess around us. I was beginning to think that Mr. Glen was my guardian angel. He was a good-looking fellow, with wrinkles around his eyes, and dressed as if we were still in the 1950s. He was one of the lucky ones who had aged well, which made it difficult to guess his age. His wife was another story. The years had not been kind to her; she looked like a hag with a bad attitude. She had a short, no fuss, snowy white hairdo. With a flair for fashion, she stood cross-armed, wearing a yellow raincoat and fitted jeans with baby blue moccasins.

"I would really appreciate it. I was going to try to make my way up to Michigan, my home state, until I found that my car had been stolen," I said, and reached to take Mr. Glen's hand. "My name's Henry Rickner."

Mrs. Glen's stare could burn a hole through anything. She didn't lift her hand to meet my extended palm. Instead, she turned to her husband, continuing her tirade, "Don't you dare use the Bible against *me,* James Howard Glen! Jesus certainly would take anyone in, but I don't think he would be so trusting at a time like this!"

I wondered if she really paid attention in church.

"This is the perfect time to help someone in need, Roxanne," Mr. Glen said, putting his arm around her narrow shoulders. "I'm not hearing another word about it. Henry will come with us to Ohio. I hope that works for you?" he asked, looking embarrassed by his wife's behavior.

"Would that work for me?" I muttered back. The sheer hope of being reunited with Kayin made me smile. "Oh, that would be wonderful, Mr. Glen. I can manage the rest of the way. Thank you so much! I'm forever indebted to you and so grateful!" I jumped on him, enveloping him in an enormous bear hug.

Mrs. Glen groaned, walking away from my crazy antics. Jim rolled his eyes and gave me the signal to follow.

10

"Where were you when you first found out about the aliens?" I asked, kicking a stone out of my way, walking toward their vehicle.

"Let's see ... it was a Sunday, right, Roxy?" Mr. Glen asked his wife.

She looked at him from the corner of her eye. "Yes, it was, we were just getting home from dinner with friends when Sarah called." She was good at adding her two cents here and there when Mr. Glen would get a detail wrong.

Mr. Glen had a way of making me feel like an old buddy. He was an easy man to talk to, and our conversations flowed easily.

"Who's Sarah?" I inquired.

"Our daughter," Mrs. Glen snapped.

"Where were you?" Mr. Glen asked, returning the same look his wife had given him.

"I was out, too," I swallowed hard. "I was at a bar." I didn't mention it had been on a date with someone other than the woman I loved, but it was that same night I realized I'd made a terrible mistake. "Why were you turned away at the base?" I asked.

"I'm too old, and they didn't have accommodations for Roxy. Being totally honest, I wasn't sure I wanted to get involved, and I sure as heck didn't want to see her get shipped somewhere alone."

"I wouldn't have let them take me!" Mrs. Glen stated. "Let them try and separate us. Good luck with that."

"If you didn't want to get involved," I interjected, trying to avoid a fight, "why did you try?"

"I fought in the Vietnam War—drafted, unfortunately. I wasn't a very good soldier then, and I'm certainly worse now. Hippie first, soldier second. We believed in freedom and love for everyone. We had a lot of, um, *fun* back then." He laughed; he had a hearty laugh. "I did my duty because it was the right thing to do—just like now. I didn't agree with the war or the reasons we were there, but it didn't matter. No one asked us, they just sent us to meet our fate." He sighed, pondering his memories. "Thought I would try and do my part if they'd have me."

"How did you two meet?" I asked, quickly changing the subject.

Mr. Glen snapped out of his memories, "We met back in high school, though we didn't travel in the same circle. I think Roxy told me once she hated me? Do you remember that?"

"Of course I do," she yelled behind her, while walking a few paces in front of us.

It was a shame she didn't have a better attitude, but I wasn't going to push the issue with her or her husband, remembering how a few short hours ago I was in a foul mood too. Stress does weird things to people.

"You never paid attention in school—always mouthing off to the teachers," she continued. "It wasn't until you went away to Vietnam that you came back a changed man."

"Hey, look," Mr. Glen whispered, pointing ahead to two people dressed in the same dark colors. "They're wearing that Shelter uniform. We should ask them if they know anything new. It isn't smart to be out of the loop for too long."

"Good idea," I muttered.

"Roxy, wait up!"

Mrs. Glen sauntered away from the two of us. "I'm not waiting for too long—don't try to squeeze them into our van, either!" she hissed, turning on her heels.

"Excuse me," Mr. Glen shouted to the workers. "We're on our way home, do you have any news about what's going on up there?"

The pair glanced at each other.

"We don't have much," the female said. "Nothing's really changed over the last twelve hours."

"Workers like us have been trying to evacuate as many people as we can into the shelters, but no one seems to have much luck," the other told us.

"Civilians aren't concerned with the war that's about to take place," his female companion added.

"Everyone seems to be under the impression that the Shielders will take care of everything, and the Temorshians will not make it to Earth. Of course, this isn't the case," he murmured.

The female he was with paled at his words.

"What do you mean?" Mr. Glen asked. "It can't be as bad as all that. The rumors—"

"Are real," the male volunteer stated. "The Temorshians are going to reach Earth in a matter of hours."

"The Shielders' first line of defense has already been destroyed," whispered the woman.

My stomach dropped as the Glens reached for each other. My chest tightened, causing my heart to skip a beat. I couldn't breathe. We looked at each other, unable to form coherent words.

"Come with us," they begged.

"No, thank you," Mr. Glen said with a sad smile. "We are not going to forsake our families for the slight chance of being safe in a shelter. Besides, I think it would be safer to stay in our own little group."

Than to stay in a shelter with hundreds of other people, I added in my head. Mrs. Glen didn't give the impression she was fond of that idea either, so we continued on our way at a quicker pace.

"I'm pretty surprised the Shielders were defeated so quickly since their advanced technology seemed to not have any limitations," I whispered to Mr. Glen. "Earth can't stop an invasion of this magnitude. There's no way we can slow the Temorshians down."

"We're in a terrible position, Henry," added Mr. Glen. "We have to keep moving and hope for the best. Let's just focus on getting out of here."

My feet ached with blisters by the time we reached the Glens' van. Their van was in good condition, a Chrysler Town & Country, dark green and packed full of their most valuable treasures. It was parked in an alley close to the highway—a smart and safe idea.

"Let me just move some things around to give you some room," Mr. Glen said, opening the door to shift boxes around.

While he worked, I looked at Mrs. Glen, who was eyeing me as though she might be releasing some of her anxiety about me. She gave me a small smile as she got into the front seat; so small, in fact, perhaps I imagined her newfound kindness.

It took Mr. Glen five minutes to get everything where he liked it, making sure I'd be comfortable.

"I'm not worried about being comfortable. I'm just grateful to have a ride," I said over and over.

"We've been coming this way for years. Sarah and Howie—that's her husband—live just outside of Columbus near Lancaster." Once we made it to the rural areas—filled with countless farms and wide-open fields—Mr. Glen didn't mind doubling the speed limit.

"Since our grandsons were born," Mrs. Glen explained, "we've been making this drive countless times throughout the years." The only thing Mrs. Glen wanted to talk about, I discovered, was her family—especially her grandsons, five-year-old fraternal twins.

Before I knew it, we were about to leave Maryland and make our way through Pennsylvania. The sky turned from a pale pink to a dark navy as stars began to dot the horizon. Mrs. Glen was settling down, too.

She would take the second shift of driving since she knew the way so well, and then I offered to take over sometime after that. I caught a glimpse of the two Glens eyeing each other. It was obvious they didn't want me to drive.

Accepting my fate as a passenger, I lay down, getting as comfortable as I could with the small space I was given.

The sun was low in the sky; so low, in fact, that I could barely see it. Beautiful colors of gold, pinks, and oranges made the sky look heavenly with the radiance from the last few rays of light. It took my breath away with the ebb and flow of subtle colors blending into themselves.

I relaxed, watching the last few rays of sunlight fade. As darkness started to envelop me, I began to think of my loved ones. I thought of my parents. I wondered where they were and if they would stay safe during the fighting. The last time I'd spoken with them, they were doing well and planned on staying home in their safe house. I knew they'd invested in a small one, but they'd never given me enough details to make me truly feel comfortable. For all I knew, it was a cheap copy. There were a few terrible souls out there that sold knockoff safe houses to countless buyers. I prayed they would live through this; that, somehow, planet Earth itself would live through this, too.

Kayin made her way to the forefront of my mind. I thought of her smile, her laugh, and the way her hand felt between my fingers. All the memories of her made it easy for me to dream about the past.

A new dream emerged through the chaos of my mind. When the war was over and the aliens left us in peace, I was going to ask Kayin to marry me.

In a deep, dreamless sleep, I was jolted awake by the hurried swerving of the vehicle. My eyes struggled to focus as my body felt stiff from my sleeping position. Adrenaline pumped ferociously throughout my veins, igniting my panic and will to survive.

Sitting up, I was restrained by my tight seatbelt, and the violent motion of the van caused me to flail around. Empty cups hit me in the head while bags smacked into me.

Screams, along with loud popping noises—reminding me of the shriek of fireworks—filled my ears. The popping noise grew louder and louder as the van hurled itself this way and that.

I tried to get a look outside, but the pitch-black view with flashes of light illuminating everything around us made it difficult to get my bearings. Through the flashes, I could make out the interstate laid over open fields. The vehicles on the other side stopped to watch the chaos outside.

"What's going on?" I yelled over the commotion.

I glanced over to the driver's seat. Mrs. Glen was now driving—well, trying to drive without hitting anything. She was screaming at the top of her lungs as Mr. Glen tried to calm her down.

"You're all right, Rox, just take your foot off the pedal!" he yelled over the noise. She kept screaming, driving faster.

A huge explosion erupted overhead, lighting up the world like the sun, ending in seconds.

A chill ran down my spine. *That's not good.*

"Roxanne, stop! You are going to kill us all!" Mr. Glen yelled, "Stop now!" The van came to a screeching halt as the popping noise and flashing lights stopped at the same time.

We sat in silence for a few moments trying to calm our beating hearts. I focused to control my breath and formulate a coherent sentence, while Mrs. Glen panted heavily; tears fell down her cheeks. Mr. Glen held her hand, stroking it gently.

"W-w-what just happened? What is going on? What did I miss?" I asked, pushing panic away as hard as I could.

It took a moment for Mr. Glen to answer. "I'm not sure," he said, still holding his wife's hand and turning toward me. "I believe that's the Temorshians starting the fight, but I can't tell. It happened so quickly."

"I'm sorry," Mrs. Glen whispered softly, looking down in disgrace. Her energy had changed. She wasn't the hard bitch I had met anymore.

Mr. Glen pulled out a hanky for her. She smiled and wiped her tears away, eyeing me through the rearview mirror.

"Honest mistake, Roxy. Let's change seats, shall we?" he asked his wife lovingly. As they did, I looked around. I had no idea where we were or how close we were to Ohio. Once you leave the coast, every tree and field begins to look the same.

"If it was the Temorshians and the war has started, where are the Shielders? Where are our troops?" I asked no one in particular.

No one answered.

The three of us looked around for a clue. It was dark outside, the grass rustling in the wind as the breeze passed by. Traffic had become almost nonexistent.

Mr. Glen looked into the rearview mirror and met my eyes. "We are going to continue. We'll be crossing the Ohio border in about an hour or two. The sun will be up by then. But we have a little problem ..."

"Okay?" I questioned. "What is it? Is everything all right? Are *you* all right?" I asked, looking from Mr. to Mrs.

"Oh, son, I'm fine, it's not about me or Roxy. It's the van ... We may run out of gas before we make it to Sarah's house. The tanks we brought with us, well, they didn't hold much, did they?"

"It's been so hard to get gas these past few weeks. How did you manage?" I asked, amazed by the little luck we'd had. "Almost everything was reserved for the military, and the price had skyrocketed."

"Give an old man some credit, son. I have my ways."

"How far do you think we can go before we reach empty?" I asked.

"It depends. If we miss a lot of traffic, we could make it there in no time. Then we can say we worried for nothing, but with what just happened, who can say what we will encounter?" Mr. Glen said flatly. "All we can do is try and get through whatever is in front of us. I have one other small container of gasoline but that's if we can make it without encountering any more ... *problems*."

Shit, we'll be making it to Sarah's on foot.

"All right, let's do this!" I exclaimed. "I'm ready when you are."

With that, we continued on our way.

I wasn't interested in sleep anymore, my thoughts focusing on the explosion overheard. What was it? What did it mean for Earth? I kept thinking it was the Shielders practicing some war tactics, but that didn't seem right. Why waste energy and power for a few drills? I knew it wasn't the start of the war because there was no resistance from the Shielders nor was there any action from our end.

At least, I hoped it wasn't the start ...

I looked up. Stars dotted the sky as wisps of clouds passed slowly across the moon. I thought I could just make out the outline of a spaceship. Whatever had happened was not a good sign. I hoped we still had time to find somewhere safe to hide.

I was so consumed with my thoughts of the explosions and how to get back to Michigan that I hadn't realized that we had crossed the Ohio border without running out of gas. It was early morning. The sun was shining against the pale blue sky.

The Glens were making plans for the eventual early stop we'd make, but they were happy. I was happy for them too. I was glad they'd be reunited with their daughter and her family soon.

I was hoping with every ounce of my being that I would be as lucky as they were.

11

"**I** am so happy we made it!" Mrs. Glen shouted, bouncing in her seat.

"We're not there yet, dear, another twenty minutes or so," Mr. Glen responded; he didn't seem as thrilled.

All through the journey, Mr. Glen had been calm, cool, and collected. Not to mention optimistic, even when we were faced with immeasurable odds. Now he was silent, looking around every so often. If Mr. Glen was on edge, something wasn't right, and I wasn't going to ask to make things worse. Selfishly, I liked the change in Mrs. Glen; I didn't want to bring the mood down if she wasn't aware of the change in her husband.

Time crawled as we drove mostly in silence. Mrs. Glen periodically made remarks about certain landmarks or businesses they'd frequent when visiting in happier times. I tried to act interested, but Mr. Glen's silence kept me alert and concerned.

The van sputtered, chugging out a few bursts of energy, then slowing down as smoke bellowed from the hood. Jim managed to stop the van on the side of the road.

The smoke thinned as we came to a stop. Mr. Glen coughed

some of the polluted air out of his lungs. "Well," Jim sighed, "thankfully, we are not too far away from Sarah's home. We'll take what we absolutely need ... *right*, Roxy? And come back when we can for the rest. Scout's honor!" He got out of the car and stretched his arms.

I held my breath, waiting for her rebuttal.

Mrs. Glen unbuckled to jump out of the car. She pranced around as she grabbed her handbag with another small bag.

In a singsong voice she announced, "I'm ready! This is all I need—I can do without the rest. I can't believe we made it in such good time!" She walked away humming "These Boots Were Made for Walking" as she went.

Jim and I gaped at her as Mrs. Glen joyfully walked toward the home of her only daughter—without a word of protest.

I liked Mrs. Glen, but I finally realized she might not have a good grip on reality. In her fantasy world, this was just another trip to visit her family, and this war would not affect her small corner of the world. On the other hand, I didn't want to skip or sing. I wanted to *survive*.

I grabbed my bag and hopped out of the van, pushing the last twenty-four hours from my mind.

A cool morning began with the sun rising over the treetops. It was one of those mornings on which you and your loved ones would want to have a nice brunch on a beautiful terrace sipping bottomless mimosas.

I stretched, breathing in the sweet scent of grass. I tilted my head to examine the blue cloudless sky. My eyes widened, causing me to almost fall over from the awful scene ahead.

Dotted around the sky were outlines of black ships, the blackness engulfing everything around it. I could barely see the pale moon fading into the horizon.

I gasped, my heart stopping as I began to taste bile in the back of my throat.

"It's looked like that for the past forty minutes," Jim said next to me. "I didn't say anything because I didn't want to panic Roxanne or worry you, but it's starting."

"So soon?" I asked, trembling on the inside. "Everything that has happened in the last twelve hours pointed to war, but seeing this—*shit!*" A shudder made its way down my spine. "I wasn't expecting a real war."

"I don't know what I expected, honestly. But look," he said, pointing, "those ships are not La'Mursian."

Instinctively my fists clenched, digging into my sweaty palms.

"We have to hurry. We can't be out in the open when it begins." Jim turned to face me, looking me straight in the eye. "I read somewhere that the Shielders recommend the shelters or a safe house. Sarah has one—there's plenty of room."

"Do you think those two options will protect us from whatever is about to happen?" I asked. "Look at the sky, Jim. This is not what they told us about! There's no way. There's just no way we can survive this."

"I have no idea whether or not we can survive or if the house will hold," he professed, looking back at the sky, "but it gives us hope, doesn't it? That's all that matters right now. I have faith in the Shielders—I know they will protect us. If they can't, then I know my son-in-law and I can protect our family."

My heart sank. I owed him a lot for taking me this far, but he needed to know the truth.

"I'm afraid I haven't been quite honest with you or Mrs. Glen," I started, beginning to share with him all I knew from Kayin. I told him about the ships getting everyone off the planet and the real possibility the Shielders were useless.

Mr. Glen pondered and chewed over my words. We stood in silence watching the movement of the smaller ships in the sky.

Slowly, James Glen turned his attention to me. With sad eyes, he said, "I had a feeling something like that would happen. I wasn't sure what the government was thinking, but I knew it had to be sneaky like that. With all the time they had left you would think they would come up with a better plan." He sighed, patting my arm. "As for those other *aliens*, God help us all."

"Do you think we will have a chance to get on a ship?" I asked, the two of us following Mrs. Glen to their daughter's house.

Jim was silent for a while. My question, I could tell, weighed heavily on his mind.

He finally answered, "I would like to hope so, but if they're going to the big cities, our chances are low. Even if they did make it close to here, there would be no way to get there in time." He sighed. "Sarah's husband told me the other day that he is fully equipped to protect the family, if you know what I mean. He has guns—plenty of them. I know they won't be much against these Temorshians, but it could buy us time ... "

I digested Mr. Glen's words. His son-in-law had a solid plan but the thought of fighting one-on-one with aliens frightened me—the chance of surviving that type of attack would be grim.

"I'll help as much as I can," I said. "I need to get back to Michigan, but I will do what I can for you and your family. Especially after everything you have done for me."

Mr. Glen smiled, "Thank you, young man. You are a caring individual—rare in today's world. I know this must be hard for you. I'll hold you to nothing and give you what I can for you to reunite with your loved ones." He squeezed my shoulder. "We'd better hurry. Roxy is on a mission, and by God she's going to do it with or without us."

I laughed as we quickened our pace.

Everything around us was still giving off an eerie feeling. It could have been a beautiful little town, but with galactic war hanging over its head, it looked more of a ransacked ruin. The buildings were freshly painted, but scavengers had broken doors and windows while ripping off signage. Valuable goods were thrown out into the street in tatters.

"Is this place always this quiet?" I asked, trying not to be disrespectful.

"No, this is Main Street. It's usually busy. Let's hope people made it into those shelters and they're safe," Mr. Glen said, looking up and eyeing the sky. "This place was bustling with life—full of families on weekends. Now it looks like a ghost town."

With every step, more ships came into view. We moved through debris and parked cars, trying to avoid the constant need to watch the sky.

Jim continued, "I think because of the rumors, and now the ships, perhaps reality has finally scared enough people into realizing that war is imminent and the outcome will probably not benefit Earth." He sighed. "Our world will never be the same."

We walked in silence for half a mile, barely catching up with Mrs. Glen, who was blissfully unaware of her surroundings.

"Wait ... " Mr. Glen whispered. "Do you hear that?"

"I hear the wind?"

"No, listen."

Before I could answer, three men leaped out of nowhere. My heart jumped into my throat, causing me to choke on my breath. My mind raced but slowed as I watched in horror. They attacked Mrs. Glen with a blow to the head, grabbing her and knocking her body to the ground, her limbs flying helplessly around her small body.

Two of the men turned toward us, their eyes filled with a fury I'd never encountered before. I shuddered from their glare. The biggest of the three snickered at Mr. Glen and me.

Mrs. Glen's screams turned to cries of terror.

Something within me snapped. I pushed away the helplessness and without thinking, I lurched toward the group while Mrs. Glen yelled for her husband.

"Stop, Henry!" Mr. Glen shouted. "*Stop!*"

I stopped feet from the horrific scene, roaring, "We can't just let them—"

"Let me handle this, please. And calm down, this is no time for hysterics!" he hissed in my ear, walking slowly up to where I'd paused. He looked apprehensive, but his features settled into a determined, though pained, expression. "Please, we don't want to see anyone get hurt," Mr. Glen implored, turning his gaze to the men and then to his wife's face.

"We don't have anything you'd want!" I yelled. My fists curled into tiny balls, nails cutting my skin, while I resisted every impulse to run at the men.

Held tightly by a stocky man, Mrs. Glen was whipped around to face us. She looked ill as tears streamed down her face. Her eyes were large with fear, but they never left her husband.

My stomach dropped while rage filled my body, sending tiny shocks of electricity through me while the adrenaline pulsed through my limbs.

The smallest man in the group laughed, taking two steps toward me, playing with a knife in his hands, dry blood covering his clothes. The others looked the same, but somehow less intimidating.

"What brings you to the neighborhood?" the leader asked, pointing the blade toward me.

Mr. Glen stood to my left, standing tall, emboldened by his mission to save us. I hoped his army training was rushing back to him. I had no plan, I just wanted to save Mrs. Glen and get away from the assholes in one piece. We didn't need this bullshit, not when something much worse hovered in our atmosphere.

"We are only passing through," Jim said. "Our van broke down about a half a mile back."

"If you are looking for valuable items or guns, that's where you'll find them," I added. "If that's all you want. Keep the van."

"Just give me back my wife," Jim implored.

"You think we want your shit?" one of the hoodlums spit.

"Or your old hag of a wife?" laughed the other.

"That's enough," the leader hissed to his cronies. "You have nothing of value on you now? I can't imagine you fuckers would walk around without any kind of weapon. Do you have *food*?"

"There's money in my purse!" yelled Mrs. Glen. The man

holding her tightened his grip around her tiny body. She yelped in protest.

The man clenching the purse looked inside. He pulled out her wallet and pocketed it, smiling. He rummaged further, finding a small handgun hidden within.

"Where are the rounds?" he asked her.

"She doesn't have them," Mr. Glen answered. "She's afraid of guns. I put that in there just in case. The bullets are back in the van."

"We're supposed to believe *that*?" the leader sneered. "You look like you carry." He eyed me, his face reddening.

"I don't have anything like that," I said, grinding my teeth. "Go back to our van and take whatever you want. We don't have any of that shit on us."

"A likely story, asshole."

"He's not lying. We found him unarmed and ill-prepared on the road," Mr. Glen explained, reaching into his pocket. "Here, take this," he said, and pulled out a small Swiss army knife, tossing it to the ground at the leader's feet. "And this," he said, reaching into his back pocket and drawing another small handgun.

In one motion, Mr. Glen fired at the leader, hitting him in the chest. Blood exploded onto his companions, the dead body falling to the ground in a heap. He turned his focus to the man holding Mrs. Glen's purse, shooting him in the leg. The man let out a yell and fell sideways, dropping everything he'd confiscated. Mr. Glen repeatedly hit him over the head with the gun.

I threw myself at the other man, my fist colliding with his jaw. Mrs. Glen howled, using all her strength to pull away from her aggressor. The veins of her neck tightened as she escaped her captor. He was now free to turn on me.

Blood flowed freely from the side of his mouth as he threw his weight to yank us both to the ground. I hauled him down, trying to stay on top, but he was too heavy. We landed in a pile of limbs as we beat and scratched our way to victory. Neither of us could get a good handle on the other, which caused us to roll away from the others.

A gunshot rang out.

We froze for only a moment but continued to wrestle after the sound faded. He flung my head back, cracking it against the concrete. I lost focus as he wrapped his chubby fingers around my throat, squeezing my neck, inching closer to collapsing my trachea.

The world slowed as my vision blurred. The pressure closed my airway, while my heart beat wildly in my ears, air escaping my open mouth as I tried to gasp my last breath.

It stopped.

My vision cleared enough to see the man's shocked face. His eyes rolled back into his skull as blood spilled from his lips onto my face. I pushed him off, disgusted by the sight, the copper taste stuck in my mouth.

Gaining my breath, I looked up to see a familiar face.

Mrs. Glen reached out to help me up. She was breathing wildly, her eyes aflame from the adrenaline. I tried to speak, but the swelling in my throat had already begun.

"Don't try to talk," she murmured. "You'll only make things worse." She offered her hand again.

The two of us worked together to get me standing on my feet as the blood rushed to my head. I teetered for a moment until my vision returned to normal. I finally looked at the woman before me.

She was covered in crimson, a bloody knife held tightly in her other hand.

I stood there, mouth open, heart racing, the shock leaving my body.

"You ... you saved my life?" I whispered.

"We're running out of time. Don't you dare think I didn't notice those ships, James Glen, I saw them," Roxanne Glen said to the two of us.

The matriarch of the Glen family looked like a different woman: strong, daring, and able to take on the world with nothing but her own two hands and a knife. I could only admire the once frail-seeming grandmother who had turned into my savior. My respect for her grew tenfold as I appreciated every fine line on her face: a map of all the battles she had won in her life.

"We need to clean ourselves up. Give me his shirt to wipe my hands off," she ordered.

Without thinking, we did as she asked, doing the best we could to take care of the blood, though it was obvious we'd been in some kind of fight.

My throat was sore, but I could move my limbs—nothing had been broken. My head hurt, but I could handle it. Mr. Glen looked tired but relieved none of us were nursing wounds we couldn't mend. Mrs. Glen was, I couldn't believe it, glowing—peaceful even.

"You okay?" Mr. Glen asked me.

"A little shaken, but I'm fine," I murmured, trying not to strain my vocal cords.

"Good. That's good. We're lucky," Mrs. Glen observed, trying to wipe the rest of the filth off. "Let's try not to mention this to Sarah and the boys."

"Let me handle the family, all right?" Mr. Glen answered. "We should be able to explain all this and not cause a panic. But look, we need to hurry. The sky isn't getting any better."

"That's fine with me," I wheezed, still in a daze. "I still can't believe—"

"Let's go. We still have another mile to go!" Mrs. Glen interrupted.

"I have to thank you … "

"No, you don't, young man. I am quite positive you would have done the same for me—for either of us."

"That's true, but thank you. Thank you for saving my life."

Mrs. Glen tilted her head as she examined me. Her eyes looked sad, but held a sparkle of hope. She inhaled, finally saying, "You're welcome. I'm not proud, but these are difficult times. We do what we have to do."

I nodded, following the powerful matriarch until we finally reached Sarah's home. Two little boys looked out of the big window in the front of the house. The house was a ranch style from the early 1990's with a white fence and big front yard. The safe house waited in the backyard.

Sarah answered the door with tears and a smile, but faltered when she saw me. Mrs. Glen let go of her daughter just long enough for Mr. Glen to get in a quick hug. Sarah's grayish-blue eyes pinned me to the spot, her pixie cut clear of her glare. She eyed the blood on our clothes but said nothing.

When I was introduced, Sarah shook my hand with force—she definitely had parts of her mother's personality. "Nice to meet you, Henry. Let's get back inside. Being out here gives me the creeps." Sarah gestured for us to enter. "The boys have been glued to the window since they've been up," she told us as we walked to the house. "I thought Howie and I could keep them focused on something—*anything*—at least for a little while, but Matt ran to the window first.

"I've been a fucking mess waiting for you guys. What *happened?*" she asked as the boys ran to their grandparents. Again she eyed the blood, then me.

"So dirty!" squeaked one of the twins.

"Mom swore!" laughed the other innocently.

"Let's get inside," Sarah said with motherly authority. "And Mommy's sorry she said a bad word." She turned back to her parents, "You're so late, I was afraid ... "

The Glens tried to explain, but they were too focused on their grandsons. Matt and Mark were good boys but still young—naively excited about the situation, as children would be. They were too young to understand the dangerous predicament we faced. I thought the boys looked like their mother, but when I saw the husband, Howie Heggin, I changed my mind. He was a big guy with jet-black hair. He was intimidating but hospitable. The boys were built like their father, but had their mother's soft hair and eyes.

After all the hugs and kisses, we settled into their living room. A large couch faced the big window with a rocking chair in the corner.

There were plenty of ferns around the room, and even a small piano on the far wall. Various paintings of still lifes and landscapes lined the walls, alongside the smiles of wedding photos, baby pictures, and vacations. This was middle-class America at its best. It almost made me forget about the war, but looking outside, the ships were still visible, a harsh reminder of our new reality.

I sat on a chair near the piano, feeling like an invader while the family chatted about our misadventures. I felt as though I was ruining what could potentially be their last few moments together. I was grateful no one seemed to notice me in my small little corner of the room.

"Did you see the explosion last night?" Jim asked.

"Yes, we did," Sarah said. "Though we're not sure if it's a good or bad sign."

"I can only speculate," Howie answered, "I would say practice shots? We hoped it was just a false alarm. What do you think, Henry?"

"I can't say. Luckily, it wasn't the start of the fighting," I said. The Glens and Howie nodded.

"Why didn't anything happen here on Earth?" Howie asked, looking at his wife. "It's odd ... "

We sat in silence, letting the theories swirl around us.

Matt, who was sitting with his grandmother, interrupted our grim silence, "Did you paint, Pappy? Why are you all red?" he asked.

Mr. Glen continued, avoiding the reference to paint. "We left the van a mile or so back. We'll get it when it's better outside."

"I'll go get the van tomorrow," Howie said.

"I'll go with you, if you need help. Though if there's no fighting today, I plan on leaving early tomorrow morning. I hope you don't mind," I stated, looking at Jim.

Mrs. Glen and the Heggins looked at me in horror.

"You actually *want* to travel some more?" Howie asked. "I mean, I'm sorry, I don't know your story, but to actually leave security and venture out? You got balls, man."

"Let me explain," I said, continuing to tell them about my mishaps.

"You're more than welcome to stay with us for however long it is we're stuck here. That is, if you change your mind or can't leave. We have plenty of provisions," Sarah said with a sad smile.

Mrs. Glen nodded in agreement.

"You have all been so kind, but I have to do this. I'm so close to being reunited with my ... family—"

Explosions burst overhead.

The noise was loud—reminding me of fireworks—the shrieks filling my eardrums. The house shook as things fell off the walls. The boys began to cry. Mrs. Glen picked up Matt and Sarah ran to grab Mark. Mr. Glen, Howie, and I were up and at the window within seconds.

Sure enough, the sky was filled with bright lights and dark, black clouds. Pieces fell from the destroyed vessels and began to enter our atmosphere. The burning debris looked immense even from our distance. On the horizon, I could see other, smaller ships rising up to meet the ones doing the fighting, and others hovered above the tree line.

"There's a Shielder base not too far from here," Howie explained, yelling over the noise. "We were afraid this would happen. All this shit overhead."

"This is how it starts," Mr. Glen affirmed, heavy with worry. "Come on, gents, let's join the rest of the family in the safe house," he said, then turned and quickly walked out of the room.

Howie and I stayed for a few more seconds. "I have guns, Henry. Do you know how to work a weapon?" he asked me.

I turned to face him as a large explosion popped my eardrums.

"Do you think it will come to that?" I countered, rubbing my ears. The bookshelf fell over, smashing all of the family photos.

"Yes, yes, I do. Just look at it up there," he yelled back, "It looks like a mess. Plus," he paused, "we should be prepared for anything."

He had a point, I thought, my stomach dropping. *I hope Kayin is safe.*

"I will help defend your family to the best of my ability while I am here, but as soon as I can ... I'm leaving. I have my own family to think about; I hope you understand."

The battle grew louder by the second. Explosions of various colors—orange, green, and dark blue—thundered overhead.

"Trust me, I understand," Howie yelled back after the noise died down. "I would feel the same way, if I were in your shoes. Come on, we better get in the safe house—I hope it holds up. Just look at all that debris coming down!" He pointed to the falling pieces.

One came down, smashing a tree and causing it to crash down. The house shook again as the last painting hanging on the far wall shattered to the ground. Up above, a small ship exploded into a million pieces. Bits of debris fell across the street, splitting a nearby tree into two.

I turned to follow Howie and the others into the safe house. As I went, I prayed my family and friends were as safe as they could be. I pictured Kayin with her family in their safe house: safe and calm.

I knew she was safe—she just had to be.

12

There are certain situations in life in which you should never find yourself alone with strangers—it complicates things. When shit hits the fan, you have to try to react calmly or, at the very least, not lose your mind too horribly so that others think about voting you off the island.

Having your world fall down around you in a chaotic, undefined mess is one of those times.

I fought my natural instincts to cry like a baby, covering my mouth with my hand to avoid screaming. My lungs fought to keep themselves full, while my insides twisted with every explosion, thump, and crack coming from outside. I was using every ounce of my being not to freak out and lose control.

Howie and I barely made it to the safe house before the war erupted outside. After we closed and locked the door, everything started to crash down around us, leaving the feeling we were going to open the door to a new world just like Dorothy, but it wouldn't be in bright Technicolor.

The bangs caused by the chaos outside made sounds with such force it was hard not to jump every time something smashed the safe house. Debris kept hitting the walls with thumps and crashes against the metal. I was sure we faced certain death. Shortly after every bang or scrape on the side of the house would be a swishing noise. This was frightening because the swishing—a sharp sound with angry undertones—confused us.

"What is that?" Sarah yelled over the noise.

"I don't know! Metal? Some type of debris?" Howie answered.

"It's producing such a sound—it was *not* manmade," shouted Mr. Glen. "Let's just be thankful we aren't outside to witness it!"

My mind started to race. *What was happening with the Shielders? Who was winning?*

The noises and bangs from outside of the safe house terrified the rest of the family as they reached out for one another, but the noise pierced my soul. They had each other; I was alone. I tried to remain as calm as possible, but it was no use. My heart raced, sweat flowing like a river, while my body shook violently. I could barely use my limbs to keep myself upright when the whole structure moved with a crash of debris.

As the chaos raged on, I tried finding peace, knowing I was in a *safe* house. Truthfully, however, it reminded me more of a small tin can instead of something that was built to protect. It was filled with all the basic needs to live through anything, but with limited space— made for two adults and maybe one child. The space was cramped but it was doing its job for now—saving us from the terror that awaited us outside of the four walls.

The shelter was crammed full of dry goods to last several months, each can or box labeled to depict the prize inside. I noted the far wall was lined with shelves of ammo. Close by, various guns dangled. In each corner stood a slender tube from ceiling to floor. On the side in neat letters read the word "Water". Sarah and Howie had done a good job at stocking up for whatever awaited the family in the future.

As time crept slowly ahead, we waited, the war raging on. No one spoke inside the tin can—not that we could hear over the roar from outside. All we could do was wait and pray we'd make it through.

The lights flickered on and off periodically, causing whimpers from the boys, clutching whichever adult they could cling to for strength, for love, for what little protection the adults offered—waiting and listening to the chaos around them.

A few times the lot of us jumped and screamed when there was a large thud against the side of the safe house, but quiet returned, as the madness thundered on. By some great miracle, our sanctuary held.

Mrs. Glen prayed under her breath, stroking Matt's hair. For the first time in a long time, I wanted to talk to something greater than myself. I wasn't a religious person, but it was as good a time as any to get back in touch with God.

I didn't think it was appropriate to ask to be saved. Who was I to ask for something like that? Besides, this was no time to be selfish. I only wanted God to protect the people I loved.

Kayin. It always came back to Kayin Aves.

I thought of her smile and her indecent sense of humor, which she held captive unless she was with the right kind of people. I tried to picture what it would be like if she were here with me. How I would hold her tight, wipe away her tears, and make sure nothing hurt her. She would have looked up into my eyes and smiled—a smile only she could offer—to reassure me that in the end everything would be fine.

"It'll be okay, Henry," she would say, reaching up to touch my cheek. "It always ends the way it should."

My heart broke.

She had said those words to me the last time we were together before I had driven far, far away. I'd left her all alone and if anything happened to her ...

My eyelids grew heavy with exhaustion. The racing thoughts that took up every part of my consciousness began growing quiet as I tried to focus on the prayers Mrs. Glen had recited for the hundredth time.

The little boys had already fallen asleep, signaling everyone else to do the same.

It was amazing how quickly the sounds of the chaos outside

slipped away as dreams evaded me. As frustration threatened to take hold, a memory crept into my consciousness. The last day I'd spent with Kayin played out in vivid detail. Already, I'd spent the last several hours hating myself, so this was a welcome memory. The relaxation washed over me as I allowed the thought to enter my awareness.

Kayin and I had spent the whole day together in our tiny one room apartment near Detroit. Remembering her beautiful face and the smell of her luscious skin filled my senses.

"You know I'll miss you ... " she'd told me, caressing my lower back.

"I'll miss you, too," I'd confessed, lying on my stomach and not looking at her. "But we'll see each other and I'll be back often," I'd said; I'd felt the lie slip out before I could stop myself. "You know we will, don't you?"

"Right ... I *could* always go down and visit you, too," she'd said, trying to reassure herself. She'd avoided my eyes as she kept caressing my skin. I could feel her sadness around me, but I'd continued to brush it off.

"Of course, I'd love that," I'd murmured, turning toward her, taking her hands. Her hands were small and smooth. Her beautiful dark skin looked bright compared to my dark tan.

I'd looked into her face, trying to remember every line, every dimple, and every freckle. Her dark green eyes had been serious, sparkling with tears. I'd known she was hurting more than I could ever imagine. I had pushed the same feelings deep down, where I could avoid them until I was ready. I would think about them tomorrow.

"We could meet up and go see the sights, take a mini-vacation or something. We'll have a wonderful time. We can do *this*. We can do a long-distance relationship. Everyone does it nowadays," I had tried to convince us. Even then I'd known the lie was growing out of control. "It's average for people to date long distance for a few years, then come back together and spend the rest of their lives together; that will be us. If anyone can make a long-distance relationship work, it's us. Don't you think?"

She hadn't answered.

"I love you. You know that, right? I love you very much," I'd told her, holding her close.

She'd looked at me, giving me a sad smile. "I *do* know that. I love you too, but I can't help feeling that it's the end. What we have is special. Now it feels like you are walking away from everything we have together. We could be ... so much more ... " she'd trailed off, looking down at our clasped hands.

I'd known what she was trying to say. We would have gotten married and had babies together if I had stayed. Even if she wasn't that type of woman, she knew she wanted those things with me. I wanted those things with her as well. But I needed to settle my ambition before I could even think about marriage or children.

I'd never met a woman like Kayin. She was strong and smart. She could light up a room with one tiny smile but put you in your place if you got out of hand. She'd let people cut in line, pay for someone's coffee just because, and was always there to cheer on her loved ones. Loyal to a fault, but she respected herself enough not to let anyone take advantage of her. She'd be hard to forget.

We'd looked deeply into each other's eyes. Studied each other's faces. Allowed ourselves to truly understand what we'd been avoiding all this time. We'd known at that moment that things wouldn't work out. We might see each other during the holidays, but as a couple, we were over. Our journey together was at an end.

Instead of getting angry, we'd held each other tightly and taken in the last moments we were going to have together. The love we'd shared had slowly turned into a beautiful, loving memory.

I awoke suddenly, everything hitting me at once: the war, the sounds, and the terror. I shivered from the fear.

It was dark in the safe house, and no one was moving. I tried to look around but it was pitch black; I was barely able to make out the forms around me.

The silence was deafening. I realized it was what I wasn't hearing that was making me so uneasy. After twelve-plus hours of nonstop noise, it was finally quiet.

I tried to move a little to get out of the weird position I found myself in: legs spread out and my upper body in some strange zigzag-like pattern. Something heavy was on my right leg, and it was making my entire leg fall asleep. I pulled my leg out from under a large lump and attempted to stand up.

"Henry, stay low," whispered Mr. Glen in a low, soft voice. "I'm not sure what kind of shape this shelter is in. We have an hour until sunrise. Try to get comfortable and wait. I don't want to wake the others just yet."

"What do you think we'll find when we get out?' I asked in a whisper, hopeful we still had some sort of planet left.

"I'm not sure. I suppose not much," he said in a whisper equal to my own. "Not much at all, really. With what happened earlier, I would be surprised if my daughter's house is still standing."

As we waited for the sun in silence, the others slowly began to awaken. The little boys were hungry, so Sarah and Mrs. Glen got a little breakfast ready for everyone. The rest of us surveyed what we could see inside the shelter. There were parts that were severely indented; others shook as we moved around. The ceiling didn't collapse, but it was definitely lower than it had been.

"Well, at least it held," Howie chuckled lightheartedly. He touched a part of the wall that was shaky, "We are very lucky."

"We are indeed," Mr. Glen said solemnly. "I just hope we aren't alone in our luck. And that there won't be a round two anytime soon." He tried to stand up, but couldn't because of the caved-in ceiling. "When we finish eating, we have to go look for other survivors."

Howie nodded in agreement.

"I can't," I said without hesitation. "*I am leaving*. I've waited long enough. I need to get to Michigan, and I need to find Kayin."

Everyone stopped what they were doing and stared at me in silence.

"We won't hold you back any longer," said Mr. Glen before anyone could object. "We'll try to give you all that we can to help you get home safely."

"Thank you," I told him. "I really appreciate it. I don't want to burden your family any longer. You've been nothing but kind and supportive."

The family and I ate breakfast silently—water, dried fruit, and oatmeal. Simple but enough to give us sufficient energy to overcome whatever the day brought us. I knew the Glens would stay with their daughter until everything was back to normal—if there was a normal. They had the whole family unit intact and together; in my eyes, they were the lucky ones.

"All right, everyone ready?" Howie asked.

Mumbles from the group convinced him to open the door. Using all his weight, he pushed it open.

The sunlight was bright against the dark, dead sky. My eyes, not used to the natural light from the sun, burned as I strained to take in the wreckage. The outside of the safe house looked like a deadly wreck; every part of it was scratched and torn from the original frame. It had looked like a tin can before; now it looked like a bunch of scrap metal in a junkyard.

As Mr. Glen had predicted, the house had been destroyed. Only a small fraction of the framework stood. The rest had been blown up or smashed by falling debris.

The Heggins climbed out of the safe house, collectively letting out a moan as they saw that their beloved home was gone forever. Sarah began to cry as she walked toward the pile of wood and metal that was once her place of residence. Their cars seemed to have survived a little better, but there was a chunk missing from the side of one and a tree covering the hood of the other.

Their neighbors had fared the same, but murmurs from Mr. Glen and Howie explained they didn't have safe houses—some had been staying home all together.

Shivers went up and down my spine.

"Many people stayed in their homes because no one thought it was going to get this bad," I sighed. "No one thought the Temorshians would get as far as they did into our atmosphere."

"We've all been fools. How many people lost their lives because no one took this threat seriously?" Howie asked, kicking a branch out of his way.

We walked around slowly surveying the damage. Bits and pieces of metal were scattered around the yard. Trees and plants had been completely uprooted and tossed aside. The air was thick with ash from burning debris. The sky was dark with smoke. When we looked down the road, the scene did not change. Destruction was every-where. We still had a planet, but it would take months—no, probably years—to get it back to how it was before. Unless ... I pushed the thought away. I couldn't bring myself to imagine the other possi-bilities.

"We are going to need to search the debris for anyone who is still alive," Mr. Glen said.

"There's a good chance everyone left," Sarah stated.

"No, I don't think so, honey," Howie added. "You know who stayed ... " He eyed the direction toward close neighbors.

"We don't have the medical supplies to help everyone," she whis-pered back.

"By the look of things, I doubt very many of them would be alive," he said.

Mr. Glen and Howie started for the closest remnants of a home.

"It's true that we need to find survivors and regroup, but I really don't have time to help," I added. This was not my fight—not here and not now. I had a plan and a purpose, and it didn't involve anyone else but Kayin.

"Honey, I think now is a good time for you to get going and get home to your family," Mrs. Glen told me, softly resting her hand on my shoulder.

I turned to face her. Her eyes were filled with understanding and compassion. She was a far cry from the woman I'd met before—that woman was a lifetime away.

"Yes, thank you. I know this isn't a good time to leave, but with all this, when is a good time?" I asked pointedly, already feeling defeated. "I just hope my family fared better than what I am seeing now. Do you really think there are people in those homes?" I asked her, pointing to the sad remains of houses around the neighborhood. I had a hard time believing that someone could actually survive what had happened to us in just a regular home.

"Who knows, dear? We at least can hope no one is trapped. I believe we are all going to need a huge batch of hope in the next few days. Hope and prayer," she said sadly.

As we both watched Howie move a battered-down door, Sarah came up behind us. She held a large sack in her hands. She watched her husband and father move debris around her neighbor's home.

"I don't think they will find anything over there. They left a few days ago, before all hell broke loose," Sarah said calmly. "The ones they should be checking are down the road ... " She looked at her sack and turned to face me, "Henry, this isn't much, and I'm not sure if you'll have everything you'll need, but this is all we can offer you," she said, handing me the heavy bag.

"Thank you so much, whatever it is you have to offer is great. I feel awful just leaving, after everything you've done for me. I don't know how I'll ever repay your family ... "

Sarah put her hands up to stop me, saying, "All you have to do is get home and live through this *war*. This is our new reality. We just all have to focus on today and today alone. Don't talk about the future. After what happened yesterday, who knows what we could face tomorrow?"

"We could face our savior, Sarah!" stated Mrs. Glen, trying to lift

the mood with a poorly timed joke. "Please, you must be more positive. We made it this far, we can make it through anything."

Saying goodbye to the Glens and the Heggins was one of the
hardest things I have ever done. We'd shared a very personal experience together, something that no one else can ever understand or
imagine. I felt as though they were dying in front of me, and there
was nothing I could do about it. I couldn't stay to protect them and
make sure they survived; that wasn't my job.

My guilt was growing by the hour.

I had this horrible feeling that I would let them down with any of
the choices I could have made in this situation. I even lost my desire
to find my parents because my heart was aching to see the love of my
life. No matter what happened and what I found on my way, Kayin
was my only priority. Nothing in the world mattered more than her
safety.

[13]

Perhaps the more prudent option would have been to find some type of vehicle or bike to travel across the state. It was too late now. I doubted my decision, but looking around at my surroundings, wheels would have been impossible to maneuver and probably would have held me back even more.

I sighed, pushing forward. Every fiber in my being ached with each step; I wanted to rest, but I couldn't—not yet. I needed to keep pushing on and if there was, by some miracle, a place to stay safely, I would. Looking around, I didn't feel safe. I quietly doubted I would ever feel safe after last night—the terror was still fresh in my mind.

I walked for hours without meeting another soul. Nothing stood after the blowout from the night before. The world was destroyed, a wasteland of rubble.

The scenery didn't change as I walked along: destroyed buildings, remains of homes with cars smoking from explosions, debris in jagged shapes, and very few trees left standing, a dismal sight. I shuddered from the silence.

The feeling of being completely alone was terrifying. I couldn't avoid the truth any longer: people were dead. Because of lack of preparedness and stupidity, people had lost their lives. There was a good chance entire cities were now gone. The world as we knew it was simply a memory. This was Armageddon at its finest.

I pushed those thoughts deep down inside me. I didn't have time to wallow in self-pity.

It'd been six hours since I'd parted from the Glens. The fighting was nonexistent, but the occasional explosion or crash from somewhere in the distance would catch me off guard. Thankfully, the fighting we'd experienced in the safe house was over.

I began to lose steam. Exhaustion threatened to take me down. My limbs ached, my clothes were soaked through, and my eyelids lurked over my eyes. I fought against it all.

Sarah had been smart enough to include a map of Ohio in my care package, along with food that could last for days if I was careful and a blanket. Even Howie had snuck in a handgun with ammunition. I knew it wouldn't do much, but it gave me peace of mind.

By the time the sun set, my fatigue had worsened. I needed to find some place to spend the night. Who knew what kinds of things I could encounter in the dark?

In my sad attempt to find a safe path, I managed to find the highway and followed what was left of it. From the trashed and empty road, I realized I was in a small town just a few miles away from the Michigan border. I would've loved to reach it before the sun went down, but I doubted I could make it in time before the blackness set in. I didn't want to gamble my chances of successfully joining Kayin by doing something stupid.

I got off the road, trying to get a better idea of the area. Debris and parts of buildings were strewn everywhere, throwing an eerie shadow on what was left standing. Large chunks of bricks were scattered in my path. Through the mess, I knew there'd be something I could use to make shelter. I had been excellent at building forts when I was younger, how hard could it be to make something now?

Finding part of a brick wall still standing with bits of it thrown around the shattered metal debris made the area look as inconspicuous as possible——it would serve me well. The wall looked sturdy enough to make some sort of shelter and not be spotted. It gave me a false sense of security, but it was better than nothing.

I looked around, making sure I was alone. *This could work.*

Metal scraped the ground as I dragged the heavy beast toward the wall, stopping every so often to avoid detection. I propped up the metallic slab against the brick, hoping it would hold– it did—and added the other piece of metal to create a triangle. Once the structure settled into place, I placed the blanket on top, calling it a day. It wasn't cold out yet, which meant the clothing I had on—jeans, t-shirt, and hoodie—would be adequate to survive the night.

The sun had already set by the time I finished my sad excuse for a shelter, causing everything to become even quieter. I stood back to examine my work, thankful it blended in with the scenery. It might be obvious to someone looking for signs of life, but only if they were smart. Most people aren't that bright.

I crawled into the heap of junk and tried to get comfortable.

I opened my pack, selecting a delicious-looking protein bar. With one bite, I lost all desire to eat. I had been succeeding at ignoring my feelings, but like a load of heavy bricks, everything hit me at once. The inevitable loss of my country, maybe the world, and the many people I loved was too much. Everything was gone, and I was never going to get them back. My world only existed within this cold, dark, little shelter I'd created with my own two hands.

Alone and scared, I was flooded by different memories in fragments. I longed for the long nights I would spend wrapped in Kayin's arms. I remembered how my mother's singing voice filled every room of my childhood home: crisp, clear, and beautiful. I remembered how I loved all the lullabies she would sing to Nick and me. I could smell the warm aroma of freshly baked muffins just coming out of the oven. I recalled how the sun sank low on Lake Michigan after a long day on the sandy shores—all the variations of pinks and purples swallowing the bright sun as it dropped into the horizon.

I fell into a pit of despair, tears gradually falling from my eyes.

My heart broke with no way to pick up the pieces. There'd be even more pain once the Temorshians landed, if they weren't already here.

Sleep escaped me.

After hours of tossing and turning, I exhausted myself and wandered into a fitful sleep, waking only occasionally to monitor my surroundings, then drifting off again. The cycle continued throughout the night until a humming noise barged into my psyche.

I almost didn't notice since the hum fit well into my subconscious—the dreamless blackness I could always count on for relief. The noise was peaceful, but menacing, unfamiliar to my senses. A higher pitch than any manmade craft, it sounded as though it was going way too fast for anything remotely human. Louder, louder, *louder*—so loud I awoke with a jolt. The startled realization that it was outside of my shelter paralyzed me with fear.

I am not dreaming.

Staying as still as I could, I listened to the noise as it crept closer.

I shook uncontrollably and could not will myself to move to look. *Okay, snap out of it. You need to move slowly and look outside.*

As if responding to my pleas, another Henry took over. In survival mode I forced myself to move, slowly making my way to the small opening I used for a door and peering out into the still morning.

The sun rose in the distance, giving off a sense of warmth with the bright pinks and oranges it was creating in the cloudless sky. A light fog covered the ground, and the sunlight was dancing in the dew. Everything looked as it had last night: debris everywhere and a building half blown away, although the smoking from the car a mile away had finally died down.

The humming strengthened as I surveyed the scene, the sound floating to my ears from the opposite direction. A chug pierced the stillness, signaling a change in speed.

Dear God.

I made myself crawl a little further out of the opening, slowly looking around the corner toward the scream of the engine.

Sure enough, it was a space ship.

I'd only seen a few Shielder ships from the previous Army-based encounter, but this one was bigger with no markings. Large and colored gray, with rocket-type engines, it burned a blue-green flame. It almost looked like a dreidel from the side, with a tower on top and rounded edges.

As I watched in horror, it crawled to a slow stop, hovered a little, and finally landed with a thud, blowing debris out of its way.

The animalistic side of my brain screamed to move—*to flee*—but I couldn't pull my eyes off the stilled ship. If I ran, I'd be seen. Yet I couldn't just sit there like an idiot either. I reached for my gun, just out of reach.

Whatever was inside was about to make its entrance onto the Earth's soil.

Steeling myself from any thought beside survival, my heart raced—blood pumping in my ears.

A side door flew open, and metal crashed on the ground. A bright light glared against the doorway, almost blinding me. I squinted, trying to follow the movement coming from the ship. A large figure treaded guardedly onto the platform, its armor shimmering in the morning light.

A Shielder stepped out of the ship.

I let out a sigh of relief, though I quickly regretted it. I stayed where I was, watching the movements of the large creature.

It first cautiously looked around, holding its weapon in a ready position. The giant body stepped off the ship, walking a few feet away from various others who slowly followed with the same amount of caution. A handful of Shielders made their way toward my hiding area, surveying the area and ignoring my presence.

When the Shielders were on TV, they always wore fancy clothes and looked put together. These Shielders looked completely disheveled, hair half pulled back in messy up-dos, wearing very complicated-looking shiny armor. They seemed tired, with bags under their purple eyes, and nervous—more nervous than I had ever noticed before. They were on edge in a big way. The Shielders slowly walked out into the open in formation.

I hadn't moved a muscle while the Shielders came out of their ship. I held my breath as I watched. I didn't want to startle them; I was even unsure I wanted to be found.

Remaining silent, I looked over their ship. It'd been through some serious combat. Holes dotted the sides, while panels had been blown off completely. The structure looked like a strong gust of wind could blow the whole thing over.

A chill ran down my spine.

Maybe they could help me, or at least inform me of the status of this galactic war if I reached out to them?

Quietly grabbing my supplies, hoping they didn't catch my subtle moves, I crawled out of my hiding spot.

One of the Shielders yelled in La'Mursian in my direction.

I froze, half of my body exposed to their weapons.

The air tensed and fell silent.

Looking in the direction of the voice, I attempted contact. "It's all right ... I'm Human. My name is Henry Rickner."

Silence.

"I promise I have nothing that'll hurt you." *Was this a mistake?*

"Come out where we can see you," a female voice called out.

Following her orders, I slowly made my way out. The whole of the small group had their large weapons pointing in my direction; I instinctively raised my hands over my head.

"There will be no need for that, sir," the female said matter-of-factly. She turned her attention to her people, telling them something in La'Mursian. Immediately they dropped their weapons, barely relaxing.

I followed, putting my hands down. I stood up straight and walked closer to the group. Apprehensive I was doing the right thing, I made my way over regardless.

Some eyed me suspiciously as others went off in the opposite direction. I continued toward the group that stayed near the entrance of the ship. They guarded the female that'd spoken.

The impressive female took me in with her purple eyes. "How did you survive? Were you here when this happened? Are there more of you?" she asked me, coldly looking over my head. "Do you need medical attention?"

She was attractive for a Shielder. Slim, but extremely muscular and tall. Her medium-length hair hung in thick braids around her head; some had fallen out of their binds. Her eyes were light purple and her teeth pointed, giving her a menacing look. Her clothes were different from the others, along with the markings on her visible skin—more extreme and pronounced, but still intriguing.

"No, ma'am, I'm traveling alone—only me. I'm not sure about the area," I responded respectfully. I knew better than to mouth off to a Shielder. "I don't need any medical care; I'm fine, thank you."

"You are traveling?" she questioned me in disbelief. "You were not in a shelter?" She narrowed her eyes, looking me over more closely.

"I was in a safe house, but when all the fighting ended I left, and now I'm trying to reconnect with my family," I explained.

Her wide, puzzled eyes searched for answers. She seemed to be struggling with my choices. I was uncertain how to proceed. Not a soul was breathing. I stiffened at the realization.

"Is that a problem for you?" I asked flatly, trying to hide the concern that was beginning to boil within me.

"No, but you do realize it is extremely dangerous to be out here without any weapons—*alone*," she told me, regaining her stern exterior. "It is obviously not safe for you to be about ill prepared. What were you thinking?"

"No, I didn't realize—I mean, I didn't think about it. I've been traveling for a day on my own, and my only concern has been to reunite with my family—regardless of the danger."

She eyed me up and down.

"I guess it's rather crazy that I was alone and walking around—"

"You cannot continue," she announced flatly. "The Temorshians have landed and are attacking everything in sight. It is not safe to be out in the open—especially without any type of weapon. Not that anything *Human* could save you now ... You are going with us to find other survivors, and then we will all head back to Selucia." She turned around and walked toward the ship, speaking to another Shielder in La'Mursian.

Her incredible bluntness was rude as hell and completely took me for a loop. *The Temorshians were on Earth?* This was not good.

"I'm not going with you!" I shouted at the female's back, regaining my composure. "I have come too far to get off track. I survived the first attack, I'm pretty sure I can survive whatever else gets thrown in my path!"

The female Shielder stopped walking and turned sharply in my direction, her braids flung behind her. If I'd thought she was menacing before, the soul-crushing look she gave me now made her look much worse. I braced myself for battle. I wasn't going to back down, Shielder or not.

"Excuse me?" she asked. "I must not have understood you correctly ... "

"No, you *heard* me correctly. I will not go with you. I cannot go with you," I told her in a huff. "I'm not really sure if you understand the concept of love and honoring that love, but I have to find my girlfriend, and I have to make sure she's safe. It's something I have to do, and no one, not even you and your gang, can stop me!"

"You are very brave, but that bravery will get you *killed*. You need to follow my instructions and come with us," she said, coming very close, her shadow engulfing me.

I almost stepped backward, showing my vulnerability, but I stood my ground. The Shielder was large and could easily kill me with one blow to the head, but it didn't matter. I was going to stand up to her and fight if I had to.

"I am sorry for any losses you must have suffered," she continued, "but trust me, your family and this woman of yours are dead. You would be wasting your time. They are gone—just like the rest of your world."

"Excuse me?" I questioned, my voice edgy with anger. "I'm not really bound to you by any law, so I'm pretty sure I can do as I please. There's nothing you can say or do to stop me from finishing this journey. I am in love with this woman; can you understand that? I *need* to be with her, and I *need* to make sure she's safe. Even if there is the chance that she didn't make it through the first attack, I'm still going to try. It's something I have to do, and I don't care if you understand a word I'm saying!"

I stared her down; her lavender eyes filled with rage. After all, how could a small human talk to her in such a manner?

I continued, "Do you know what the English word *compassion* means? It means to have sympathy for the distress other people experience and to want to help them make it better. Does this make sense to you? Do you understand what *I'm trying* to tell you?"

I let my words sink into her thick skull.

The Shielder in all her finery stared back at me. Her eyes were blank, her mouth a thin line, her cheeks burning a deep mauve. I noticed the others circling around us, quiet, listening intently to our conversation. I could sense that none of them had ever tried to confront this monster of a Shielder before in the same manner. This was as new for them as it was for me. I glanced back to the burly Shielder bitch. She was still silent, but the wheels in her mind were spinning.

I shrugged my shoulders and turned to walk away. I was wasting time.

"Why were you not with her when this all started?" she questioned in a thick accent. "If you love her so much, why did you wait to reunite with her?"

I stopped, turning back to her, my heart cold as ice. Her eyes were piercing as her question hung in the air, swirling about me. I looked down at my feet. My shame hung on my shoulders like a thick cloak.

I avoided the general's eyes as I tried to explain. "I wish I could answer that myself ... In the end I was selfish. I left her to try to create some self-satisfying career as a lawyer. Obviously, if I would have known all this was about to happen—"

"This is the problem with you Humans," she interrupted sharply. "You only think of yourselves, and when it is too late, you cry like infants. You crave companionship, but when it stares you in the face, you push it aside for something *better*. What could be better than love is beyond me."

She walked around me, letting her words cut me, tearing into every bit of my soul.

"You think better is always right around the corner, when perfection is always at your fingertips, right in front of you. The ones you love are always around you, supporting you, and caring for you, but in the end, you leave it for what might be, instead of what is. What is within reach is never, ever good enough," she paused. "This is where your species *fails*."

All eyes burned into me for a retort, some type of intelligent banter, but I had none.

She was right.

I had left to better myself, in hopes of finding a better partner and a better life. I hadn't given my family much thought, and I had the notion that if Kayin loved me enough, she would wait for me. My selfishness had put me on this path: a path away from all the people that cared for me most. This was why I was alone.

"You did this to your woman, your family, and to yourself," she continued. "How am I to feel compassion for you, when you could not do the same for your people?"

I looked up into the Shielder's face. "I'm trying to mend the error of my ways. I know I did this—I'm trying to fix it," I explained meekly. "I'm trying to do what I should have done a long time ago ... "

"What exactly *is* that?" she asked, her eyes beating down onto me.

"To show her how much I *do* care and that I would do anything for her ... make things right, instead of focusing on the past that I have no control over. I made a mistake. Do you understand, I made a mistake, and I need to make it right."

The Shielder smirked a little, but then looked distressed. "Do you really believe that she is alive? That she somehow survived all this?"

"I ... I just know she did," I said firmly.

"You Humans and your feelings. If I did half of what I do on feelings, I would not be here right now," she said with a shake of her head.

She looked to her left, saying something in La'Mursian to a comrade. He nodded and quickly returned to the ship. She said something to the others; they quickly went off to search the area.

Finally, she set her sights on me. "Against my better judgment, I will do what I can for you and your people. If you help us find other survivors here, I promise to take you to wherever it is you think you need to go. I cannot guarantee a happy ending, but I can offer transport. After that, we will see."

I was speechless, unable to form words with my mouth. Overjoyed, but surprisingly stunned.

"Deal," I stuttered as I extended my right hand to her.

She reached out to take it and shook it fiercely, her large hand enveloping my own. She didn't look happy.

14

I had no idea what kind of devastation and death awaited our small party, but I wasn't prepared for what I witnessed in the destroyed shopping area. The stench of decay filled my nostrils, causing me to gag as I looked through piles of debris. Pieces of buildings crumbled on top of Human bodies, as did safe houses that had done nothing to stop the carnage.

The female Shielder who barked orders left and right was a high-ranking general. Her name was Beenishia Tora. She was a skilled warrior with a very good reputation for killing. As I learned from another Shielder, Zaforous, she was directly appointed by Prince Naluba to fight on Earth and was his second in command.

"You do not understand," Zaforous explained in a heavy, sometimes confusing accent, "it is an honor to be in her presence. We are fortunate to work under her."

"Okay, man, I get it—she's a big deal—but what happened? How did we get into this mess?"

The young Shielder sighed. "Our platoon fighting on Earth had been separated from the rest of our forces in Space after the fighting began. Communication between our two groups was cut off almost instantly, which caused major problems and losses. It was a shock—that's never happened before."

The gun he was holding shifted in his hands as though he were uncomfortable with admitting defeat. "Once the fighting stopped, we discovered that our forces in Space had either been destroyed or left because of heavy mechanical issues," Zaforous told me, looking sad. "It was a mess and ... well ... now I am not sure how it will be. We suffered so many losses—a rarity."

Zaforous's markings were less elaborate than Beenishia's and the others. He had shorter hair, meaning he was young and inexperienced. His deep purple eyes were alert with the naiveté only young beings can have; he had blunt teeth that had not been sharpened yet. He was thin, but his muscles were visible, as though he hadn't eaten in a few days. He was a large fellow but not as large as some of them. I liked him immediately for befriending me. I was grateful to him for seemingly taking me under his wing. Friendship, Human or otherwise, was something we all needed at this time.

"When we found out what had happened to the rest of our forces, we had to make a decision: try to break through the Temorshian barricade or stay," Zaforous whispered in a low voice so the others wouldn't hear us.

"Is this all that is left of your kind on Earth?" I asked.

Zaforous didn't answer. He looked distracted and pained.

"No. We are not the only ones," he said. "There are more elsewhere, but we are the only ones who survived in our platoon. *Mezda* Beenishia sent others along to search other areas and, of course, there were bases around the world, there have to be survivors there ... "

We continued our search, moving farther away from the group.

"Communication has been limited, however, because the Temorshians have infiltrated our systems. We cannot be certain what kind of numbers we have left." He lifted a chunk of a fallen tree that had collapsed, blocking our path.

We entered into the remnants of a Burger King, pushing aside various bits of metal and debris. Half a wall had been left standing and the kitchen had caved in—it was a pile of junk now. We should've gone in and out quickly, as there was no way there were people left in the building. I stopped him.

"Tell me more, please," I begged. "I've been in the dark for too long, and if General Beenishia had her way, she'd keep me there. But you and I both know that's not right. Why can't you share with me anyway?"

Zaforous looked around before speaking. "The original plan was to regroup somewhere near Washington, DC, but unfortunately there is nothing left of your capital," he explained sadly. "When the fighting started, our ships went this way and that—all of them confused—running out of ammo in no time. General, or *Mezda* in La'Mursian—weird to hear you call her *General* in English— anyway, *Mezda* Beenishia tried to reconnect with a few other platoons but ... but we were unsuccessful ...

"It was like they were all blown out of the sky—completely gone—just like that! With communication as it is, we are not sure what happened to the others outside of the States. Hopefully they are a lot better off than we are." He paused as he caught the eye of one of his companions. "As for not telling you, a shame really, I do not know. I just do what I am told, and we did not expect to find many Humans—"

"Alive," I finished for him.

The other Shielder who had held Zaforous' gaze walked off after a quick word in La'Mursian to us. Zaforous motioned for me to follow him out of the rubble.

"No one could believe how prepared the Temorshians were," he whispered. "It was like they knew our strategy before the fighting began. They destroyed many of the bases we had set up in Europe before we could even reach our ships." Zaforous kneaded his eyebrows together as if he were unable to believe his kind could fail so badly.

I shivered regardless of how warm it was outside.

"They knew?" I asked. "These Temorshians knew where to find large groups of Humans and Shielders?"

Zaforous nodded, looking as though he might be sick, his cheeks flushing a light purple.

I watched Zaforous move on to another pile of rubble. "So, then what? Your crew is just flying around and searching?" I followed him into another half-destroyed building.

He sighed, continuing, "We landed to refuel with what we could—which was hardly anything. We came up with a plan to try to make it to the other side of your country to see how things were going. Maybe we could reconnect with others outside of North America, but as you see, we only got this far."

He stopped talking as he entered a burning building on the other side of the restaurant.

My eyes followed. The smoke and stench of death didn't seem to bother him. I let him poke around as I waited patiently. He came out moments later.

"All dead ... " he uttered softly.

"I could have told you that ... Didn't you smell that?" I asked, wondering who had lost their lives.

"I do, but I need to check. You never know if there is one that can be saved," he responded, looking around. "We have to be certain. I do not think you understand the severity of the situation."

"I guess I don't. I'm not used to this way of life like you might be."

He nodded, frowning.

It was a dismal sight even in the morning light. Buildings had crumbled under the weight of the debris, while some trees still stood. Bushes swayed in the breeze, their buds the only sign that Mother Earth could take care of herself.

"Our orders are to keep moving; save as many as we can ... " Zaforous continued looking around as he spoke. He glanced back at me with a hint of a smile, motioning me to follow as he continued to fulfill his mission. "We are trying to save anyone at this point. That is why we cannot let you travel alone. It is not safe, trust me."

"How bad was the fight?" I asked, trying to search the twisted remains of a fake Safe House nearby.

People would do anything for a buck even during the end of the world, I thought angrily as I examined the house. It was disgusting that so many people trusted others yet lost their lives in the process.

Zaforous stopped. He swallowed as he answered, "The Temorshians were not supposed to be as prepared as they were. They should not have known our tactics or known where all of your army strongholds were. We have a system in place to avoid such dangers. It is next to impossible for them to know ... impossible for anyone to know outside of command and our communicators to know exact locations—it is safer that way. Honestly, it has worked for millennia, why would it fail now?

"We are not sure where they got their information from ... " He paused, turning toward me. "You have lost a lot, I am afraid. Many of your kind have died, and I believe we have lost almost half of our forces. The damage is astronomical. Nothing could have prepared us for this ... "

We acknowledged the loss in silence.

I let my new friend continue his mission. I wanted no part in searching. If I was only going to find the remains of bodies, I did not want any part of it.

Grateful to be left alone for a moment to process, I found an open piece of grass unharmed from the brutal attacks of the previous day. I sat down, trying to clear my head. The grass was cool to the touch: moist, green, and full of life. We'd need the environment to replenish itself at some point, but today Mother Earth would grieve for her loss.

"This war is not over," said a voice over my right shoulder. "You and your kind will not be safe for many months, maybe years to come."

Beenishia, the voice of reason no matter how hurtful.

"What are you talking about?" I asked her, annoyed that I was unable to get just a moment of peace.

"They will not leave easily, the Temorshians. Worse, they may bring allies to their cause ... We cannot be certain, but this fight for your planet is far from over ... " She bent down next to me as she spoke. As quick and as gentle as a cat, she caressed the grass beside me.

"Grass is so interesting," she stated, feeling it beneath her fingers, acknowledging its simple beauty, yet its strength and endurance. "We do not have this on Selucia."

I ignored her.

"You will be called upon to help build relations with your people," Beenishia told me calmly. "We acknowledge that we have failed you. We will not stop protecting your planet just because we failed. We will do what we can and now, more than ever, we need to work together.

"I know what you are thinking, but we have put things in motion to get your planet back," she told me. "Will you help? Can you help us?"

The way she spoke grated on my nerves. I could not contain the rage I felt inside toward her people. "Help? Help with *what?* This mess? Fix this? You and your kind let us all down, that's for sure," I shot back in her face. "All of you act like you have the answers and you know how to help everyone and anyone. The sad fact is you don't. This is painfully obvious, especially looking around at this mess. Look at what you did!" I gestured to the wreckage surrounding us. "It's fucking destroyed! Our home is gone!" I stood up, causing the general to fall back onto her bum.

I looked down on her—the symbolism not lost on me. "Yes, I can help. Though I'm no fool, I know we both need each other's help and support, but do not think for a moment that I'm going to allow you or any other alien species to take over again and keep us in the dark. You need to be honest with me, and I'll be honest with you. I'm going to share any details I get from you or your soldiers with my people. Is that clear? We are equals, and you'll treat us as such!"

The rage burned inside but settled. If this bitch wanted my help, then by God, she'd get it. I'd be the thorn in her side she never saw coming.

"How did they *know*? How did they know where to find you?" I asked bitterly.

The great general gazed at the grass, taking in the beauty of its quiet strength. Slowly she looked up into my eyes. Beenishia had taken the war personally, and it showed on her face. It wasn't just a great loss for her, but a sheer and utter disappointment. She'd let down not only her commanders and people, but also Earth as a whole. The fine lines around her tired eyes mapped out the bitter regret she buried deep within her.

Beenishia let out a long, deep breath. "I would not expect any less from you," she retorted. "This will not be an easy road ... "

"No," I said, filling the space between us. "It won't be, for both sides—for both of us. But we can't give up. We just keep moving forward."

I looked around; the other Shielders were finishing up, making their way back. "Do you know how they found you?" I asked again, kneeling down closer to her large frame.

"No."

"You have no idea?" I kept pushing.

"I cannot possibly know." General Beenishia stood up, rubbing her long, bony hands together. "We have no communication with anyone in Space or Selucia. I can only speculate."

I stood with her, trying to increase my size with a straight back and puffed out chest, though it was pointless, as she was a foot taller. We stared each other down for a few moments.

"Do you know where your love is?" General Beenishia asked, placing her hands on her slim hips.

She was changing the subject. I wasn't going to let the subject die, but it was no longer an appropriate time to have this discussion. Her comrades had made it back from their searching. The general and I needed to have this conversation in private. She didn't come across as a Shielder who would disclose information freely to openly cause panic.

"I've some type of idea of where she could be," I finally said. "Just get me as close to the area as possible, and I'll do the rest."

"I will do my best. The Temorshians are everywhere, and it's not safe."

"I thought they'd gone?" I asked her, confused.

"They left for now. There are still large ships in your orbit. Last we knew, most have not landed yet, but they will, and when they do, there will be more of them, more than you can imagine."

Beenishia motioned for me to follow her and I did quietly.

"I hope for your sake this woman is where you believe and that you will not find disappointment," General Beenishia said as we neared her ship.

"Sometimes it is better to be disappointed than to never know at all," I responded.

Beenishia turned to me and unexpectedly placed her long bony fingers on my shoulder, patting it ever so gently. "Come, we will see what we can find ... *together*."

Needless to say, we never found any survivors.

I watched silently as the crew worked to take off. Beenishia barked orders from the front of the ship, while her inferiors carried out her wishes. I sat in the back away from the action. I wasn't any help, but I was fascinated watching the crew work in perfect unison.

The ship was a little tighter on the inside than I'd imagined— cramped, but not suffocating. I had freedom to move and get comfortable, but they had packed a lot into one tiny ship. Seating for various functions lined the walls, and at the helm sat Beenishia and her first lieutenant. Flashing buttons dotted almost every part of the ship. The shouts and frustrated voices came from the working Shielders all around me.

"It doesn't look like much, does it?" Zaforous asked, smirking at me. "Trust me, this ship has a lot of fighting power. It's fast, too."

I shrugged, returning his smirk. "If you say so."

I wasn't in the mood to see the thing in action; I just needed them to get me close enough to Kayin so I could make it to her by nightfall. My heart skipped a beat at the thought of being reunited soon.

Shielders tensed and began yelling at each other throughout the ship. Alarms sounded as lights flashed in perfect unison. Something was the matter. A cold sweat formed on my temple as I watched, trying to catch what they were yelling about, but since I was shit at languages I could only watch, twisting my hands together to keep from interfering.

Beenishia barked another order in La'Mursian to a Shielder sitting close to her. The Shielder went into action, hitting this button and that. With a shake, the ship began to lift and vibrate. An ugly scraping noise pierced my ears. The ship stopped moving.

Beenishia turned slowly to the Shielder; all eyes were now on the two of them. They exchanged a few words, and the Shielder tried again. The ship moved, vibrated violently, and then the ugly sound rang out into the silence.

They tried a third time, with no change. The crew and I waited, holding our breaths.

Beenishia ordered a few others next to me. They silently exited the ship.

"Everything all right?" I asked. "I know I don't speak your language, but I can help if you need anything."

"It will be fine," the General said, avoiding my eyes in the small mirror above her head. I could tell she was trying to stay calm and use her training to get them out of this dilemma. The lines of her eyes deepened as bits of free hair whipped around in the fury of her motion.

"We are low on fuel, and sometimes when that happens, it takes a moment to get the ship online," Beenishia told me as the two Shielders returned just as quickly as they had left.

Beenishia stood up and met them in two strides. The three spoke in La'Mursian quickly as a small smile crept onto the general's face.

"All right, everyone," she said in English, "please take a seat. We are good to go. Henry, where are we headed?"

I couldn't help but smile too. "Yes, right, well the last time I spoke to Kayin she was headed back to her family's home. I believe that is just outside of Grand Rapids. Just get me as close as possible."

"Fine," Beenishia agreed, sitting down as the others readied themselves for takeoff. "You heard him, get the coordinates and set the path. Zaforous, scan for life as we travel. I want to get an idea of how many Humans are alive on the ground."

"Will we be able to help any of them?" I asked.

"It depends on what kind of shape they are in and how much fuel we have left," Beenishia responded rather coldly. "Our fuel supply is very low, and I need to regroup with the other platoons. That is more important at this time."

I knew she was right, but I couldn't help but become bitter at her words. "Like I keep saying, just get me as close as you can to Grand Rapids, and I can do the rest."

The ship began to shake. The Shielders, talking in La'Mursian, flipped switches and pushed buttons. As they did the ship started to stabilize. With one quick motion I felt the ship leave the ground, taking off so fast my whole body was flung backward into my seat.

"Don't worry, Henry, we will make sure you are reunited with your *love*," Beenishia said. "We will be there soon. Try to remember—"

"Mezda," interrupted a Shielder to my right.

Beenishia turned her head in the direction of the voice. The Shielder, a large fellow with deep markings and long hair, began speaking rapidly. The rest of the crew turned in his direction. I noticed the others were having a hard time understanding him too, their eyes darting back and forth to their comrades. The fellow speaking looked nervous and unsure of what he was seeing, pointing at various maps and screens. He broke off to rub the exhaustion from his eyes.

"Are you sure, Ralphan?" Beenishia asked him in English.

The fellow nodded.

"If that is the case, we will help Henry and then follow the signal," Beenishia ordered, still in English. "Good news, Henry. There seems to be a signal from a few of our survivors in the northern part of Michigan. The signal is weak, but we can still track it."

"That's great! Do you think Humans can find the signal and follow?"

"If they have one of our systems or are in a shelter with others who can distinguish the signal from static," she said. Her demeanor changed slightly with the slump of her bony shoulders; she was obviously relieved there were more Shielders out there.

"If we can regroup and get backup forces from Selucia, this war could turn," the general stated to no one in particular.

I sat back, happy to have some luck on our side. Looking out of the small window next to me, it was apparent that Earth was devastated. Things looked much worse from the air. Trees were all but gone. Houses were demolished, and there was black, thick smoke that still lingered just above the ground.

My stomach sank.

"Let's just hope the Temorshians don't find them before we do," Zaforous said to me quietly.

"Yes," I agreed, "let's keep the faith and hope our luck holds."

15

"**A**re you sure we are here?" Beenishia asked skeptically, as if my vague directions annoyed her.

We'd been searching from the various windows for almost thirty minutes and saw nothing that would give away Kayin's location. Her grandparents' farmhouse should be within the area, but the wrecked trees and battered homes left me second-guessing myself. No landmark had been left untouched, which made it hard for my already blurry memory to pick out the spot—everything was either burned or leveled to the ground.

"I think so ... " I told her, peering out of my small window.

I strained to gaze harder but it was no use. I could've been flying over Canada for all I knew.

"Henry, come up here and look," Beenishia offered.

The monitors combing for life hadn't gone off in some time, which could've been worrisome, but we were in a remote part of the state where the population thinned.

While I struggled out of my seat, the rest of the crew kept looking out of their peepholes, scanning for anything that could give me a clue. I hovered over the general's shoulder, peering out of the large window, while the rest of the crew slowed the ship. They managed to lower it down even further so I could get a better look.

"I know it's hard to distinguish where we are," Beenishia said in a low voice, looking just as hard as I was for a sign. "If you see anything, anything at all, just say so and we will stop."

"Perhaps we can land and I could look around?" I asked her.

"I'm afraid not," she stated, "If we land we may not get the ship started as quickly as we did before. I only want to land when we see life."

The view of destruction hadn't changed much from the view we'd seen on our flight up to the small town. Homes had been hit harder in this area—*much* harder. Some safe houses still stood in good condition; people could be inside them—alive. Yet our life-detecting machines made no sound.

A tree came into view I recognized immediately. It was missing a few branches, but the old thing was as sturdy as ever.

"There!" I shouted. "That tree is on Kayin's grandparents' property! We're here!"

The crew maneuvered the ship to hover around the area. Again we began looking out the windows for the family's safe house, my face pressed against the glass.

Soon the foundation and basement of the farmhouse became visible. The rest of the house had been blown away as if picked up by a tornado. A few feet away stood the safe house, intact, with little damage.

In unison, we let out a sigh of relief.

I did it! I thought, my heart beating wildly. It felt as though a huge weight had been lifted from my shoulders. The thought of holding her became too much, causing me to shake, my body vibrating with anticipation.

"All right, now what? Can you land, or do I jump out of the ship?" I asked Beenishia, becoming increasingly anxious to get out of the tin can.

Beenishia rose from her seat, turning to look at me. "Have a seat, Henry," she said, pity in her eyes.

I did as she asked and sat.

As I sat, Beenishia followed, stopping by Zaforous. They exchanged a few words in hushed La'Mursian, stopping to turn their attention back to me.

The sick feeling of the reality of the situation dawned on me.

I'd completely forgotten that Zaforous was in charge of finding life. The monitors had been silent all this time—even here, at the farmhouse.

Beenishia made her way to my seat in two quick strides and bent down in front of me. I avoided her eyes—I knew what was coming.

My body stiffened.

"As you can guess," she said softly, "we have not picked up any movement on the ground ... I am sorry. I am *so* sorry, but I do not think anyone is down there ... " She put her long, bony hand on my right shoulder, squeezing it slightly.

A rush of sickness overwhelmed me. I put my head between my knees in an attempt to quiet the violent throbbing and painful turn of my stomach. My vision blurred as my whole world crumbled. For the first time in my life I had no feeling. My mind was blank while my heart slowed itself, causing my veins to scream in protest. I welcomed the waves of grief.

The silence of the ship enveloped me.

"Are you all right?" Beenishia asked, holding my shoulders gently, trying to steady the shaking. She said something in La'Mursian, and soon a glass of water appeared in front of me.

"Where ... " I tried to ask after taking a sip of water. I felt weak, as though I had been carrying twice my body weight. Unable to focus, the lights in the ship stung my eyes. "Where did they all go? They couldn't all be ... They couldn't be ...." The words choked me.

"There is a trail," added a Shielder I had not yet met. "From the look of things, it's Human-made."

Beenishia sighed. "Thank you, Gorgen—that's true, but we are not sure," she patted my back as I stayed in my hunched position. "There are some indications—some traces—of Humans heading north, but we cannot be certain until we follow the trail they have been leaving behind. And even then it might be nothing.

"We did find some left in their houses previously," she continued, "but there are too many homes left in some semblance of order to have them all disappear. They could have heard our signal."

"Could they have followed it?"

"I doubt it. There is no way to interpret our codes unless they had a vast understanding of how they are created. It is difficult for most of our soldiers, since only a few crew members are trained as communicators."

"But there's a chance?" I asked, sitting up. "There've been Shielders on the planet for months now, maybe, *maybe* the Humans learned La'Mursian?"

"It is possible, but not probable. We should not get overly excited one way or another," Beenishia added. "It would not be wise to follow such a signal."

"Why?"

"My communicator, Vira, is not certain if it is one of ours or a ploy by the Temorshians."

For the first time, she looked tired. The lines stood out on her gaunt face, while the skin around her eyes glowed pink from lack of sleep.

"You said yourself people needed someone to interpret the code? Fine, but how could they have known it was safe to travel north otherwise?" I asked.

"We do not know," she said. "It is the only logical theory we have right now. Either they figured out the signal, or they decided to leave without a reason we would understand at this time. The trail we found could be fresh or used before the attack. We cannot be certain from up here."

"What about the Temorshians?" I asked in a hushed voice. "They couldn't have taken them ... "

Beenishia looked at me with wide, horrified eyes. Her mouth slowly opened but closed as if chewing on her words as she thought about how to proceed.

"Mezda," Zaforous interjected, "what if ... what *if* the Humans heard their own signal?"

The whole ship turned to stare at him.

"You're right, Zaforous," I said, hope beginning to return to my deflated heart. "The safe houses were equipped with emergency radios and communicators; it could be possible. Hell, it's even possible that they are all heading toward the Shielders you want to connect with! Where else could an entire town disappear to?"

A slight smile showed on Beenishia's face as she stood up. "Perhaps," she said, and the smile vanished as quickly as it came. "Either way, we need to move on and see if we can connect with them or my comrades before sundown." She turned to her crew and continued, "I do not want to be in the air come nightfall. We all need to rest and prepare for the next several days. We also are going to need to look for supplies. I need you to be on the lookout for a place to land for the night if we begin to lose daylight, understood?"

The crew agreed and prepared to move on.

"Vira, update us at once if there is a change in the signal or if we can gather any Human communication as we go."

Beenishia moved toward the captain's seat and sat down, catching my eye in the mirror. "You and Zaforous will continue to look for survivors or any hint of where the Humans are traveling. Can you do that?"

We agreed we could. Zaforous went back to work, and I settled myself in my seat and prepared to keep looking.

My head spun trying to think of the reasons her family had disappeared.

The ship vibrated as it kicked into gear. It zoomed faster and faster as we continued to head north. We could've been able to make it to the other Shielders in a heartbeat, yet the decision was made to try to save my people. It was touching, all things considered. Not to mention fuel was now a top priority. Going fast would deplete our supply or worse, destroy an engine that was already running on fumes.

"General Beenishia, what happens if we meet up with more Humans?" I asked. "What are we going to do? There isn't enough room to fit them all in here."

"I know, Henry," she answered promptly. "I figured we could decide what to do when we see the numbers. If there are too many, we follow them and guide them to where the signal is being distributed, or we set up camp safely out of the way."

"When we all regroup, what then?" I asked. "What will we do when the Temorshians come back?"

The threat of the Temorshians returning was very real. It was going to happen whether we liked it or not. Everything depended on Beenishia and her team being ready to help defend the survivors. I had given my word that I would help her and I meant it, but the others? What would happen to them? We *needed* to be prepared.

Beenishia sighed. "You're asking such hard questions, Henry. I cannot say. It depends on what we have in front of us when we do regroup. We could have more soldiers and ammunition. We could have a defense set up and in place. Or we could have nothing," she stated.

She was so good at pushing her emotions aside to further the mission. No wonder she was second in command.

"I know my comrades are prepared. They have been trained well. I trust that they will do what they have been taught to do, and that is what matters right now," Beenishia told me, a little louder so her crew could hear her clearly.

"Makes sense, but what can we do? The Humans, I mean … "

"Depends," she answered, turning her head to the left so one eye could see me better. "Are you willing to fight?"

"Yes, of course. I'll do whatever it takes."

"Then, if more of you have the same mentality, we will be all right," she said with a hint of optimism. "Your kind will need to help now that our numbers are so low. We will need each other in the next few days. The way is simple: fight or be taken."

"Trust me, we will fight," I stated. "Humans fight for what we believe in—and much more. This is no different. Our survival is at stake."

The view was getting better the more we traveled north: less devastation and more trees, which gave the whole ship hope. Everything appeared to be untouched and preserved—like the battle had never happened in this small corner of the world. Zaforous found Humans in their homes or outside looking around. They were small clusters of people, but not the ones we were now tracking.

Maybe this is why Kayin's family left their destroyed home?

We didn't stop when we saw the small groups in their safe houses. It would be dark soon, and we didn't have enough fuel to stop and restart so many times. We had to be wise and calculating. They might be safer in their safe houses compared with the others who were blindly walking out in the open. I felt selfish for only looking for the people I cared about, but I had come this far. There was nothing else I could do except finish my mission. Besides, the groups we flew over were safely secured within their homes and safe houses. There was no sign war had reached their doorsteps. We felt comfortable leaving them be.

Unfortunately, we weren't going to make it to where the other Shielders were located this evening. The rest of the ship wasn't too happy, but I was. The Humans needed more help. The leftover troops could manage far longer than a small group of inexperienced Human civilians. Besides, tomorrow was another day.

As we traveled, one of the Shielders noted that outside of our atmosphere, more Temorshian ships gathered. Just as Beenishia predicted, their numbers were growing. We were sitting ducks being out here alone.

It was late afternoon by the time we made it to northern Michigan. The crew lowered the ship, pausing briefly before the crew seamlessly landed the vessel.

Beenishia, in a hurried conversation with one of her lieutenants, powered down the ship with the help of several others. "Me leio falta megour," she hissed. "Gatharck sem bled, me leio."

The same lieutenant barked the same orders to three other Shielders as he made his way to the exit. They copied his move, grabbing their weapons and following him outside.

"Where are we?" I asked as everyone started to prepare to leave the ship. "Can I help with anything?"

Zaforous took off his headset and scratched his head, turning to me when he was done smiling. "Well, I guess we are camping here for the night," he said. "Would you like to come with me and see what we can find in the houses nearby?"

I nodded, undoing the latches to my seat. Once free, I stretched, getting the kinks out of my spine.

"What do we need?" I asked.

"You will need to look for food and anything else we can use," Beenishia interjected, walking toward the two of us.

"Yeah, okay, I can help with that," I said. "By the way, any developments on the signal or the tracking?"

"Signal is still going strong," Beenishia stated, resting her body weight on a nearby chair. "We can reconnect with them tomorrow afternoon. We've had to slow the ship down to conserve fuel, or we could have made it today. I guess it worked out—we should be getting closer to the pack of Humans. They might be closer than we think."

I couldn't help but smirk. *It was working out, for me anyway.*

"We will find them, won't we?" I asked.

Beenishia looked down at her feet. She didn't answer right away, as Zaforous decided he'd had enough of waiting.

"Do not worry so much, Henry," he mused, pushing me toward

the exit. "You have done nothing but worry since we have found you. It will work out."

Gently pushed out of the ship in the direction of the nearest home, I couldn't fight against the strength of a Shielder. "I thought we decided I needed answers?" I asked him as he let go of me. I tried keeping up with his strides as we walked.

"We did," he said, "but you worry too much. Everything *will* be all right. The Humans are close ... How do I know this? I thought I saw a large pack on the screen."

"Wait! What?" I cried, trying to grab his arm to slow him down. "Wait a minute!"

He stopped to look at me, a small smile on his face, but it quickly vanished.

"I *did* think I saw something. It did not stay present on the screen long enough for me to be certain," he said. "I did not say anything because as soon as I saw it, I lost it. *Mezda* Beenishia does not do well with failure." He paused. "I did not want to ... I did not want to say anything to get your hopes up or to upset *Mezda*."

I sighed, walking toward the house with Zaforous in tow.

"It's okay, it was probably nothing," I told him, my stomach settling.

The front porch of the home was attached to a large house, but it didn't have a safe house anywhere on the property. The white siding looked crisp in contrast to the greenery surrounding the area. The various windows sparkled in the sunlight.

"A shame," I sighed.

"What is a shame?" Zaforous asked as he checked around the perimeter of the home, walking back to me when he saw nothing. He signaled to me to enter the home.

"Well, it just seems like if you have so much money to own such a nice house, you'd pay for a safe house?"

Zaforous shook his head. "Humans ... "

The outside had been neglected for several months, with weeds and wildflowers sprouting up wherever they pleased. The grass was not trimmed or watered either. Even with the lack of care, the house was picturesque. Zaforous let me climb the stairs first. I reached the impressive door while admiring the furniture on the porch.

"Nice place," I said, opening the door easily. "That's odd."

"What?"

"The door. Normal people lock up before leaving."

The inside of the home was just as impressive as the outside. The owners had decorated it heavily with photographs from their adventures through life. Wedding photos along with images of children and grandchildren and other life events decorated the walls and mantles of the fireplaces around the home. It was very homey, but empty. The family that had lived within must have fled many weeks ago. Others had ransacked the place in their absence, for it was dirty and various unnecessary items were broken on the ground.

"Perhaps they found a better option," Zaforous suggested, looking around and frowning. "We may not find anything useful in here. Everything's gone."

"Let's check the kitchen," I offered. "You never know, maybe they looked past practical needs for material goods?"

We headed through a large entryway, passing a staircase. A hallway ran the length of the house and opened up to different rooms: TV room, bathroom, and closet space until we reached a dining area opening to a breakfast nook. After a few wrong turns, we ended up in a giant, gourmet kitchen. A large granite island sat in the middle of the room with its own sink. Dotted around it stood a few stools, while others had been thrown around the room. The cupboards were open, one door hanging by a bolt.

On the far side of the room two French doors stood undisturbed by the invaders. I walked up, pulling the metal handles. As expected, the pantries were still full of edible food.

"Great, look what I found!" I yelled to Zaforous as I entered a large and spacious pantry filled with plenty of usable food.

Zaforous poked his head in. "It is Human food," he grimaced, obviously disappointed. "It will have to do for now."

"Oh, come on, don't be such a sourpuss! It'll hold you over until you can get rations from your kind," I reminded him. "This stuff looks pretty good even if it is on the organic side."

Zaforous shrugged, turning to put his weapon on the counter in the center of the room. He scanned the room, his eyes landing on the field outside of the big window.

"Do you need water?" I asked as I gathered some items into a big plastic bag I'd found inside of the pantry. "Do you even drink water? I know I'm going to need some water. Isn't there some tea or something you guys drink? Do you create that with water?"

I waited for an answer as I packed bags.

"This cereal is pretty good," I insisted, inspecting a box of Captain Crunch. "Though, let's be honest, I haven't had any of this sugary stuff in years."

I stopped, glancing back at Zaforous, who was obviously ignoring me. I left the pantry with several stuffed bags, finding him looking out the window in a trance.

"Hello, buddy? Did you hear anything I just said?"

I left the bags of food on the island to walk over to him.

"Zaforous? What's wrong?" I poked his arm. He flinched.

"Something is out there ... " he sputtered, not looking away from the window.

I slowly turned toward the window. The breeze danced among the blades of grass, and the pine trees swayed in the wind.

"I don't see anything," I told him quietly. "Are you sure?"

Zaforous pushed a button on his suit of armor, quickly speaking La'Mursian. I watched as his jaw articulated his words, though I hadn't a clue what he was saying.

I turned my attention back to the field. I saw nothing, but then again, I didn't have the eyesight of a Shielder. I scanned the tree line but didn't see any movement. Zaforous was thoroughly freaking me out by his sudden change in demeanor. My heart raced, my mind spun, but all I could do was stare out the window, trying to see what he saw.

We stood in silence.

This is not good, I thought, *what scares a Shielder?*

Sudden noises from behind startled me. I turned quickly, coming face to face with Beenishia's lieutenant and shortly after, Beenishia herself. Others followed behind with more weapons than I thought we had with us.

"What's going on?" I asked.

The lot spoke in La'Mursian, ignoring my question. Some went running outside as others set up machines in other parts of the house. My words hung in the air.

Staying out of the way, I stood there useless and afraid.

"Beenishia," I yelled over the chaos, "what is going on? What can I do?"

She looked up from her gun, "You need to go back to the ship."

"Are you sure? I could stay and help—"

"No, Henry, not this time. Go back to the ship now and stay there," she stated, as stern as ever.

"But you said—"

"I know what I said!" she snapped. "But now is not the time. Go to the ship."

I could taste the dread in my mouth. It threatened to show itself, but I forced it down.

"Fine, but tell me what you see ... " I pleaded, pushing panic aside.

"They are here," one of the soldiers said next to me.

"Who ... ?"

Shit.

"How did the Temorshians get so close without us knowing?"

Beenishia's words rang through my ears—I needed to get to the ship and fast.

I ran down the hall through the entryway and out the front door as quickly as I could. I left the door open as I raced down the stairs, jumping off the last porch step. My body struck something hard. A raging pain shot through me, splitting my head along with it. I tried to stand, but my vision blurred, the world spun, and I crumpled back to the ground as voices rang out.

Gurgling sounds left my mouth; my tongue was unable to form words.

"Are you okay?" someone asked in English.

"Give him some room," said another.

"Oh, God, he's bleeding from his forehead. Go get Harrison, he'll have something for the wound," said another, touching the side of my face.

"Wait, let me see him!" squealed a girl's voice. "Oh, my God! *I know him!* Henry, Henry, can you hear me?" the girl shrieked.

"Y-y-yes," I stammered, my tongue doubling in size by the minute.

My head throbbed. I tried with all my might to open my eyes and focus, but the sensation felt wrong; my eyelids were heavy. A face came into view through my distorted vision. The face was distorted but I caught the outline of a young girl with large dark eyes and flowing brown hair.

"Kay ... Kayin? Is that you?" I choked.

My vision focused, the sunlight bright against her outline. My eyes watered, but the lush green of the world around me engulfed my sight. The flowing brown hair blew gently into my eyes.

Pain stung the inside of my head, but the dizziness subsided just enough for me to look up into the girl's face. She spoke, but I couldn't make out the words.

My heart sank. It wasn't Kayin, but her younger sister, Layla Aves.

16

"What on Earth are you doing here?" Layla asked breathlessly as she helped me sit up. "How did you get here?"

Layla was just as beautiful as her sister. The only indicators the girls weren't twins were her medium-length brown hair, lighter in color than her sister's, and a difference in height. She had a dimple on the left side of her mouth that stood out when she smiled and disappeared completely when she was angry—which was rare.

I only stared at her, soaking in the surrealism of the moment.

My head was spinning more from the turn of events than the pain. I'd smacked my skull hard on the ground, managing to run into a big fellow I didn't recognize—someone from Layla's crew. Everything was slowly coming back into focus, but my head buzzed as images barely registered.

"I came to find Kayin," I told her. "I met up with Shielders, and they took me to your family's house. It was empty, so we found some trail we thought you'd be on. We decided to follow it. Looks like I was right. But what were you thinking leaving the safe house? It's not safe out here!"

I finished as the others joined us. There weren't many of them, maybe twenty people, including some of the relatives I recognized from family gatherings. I looked around at the faces staring back at me—just as confused as I was, though perhaps they were relieved in some small way that others existed outside of their small bubble.

"Where's Kayin?" I searched frantically for her through the growing crowd. My racing heart made my head throb harder, and a thin stream of blood trickled down the side of my face, but I ignored it, searching for her familiar face.

"Where is Kayin?" I asked again as someone came down to my level. It was a man in glasses with black-and-white peppered hair, his hands full of gauze and a med kit.

"Let me take a look at your head," he insisted. "I'm a doctor—my name is Harrison Rhodes. Do you have any pain or dizziness? How is your vision?"

Harrison examined me. He was quick and seemed to be good at his craft: cleaning, examining, and asking frequent questions.

"Thankfully the gash doesn't appear to be too deep or you'd need stitches," he murmured. "Here," he said, handing me more gauze. "Keep pressure on the wound, but it should stop shortly. You're lucky it's not bigger. If you feel unusually tired or anything out of the ordinary, please tell me. I don't have the equipment to do a head scan to examine further, but you're lucky. It's probably just a slight concussion."

I smiled, letting a sigh escape my lips. "Thank you, I'm Henry—"

"I gathered that from Layla," he said flatly. "Just relax for the rest of the night. We can set up a campsite for you to rest—"

"No! You don't understand!" I yelled, gathering my strength and forcing myself up. I managed to stand, a little shaky, with some help from Layla and the doctor. "We have to get to the ship."

Again, I counted the number of people around me. It'd be tight but we could fit in the ship. I had wasted valuable time nursing my wound.

"You're not making any sense," Harrison said, not letting me go. "Are you sure you're not feeling—"

"No, listen!"

"Henry, how did you get up here?" Layla asked, ignoring Harrison. "There's no way the Shielders stopped what they were doing and helped you get here. Are you with Kayin?" she asked me, holding onto my shirt. "Did you two meet up somewhere?"

"Am I with *her*?"

"She said she'd make it to her grandparents' house, but she never did!" shrieked the girls' mother, Mrs. Aves. "How are you here and she's not?"

My words turned to dust on my tongue.

"She's not here with you?" I asked slowly, bile forming at the back of my throat. "Kayin told me she was heading to your house, too."

I moved away from Layla and Harrison. I let my words hang in the air as I watched Mrs. Aves crumble into her husband, her wails echoing through the trees.

The group remained silent.

"I'm sorry," I said, pushing my heartache aside, "but we have to get out of here. You see, they're—"

"Where are the Shielders?" someone behind us asked.

"They're inside the house—they're busy. If you could all follow me, we can talk more in their ship. Come on."

Causing panic was the last thing I wanted. Walking in the direction of the ship, no one followed me. I stopped, confused and annoyed we were wasting more time.

I turned, "Come on, we really need to get out of here. *Please.*"

"We don't need to follow you, Shielder lover," a big, overweight man yelled, stepping out of the group of people.

The rest of the group, including Layla and her family, looked from me to the fat man, eyeing their companions as they went, each slowly inching toward their loved ones.

"You don't understand," I pleaded. "They're *here*. We need to go—it's not safe standing out here."

"Yeah, we know they're *here*. We aren't listening to you or any other Shielder anymore," said the fat man. "They got us into this mess, and we're not taking any more idiotic orders from those scumbags."

Great, I thought, *opposition from a dumb ass.*

I looked around, trying to find someone to back me up. None of them made eye contact with me. I was getting the impression that he'd been the one to make these people leave their safe houses and trek all the way up here.

I might've thought the way he did, but not now, not when I'd seen the terror in my new friends' eyes.

I took a deep breath, preparing myself to talk them into following me. We were going to be caught in this mess whether we liked it or not, but the safest place was in the ship. Hell, I was a lawyer, after all—I could talk anyone into anything.

"First of all, I don't know who you are or what your game plan is, but you need to listen to me," I stated as calmly as I could, clenching my fists to keep from exploding. "I'm not the enemy here and neither are the Shielders inside. Trust me, I've spent the day with them. They're here trying to protect you—*all* of us. "

"Oh, yeah, like they did a few days ago?" the fat one retorted with a snarl.

Murmurs of agreement and defense quickly erupted from the group.

"Please, you have to keep it down ... " My biggest fear as the voices grew louder was that they would unknowingly bring attention to us. "I can explain more if we could just—"

"Shut the fuck up," the fat man said, silencing the others at once.

He'd gotten unbelievably close to me while I tried to quiet the others. I took a step backward.

"Who the fuck do *you* think you are?" he asked. "We don't know you and don't give a shit about what you think."

"I know him, my family knows him. Let him explain," Layla tried to reassure the man as she stepped closer to the two of us.

"Bitch, no one is talking to you," he snarled back in her face.

"Hey!" I objected, the anger starting to get the better of me. "Don't talk to her like that! If you have a problem with following me, fine. But I'm going to take my girlfriend's family with me. You want to walk straight into the Temorshians' arms, so be it. Anyone interested in following me to safety can come with us."

I stared directly into the fat man's face, yet he didn't move a muscle. He looked back just as fiercely. It was obvious he wasn't going to back down. This man may have been able to dominate the others and talk them into this foolish mission, but he wouldn't be so lucky with me. I continued to stand my ground.

"I thought *Mezda* told you to go to the ship, Henry. What is all this noise—" Zaforous asked, coming out of the house in a huff, stopping once he saw the group of Humans waiting by the porch. "Oh," is all he could manage to say once he realized the situation.

The fat man spun around as Zaforous spoke, glaring holes into his skull.

"They found us—you were right, Zaforous," I told him casually.

He didn't answer me. He stood as still as he could, his mouth twisting as though he was calculating what to do next.

Tension hung in the air, tickling my skin. His presence only upset the others, and their energy immediately changed once he stepped outside, the intensity bubbling over.

"Don't worry," I reassured him, stepping in before he made things worse, "I was trying to explain to them that they needed to follow me." I made eye contact with Zaforous, pleading with him to turn around and get back in the house.

"We should kill you," the fat man said, not letting his eyes move from Zaforous's face. "We should kill you *all* ... "

Zaforous' mouth opened slightly, only to close again into a thin line. His eyes were wild as he looked from me to the fat man in confusion.

"I ... I do not understand," he muttered, looking down at his feet, glancing back up to me. "Henry, did you not tell them?"

"I've been trying. This one thinks you're the enemy—not *them.*" Pushing the fat man out of the way, I walked back toward the house.

I turned to the rest of the group. "Look, I know you don't know me or understand what's going on, but I'm asking you to trust me and let me explain in a safer place. Please, you have to come—it's for your safety. They've made it to Earth—they're very close. The Temorshians are *here!*"

The crowd gasped collectively as my news hit a nerve. Only the stubborn pig stayed silent, keeping his gaze on Zaforous. Kayin's family looked to each other as if silently communicating their next move.

"Are you sure, Henry?" Layla asked in a shaky voice.

"Trust me, I'm sure. These Shielders are my friends, and they know what they're doing. We need to move."

"Where do we need to go?" she asked, as she reached out for her mother's hand.

"To their ship."

Murmurs of agreement followed.

"How far is the ship?" asked another.

"It's not far, trust me. Come on!" I yelled, walking briskly to direct them where to go. "Tell Beenishia we found the others, Zaforous. We'll be in the ship if you need us. Good luck!"

I waved back to him, but he missed my motion. "It's one thing to hide one Human, but a large group of adults?"

"It'll be okay!" I yelled.

He looked up and smiled. "Stay in the ship, Henry. I'll find you when it's over." He turned quickly to report to Beenishia.

I'd formed a friendship with young Zaforous, and I'd started to care about Beenishia, whether I liked it or not. I wanted them to be safe almost as much as I wanted Kayin to be safe, wherever she might be. I had a responsibility to these people, especially her family, now. I'd get them to safety and protect them just like I would've protected Kayin.

"I don't know how you managed it, Henry, but I'm glad you're with us now," Layla told me as we approached the ship. "I'm sure Kayin would have wanted it this way, wherever she is. She's alive somewhere—I just know it."

I gave her a small smile. "I'm sure of it, too. We'll find her. When things settle, we'll figure out a plan to find her."

I turned toward the others as we slowed down at the entrance of the ship. The group eyed the ship skeptically, hesitating to enter.

"Now, it's a little cramped in there," I told them, "but this is our best bet to stay out of the way while the Shielders do their thing, okay? Who's first?"

Kayin's family volunteered to show good faith and soon the others followed. Layla, Harrison, and I managed to get everyone inside easily. It would be tight, but it was going to have to do for now.

Before I followed the others with Layla and Harrison, I noticed the fat man stayed behind with his family, wandering off into the distance and heading right toward where Zaforous had spotted the Temorshian gang. A shiver ran down my spine.

Layla followed my eyes to the family. "Good riddance," she said. "That man was a monster and had no idea what he was doing. He tried to get us to leave earlier before the fighting started, but *Abuelo* told him to take a hike. Once the fighting ended and everything was destroyed, we decided to leave on our own. There was a faint signal we picked up. We knew we had to get out of the devastated area and find another place to stay. Nothing was left for us at the house," she admitted sadly. She looked down; the corners of her mouth faltered, but she shook off her melancholy. "We had the unfortunate luck to run into Pat—that's his name—and his family out in the open, so we were stuck."

"How did you get all the way up here so fast?" I asked her.

"That's where I came in," Harrison interjected. "I had a huge van that, luckily, fit all of them. Only trouble was that we ran out of gas a few miles back. When you ran into us, *literally*," he chuckled. "We'd been looking for a place to stay the night. We'd heard your ship but, of course, Pat was against connecting."

"Pat didn't like the idea of staying put or Shielders, but he was hungry so he *allowed* us to search for a place with food," Layla continued. "That's when we tricked him into getting close to the ship."

"But how did you know it was safe?"

"We didn't," Harrison answered, "but it was better than walking around like chickens with our heads cut off."

"You're lucky, because the Temorshians are in the area too."

"Yes, we are," Harrison added, giving Layla a side eye.

She ignored him. "I'm glad Pat's gone. He wasn't nice, and his family was a bunch of whiners. No one needs that at a time like this ..."

"You realize they are walking to their death?" I asked.

"Let karma take care of business," she purred.

The three of us stood in silence as we watched Pat's family disappear into the tree line. The sun was beginning to set, and it cast an orange glow over the landscape. It was beautiful—something I could have enjoyed, if it weren't for the threat of Temorshians.

"Do you really trust them after all this?" Dr. Rhodes asked, after watching the sun set behind the trees. "After everything that's happened?"

"Yes," I stated flatly, "I do. It's hard to believe—even for me. Before I met them I hated them—especially that prince. The ones I hooked up with are nice, even if they are tough and blunt. Sometimes they keep information to themselves, but I think they do it because they think they're helping. They're strange but mean well. I'd like to think we're friends now." I paused at the absurdity of it all. "They seem to feel awful about what happened, not just because they had tremendous losses on their end, but because they let us down—they know they failed us."

Harrison sighed, scratching the side of his face.

"Well, we'd better get inside. We have some food with us from our safe house, Henry. Let's eat and rest up a bit. What do you say?" Layla asked, with a sweet smile on her face. She walked into the ship shaking her head. She stopped, taking one last look at me. "I can't believe you're here—all *that* way. A miracle!"

Harrison chuckled, patting me on the back. "Or dumb luck." He entered the ship after Layla.

I stayed outside, taking in the last bit of sunlight. The sun's light bathed the ship in a warm wave of color. I breathed in the spring air and allowed myself to enjoy the peacefulness the area offered. Even with the danger just beyond the trees, the land grew a lush lawn and solid trees.

I didn't want to think about my disappointment. I had to be content with the fact I was still alive—today, *now*, here. I didn't know what tomorrow would bring, but I felt relief knowing I was in the best possible position I could be. I was grateful for the small miracles that had led me to where I was at this moment.

"I'll find you, Kayin. I promise."

Our small group was made up of doctors, teachers, college students, farmers, fast food workers, from all walks of life. We were a delightful bunch of random people all brought together by tragedy—a new type of family with a different kind of bond.

It was a very tight fit getting all of us in the ship. No one complained or made any trouble; instead, they helped each other and made sure everyone was as comfortable as possible. They shared food and supplies, and even made a few jokes here and there. Under such circumstances, I would have thought everyone would be on edge, but they were pleasant and calm.

I rubbed my temple; the pain still lingered, but the dizziness had subsided long ago.

After everyone, including myself, got something to eat and drink, we settled into our respective corners.

"I was getting food from the grocery store when the sirens went off. I didn't have time to think—I just dropped my bags and ran.

Mind you, I've never been athletic in my life! But I didn't stop—I just ran as fast as I could to the house," an older gentleman told us. "I made sure I got the family into the house in time—we were lucky."

"*Mamá* had us all in the safe house before everything started. The moment the ships were visible, we were stuffed—" Layla explained before her mother playfully hit her arm. "What? It saved us, didn't it?"

"*Si, mija, pero basta!*" Mrs. Aves retorted.

"Excuse me," a small child's voice rang out. "Henry, could you tell us more about the Shielders?"

"Oh, sure ... Well, they're cold at first ... "

I told them of my experience with the Shielders. Some fell asleep as I spoke, but most stayed awake, listening and asking questions.

"What do you think is going on outside?" asked a young man, a few years younger than me.

"I don't have the slightest idea," I said.

"The Temorshians could have realized who they were up against," added an older woman of color.

"Maybe," said another, "but I think they're waiting to get more of us."

"Hush, you'll scare the kids," a father of four pleaded. "I almost had them sleeping."

"They need to realize we're at war. You can't save them from everything. It'll be better if you let them be afraid," a man chimed in.

"Not much use to worry about it now, is there?" asked Harrison, halting the panic before it could grow. "I'm sure the Shielders know what they're doing and are making the best strategic decisions."

"Yes, I guess so," piped Kayin's grandfather, a wise old man, with few winkles for his age. He still had his dark hair with very little gray—he'd hit the aging jackpot. "Let's get some rest. I'm a light sleeper, so I will wake everyone if I hear anything suspicious. G'night, all."

We said our goodnights and settled down to get some rest. As soon as I closed my eyes, I entered into a deep, dreamless sleep.

As my body restored itself with a much-needed rest, a buzzing sound stirred my consciousness. It wasn't loud, but it was annoying. I opened my eyes slowly while the rest of the ship slept quietly. The occasional snore met my ears.

The sun was beginning to rise, and its glow caused frightful shadows along the walls. I might have been sleeping longer than I thought, but the ship was still dark, which meant it was early morning.

Everyone was still sleeping except Kayin's grandfather. I found him sitting in Beenishia's captain's seat, an odd image compared to the sight I was used to seeing. The thought of Beenishia made we wonder why none of the Shielders had come to check on us during the night.

With enough room to stand, I made my way carefully over to Kayin's grandfather, making sure not to wake anyone. As I approached, I noticed Harrison and Layla stirring.

"Shhh," shushed *Abuelo* quietly. "I started hearing that noise about thirty minutes ago. It keeps getting louder, but I don't see anything."

"What do you think it is, *Abuelo*?" Layla asked in a low voice. "Is it—is it *them*?"

"Where are the Shielders?" Harrison added. "If it's them, wouldn't the Shielders be out here?"

Paralyzing fear plagued my system. For the first time, I was without ideas. "I don't recognize that sound," I said, trying to control the pitch of my voice.

"I haven't been close to an extraterrestrial ship before, so I can't distinguish the sound myself," *Abuelo* said. "It's not ours, that's for sure."

The buzzing noise grew louder the longer we watched from the cockpit. It'd turned into a low hum. Whatever it was, it didn't sound good, yet nothing moved on the horizon.

By this time, the rest of our party had woken up. Whispers erupted behind us.

"Quiet, please, everyone shut up!" Layla hissed.

"It's going to be fine. We're in the safest place," Harrison added, trying to keep the group from getting out of hand.

It helped quiet down the group, but the panic in the ship was building.

Movement directly in front of me caught my eye. The tree line before the ship started to sway in the breeze coming off whatever was coming for us.

"Everyone stay away from the windows and the door! Move to the back!" ordered *Abuelo*. "Henry, do you know how to work this thing? Lock it or use its power?"

"No!" I yelled over the clatter of everyone moving to the far side of the ship. "No, I don't!"

"We'll be fine, *Abuelo*! Just come over here with us," pleaded Layla, as she hugged her mother. He did as she wished, coming to hold his wife and what was left of his family.

I noticed Harrison get as close as he could to Layla, both locking eyes in a silent show of affection.

It was the second time in days that I felt like an outsider. Looking around at the families huddled in the ship holding onto one another, I was alone.

I made some very wrong decisions in my life.

As I squatted down with the rest, I realized that was what life was all about: love. It was all that mattered and all that ever counted.

I peered out of the large window the best I could. The trees swayed more violently now, and the birds had long since flown off. A ship came into view just over the trees. It was as large as ours and similarly shaped, but rounder and flatter. It had undergone severe damage to the point I could not understand the markings on the sides. As I watched, I noticed it slowed to hover close to our hiding spot.

I waited for the fight to begin. Instead, the ship lowered itself a few feet away, landing with a thud.

"Why isn't anything happening?" asked Harrison in a voice just above a whisper.

We all kept still, holding our breaths as we watched the ship land on the ground.

"Can anyone see what's happening from where they are?" I whispered, straining to see anything.

"No, Henry," Layla whispered back. "I can't see a thing. Should one of us move closer? I'm small, I can do it."

Layla didn't wait for an answer. She made her way slowly toward the front of the ship. She stayed low, trying her best to go unseen by anything that could see through the window.

"Be careful," I reminded her, "we don't know who's in control of that ship."

Layla made her way to Beenishia's chair, stopping to take a deep breath, and finally making her way around.

"What can you see?" asked Harrison quietly. Again I noticed how his eyes never left her small form.

"Nothing, really," she told us. "Nothing has come out of the ship. Wait! *Oh, my God!* The Shielders that were with Henry are coming outside with weapons."

My stomach sank.

Layla gasped. "The ship ... the ship's doors are opening. *Oh, God ...* "

"Layla, I think it's time for you to come back over here," her grandfather pleaded.

"No, we need to see what's happening," she whispered back. "Something is coming out of the ship ... "

The silence hung in the air as we waited.

"The suspense is killing me! What is going on?" Harrison interrupted the silence, moving forward, but I stopped him.

"Too much movement could force us out in the open," I hissed.

Layla didn't respond right away. She seemed to be in a trance, lost in her own world.

"Layla," I pleaded, "what do you see? What is it?"

"Good news ... " she said, standing up. "It's not *them*, thank God. It's more Shielders!"

[PART 3]

Melissa Pebbles
Detroit, Michigan
Earth

[17]
APRIL 29TH, 2013

My lungs burned as I inhaled a cloud of smoke. The heat of a distant flame warmed my dry skin, causing me to fight to open my eyes. Though the smoke was thick and burned my lungs, my body tried to move. I strained to make out the sounds around me, but the ringing in my ears wouldn't allow me to hear over the hiss. I remained motionless, and my hearing came back, the ring never breaking its roar.

I grew cold as my limbs rebelled, shaking violently, prickly bumps dotting my skin.

You're going into shock, I screamed internally. *Focus and get up! This is not the time to sit here.*

I fought to stay calm, continuing to lie where I was, working to bring my heart rate down. The humming of various voices pierced through the hiss, the ringing drifting away as their voices grew louder.

Though my memory was hazy and distorted, I knew I was in a shelter with other people, but exact details blurred together, creating unrecognizable images. *I'd made it to my parents' house where my entire family was waiting and taken them all to the nearest shelter. It was hard to enter, but we made it inside—we found safety.*

The terror I felt as I listened to the chaos outside of the shelter rushed back to me, ripping throughout my body. I bolted upright, barely missing the beam hanging inches above my head.

Shit, I groaned, *the war has begun.*

I strained to accept the light meeting my eyes as they created shapes out of my surroundings. Various forms ran, encircled in clouds of smoke, making it hard to see. The occasional spark from broken or cut power sources sizzled.

Just as my eyes took in the horrific scene, my hearing came back all at once. Screams on top of screams, cries on top of heartbreaking cries; my body shook violently. Their pain sent shivers down my spine.

I tried to block out the sound, jamming my fingers in my ears, but it was too late. The screams stayed with me and rang loudly in my head.

I tried to get up to run away from my horrible surroundings, but my body was stiff and too heavy to move.

I pulled my left leg into me as the pain of trying to move my right shot through me. I looked down to survey the damage. My right foot had been crushed under debris that had fallen during the attack.

I had no choice but to gather what was left of my strength to push the twisted metal off my leg. I threw my weight against the beam. Slowly the metal started to give, moving at a snail's pace. Giving up on moving the whole thing, I lifted the rubble just enough to pull my foot out from under it, fighting the pain racing across my extremity.

Before this mess I'd put on my favorite pair of boots and, to my surprise, even after being smashed under such heavy metal, the boot was intact. I could only hope that it had saved my foot from any further damage, though the pain did not offer such an optimistic view.

I reached down, unlacing the strings of the boot, slowly beginning the process of removing the shoe. The same sharp pain ran up my leg. I couldn't bring myself to continue—it was too much to do it alone. I looked around for someone who could help.

"Mom?" I asked. I'd lost sight of my parents when the fighting began and now didn't see anyone I knew. "Mom, are you there?" I waited for a reply, keeping my frantic thoughts at bay.

"I'm here, honey," she said in her soft, reassuring voice I knew and loved. She pushed her way through the rubble toward the sound of my voice, the thick smoke hiding most of her frame.

"Mom, over here!" I called. I watched her struggle her way over to me as parts of the building begun to crumble, causing the screams to intensify.

"We need to get out of here. Where's Dad?" I asked her as she bent down to reach me.

"I got them out, honey. They're fine. How are you feeling?" she asked in her sensible way. She wasn't a doctor or nurse, but she had a way of knowing what was wrong even without fancy degrees. She looked over my body as I told her about my foot.

"You'll be fine, but your foot may be broken. Let's try to get you out of here. I can't look at it now," she said as she laced up my boot. When she was done she placed her arm around my shoulders to help me to get up. "How does that feel?"

I stood and a searing pain shot through my ankle. "When I put too much weight on my right foot, it kills, but I can make it."

I looked around through the smoke. Death and devastation met my eyes: half the building had been blown away, leaving countless dead. I slammed my eyes closed. My mother tensed as she watched me.

"Try to keep your eyes down, Melissa," she suggested to me quietly. "Many people lost their lives ... "

I could tell through the screaming that persisted that things had gone poorly for all of us seeking shelter in this destroyed safe space.

"I won't look," I told her, moving slowly around the obstacles in our path. "Where did you take everyone?"

"Just outside. Far enough away so when this thing finally decides to fall down we won't get hurt and close enough to stay in the know of what's going on," she said quietly as she helped me over the fallen beam.

I was suddenly overcome with emotion for my strong and fearless mother. My mother: fun, capable, strong, and loving. I looked at her, finally seeing her—the real woman—for the first time. Her skin showed signs of age but still held its radiance even hidden under the filth, while her dark hair, streaked with white, stayed put despite the breeze. She didn't seem as shaken as the rest of us, and thankfully, she wasn't hurt. What had happened to us may have broken bones and stolen life, but with my mother by my side, I could get through anything.

After carefully making our way outside of the devastated build-ing—fighting to push our way through the survivors—we reached the rest of my family. I saw my father first, who ran over to help me get settled down. My mother bent in front of me to assess the damage. I tried to look anywhere but at what my mother was doing. I couldn't stomach the disfiguration that surely awaited me.

I saw my grandfather and my sister, Mabel, standing over my grandmother. Grandfather was brushing her hand slowly but lovingly. I couldn't see my grandmother very well, but she was lying down and not moving.

"Is Grandmother all right?" I asked my parents.

They glanced at each other, and then went back at what they were doing. My mother lifted my boot off my foot, and instant relief flowed through the swollen area. My father sat next to me and held me close. Neither spoke.

"Well?" I asked again, "What happened?"

"Your grandmother didn't make it, Melissa," my father uttered, holding me tighter. Somehow he looked older. His hair was thinning, and what was left was snowy white.

I'd been extremely close with my paternal grandmother, and the agony from the news broke my heart into tiny pieces blown away by the wind. I gulped for air as I sobbed into my father's shoulder, unable to stop the ferocious shuddering. I allowed all the emotions I'd been feeling over the last few days to bubble up inside and spill out. My father and I embraced as my mother worked on my foot and patted my other leg lovingly when she could.

We didn't speak for a long time. The sound of my howls vibrated off the surrounding buildings as distant cries matched my own.

As my mother finished wrapping my leg, she said, "Well, thank God it's not broken, Melly, but you'll need to take it easy. It's definitely sprained."

I sighed. I could deal with an injured foot, but my heart hurt far worse than anything physical.

"Can I see her?" I asked, ignoring my mom.

"Of course, honey, of course. Let me help you up," my father said as he shifted his weight to help me. He gently propped me up on his shoulder as the two of us slowly made our way to the body of my grandmother.

Mabel, the younger of the two of us, caught my eye. She looked a little worse than I did with grime and dust covering her body, but she appeared healthy. I sighed, letting relief surge through me. I don't know what I would've done if anything had happened to her. She was my best friend and greatest competitor. It wasn't that I didn't love my grandmother, but it was because Mabel was in my generation. I needed her in my life—I wasn't ready to lose her. It'd been a secret fear of mine that I would lose my sister at a young age.

I shuddered. *I'd been so close to losing everything, family and all.*

I could tell from Mabel's tearstained cheeks she'd been silently crying. Her face didn't change as we crept closer to the body, but I knew she was grateful for my safety as well. She reached out for me, and when our hands clasped together, she gave mine a squeeze.

Mabel looked down at my foot, her dark hair sliding over her shoulder. "How bad is it?" she asked.

"Not bad," my mother answered, walking around my father and me to help my grandfather sit down on a nearby box. "Come on, Will," she said quietly. "Why don't you come have a seat? Can I get you anything?"

My brave, strong mother moved Grandpa slowly. He was reluctant to move, his mind crumbling just enough for him to be managed and taken care of by Mom. I watched them while Grandpa started to mumble something under his breath. If my heart had any pieces left, they were turned to dust watching my grandfather become lost to us.

His tearstained face contorted in agony. I willed myself to look away and pay my last respects to my idol, my grandmother.

I felt my father leave my side as I slowly bent down to hold my grandmother's hand. I looked at her one more time. Even though most of her body was wounded, her face was peaceful. She looked calm and relaxed, as if she had known she wouldn't make it through the war but was content to have lived her life as she did. She'd lived a long and happy life with my grandfather for many years. She had fought for women's rights in the '70s and had been active in her community. She'd had many friends and lit up the room when she entered. I knew I wouldn't be the only person sad to lose her.

"You have to help us now from heaven," I implored as I choked back tears. "We need you. We need you more than ever. Please, Grandma, please send me the strength to make it through this and give me the ability to save our family." I paused. "I'm so sorry I couldn't save you ... "

I've always believed that tears do not ask permission. They'll come when they come, and it's hard to hold them back. It's the body's way of removing emotion it can no longer contain. At this moment, overwhelmed by all the emotion of loss, confusion, and depression, I cried myself into a stupor. My heart was a fraction of what it used to be.

After we did our best to say our goodbyes, we faced the challenge of what to do with her body. As Dad and Grandfather went off to inquire about any possibilities of disposing of the dead with dignity, Mom, Mabel, and I sat around eating what we'd managed to save from the shelter. It wasn't much, just a few snacks, crackers, and nuts mostly. Everything we owned fit into the four knapsacks Mom alone had managed to save.

"We're going to ration the rest," Mom told us. "Who knows when we'll find anything else?"

I looked around as I munched on a Nutri-Grain bar.

Buildings were now piles of rubble, the air was thick with smoke, and the smell of death hung about. It was hard to tell what time of day it was because the smoke blocked out any sunlight that might have reached us. Cries still rang out from time to time, but they eventually died down. Death was imminent for most of the survivors.

My family had been extremely lucky. Mabel had a few bumps and bruises, Mom and Dad were fine from what I could tell, and Grandfather had a large gash on his arm, which Mom bandaged as best as she could. It seemed the only person with a deterring wound was me. Even though it was still tender, I could walk. I would be slow moving, but we needed to leave, which was all the motivation I needed. I wasn't going to stay around any longer in this mess.

I thought back to Joel, my boyfriend. We'd had a huge fight before my family and I left because he'd wanted us to come with him to his parents' cabin. My parents didn't think it would be a good idea—Dad thought the shelters would be a lot safer with the Shielders around.

Oh, how wrong you were, Dad.

If Joel was right, the fighting would be worse where there were Shielders. We had gone right into the fighting and witnessed his theory come to life.

"We need to leave," I stated. Both my mother and sister turned toward me, jolted out of their own thoughts. "After we take care of Grandmother, we need to take everything we can and get out of here."

"And go where?" Mabel asked in shrill voice, catching on the last syllable. "Everything is like this!"

"We don't know that ... "

"We know that there's nothing left. We should stay with the Shielders and hopefully they'll protect us."

"Oh, because they've done such a good job to begin with?" I snapped back.

Mabel had been one of the many who had fallen in love with the Shielders and had her bedroom walls covered with posters of them, especially Prince Naluba. I'd even caught her in a T-shirt once, but after I'd laughed for hours, it never saw daylight again. I, too, had fallen for their gorgeous eyes, long hair, and slender bodies, but not now—not after this.

"Girls, enough," Mom said, stepping between us. We were notorious for our sisterly fights and she knew it. She didn't have the energy to deal with us and get us to safety. "You both have certain points," Mom continued, "but I agree with Melissa—we need to leave. There isn't anything left for us here."

"What about Grandma? We can't leave her," Mabel asked. Her eyes were round as saucers, tears threatening to spill over.

"We aren't leaving her; she'll always be with us," Mom said. "Your grandmother would've wanted you to live, Mabel Lynn. She wouldn't have wanted you to stay in a place just because it was once safe."

Still shattered from our loss and dealing with survivors' guilt, the three of us sat in silence.

I noticed Dad and Grandpa in the distance. They were coming toward us looking sullen and useless, their arms hanging in defeat, heads bent. Dad carried what looked like a large tarp. Mom noticed them too and stood up.

"I'm afraid I don't have good news, girls," my father said once he reached us. "The only thing we found for the body is this large bag. We'll—we'll have to wrap her up and ... "

"And what? Bag her like trash?" I hissed.

"Melissa Ann, that's enough!" barked my mother.

Grandfather looked devastated, with tears running down his cheeks. He wouldn't look up, just down at the ground, avoiding everyone. Mom made her way to him and helped him sit down. In one quick glance to Dad, she shared some unspoken orders with him.

"Come on, girls," he said quietly, "follow me."

We followed him. I limped as best I could—to where Grandmother was lying. I wasn't afraid of touching a dead body, especially the body of someone I loved, but I was apprehensive about moving it.

The three of us looked down, unsure how to begin.

"What's the plan, Dad?" I asked. I fought hard to keep resentment from creeping into my voice. I didn't want to blame him for this, but a small part of me thought we could've avoided such a loss if we had gone with Joel.

"We need to wrap her up and then find a place to store her," he stated bluntly.

"*Great* plan," Mabel interjected. "Just wrap her up like a burrito and leave her for who knows what! We *can't* do that!"

"I don't have the tools to run a full funeral service either," Dad roared. "This is the best we can do. I'm not happy about it, but what else do you expect at a time like this?"

As my father and sister argued, a small movement caught the corner of my eye.

We were being watched.

I stopped listening to my sister shriek with all the protest she could muster and watched as two lavender eyes examined us from a dark corner. The eyes caught my glare, locking onto my own. We stared each other down for several seconds before the eyes left the dark, silently creeping out into the open.

The lavender eyes belonged to a Shielder male. The enormity of a Shielder body was breathtaking and yet intimidating. I felt myself shrink as he walked up to my agitated family.

The Shielder's hair was tied back in intricate braiding and his deep-set markings, almost like tattoos, shown in the rays of sunlight coming through the clouds. His presence stopped the argument with a jolt; they watched as he walked up to us.

"I can do this," he stated, gently grabbing the bag from my father.

"I know of a safe place to hold the body until...." he trailed off as he went to work wrapping my grandmother carefully in the bag.

The three of us only observed as he quietly and easily took care of the body. He wrapped her frail form with such care I was truly touched.

I glanced over to my sister, who was silently crying as she watched the Shielder do what we could not. Dad stood dumbfounded, muttering to himself. I snapped my head back to the odd sight as the Shielder finished his task.

He stood up, looking to the three of us. "I heard what you were saying," he started. "I wanted to help. I ... I am sorry for your loss. If you are ready to say goodbye I will finish the job."

By this time, Mom and Grandpa had joined us. The Shielder looked around and waited patiently for one of us to say something, but no one spoke. The family was still in shock from his kindness.

Finally, my father shook his head in agreement. We watched as the Shielder carried the body out of sight.

"Wait," Mabel called after him. "What's your name?"

"Clairfic Munal," he said, turning around slowly. "I will make sure she is in a safe place where you will be able to claim her after ... "

He walked out of sight, taking our beloved grandmother with him.

No one uttered a word. I felt a tug at my sleeve as Mabel and the rest of the family came together to grieve as one. We embraced for a long time, the tears flowing freely.

My family might have been thinking about our loss, but I soon turned my attention to our escape. We needed to get out of here *alive*.

18

"We need to leave, it's as simple as that," I tried explaining for the fourth time to my stubborn father. "It's not safe here, and *look*—look at everything! It's dead. We need to keep moving. There's nothing here for us now."

My father sighed, waving his hand, ignoring my plea.

I knew I was winning him over with my logic, but he obviously held on tight to his own idea of what the family should do.

The five of us had been standing in a circle for nearly an hour arguing about what our next move would be. Mabel and Dad agreed for the first time in their lives; both wanted us to stay and try to work with the Shielders—wherever they were at this time. Mom and I wanted to get out of the city as quickly as possible or, at least, far enough away from the destruction to rethink a next move. Grandfather just swayed side to side, not paying attention to the words being thrown about him.

"Getting out is the best option," Mom said. "We're no use to Shielders in this state and remember, the only one we met walked off. I didn't see a single one the whole time I was getting us out of the burning shelter!"

"Making it further than the city limits would be next to impossible," added my father.

"We have to try," I said, my anger boiling over. "We're wasting time standing around arguing."

"I change my vote," Mabel interjected. "I want to go somewhere safer."

The three of us eyed Mabel. She was just as stubborn as our father; it was highly unlikely she would change her mind so dramatically.

"We might not have to go too far, but at least we'll be somewhere else. We can always make another choice once we've reached a safer place."

"Fine," Dad sighed. "Let's pack up what we can and regroup outside of the city."

I watched as they packed the few items left and formulated my own plan. We needed to get as far away as possible from other Humans. I also wanted us as far away as possible from these lunatic Shielders and whatever else came from the sky!

I'd been a fan of these beautiful creatures, not as obsessed as Mabel, but I enjoyed the way they held themselves, their long braids and tattooed skin. The kindness they emitted was admirable, but now, after all the death and loss? I hated them. I wanted them gone and off my planet.

Dad went to see if he could find any other supplies that would be useful, while Grandfather, Mabel, and I helped with what we could, going through our stuff. Mom organized the contents.

"What do you think of the whole Clairfic thing?" Mabel asked in a low voice so only I could hear.

"I don't think anything," I told her flatly. "He thought he was helping and took Grandmother's body away. That's that."

"Well, he did help. We wouldn't have been able take care of her or find a safe place for her to rest in peace ... "

I already knew what was coming next.

"He did what he thought was right and really did us a great

favor," she continued. "I wonder if we'll be able to thank him before we leave," she finished, looking in the direction of his disappearance.

"I doubt it, he's long gone."

"You never know, it could be nice to find him and thank him," she confessed quietly.

"Why? He did this—*they* did this! If they'd done their job, we wouldn't be in this mess," I said, almost raising my voice at her words. "How can you want to thank someone for doing something that could've been prevented?"

Mabel snapped her head around, staring me down. Her eyes were angry for a minute but turned cold with sadness.

"I know you're right, Melly," she finally said in her low voice. "They did do this, but aren't we no better than them if we hold it against them? I mean, they tried, that's something in my book. You saw how hard it was and how those Temorshians came out of nowhere. Something could have happened we don't even know about. They weren't prepared and even with the warning, many of us weren't ready for the attack."

"I understand, but I'm still angry—"

"So be mad," she said, packing a sack full of food. "I'm mad. Mom and Dad are mad. Be *mad*. But I know you remember the short notice we had to get to a Shelter. No one was ready; not even the Shielders. All of us—yes, Mel, *all* of us—thought we had more time."

I swallowed my words while letting out an exasperated sigh. Mabel did have a point. I didn't want to admit it, but she was right.

"Well, girls," Mom interrupted our sisterly moment. "I think we have enough to get us through the next week if we're careful. I'm hoping your father has found other things. Weapons would be nice."

"Weapons, Mom? Really?" Mabel asked in shock. "I thought you didn't condone violence?"

"When it comes to life and death, girls, I will always choose life," Mom admitted, sitting down next to Grandfather.

"Look!" I yelled, pointing to the distant horizon.

Our father was walking very slowly with a bag of some sort on his back. Next to him was a Shielder—the same one who had helped us earlier, Clairfic. The two unlikely acquaintances looked like they were gabbing like old friends while walking in our direction. Clairfic had two larger bags on his back and two weapons at his side. As they approached, I noticed they had more weapons than I thought were necessary. Mother would be pleased, but the sight made me uncomfortable.

"All righty!" Dad exclaimed as he reached the group. "Look who I found! Clairf—*Clair*—Clairfic? God, you all have such hard names! Clairfic has asked to join us. Isn't that nice of him?" he asked, then paused to look each of us in the eyes, daring one of us to oppose him. None of us did. "Come here, girls, you'll get one of these guns, and he'll show you how to use it."

I eyed Mom. She was pleased Dad had done his job, but apprehensive. Guns she meant, but *Human* guns were what she wanted.

I glared at the Shielder, my eyes never leaving his. I didn't want this thing's help, but I wanted protection more than I wanted food. I'd seen enough devastation to understand that in order to live through this, I would have to get ruthless. I was ready to fight for my family—no matter what. If he would be my gatekeeper, then I could make the best of it.

"Do we have time for this?" Mabel asked.

"Sure we do," Dad responded.

"Let's be quick about it," Mom said, looking around. "No need to waste any more time, Viktor."

"Okay, Mr. Clairfic, show me what I need to know," I volunteered.

Clairfic was a patient teacher. He answered all of our questions as he showed us how to use the various weapons by explaining the buttons and levers associated with each function. Even though the machines were complicated, pulling a trigger was not.

"Push here and here," he said, gently holding the gun while I watched his hands move around pointing to various buttons.

"When we are outside of the city, we will need you to shoot a few rounds," he explained. "All of you must be comfortable using these weapons. We do not have that type of time, but once we are in a secluded space, I will make sure you are each comfortable."

"No problem with me, Clair," I told him. "Now that we have what we need, can we go? We've wasted a lot of time, and it'd be nice to find a place to sleep tonight *outside* of this mess."

"Yes, you're right, dear," Dad said, obviously relieved to have Clair with us. "Let's pack up and move out!"

I took one last look at the ruin that lay around me.

It broke my heart to see my beloved Detroit turned to dust. It was dead before, barely any business or life left, but it had been fighting back. People my age had moved back into the old homes and turned the once lavish city into something we could all be proud of: a happy and healthy community. Now, no one would get the opportunity to see the city restored. It was gone and the only thing left was a fragment of the lost.

"God, it's so hot," Mabel complained to the group. "We've got to be out far enough to rest or something?"

"No," Clairfic and I said in unison.

I looked at him, startled that we shared the same feelings about getting as far from the city as possible by nightfall.

He was a male of few words, yet he was a great listener. He heard all about our life and family history from my father as we made the hike out of the city. Clairfic was the calming presence we desperately needed.

We moved slowly because of Grandfather and my foot. It hurt with every step, but I pushed forward—I knew the stakes. Clairfic offered to carry me, but I couldn't allow that to happen. I was mortified when he originally asked and still felt embarrassed thinking about how my sister giggled herself silly at the offer. Occasionally,

Clairfic would eye me, almost asking if I was holding up, while we walked; I ignored him.

Who did this guy think he was? I thought bitterly. *First he saves the day by helping out, and now he wants to carry me like some princess? Hell, no. I won't let myself be put in such a vulnerable position—no matter how much pain I'm in.*

"God, my feet *hurt*, Clair. Why can't you pick me up?" Mabel asked, annoyed as usual when things didn't go her way.

"You are not injured," Clairfic stated pointedly. "You need to build your strength if you are going to make it through this war."

"Bah," she replied with a wave of her hand. "I'm strong. I just don't see how it's fair you ask Melly and not offer anyone else."

"I did offer others."

"If you say so—"

"Lay off, Mabel," I interjected. "You know he asked Grandfather—not just *me*. We only have a few more miles to go before we can rest."

"Whatever." Mabel stopped walking to turn to face me. "You always get the attention. And—"

"You know what? I will take you up on that offer if you don't mind, young man," Grandfather interrupted.

Clairfic made his way over in one swift motion to where Grandfather stood. We watched in silence. As if Grandfather were light as a feather, Clairfic scooped him up in his arms. He walked right past Mabel, whose mouth was gaping open.

"See," I said to her flatly, "I told you he offered." I smirked as I followed Clairfic and Grandfather.

"Girls, is there any way you could not fight with each other?" Mom asked. "You would think at a time like this, you would be more loving toward your sister."

Mabel rolled her eyes as she began walking. I shrugged, trying to keep up with Clair. The rest of the family followed behind as Mom and Dad tried to talk sense into my younger sister, though she was obviously not listening. I could hear my father and sister go after each other like old times, while Mom interjected where she could.

"You have got to hold that tongue of yours," Dad yelled.

"Or what? You'll send the aliens after me? Send me to my room without supper? Please, you can't stop me," Mabel sassed back.

"Mabel, for once in your life, please try to be respectful *and* try to control that attitude of yours!" Mom exclaimed.

It's going to be a long walk to safety.

The fighting grew louder with every step.

"Is it always like this?" Clairfic asked in a hushed voice.

"Yep. Aren't you glad you picked such a fun family to help?" I answered with a wink.

"It does not bother me. I enjoy learning about your family and will accept all of you as you are."

"Well, thank you," I uttered, relieved and even a little shocked. "Clairfic, do you mind if I ask you something?"

"You may ask what you wish ... "

"Right, thanks. Well, it's weird that ... wait. What is that *noise?* Grandfather? *Grandpa?* Is he all right?" I asked in a panic.

Clairfic did not slow his pace.

"He is sleeping, I think," he said, looking down at the grown man in his arms. "He is comfortable and needs his rest."

"Oh, yeah, I guess he snores in his sleep," I laughed. "That's pretty funny."

It felt good to laugh, despite everything.

"He has had a hard day."

My cheeks grew red with embarrassment. "I wasn't trying to make light of our situation. If I'm going to make it through this tough time, I'm going to need to laugh and make jokes."

He ignored me.

I moved away from him and didn't continue to talk to Clairfic. I'd offended him by laughing, but I was also unnerved by the stoic nature of this Shielder. He needed to loosen up. He was large and intimidating—his quiet nature did not help the matter, either.

We walked in silence for another half a mile, the suburbs slowly coming into view. The area didn't look good; things were still destroyed without a soul in sight. I began to think leaving hadn't been a good idea, especially if things were still this bad, but it was our only option. I had to keep the faith there would be more further along.

"You were going to ask me something," Clairfic gently reminded me, interrupting my dark train of thought.

I jumped a little at his words. "Yes, you're right. I was going to ask you ... well, you see ... "

"Why am I here—with *you* and your family?" Clairfic asked without emotion.

"Clairfic, you don't need to tell me anything you don't want to, I hope you know that, but I was wondering why you didn't stay with your people, um, your kind? Won't they miss you? Don't you have orders?"

Clairfic didn't answer.

My family caught up with us, their curiosity getting the better of them as well.

Shielders were phenomenally trained soldiers. They normally followed through with orders until success or death. Clair being alone wasn't a good sign.

He avoided my eyes and kept walking. "My orders are to protect and defend the Humans," he finally said without emotion.

"Right, of course. We understand that, but ... why didn't you stay back?" I asked, trying not to push too much but just enough to erase my nagging suspicion that he knew why my planet was now in chaos.

"You needed help. I wanted to help."

I realized I was getting nowhere with this Shielder in this fashion. I changed my attack.

"We would've managed without you, you know. We aren't a weak family. We're capable."

"I do not need to argue that point, Melissa," he said, and looked at me out of the corner of his eye.

I felt my cheeks redden and my heart skip a beat. His informal use of my full name caught me off guard.

"It was not that I thought your family could not survive without my help," Clairfic continued. "It was more ... more personal than that."

I shivered as I gathered his meaning.

"Clairfic, what happened? Why were you near the shelter after the attack? We never had Shielders in the area before ... Clair, stop walking. What happened?"

My family held their breath behind the two of us.

"We should not stop here," he said. He quickened his pace.

I turned to look at my parents. They shrugged, and Mabel gestured to follow him.

"Wait, Clairfic!" I called after him. After only a few steps he was already a few feet away. "Wait up. Okay, fine. We won't talk about it here. But, look, we need to know what you know at some point. Just take all the time you need, okay?"

"It is getting late. Do you see that building?" he asked, completely ignoring what I'd said to him.

"Yes, I do. Do you think it's safe?" I asked, looking into the horizon. I could barely make out what he was looking at, but I saw the outline.

"It seems to be. I will check it out when we get closer, but I think it will do for the night. We need to look for more supplies anyway."

"All right, everyone, you heard him. Let's make our way over to that building," I yelled to my family.

They let out a sigh of relief.

"Thank God!" Mabel exclaimed, increasing her pace toward the distant structure.

Everyone started walking faster. I stayed behind. My father looked back at me with an inquisitive look on his face.

"I am fine, Dad. I just need a minute. I'll catch up with you in a bit."

He nodded. "Don't take too long, Melly. It's not safe."

"I won't. I'll be fine—you worry too much." I smiled, trying to stay positive.

Though I knew I'd hidden it well, I couldn't shake my worry about the silence of our new Shielder friend. Clairfic didn't want to share what had happened to him or his people.

Even if I couldn't trust Clairfic fully—not until he told me what he knew, I felt the responsibility of keeping my family alive weigh heavily on my shoulders.

I felt tired and out of sorts; but I couldn't let it win. I pushed it deep down. I took a moment to get some water and looked down at my swollen foot. I sighed, but I knew I had to keep fighting. My life and the life of my family depended on it.

19

"The building is deserted," Clairfic stated as I walked up to him. It seemed he'd been waiting for me. "It will be fine for the night."

By the time I arrived to the half-broken, half-standing building, Clairfic had the whole family working. Dad and Mom were looking for food and medical supplies, while Mabel set up a place to sleep in one of the sturdier rooms. Grandfather was still asleep, which was what he needed. It's what we all needed at this point, but we had jobs to do. We pushed through the exhaustion until we could fall into makeshift beds come nightfall.

"It didn't take you long to get everyone working, Clair," I admitted, impressed by his leadership. "You must have a great pair of eyes to see this pile of rubble from so far way. You sure it'll be safe?"

"I am or I would not have let any of you near it," Clairfic said flatly, holding sheets under his arm. "The place is secure and will be fine for a day or two. Your family cannot make the trip to a safer place as quickly as you think, Melissa—especially your grandfather. Even your foot hinders you."

"Don't say that," I replied angrily. "I can walk just fine, and I don't feel pain anymore."

"It is because you have been on it for too long," Clairfic stated, turning to leave.

"Not so fast, hot shot," I said, and grabbed him by the arm, my hand looking silly on his long, muscular limb. "I need a job, too."

I felt Clair tense at my touch, but I left my hand there, my fingers scarcely long enough to envelope his bicep.

He turned slowly, leaning toward me. His movement almost made me jump back in alarm, but I kept my stance and allowed him to get close enough to whisper in my ear. I breathed in his scent, smelling incense and sweat. He smelled good; it was intoxicating.

In a quiet voice, he whispered, "There are dead Humans on the third floor."

All sexual feelings disappeared in an instant.

"W-w-what did you say?" I asked in shock, pulling my face away from him.

"There is a small family of dead Humans—"

"No shit, I got that part," I said. "Why are you telling me this?"

"I intend to bury them. Just like I did for your grandmother. It is Human tradition, is it not?"

"Right, okay, that's good. Good idea—very *kind*. Um, so what do you want me to *do*?" I asked, feeling a little sick to my stomach; my words were devoid of all emotion.

"I will need your help," Clairfic responded. "Are you up to the task?"

I couldn't let him see my discomfort. In our short time together, he'd realized I never turned down a challenge.

"I will do my best, Clair. Just tell me what to do."

"Follow me."

He turned to climb the emergency staircase just behind us. It was still standing, although debris covered the steps and half of the outside wall had fallen into heaps on the floor. I followed quietly behind him, mentally preparing for the task.

We made it up the first flight of stairs just fine, but the second was more challenging.

"Can I help you?" Clairfic asked as I tried to maneuver around a large, fallen piece of drywall.

"Sure," I said, taking his outstretched hand.

With no effort at all, he lifted me up and over the debris.

"I could carry you the rest of the way. It would be no problem. We do not have very far to go," Clairfic kindly offered. He stared deeply into my eyes, almost pleading with me to allow him to help me, just this once.

"Clairfic, that's so nice, but aren't I heavy? I can manage."

"If that is the only reason that prohibits you from letting me help you, well, then, you do not know me. You are as light as a piece of *planqua*. It is no problem, and we are wasting time." Without waiting for an answer, he scooped me up, and we continued on our way.

I tensed in his arms, holding my breath as long as I could without his noticing. It was no use; his scent filled my nostrils again. The sweet scents of incense and sweat relaxed my tired muscles, while my hunched shoulders straightened out, no longer holding the worry they'd become accustomed to carrying.

I should be feeling solemn about what I'm about to do, not giddy.

I desperately tried to stop myself from enjoying the ride. Luckily, it was soon over, and the next thing I knew, I was placed back on the floor.

"Well, thanks," I told him. "That was fun. Let's try to do it again sometime."

"With pleasure," he smirked, walking toward the unit with the family.

I stayed behind, gathering my courage. I took a breath, looking around the vacant apartment complex that had survived most of the fallout from battle.

A small sigh left my lips. *Why on Earth would a family stay here? Didn't they know this would be the last place to hide?*

"Do not judge them." Clairfic startled me out of my thoughts, gesturing me to follow him.

"I'm doing my best, but this could've been avoided," I replied while I followed him. "Why anyone would—"

"We cannot judge what has happened. It is in the past. It is *done*."

"It's still sad and I can be angry about it—about all of this!" My voice trembled at an octave higher than normal.

"You are allowed to feel that way," he said, opening the apartment door. "You are entitled to your feelings—they are valid."

We paused before entering the room and stared each other down.

I didn't know what to expect. My innards were already twisting themselves into knots.

Again, without missing a beat, Clairfic read my mind. "You should stay here. I can prepare them, and then you can help me take them out."

"No, I can help, honest. I'm fine."

"You are very stubborn. I was not really suggesting ... "

A part of me was relieved, but I wouldn't allow myself to show him. "Oh, I see. You get to make the decisions, huh? Okay, boss, you do what you need to do, and I will be here waiting."

He chuckled softly but continued his work.

I watched him from the doorway, following him with my eyes, my curiosity getting the better of me. Clairfic was large enough to block most of my view, but the small limbs of a child, bloodied and disfigured, flopped side-to-side. Clairfic was gentle with the body as if the child were still alive. My heart softened for this strange new friend, though the scene horrified me.

After the child was safely wrapped in the sheet Clairfic had found, he moved on to the parents.

"Melissa, could you please turn away?" he asked tenderly from where he worked. "You should not be watching any of this."

"Um, sure thing, sorry," I responded, moving away, but I was too slow. I watched an adult limb fall to the floor as Clairfic went to wrap one of the parents.

My breath caught and my body tensed violently. Before I could stop myself, my stomach convulsed, and I vomited everything I'd eaten in the last twenty-four hours. No matter how I fought to push it out, the limb falling replayed over and over again in my mind. The image was seared into my memory. Every time I fought to ignore it, my stomach released what was left inside.

Focus, I demanded as the last of my convulsing ceased. I wanted to be strong—I wanted to be helpful. I was neither now. My eyes burned with unshed tears from the horror of death around me. I hugged myself tighter, trying to still my senses. That worked for a short time, but then I let go for another round of vomit.

"I have finished." Clairfic handed me a towel as he bent down to where I leaned against the wall.

I wrapped my arms around my middle even tighter, trying to steady myself instead of shaking. "I'm sorry," I whispered. "I'd never ... I never ... "

"I understand. It happens," he said warmly. "Are you all right?"

"I will be—I think. Does the image ever go away?"

"It could, but it may not. You might have to learn to live with what you saw. I am afraid this may only be the beginning."

"I keep trying to push it away and to think of something else, and it's no use! It comes back stronger," I told him, tears making their escape from my shut eyelids.

"That is the problem. You must stay in the present. Focus on me now; focus on your breathing. Think of your family, who are alive, downstairs," he reminded me.

I did as he asked, feeling slightly better. I slowed my breathing and tried to clear my mind. I thought back to my family and how grateful I was that they were alive. I missed my grandmother but the thought of her brought me more peace than sadness.

"Better?" he asked.

"Yes," I uttered. I wiped my mouth, dried the tears, and tried to stand. Weak from the violent convulsions, I stood with a little help from Clair. "Thank you. I ... I think I'm up to helping now—if you still have anything I can do."

"Can you manage taking the lighter of the loads?" he asked me, avoiding my eyes—we both knew what he meant.

"Yes," I answered. "Let's be quick about it. They deserve to rest in peace." The words felt foreign on my tongue, but I meant them.

Clairfic brought the small body to me. "Do you know what a *planqua* is, Melissa?" he asked as he placed the bundle in my arms.

"A *what?* You said it before, but I don't speak La'Mursian, sorry."

I watched as Clairfic lifted the other bodies like they weighed ten pounds, moving quickly as he went. I let him lead me out into the broken hallway.

"A *planqua* is a plant that grows delicious fruit," he continued, making our way to the staircase. "The fruit can be eaten and is known to have healing properties. Watch your step—I will help you down in a minute. The rest of the plant is also used for medicine and other things we need for healing. It is quite amazing," he told me, going down the emergency staircase without me. "Wait here."

I did as I was told. He came back, making his way to where I stood in only a few steps.

"Can you manage holding the body while I help you down?" he asked.

"I can," I replied meekly.

He reached for me, bringing me close. He was careful with the body between us. Gently, he picked me up, turning to walk down the stairs. His smell helped mask the smell of the decaying flesh that was beginning to rot in my arms.

"So, here we are again," I joked, trying to make light of this horrible situation.

"Does it bother you?" he asked in my ear.

"Would it bother you if something big kept picking you up like you were nothing?"

He chuckled. "I see your point. Luckily we are done." He put me down gently. "Follow me, please."

We walked out of the apartment and into an area untouched by devastation. It was the perfect place to lay the family to rest. We were surrounded by overturned cars, debris of all kinds, and ruins of what appeared to be other apartment buildings, but there was enough green Earth to rest for eternity.

A shiver ran up my spine, but I avoided it by doing what Clairfic had suggested earlier: I stayed in the present.

"What made you think of *planqua*? Did I say it right? La'Mursian is a difficult language to master, but I try."

"Yes, surprisingly, you did," he said, and smiled at me as we reached the clearing.

I'd never seen him smile before, and it caught me off guard. His teeth were sharp and intimidating, but the kindness radiated out of his eyes, downplaying any horror his mouth might bring.

"I thought about it because it is a very helpful plant and when you take it out of the ground, it's as light as a feather. Mind you, it is a large and cumbersome plant!"

"So I'm cumbersome?" I teased.

"No, no, no! Anything but!" he laughed.

I joined him. It felt good—natural to laugh with Clairfic. It was weird it happened as we were about to bury dead bodies, but the release was welcome nonetheless.

Clairfic continued to chuckle as he lay the bodies down. I put my little bundle down as well. He found a metal rod good enough to use to dig, while I surveyed the area to find another shovel-like object.

"I can do it," he said. "It will not take long. You should return to your family and see if they need help. I hope they found more food. We will need it."

"Me too. Do you mind eating our food?" I asked, off-topic.

"It does not taste like food back home, but it will suffice."

"We are weird, aren't we?" I asked him. He did not answer, focusing on his task.

I realized that he would not answer those types of questions. He was extremely private.

I sighed. "You know, I haven't forgotten that you promised to tell us why you were near the shelter," I reminded him flatly.

"I know this; I have not forgotten either."

"Well, I don't mean to push you. I just want you to know that I'm a great listener. I understand that whatever you saw—whatever the reason you left is painful. I understand that—we all understand that. You can trust us," I told him sincerely.

He stopped his work and turned slowly toward me. "Thank you," was all he said in a small, quiet voice.

He returned to his work.

There was no more to say on the matter. I understood that he was guarded with his emotions. Whatever had happened to him bothered him to his core, and he would not share unless he felt completely safe. I respected that and left him to his thoughts.

I also realized he had never really needed my help.

"We have found some food items. Nothing substantial, but we can keep looking as we go. Sooner than later, we are going to run out and things will go bad," Mom mentioned. She looked older in the light from the setting sun. We could read her face as plain as day, but she tried to hide her worry by keeping her hands moving items around to stay busy.

My family didn't find a lot in our building, but we had enough to eat for the next few days, like canned goods, crusty bread, and some fruit that hadn't gone bad yet. The rest were snacks and such that could be kept and taken with us.

Mabel and Clairfic had done a great job of securing a safe space for the night. We were staying in the only standing apartment building filled with enough units for everyone to sleep comfortably. Mabel lit dozens of candles that gave off enough light to see everything clearly. We filled two bathtubs and all the sinks with water that was left in the pipes. Each of us had a bed and plenty of space, a true luxury at a time like this. Mabel and my parents would be staying in the better unit while I stayed with Clairfic in another. Grandfather was happy on the couch or at least we hoped so. He was still out cold and no one wanted to move him.

Clairfic suggested Mabel cover the windows with whatever she could to make it safer to sleep. This was a brilliant idea since we didn't know what we would find outside. It wasn't much but enough to give us piece of mind. Only a small kitchen window was uncovered by anything of substance. We put up a sheet that didn't do much except give a false sense of security as it allowed the last of the sunlight to filter inside.

"We'll manage," Dad tried to reassure Mom. "We have rationed what we have, and we will keep looking. It will be okay."

Ever the optimist, my father looked determined to stay as positive as our situation allowed. He didn't know about the dead family lying several feet away from him. Clairfic and I weren't going to burst his bubble about that, either.

"And if it's not?" my sister asked bitterly, brushing her hair in the corner. Her looks were her only comfort in life. Now, she looked silly.

"Then we'll figure it out. Now let's finish dinner and get some rest."

"Where did you find all these candles, Mabel?" I asked, switching the conversation to something safe.

"Around," she said, putting her brush down and reaching for a cheese sandwich.

"Well, this place looks great." I lowered my voice so only she could hear, "I still can't believe you placed me in the same unit as the Shielder. Why didn't Mom freak out?"

"You're welcome," she smirked, ignoring me. "She did but I said you were the safest option and wouldn't try to seduce him like I would." She laughed. "Besides, who cares? I thought I was being funny setting it up that way." She smiled, giving me a glance through her thick lashes. "Do you think we should wake Grandpa up? He hasn't eaten anything since breakfast yesterday."

"I don't know, honey. We should let him sleep. He needs his rest," Mom stated, looking at the sleeping figure of her father-in-law. "We can save him a sandwich and let him eat enough tomorrow. I think he should sleep."

"Were you able to find any radios or anything?" asked Clairfic quietly.

It was easy to forget he was in the room. Even with his big body and sharp teeth, he managed to hide himself. He observed everything around him—like a cat. You could tell he thought about everything that came out of his mouth and didn't speak unless he had to, or maybe he was insecure about his English.

"No," Dad said flatly. "We looked all over and there was nothing we could use. We can check cars tomorrow? Maybe there's an emergency broadcast?"

"We can hope. We should not go much longer without any news," Clair confessed, eating his food. He had managed to down two cheese sandwiches and was already working on a third.

"Why?" I asked.

He took a minute before he answered. "War is difficult. We should know as much as possible about what is going on in the atmosphere and on Earth. If it is achievable, we will need to know where to meet others. We cannot do that without information."

"Wouldn't it be safer for us to stay away from others? I don't want to get involved," Mabel said.

"I do not want you to get involved either ... " Clairfic stated with a hint of sadness in his voice.

"I think it's a bit late for that," I said unequivocally. "Even if we don't want to be a part of a war, we're in one. We're stuck fighting for what's left of our planet."

A hush fell over the group.

I itched to ask the question on all of our minds. Looking around at the sad faces, I decided it was time.

"The Temorshians are here, aren't they, Clair?" I asked. "They've made it to Earth."

He looked away from us. "Yes."

"That's why you were near the shelter."

My parents let out a collective gasp, instinctively reaching for each other, as the world seemed to be falling apart around them.

"Yes," he said again, even quieter. Before I could probe further he got up and left.

Several long minutes passed before anyone spoke.

"You should follow him, Mel," Mabel suggested sadly. "You two talk more than any of us. You should go to him and find out what he knows."

"He obviously feels beholden to us, Melissa," Mom added, looking at my father.

"What do I say?" I asked. "I'm interested in being the Shielder whisperer."

"Do what you always do when someone is upset," Mabel offered.

"Just get him to talk and listen when he does," Mom chimed in. "He was talking to you earlier, right?"

"Not really," I tried to explain. "He doesn't like to share his ... *feelings.*"

"What man does?" my father added.

"Dad, he is not a guy," Mabel reminded him. "He's a Shielder. They're *different.*"

"Yeah, way worse," I interjected.

"Girls, please," Mom stopped us before we could go any further. "We have to know what he knows. He might not have told us about the Temorshians if you hadn't said anything, Melissa."

"You should see if he's all right," Dad added. "See if he'll unburden himself a little, and then gather as much information as you can. We need to know what he knows—no matter how painful."

"He obviously cares about us. Did you *see* his face?" Mabel asked. "He's one of those types ... "

"What?" I asked.

"You know ... the type that doesn't talk and keeps his thoughts to himself."

"Strong and silent type," Mom added.

"He doesn't want any of us involved, but he looked afraid. Like he knew we probably would be," Dad offered, ignoring the women in his life. "I definitely can relate. I don't want any of my girls fighting."

"Like I said before, I think it's a little late for that, Dad," I told them. "Look around you—this is war!"

We sat in silence.

"God damn it," I swore.

"Language, please, Melissa Ann!" Mom was shocked by my words; I usually didn't swear.

"Sorry, Mom. Fine, I'll go find him," I said. "I'm not coming back tonight. I'm too tired and it's late. Go to sleep and we can discuss this over breakfast—if it's okay with him. He might not even tell me anything. I don't want to scare him off. Don't push me—I'm looking at you, Mabel."

Not waiting for their rebuttal, I got up. I thought they would fight me on the matter, but they let me walk silently out of the room. They were convinced Clair and I knew how to communicate with one another. Maybe we could, but I hated the idea that I had to push him to get him to open up. That was not my way of going about things.

20

It didn't take long to find Clairfic. He'd ended up making his way to the secluded area where we'd be spending the night. I doubted my decision to bunk with the Shielder, but I craved space away from my family. He was a hell of a lot quieter than the rest of them.

The apartment Mabel had chosen for us had little damage. The living room was fine but trashed with random odds and ends scattered across the floor in broken disarray. The kitchen was destroyed but, strangely, still standing. The one bedroom I insisted Clairfic use was dirty but stood as well. After everything I'd seen today, I was grateful to have something decent to sleep in. The trash and half-standing walls would work for me.

When I walked into the space, my eyes rested on Clairfic's slender form. He hadn't moved a muscle even though he'd heard me walk down the empty hallway, each step vibrating off the walls. Managing to keep his gaze locked on the outside, he stared into space from the living room window. He moved the covering Mabel had put up to look out into the blackness.

We stood in silence for a moment as I gathered my thoughts. I wanted information, but I didn't want to offend my new Shielder friend. If I wanted to get close to him, I'd have to treat him with respect as I would anyone else.

Clair's words broke the tense silence. "I should not have left like that."

"We're a hard group to avoid, Clairfic," I told him gently as I made my way to the big window he was looking out. "We don't really give people a choice to avoid us. You brought up difficult subjects and, naturally, we were curious about what you know."

He didn't respond, so I kept going.

"I've told you before, I understand that it's painful to talk about the past. You don't have to—no one needs to know anything you are not comfortable sharing. We ... we just need to know the information that can help us stay alive." I wanted to reach out to him, to show him I wasn't interested in pushing him, but I couldn't bring myself to do it. Instead I waited. Silence was powerful, and I wasn't going to scare him off by abusing our budding friendship.

Clairfic sighed and slowly turned to face me. "You may want to sit down for what I am about to tell you."

I did as he asked and sat on the dirty love seat in the room flooded with candlelight. He followed suit and sat across from me on a chair that surprisingly took his weight well.

"How much do you know about the La'Mursians?" he asked.

"Uh, not much. I know what the prince told us, but nothing more," I told him honestly.

"We are the best—it is as simple as that. We are well known for our strategies, our strength, and our numbers. Our training is extensive, and we volunteer to join. Once we join, we normally do not leave. I think it is because we are not forced to do it, and we are treated well." Clair paused. "I have always enjoyed myself, if I might be so bold. Our goals normally consist of helping others—helping planets facing large odds they were not prepared for, not slaughtering innocents. We know how to kill, of course, but we are a peaceful people. There are other ways to give aid without killing."

He sighed again but went on, "We came to Earth years ago. I forget how many years, but I remember learning about Earth in school."

"Wait, *you did?* How?" I asked in disbelief.

"Before I was born—before my parents were even born. There was a rumor about a planet similar to ours. We knew enough and had the resources, so we set out to find it. I do not remember why we connected with your planet all those years ago, but for a time it was peaceful. We learned a lot about your culture and what Earth offered. It was in secret, of course, but we were excited to learn of a faraway planet that was similar to our own—that does not happen often."

"I can imagine that would be exciting. No fear of danger or anything," I confessed, a little jealous of his experience. I had been terrified when I heard of his kind. I didn't know what to do besides cry when I first saw a Shielder on TV. It wasn't until much later I accepted them as a part of my new normal.

"I knew I wanted to visit," he continued, interrupting my train of thought. "I was young and naïve, but I knew I wanted to learn English. The first opportunity I received I got the training," he stated, obviously very proud of himself. "I know it is only one of the many languages you have, but I settled on English with hopes of learning others. Even if they are primitive in nature, I enjoyed the sounds. I wanted to learn and understand your world—it was important to me."

"Your English is very good, by the way," I told him. "I'd always wondered why. Now I know," I smiled.

"Thank you! That means a lot," he said, and paused, his cheeks turning slightly mauve. "Anyway, you are probably wondering why I am telling you all this, but I have a point, I promise. You see, Selucia was excited to have a sister planet. We worked hard to bring Earth into the Galactic Royal Court—something like your United Nations—but some of your leaders did not think it was a good idea. One of the stipulations of joining is that the population of the planet in question agrees and is aware of the existence of others—other planets, other beings, you understand. Since at the time our transactions were in secret, we could not help you, and the joining was forfeit."

"So like *Humans*, huh?" I asked, trying to lighten the mood, but inside a raging bull erupted, sending violent shivers down my spine. "We could have avoided all this by joining some club?" I asked, rubbing my temples vehemently.

"It is not a joke," he stated sternly, bringing me back to the present. "It is very serious. It is the whole reason why this is happening." He gestured to our surroundings. "How many lives lost to the secrecy of our existence? Of the existence of others?"

The guilt of my outburst hit me hard in the gut, my cheeks burning a deep red.

"Because Earth was not protected by our rights, dangerous entities talked about coming. They made moves to take over your world. We were able to subdue most of them through politics, but there was one that we did not foresee making a dangerous play—"

"The Temorshians," I breathed.

"Yes, they found loopholes around the laws of the Galactic Royal Court. They tried finding your planet for many, many years," he said, sitting back in his chair, the frame creaking under his weight. "This gave us time to race to your planet and talk some sense into your leaders. It was a long process, but finally we changed their minds. But it took too much time. We hurried with our announcement, we expected there to be problems and fear, but not like what happened."

"You really didn't think that your very existence would be *shocking*?" I hissed in disbelief. "Shocking to a population that used to believe other planets revolved around them? Shocking for us to find out that we aren't the center of the galaxy? A planet that has strong ties to religions that say nothing about aliens? *That* surprised you?"

"I do not have the answers, Melissa. Maybe it is because I could not imagine thinking like your kind, so I felt it would go better. We really thought your leaders ... Well, they lied, did they not? We thought they would have done a better job at letting information slip gently, little by little, until we could tell everyone the truth."

"Obviously, they didn't," I said. "How could they keep this—*you*—such a secret?" I asked, standing up to pace the floor.

Clairfic followed me with his big lavender eyes. He looked concerned but dared not interrupt my thoughts. After a few moments of silence, he continued, "I know this is a lot, I should not have been the one to tell you, but it is what you need to know—just like you asked."

"I'm not mad at you, Clairfic. Not at all," I told him. "It's just so confusing. There are so many unanswered questions."

"There will be more, I am afraid."

"What do you mean by that?" I asked, spinning around to face him.

He physically avoided me; he turned his body away, looking far off into the distance. "Clair ... Clairfic, look at me!" I told him. He turned enough so one eye could see me. "What do you mean? Is that why you're afraid to tell us what's going on?"

"I am not afraid." He slowly moved his body so I could look into his lavender eyes. "It is painful to speak of the dead."

Breathless, I found myself falling into the love seat, unable to formulate another question. My heartbeat quickened as a cold sweat broke out over my body.

"They're all dead," he said with little emotion, his face stiff and controlled. "My crew, my people here on Earth—they're all dead."

Golden tears began to form in his eye and gently fell down his large cheek. Without another thought, I rushed to his side and grabbed his hand with my own, my small fingers trying to comfort him. My dark skin against his pale hand looked like a drastic contrast, but I wanted my gesture to mean something to him, to let him know I understood his feelings. I bent down to kneel in front of him.

As if my presence gave him a surge of strength, he wiped his tear away with his free hand. He did not move his hand away from my clumsy embrace but moved toward me to continue his story. "It was like the Temorshians knew of our plans. They knew our strategy and destroyed everything in their path. We did not stand a chance." Tears escaped, falling slowly down his face in waves of emotion. "We were ready for them outside of your atmosphere. We had enough power and ships to set up a blockade—it should have been a quick fight. It *was not.*

"As soon as our ships left, carrying what was left of your leadership off the planet, they attacked. They allowed the ships to leave, but they were shot down as if they were nothing. One escaped but I doubt—I really doubt they made it out alive. Two warships followed them, and we lost the signal shortly after." He took a breath.

The hair on my arms stood on end as I tried to clear the taste of bile from my throat. "I'm sure you did your best, Clairfic," I tried reassuring him, but my voice shook as I tried to hold back my emotions. "I know enough about you to know that you would've fought like hell to defend us. Every single one of you did the best you could."

He snorted. "No. We were simply fighting for our lives. It was not about saving Earth anymore, as it was about getting out of the fight alive. We gave up, Melissa. Do you not see that? We gave up on everything."

Clair ripped his hand away from mine with such force I fell backward. In two swift strides he was up and headed for the door. I fell back in shock, holding my hand close to my chest. I almost found myself falling into my own selfish despair, but a voice inside me forced me to stop him from leaving again.

"Clairfic! This is not going to help anyone if you keep running away when your emotions get the best of you!" I screamed. "*Stop!* This isn't healthy and ... and I want to help you!"

He froze.

"You've been through a terrible tragedy—we all have! Look around you! Death, destruction, loss—I know you can understand. I know deep down you feel the same way *I* do. If you need to take whatever time or do whatever you need to do to grieve, so be it, but you have to stop running away from it. Don't you see your actions are getting worse? What if ... what if you had hurt me when you got up like that?"

I paused to catch my breath, my heart almost dancing itself out of my chest. "You are *not* a monster. None of this is your fault. We don't blame you for this mess. You said it yourself—our leadership let us down. How could it be tied to you personally?" I asked, rubbing my hand. "How could it even be the fault of your people? As Humans we might not be knowledgeable about the Universe, but we take responsibility for our actions. From everything that you've said, we did this to ourselves. We need to live in this new world—our new reality.

"No one blames you, Clair. You've been through some awful, awful stuff. Let's work through it together."

Still clutching my hand out of fear more than pain, I wondered if I'd made any sense. I kept the faith he would understand and stay. He stood perfectly still, back straight as a board, while I spoke, and made no move to flee again.

"Let me help you, Clairfic," I whispered.

Clairfic's shoulders tensed. His fingers twitched as he made up his mind. Slowly, he turned around and made his way over to the love seat.

I stayed where I was on the floor. I wasn't hurt, but my pride was wounded.

"I am sorry. Are you all right?" he asked with flushed cheeks, avoiding my eyes.

"Yes, I'm fine. Clairfic, how are you?"

He didn't answer right away. "I am in pain, Melissa. All my friends, my crew—are all gone," he admitted. By this time, his tears were flowing freely. He made no move to hide them. "One minute we were flying and fighting, pushing back the Temorshian forces. The next we were in free fall ...

"We prepared for impact—we were ready to face our death. I

made my peace with my ending, and I did not feel any fear," he told me.

"You are so brave ... " slipped out from me. I was looking at him, finally seeing him. His markings were set deep within his skin, telling all the stories of his past successes in battle. His eyes were full of pain, the corners heavy from exhaustion.

I wanted to rush to him again, but I stopped myself. He would not appreciate my babying him during this time.

Clairfic looked past me, his eyes vacant, searching for the words. "I ... I obviously survived the crash," he professed, mentally leaving the room, witnessing the horrific scene all over again. "I broke my arm, had cuts and bruises all over my body, and I expect I had a head injury too, because when I came back to consciousness, I was lying in a pool of my own blood. The sun had fallen and I was alone. I barely remembered where I was until I looked around. My ship was in pieces and ... and you can imagine what else I found.

"After some time, I knew I had to get up and find others. Even if my crew had perished, I knew there would be others alive some-where. We had bases all over the planet," he said with such bleak-ness. It was as if he'd given up the hope of reconnection. His faith had dissipated.

"I was able to find enough medical items within the debris to help heal my arm and stop the major bleeding, but my communication station was destroyed and useless. With no idea where I was or how to connect with other units, I traveled toward the lights of the city."

"Is that where you found us?" I asked softly.

"Not exactly." He wiped the rest of his tears away. "I walked for miles, but could not find anyone. I did not expect to because the fighting by that point was horrible: explosions above and around me—things falling from the sky—just horrible. All I knew was that I needed to either find a decent shelter or connect with another unit, and that's what kept me going.

"After walking for hours, I reached the Human shelter where I found you. It was sealed so I could not enter—that was before half of it collapsed."

A tiny gasp escaped my lips. He stopped to study my face.

"I'm sorry, I didn't realize ... Please go on."

He nodded. "Things looked calm for the time being, so I settled somewhere and fell asleep. After that I connected with your family."

Tension hung in the air, but I felt his sadness lighten.

"I am so sorry, Clairfic," I told him gently. "I am so, so sorry."

"That is why I am here. That is why I followed your family ... My own is gone."

"But, Clair, you don't know that for sure. You are simply displaced. We all are. We can help you find the rest of your kind!"

He snorted. "I asked about a radio or anything that could help me contact them, to see if anyone is out there. If I could just hear some type of signal I could locate their position. We would be safe—safer than we are now with so few weapons and supplies. We are at the mercy of our luck."

We sat recovering from our conversation. Memories are powerful things and processing them takes time. The energy we spent focusing on them was more exhausting than the miles we had walked earlier in the day.

"I think ... " I whispered, breaking the silence. "I think we both need some rest."

"I agree," Clairfic responded. "I am sorry to burden you with all of this."

"Stop, Clair," I told him sternly. "You didn't do anything wrong. I'm glad you felt safe enough to share your story with me, and now we know how to move forward. We'll find something to help us locate some type of signal or create our own," I paused. "Do you believe me? Do you *trust* me?"

"Yes, I do, and I will do my best to keep the faith," he said, looking down at his hands.

I finally noticed the bruises and scratches over his body. What I had thought were all tattoos, I now recognized as wounds that were beginning to heal. I was mad at myself; I'd been so selfish and caught up in my own small world that I hadn't thought about Clairfic.

I looked at him—really looked at him. He was tired and worn out: his eyes were swollen from the tears, but deep purple bags hung just below his eyes. He needed rest more than any of us, yet he was the one doing most of the work. He might be the boss, but now he needed to be taken care of and put to bed.

"Clairfic," I said, prodding him gently, "come with me. Let's get some rest. You need to sleep, you look exhausted." I leaned toward him as he pulled away. "You deserve to rest. You need it."

I held my hand out to him. He reluctantly accepted the gesture. Carefully, he took my small hand and stood up, his tension slowly slipping from his shoulders.

"Thank you, Melissa. Thank you for all your kindness and under-standing," he said, and squeezed my hand slightly.

"Of course," I murmured, letting his fingers slide off mine. "Are you not used to having someone listen to you?"

He smiled. "It is sometimes difficult for me to be so ... so open with how I am feeling, believe it or not."

"Oh, well ... I'm completely *shocked*," I teased, feeling the mood lift.

"Thank you," he said, taking both my hands. "I feel better and can rest a little easier knowing I have made a friend today."

My cheeks burned with embarrassment.

"It looks like we are friends until the end—whatever that turns out to be," I told him.

[21]

Boom.

I lay silently on my bed, and I hesitated to move as the horrid sound of an explosion met my ears.

Clairfic had politely given up the bed, not because he was chivalrous, but because his frame would not allow him to lie comfortably in it. He decided the floor—with as many pillows and blankets as I could find for him—would be the best spot for a night's rest. We argued about it for some time before he scooped up the bedding and made a little nest at the foot of the bed.

If that is what he wants, more power to him, I thought.

I'd watched as he made himself comfortable. It didn't bother me that we were sharing a room. I was comforted by the idea of not having to sleep alone. When I'd stayed the night with Joel, I always felt better having another person with me. I wasn't interested in cuddling this strange Shielder, but his presence made me feel safe.

Now fear crawled over my body, goose bumps dotting my skin. Wrapped in a warm blanket, I stayed silent, reverting to my childhood stance whenever anything went bump in the night.

Clairfic's breathing stopped as he listened for further indication of what was going on outside as well.

"It's not close," he whispered in his makeshift bed.

Gunshots rang out through the night, breaking the silence.

We bolted upright in our beds. In mere seconds, Clair was at the window, wordlessly moving the debris that blocked the broken glass.

"Can you see anything?" I breathed as quietly as I could, clenching the covers to my chest.

"Nothing, except the fire from the explosion and the various shots being fired," he whispered. "As I expected it's pretty far—three or four miles away? They seem to be heading in the opposite direction from where we are."

In the dark, I watched his form stand in the moonlight. I didn't realize he'd brought one of the weapons he'd found back at the shelter to bed. He was holding onto it as if nothing else mattered, his survival instincts taking over and guiding him. The image should've made me feel better, but my heart beat too fast for it to register properly. I might not be trained like Clairfic, but my body was ready to respond to such a threat—distant or not.

"How can you be so sure?"

"Do you doubt my eyes?" he asked, looking at me through his peripheral vision.

"Look, we can start another argument, or we can make sure we live through the night. Which do you prefer?" I asked, making my way out of the cocoon I'd made.

"No, stay where you are, Melissa," he told me, dropping his voice. "Your parents are up in the next apartment. I better reassure them we are safe."

As he moved the debris back into place, I settled myself against the headboard of the bed.

"Could you reassure me first?" I asked, losing my line of sight from the darkness.

In a strange way the blackness made me feel better. Almost like it was the only thing keeping me safe while whatever happened outside stayed outside, visible only in the moonlight.

"It is funny you want me to trust you, but it seems as though you cannot do the same for me," Clairfic stated. "We are safe. I am not sure why they are wasting their ammo on such nonsense but the shots will stop shortly. It is only some Human battle. Temorshian weapons are not so primitive."

Humans shooting Humans, I thought, confused. *Why? Don't they understand what is happening all around them?*

Again, as if reading my mind, Clairfic answered me, "Panic makes everyone do strange things, Melissa."

"Looks as though you are right, Clair," I declared sadly, "but you're sure they aren't heading this way?"

"Yes, I am. I am certain they will not find us," he stated flatly. "If you are terribly worried, please take *this*." Out of the darkness Clairfic took my hand, gently placing what felt like a long knife in my open palm. I wrapped my fingers around the hilt. It wasn't heavy but by the feel of it, it could be deadly.

"This is my personal *katlan,* or body knife. My father gave it to me before I left for Earth. It had been in my family for generations. It is sheathed now, but feel here," he said as he took my other hand, looking for my pointer finger, "push this button, and it disappears to release the blade. Be careful with it."

Feeling around with my fingers, being extremely careful not to hit the button, I could tell it was beautifully decorated and embellished. Twice the size of a butcher's knife, but without the angular point, the knife fit nicely into the palm of my hand. I was honored he trusted me with such a personal object.

"Thank you, Clair. I'll be careful." I wished I could see it with my own eyes but I would have to wait until morning.

"We can practice with it tomorrow. Now that you are safe," he added lightheartedly, "I will go check on your parents and hope they have not done anything to attract these foolish Humans."

I felt his presence leave the room. My ears followed him as he left the apartment we were sharing and headed to my family. He moved so soundlessly it was hard to track, but the murmurs from the other apartment reassured me he'd made it safely.

The gunshots finally died down, and the newfound silence was maddening. I thought I'd be safer with the body knife, but I felt terribly alone, the darkness threatening to envelope me. I cupped the blade to my chest, listening to hear Clairfic return to the room.

I pushed myself to think of anything else besides my new solitary confinement. Still holding the blade tightly to my chest, I began to move my fingers around, learning the knife so it'd become a part of me. To have something so powerful in my hands helped me make up my mind to use it if I had to. I'd protect not only myself but also my family, which now included Clairfic.

My ears caught a sound: Clairfic was returning. I let out a breath I hadn't realized I was holding. Immediately, I felt lighter, and the exhaustion I'd brushed off at the first sound of the explosion suddenly came back. A yawn escaped my pressed lips.

"Your sister is a heavy sleeper, is she not?" he asked as he entered the room, returning to his nest.

"Is she still sleeping?" I asked, only half-surprised. Mabel had always been a heavy sleeper, and if that girl did not want to wake up, she didn't. "I bet that if she had her way, she would sleep through the whole bloody war."

"Yes," Clairfic laughed. "I have never seen anything like it. Your parents and grandfather were up and worried, but your sister was nowhere to be found. I asked about her, and they said she was still sleeping! Sleeping at a time like this ... I could not believe it. By the way, your family took my observations quite well. Actually, a lot better than you did."

"Well, of course they did. They think the world of you, and I'm guessing they think the sun shines out of your butt," I told him laughing. "You can be amusing when you want to be. As for my sister, do you expect anything less from her?"

"Oh, no, not anymore. I should learn to be less surprised by her actions. As for the sun, I can guarantee you that it does not, Melissa. I am surprised that I have to explain how the sun works to you of all people!"

I died with laughter.

"Clairfic!" I gasped between bouts of laughter. "That is hilarious! No, I understand how the sun works! It's a *saying*—it's a joke!" Tears ran down my face.

"Oh ... Ehhh ... " he muttered some La'Mursian I definitely didn't catch.

Soon he was chuckling as much as I was. I felt his eyes on me, even though I couldn't see him fully. My eyes adjusted to the darkness, faintly making out his form. He was sitting up in his nest looking straight at me.

"Let's get back to bed, you weirdo," I told him, throwing a pillow at his face. "Our *lovely* sun will not be up for a few hours." I lay back, getting comfortable in my cocoon.

"The same sun that does not shine out of my butt," Clairfic insisted.

I sighed, wiping the tears away. "Yep, the one and the same."

I listened, while he got comfortable in his nest of pillows and blankets. A surreal lightness I'd never known before entered my being. I chalked it up to feeling safe again and snuggled deeper into my blankets.

"Clair?" I asked into the night.

"Yes, Melissa?" he responded.

"Can you see in the dark?"

"Of course. Can *you*?"

"Um, they didn't cover that in your Earth classes?" I mused. "No, we can't. I mean, I can make out shapes and movement, but other than that it looks black to me."

"That is a shame. It is rather helpful to be able to see in the dark, especially when your planet is dark half of the day."

"Yes, I suppose it would be helpful, but that is simply not how we're made ... Do you ever get cold like we do?" I asked, pulling the blanket tighter around my shoulders. "I hate being cold."

"No. I guess that makes me lucky—we can control our body temperatures in whatever climate we find ourselves in. It is another reason I like being on Earth. With all of the seasons, it gives me the opportunity to adapt to the changing temperatures. It is a shame you cannot do the same."

I yawned again. "You're lucky. I wish I had that superpower."

"It is not a power, it is simply how we are made. Maybe Humans will change one day and learn to adapt ... "

I hid my face in my pillow. A part of me didn't want to go to sleep. I wanted to stay up talking with Clairfic about whatever. I wanted to forget why we'd come together and the fear of what we were going to face. I didn't want to wake up in the morning breaking the closeness we'd created in the dark.

"Goodnight, Melissa. Get some rest," he whispered to me.

"Goodnight ... "

I pressed my face deeper into the pillow, hoping whatever light happened to be within me wasn't shining out of my face, the *katlan* resting at my side.

When I woke in the morning, I was alone.

The empty apartment gave me the creeps. I dressed as quickly as possible, repacked my backpack, and cleaned up as best as I could with what little water I was given. Normally, my morning routine would've taken an hour, but today it was a solid fifteen minutes. Who needed makeup and hot tools at a time like this? Sensible clothing and a braid would work just fine.

I tucked the *katlan* under my shirt, tying the strings attached to it around my neck and torso. I fit it perfectly on my abdomen. The simple gesture of securing the knife made me feel powerful—it was a secret weapon I could use in a pinch. Plus the *katlan* was a gift from a trusted friend. It made me beam inside.

I joined my family in the other apartment shortly after getting ready, but most of the group had gone off to do various jobs. Clairfic went out with my father to search the area for some type of vehicle. Grandfather and Mom left to find more supplies closer to home. I was left with my sister to finish our breakfast. When we finished, we were responsible for bagging several lunches and dinners for the next few days with what we had. We needed to be careful with our rations. Being as frugal as possible, we packed on the side of caution.

"How was last night?" Mabel asked as she munched on her last piece of bread.

"I can't believe you slept through the gunshots and all that. It was terrifying," I told her as I buttered my own piece.

"I heard about *that* already. I can't help how tired I was! It's rough being in the apocalypse," she said. "Besides, I needed my beauty rest. I can't be useful when I'm exhausted."

I couldn't tell if she was serious or not. If she thought this was hard, it was only going to get worse. I kept my feelings to myself and let her talk.

"I want to know what you and Clairfic talked about," she pushed again.

"Oh, *that*," I replied. "Nothing, really. He talked about what happened to him, which was traumatic. I can't believe he is still pushing along ... But I think it helped to get it off his chest."

"Everyone's dead, aren't they?" she asked, looking at me with all-knowing eyes. Even if she didn't have an ounce of tact in her, she was beginning to understand the world without having me or anyone else spell it out to her.

"Hush, what if he heard you?" I asked, mortified. "How did you guess?"

What if he had heard her? Would he care that I was telling her bits of his story without him? I pushed the thought away. *She'd asked and had a right to know.*

"He's not here!" she said. "He's off with Dad looking for a working vehicle with gas. Probably hoping to find a radio or something, too. So spill: are they or aren't they all dead?"

"Yes, his crew is gone," I told her, lowering my voice. "He's very upset by the whole thing and worried most of his regiment is dead, too. He wasn't able to connect with anyone else while he made his way to our shelter.

"If you say anything, Mabel, I'll kill you myself. He said they were like family, and you should have seen him last night. He's really torn up about the whole way they handled the Temorshians."

"Gosh, I'm sorry to hear that," she said, then looked down with a pained expression. "I can't even imagine losing everyone like that. What else did he tell you? Anything that can help us?"

"Not really," I thought about telling her about the Temorshians, but I didn't want to scare her. I was in the same boat Clair was in: neither of us knew anything outside of what we'd personally experienced. So why make her uneasy?

I changed the subject, "He's really funny, however."

"Weird, a Shielder with a sense of humor. They always look so serious, especially Clair," Mabel said, eyeing me hard. "He doesn't look like he'd ever lighten up."

"I know. The first time he laughed at one of my jokes I almost passed out!" I laughed.

Mabel looked at me as though I'd grown a second head. I knew what was coming next—the light within me was spilling out, I was sure of it.

"How is Grandfather holding up?" I asked, focusing as hard as I could on the lunch I was making.

"Don't try to change the subject, Mel. Something else happened last night, and I'm hurt you won't tell me," she announced, pretending to be more hurt than she actually was by pushing out her lower lip in protest—something she did frequently when she wasn't getting her way.

"I really don't know what you are talking about. Nothing

happened. He needed to process his grief, and then we went to bed. Shortly after the explosion happened. Then we slept some more," I stated as calmly as I could, pushing the light down deep inside me. Whatever it was, it was no good to let other people see it, even if it was just my sister. If it didn't make sense to me, it wouldn't make sense to her.

"Sure, sure ... Where did he sleep?" she asked innocently.

"On the floor."

"Where?"

"In the bedroom, where else? Everything else in the place was a mess."

"In your bedroom?"

"What?"

"Did the big bad Shielder sleep in your room—*on the floor*—but still in your room?"

"Yes."

"Why did he sleep on the floor? In your *room*?" she asked, finishing up her last bag, fully concentrating on me.

"He is too big for a Human bed; we should have realized that beforehand. He appreciated the gesture nonetheless."

"Why was he in your room?" she asked again, this time searching for my eyes.

I looked up and met her glare. Mabel looked inquisitive and amused. I couldn't tell if she was judging me or having fun at my expense.

"I don't know why he picked that spot. I was fine with it *and* so was he. I forgot to ask him about it," I confessed honestly. "I'd forgotten to ask because at the time it didn't cross my mind that it might be weird. Why are you looking for something when there isn't a *thing*?"

"'Cause something *did* change last night, and I want to know what!" she smirked.

"We're friends."

"Yeah? Aren't we all? We gave him a freaking nickname! He is becoming a big part of this family, Melissa, and I just noticed something this morning with him."

"You're always noticing things that aren't there, Mabel!"

"Whatever. You want to deny it, fine. But trust me, something was different about him."

"*Probably* a good night's rest. If you failed to notice, he was really beat up from that crash he was in," I told her, anger rising. I didn't want to hear any of the conspiracy theories she was always rattling off.

"He was in a crash?" she asked me with wide eyes. "Fuck ... "

"Yes, Mabel, a really awful crash that killed his entire crew." I tried to let my anger settle. I didn't want to fight with Mabel, and I needed to get these lunches packed before the others returned.

Mabel didn't ask any further questions. Instead, she helped me prepare the last of the sandwiches and bags I was working on. Still, my curiosity burned inside me.

"He looked happier," Mabel whispered as we finished the last of our rations. "You're probably right. He was tired, and he felt better after getting some sleep. Who knows, he probably would have been happy outside on a rock."

"He was happy on the dirty floor, in the little nest be made for himself, that just happened to be in the room where I found a bed that made me happy. Okay?"

"Right. Whatever you say," she said, rolling her eyes. "Can I ask you something?"

"You can if it doesn't have to do with Clair," I answered.

"And you won't get mad?"

"Depends what it is ... is it about Clairfic?"

"No."

"Then I'll try not to get mad," I told her. "What do you want to know?"

"How did you end things with Joel?"

Oh, the million-dollar question from my little sister. I tried not grimace at her innocent question. I'd been thinking about him the whole time I was in the shelter, and even then I didn't have a good answer.

"Mabel, I really don't know. He was so angry when I told him we wouldn't go to his cabin. It was so confusing, and I was so hurt he'd react like that, but what was I supposed to do? Leave everyone to go with him?"

She let me mull over my words.

The pain of letting Joel down started to return, dimming the little happiness I was holding onto.

"No," she said quietly, "it would have killed us to let you go with him. I think you made the right decision. Family—*our family*—is important."

"He was—*is*—important to me, but after all this," I gestured to our new reality, "things feel different. I'm different."

"I know what you mean. I sure do know what you mean," she said, and then reached for my hand.

We clasped our hands together and smiled. I looked down. The memory of trying to hold Clairfic's hand rushed into my mind's eye, and the difference between the two made me giggle.

"I tried to hold his hand," I laughed.

"You what?" Mabel said, looking shocked. She pulled our hands closer to her chest, a big smile finding its way onto her face. "Okay, maybe it wasn't just sleep that made him happy!"

"Ha!" I laughed, taking my hand away from her tight grasp. "Not like that, you weirdo! He was in pain, and I was trying to comfort him."

"Oh, I bet he loved that! Look at you two—little lovers finding each other in this mess. How romantic!" she sang.

"No! Stop that! Please, dear God. You need to get that out of your mind right now," I yelled. "Joel may still be alive, and who knows if we're together or not? Besides, I don't feel that way about Clair. So stop, okay?" I felt my cheeks burn bright red. The little light dimmed by the thought of Joel quickly grew stronger.

"Who cares about Joel? He's an ass. Making you pick between

him and family. Who does *that*?" she asked. "Nice people don't do that sort of thing, Melissa. You're much better off without him."

"Don't say that! You liked him!"

"Yeah? I did and so what? He didn't treat you very well and as your sister, that does not sit well with me," she confessed. "He was fine at first, but he showed his true colors in the end. Now I say so long and good riddance."

I sighed. There was no point in arguing with her. I couldn't outright admit that she was right, and if the Shielders hadn't arrived when they did, I was sure we would've broken up. We stayed together out of convenience, not love. It was easy to pretend we needed each other when the world was falling apart around us. Kayin had even mentioned the same thing before that prince made his grand entrance into our world. Both important women in my life were right: Joel was a jerk and not the one for me.

"I know you're right, but still. You can't say that. What if he's dead? How would you feel?" I asked.

"I would feel the very same way: happy you and he are no longer together. Now my sister is dating a Shielder—that's awesome. Upgrade!"

"Mabel ... "

"What?"

"Shut up."

She laughed. "I promise not to mention it to anyone, not even Mom."

"Especially not her! She'd tell Dad and then he would—"

"Did you hear that?" she interrupted.

We froze. We listened to the voices yelling, *no*, screaming our names.

"It sounds like Dad," Mabel breathed.

"Stay here," I whispered back.

I got up slowly and moved over to the window. Someone had pushed aside the upright table that was blocking the opening so that half the window was visible. It allowed me to look out. I tried to look around but I couldn't see a thing.

The voice was getting louder—it was our father—but he was using a type of voice I'd heard only once before. The same voice he used when Mabel had fallen out of a tree when she was younger and he'd needed Mom to call 911.

Something was not right.

"Mabel, where did Mom and Grandpa go?" I asked quietly.

"They were going to the other building," she whispered. "The one behind this one. I ... I didn't check that one yesterday. I should have but I didn't ... "

I could tell she was scared.

"That's not the problem, Mabel. You're fine. I need you to do something for me," I told her. "I need you to go find them and safely bring them back here. Have them stop whatever it is they're doing and get in here. Take this," I handed her a small handgun from where Dad had left the weapons. "You need to focus, Mabel, and do what I'm asking. Look at me," I demanded, as tears formed in her eyes, and her lower lip quivered. "You can do this. All I need you to do is go out the back entrance and find Mom. You won't need to use this, but I need you to take it with you. Do you hear me? What do you need to do?"

"I ... I need to go find Mom," she shuddered.

"And what else?"

I could hear my father getting closer, with more panic in his voice.

"I need to bring them back here, where it's safe," she repeated, as one tear fell from her eye.

"Yes, excellent. Now go. Don't make a sound and go!" I told her, turning to gather my own weapon of choice.

"But—but Melissa, what are you going to do?" Terror rang in her shaky voice.

"I am going to go help Dad, Mabel. Now stop wasting time and make sure you find them. *Go!*"

234 / SAMANTHA HEUWAGEN

Without another word, she slipped out of the room and ran down the corridor. I heard her glide out the back as Father's voice stopped directly in front of the apartment building.

"Melissa, Mabel ... Girls, I need you to come outside, please," he yelled.

I set my task.

I grabbed one of the guns Clairfic had found. He'd showed me enough to use it, and thankfully, I was comfortable enough to shoot. I picked it up, turned the safety off, and made my way outside.

22

From the sound of my father's voice, something had gone terribly wrong.

I squared my shoulders, forcing all my courage to the forefront of my mind. I prayed that Mabel would keep Mom and Grandpa from doing anything stupid.

I moved ever so slowly out of the apartment, avoiding broken boards and weak spots on the floor. Crouching low to the ground, I made my way to the front door.

Through the small cracks in the deformed walls I could see the top portion of Clairfic's body. His hands rested on the top of his head. His face was tense while looking annoyed, but he seemed to be going along with whatever was being asked of him. I could tell by the crease between his eyes he was pissed.

What are you up to, Clair?

Since his large body was facing the apartment building, I decided to head out the emergency exit and double around. Staying low and being as quiet as I could, I listened as I walked. I wanted the element of surprise. Even if Clair was a trained soldier, one look could give away my position.

Dad had begun to beg again, "Girls, please, come out. We ... we've found someone to help us," he urged, his voice nothing but a shrill remnant of his normal drawl. "I've already told him you're in there, so be good girls and come out."

Holding in my snort, I opened the door quietly. The air was warm, and the sun had risen higher in the sky; it wasn't quite noon. I left the safety of the building, finding a pile of debris to hide behind. I strained to catch a glimpse of Clair. Without a good look, I moved on.

My father yelled one last time, "Please, girls, do what I say!"

I tiptoed around a car, finally taking in the scene: Dad spoke in hushed tones to a big man holding a gun to his head while also pointing a shotgun at Clairfic. Both of them had lost their weapons and looked utterly useless.

My heart skipped a beat.

"They won't come out. They're too smart for that," my father stated. The man pushed his body ahead, ignoring his pleas. "They would've seen us coming and left. Go look for yourself. Take whatever they left, but they're not here."

"Do I look like an amateur?" the man asked, pushing the gun further into my father's skull. "You said two girls, an old man, and your wife. You think I'm an idiot? They're scared shitless—they wouldn't know what to do. Get them out here right now before I blow your head off!"

A shiver of rage rippled down my spine. I tightened my grip on the gun.

"Let this family go," Clairfic pleaded. "They are harmless and need to be escorted to safety. Kill me and take them with you."

My heart skipped another beat.

"Shut the fuck up, you heathen!" the man yelled, smashing Clair in his side. The impact caused Clairfic to fall to his knees in pain. The blow caused blood to freely flow down his cheek.

My temper flared, rippling over my body as I got up from my hiding place. Beads of sweat formed on my brow as I silently made my way over to this beast of a man.

"Please, just take whatever you want. We don't need your truck, and we don't need any help. This Shielder is our friend and—"

A loud smack rang out. I glanced up in time to watch my father fall to the ground.

"Fucking Shielder lover. You people make me sick," he spat. "Look around you! What have they ever done for you?"

"Quite a lot, actually," I said, holding my gun to the back of his head and pushing my barrel into his curly mane.

He froze.

"Drop the gun," I ordered him, "both of them. Raise your hands where I can see them."

He did as I told him without a word. I kept my barrel tight against his skull, my finger itching to pull the trigger.

As swift as a cat, Clairfic was up, grabbing the gun out of the man's hand and holding the shotgun at him. "Melissa, I can take it from here."

"Not a chance, Clairfic," I snarled, anger flowing over my body. "This man has a lot of explaining to do. Get on your knees."

I looked over to the still body of my father and back to Clair. "Is my Dad okay?"

Without looking away from the man now positioned on his knees, Clairfic bent down to check my father's pulse.

"He will live. He will have a headache, but he will live," he stated, standing up, the gun firmly in his hands.

"Good. You would've been really fucked, mister, if you'd killed him." I circled around to face him.

The man was rugged with a long brown beard and brown hair peppered with white in a long, unkempt ponytail. His eyes were clear blue, but hidden under swollen sockets. He looked like he hadn't slept in days. His weathered skin, dark from the sun, stood out from under his old army gear. His body was covered with various hand weapons. Maybe if he wasn't on his knees I would have been impressed by his muscular arms and large frame, but I wasn't.

"What's your name?" I asked.

"Fuck you," he answered.

"I believe she just asked you a question, sir," Clairfic growled, pushing the man in the side with his gun. "Answer her."

"My name is Dominic Fuller."

"Why did you assault my family?" I asked. Adrenaline pumped through my body. It was a strange and unfamiliar feeling. I had the power to blow this man's head off. Could I do it? Yes. Would I? I wasn't sure.

"He was with one of them," he said, and eyed Clair with such hate I shuddered. "He talked to it like it was Human—something with *feelings* and a brain. I couldn't let the thing think it was okay for it to befriend a man. It isn't natural."

"So? What does it matter to you?"

"It matters everything to me!" he yelled. "Look around you, girl, our world is destroyed! Who do you think is responsible?"

I rolled my eyes.

"This wasn't their fault. What news outlet gave you the wrong story? You seem like the type of person who watched Fox News—what did they say?"

"I didn't have to hear it from anyone, I opened my eyes. I looked around. Do you not see what's in front of you?" he asked me with an air of superiority.

"I see it," I told him, "but I am not stupid enough to believe that these beings were responsible for the destruction of our planet. You should be mad at the Temorshians or even your own people, but not the Shielders. Especially not this one," I stated, nodding my head in Clair's direction. "He helped us escape from the city. What's your story? You think because he's what he is he's *below* you?

"There's nothing to be done to fix this mess except work together. Oh, yes, that's right—*teamwork*—to make it through whatever is coming for us, we're all going to have to work together. Or didn't that cross your mind?"

Dominic looked from me to Clairfic, his eyes almost bursting from their tired sockets, seemingly puzzled by what he was hearing.

"Why isn't he with the others?" Dominic asked after his shock subsided.

"What's it to you?"

He snorted. "It's nothing."

"Sure." I turned to Clairfic. "What do we do with him?"

"You'll never make it anywhere on foot," Dominic interrupted. "What's left of us Humans are scared shitless—attacking anything that moves. You might be prepared to handle me alone, but a gang? *Please*. Besides, all the Shielders left—he's proof. I don't know how you managed to get this one," he said, eyeing Clairfic like a piece of trash, "but I wouldn't be surprised if the rest of his kind died in the fight. They won't be back to help us. And don't get me started about the Temorshians. They're on their way, an idiot can gather that much. We'll be dead shortly. You're wasting your time trying to go anywhere else."

"You can think what you like, but we're leaving this area and heading north," I told him, holding my head high.

I caught Clair's eyes. He looked worried but pensive, as if what this man said struck a nerve.

Behind me, Dad came back to consciousness while my sister, Mom, and Grandfather made their way toward us—all three holding some type of weapon.

The Pebbles were always prepared.

"Dad! Dad, are you all right?" my sister asked, running to my father.

"Melissa, Clairfic, what's going on?" my Mother cried, rushing to Dad with her small emergency kit. "How did this happen?"

Clair and I made eye contact again, collectively sighing. He returned his attention to our captive as I gazed down my barrel. The defeated man stared at my family. His weathered cheeks turned red as beads of sweat dripped down the sides of his long face.

"See what you've done, Dominic?" I asked him. "Nothing threatening here. Just a small family trying to *survive*."

He flinched at my words.

"We were fine before you decided to come in, weapons blazing!"

"I ... I didn't think," he breathed, avoiding all of our eyes. "I didn't think ... "

"Of course you didn't think—that would have been too much for you." I tapped my gun against his skull.

In my gut I knew I was going too far. I could see through his fake pity. I didn't want my sweet family to allow him to enter our bubble. I knew my parents well enough to understand that they'd forgive him and invite him along. I, on the other hand, worried for Clairfic's safety as well as our own. Clair could handle himself, but he had blood running down his face. If he missed his guy once, he could do it again. We couldn't afford to take a chance.

"I'll let you walk out of here—without killing you," I snarled.

"Melissa Ann!" my Mother gasped.

"Quiet, Sandra," my father said. "Help me up. She knows what she's doing, let her be."

He struggled to get up, resting his body weight on my mother and sister.

"You made a terrible decision," my father remarked. "I don't know what you were thinking and frankly, I don't care. You'll leave or we'll kill you."

Dominic made a motion to get up, but Clairfic stopped him. "Are you alone?" he asked.

"Yes," Dominic whispered.

I knew what was coming next. "Clairfic, what are you—"

"How many guns do you have?" Clairfic asked, cutting me off.

"Enough," Dominic said flatly, glaring back at the Shielder.

"How many?" Clair pressed again.

"Clair, we don't need to rob him," I added. "We need to get rid of him. You're giving him an excuse to follow us."

"Five hand guns, three shotguns—you're holding one of them now. Enough assault weapons to make your head spin, one rifle, two automatics, and enough ammo to fill all of them tenfold. Plus an assortment of knives," Dominic rattled off, proud of his collection.

"He has a truck, too," my dad added.

"You know how to use all of that?" Clair asked, sounding slightly impressed.

"Do you need to ask?" Dominic boasted.

"You're alone with all that?" I asked, amazed.

"Yes," he answered.

"You are alone and well prepared. You should join us," Clairfic offered.

The six of us ogled the large Shielder.

"No," I said. "Don't you dare—"

Clairfic put his hand up. "You do not have to like me," he told the man. "You do not need to speak to me, but this family needs help. You have proven today that you are a man that has considerable skill." Clairfic pulled back his gun. "Will you join us?"

No one moved a muscle; the silence was deafening.

I broke the tension, "Clair, are you sure you want to do this? He wants to kill you ... "

"I do not."

We looked at the man on his knees.

"I'm furious at his kind, I'll admit that, but I don't believe in useless violence."

"*Really?*" I asked skeptically. "Because that doesn't match your actions here today, buddy. I call bullshit."

"It's not bullshit. I might be able to kill things, but there has to be a reason—a solid reason. What would you have done if you saw what I saw? I've been out here for the last 72 hours looking for anyone to ... *trust*. Anyone to help save me from these fucking aliens ... To find him," Dominic continued, pointing to Dad, "walking around with a Shielder like it was nothing—like they were the best of friends. It didn't sit well with me. That's not right, your father should've been with his own kind." He lowered his hands slowly. "Sure, fine, I can admit when I was wrong and that I might—*might*—have overreacted. But I still believe this is my country, my planet, and I want these fuckers out!"

"Yeah? Don't we all?" Mabel interjected with as much sass as I've ever heard. "But you don't see us losing *our* humanity, do you?"

Dominic's eyes widened at Mabel's words and the audacity that a woman should speak to him in such a fashion.

I mulled over Clairfic's desire to bring this crazy man with us. It made sense if Dominic had the number of weapons he said he did. Having another person to defend us when the Temorshians attacked was good planning, and Clair always thought of the big picture. It might make me uncomfortable to have Dominic along, but it was the right thing to do—the *smart* thing to do.

I sighed. "Clairfic's right. We may not be happy about it, but we could use Dominic's help."

"We'll have some rules before we move forward," my father added, looking like he'd murder Dominic if he tried anything funny. "Don't hurt Clairfic or anyone else in this family for that matter. Is that clear?"

Dominic leisurely nodded his head.

"We work as a team. No one has the final say; we work out issues and problems together. We don't have to agree but we'll do what's best for the family—for the group as a whole."

Dominic winced but agreed with another head nod.

"You don't have to consider us friends, but we're the only thing you have left in terms of companionship," he mused. "Lastly, we all work. It doesn't seem like you're new to the idea, but we each have jobs to do."

"Fine. That sounds fine," Dominic said.

"Am I missing anything?" Dad asked the rest of us.

The rest of the Pebbles shook our heads.

"You will keep your anger," Clairfic stated, reaching out his hand to Dominic. "You will need it when we come across the Temorshians."

I held my breath as I watched the defeated and outnumbered Human take Clair's hand. He didn't look pleased, but I could've sworn he was relieved to no longer be alone, his eyes scarcely hiding his relief at his reprieve.

"Where's your stuff?" I asked.

"Two miles south in what's left of my place," he said, looking me over.

"Fine, Clair and I will go with you and bring it all back here," my father declared. "We're going to lose daylight, so we'll start the trip tomorrow. We'll spend the rest of the day checking to make sure we have what we need."

"Oh, no, you don't," my sister interjected. "You two got us into this mess. You're not going anywhere with him."

"She has a point, Viktor," Mom added, looking worried. "You need to rest and make sure that you don't overexert yourself with this new head injury."

"Yeah ... sorry about that," Dominic uttered, rather embarrassed.

"We'll go alone then," Clairfic answered.

"Hell, *no*," Mabel and I yelled together.

Grandfather broke the awkward silence as he cleared his throat. "If I might say something," he interjected. "It seems to me that throughout this whole ordeal, the girls have shown that they're more than capable of taking care of themselves. Especially while the rest of us ran around like chickens with our heads cut off. Why not have them go with Dominic?"

"I like the way you think, Gramps," Mabel beamed, practically skipping over to him to give him a kiss on the cheek

"Works for me," Dominic said with a shrug, looking at Mabel and smirking.

"No, absolutely not," Clairfic all but yelled, making us jump by the sound of his thunderous voice. "This is ... this is not a job for—"

"For what, Clair?" Mabel asked sweetly, with eyes hard as steel.

"Please say for ladies," I goaded.

"This is not a job for *girls*," he professed, slanting his eyes to drive the point home.

I sucked in my breath, feeling the feminist in me prepare for battle.

Dad and Grandfather shook their heads while Mom rolled her eyes. They didn't raise their daughters or granddaughters to stand down when feminist principles were being questioned. Hadn't we just proven what we could handle anything, regardless of our gender?

Out of the corner of my eye I noticed Dad and Mom walk toward the apartment, my father leaning his weight against my mother. They knew who would win this fight.

"Oh, would you look at that, Mel —he said *it*. He said we couldn't do it because we have vaginas," Mabel quipped. "Tsk, tsk, Mr. Clairfic."

"I guess he'll just have to learn the hard way, Mabel, that we silly girls can get the job done *without* a gun to our heads. Come on, Dominic, let's go get your stuff." I turned toward the man who was looking at us in disbelief.

"Unless you can't be seen walking with girls?" Mabel added with a smirk similar to the one she'd seen on his face moments before.

"Oh, no, ladies," he said with emphasis on the last word. "I would be honored to travel with such ... such—"

"Remember to choose your words wisely, Mr. Fuller," Mabel teased. She gave Grandfather one last hug and took the shotgun from Clairfic's limp hands, making her way closer to the two of us.

"I would never forget, miss?"

"I'm Mabel Pebbles," she said, then reached for his dirty hand and gave it a good shake.

"I'd never forget, Miss Mabel," Dominic smiled, slightly bowing his head in her direction. "I was going to say, I would be honored to travel with such accomplished women with such strong personalities." He was enjoying this.

"Wonderful! Let's get started. Don't wait up, Gramps!" she yelled, waving absentmindedly behind her and taking Dominic by the arm. "After you, Mr. Fuller." The two began walking arm-in-arm to his hideout.

Mabel sure knew how to defuse tension and prove her point all at the same time. Girl had style.

"Oh, I won't, dear," Grandfather laughed, waving back. "You better catch up to her, Melissa. She held her own here, but we don't know that fellow well enough to let them go on alone together."

"Exactly my point!" Clairfic groaned through gritted teeth.

"Stop it right now, Clair," I said to him, not forgetting his sexist undertones. "You could've been killed if we'd let you go alone. Mabel calmed that guy down—at least give her *some* credit. She didn't want to see you get hurt or worse!"

Clairfic tried to argue but I stopped him, lifting my hand to silence his qualms. "Not another word from you!"

I turned to follow my sister as I caught Grandfather saying, "You were going to learn eventually, son. Those girls are strong-willed and can hold their own. Might as well honor it and respect their decisions."

Clairfic only responded in La'Mursian.

———

"This is all yours?" Mabel asked in disbelief.

Dominic's hideaway was nice but lacked imagination. As unimpressive as it was on the outside—a bare-bones shack with little to no vegetation—the inside made up for it. Guns lined the walls, and the shack contained rations enough for at least six months for twelve different people.

"Yes, it's mine. Either I bought it or found it," Dominic told us, hiding his pride.

"Even before this whole thing? Before the aliens came?" Mabel asked.

The whole time we'd walked, Mabel hadn't stopped asking Dominic questions. Her curiosity was evident on her face as she examined the stranger, eyeing him through her thick lashes; she was not afraid of him in the slightest.

"I got a few more after they showed up. The world was falling apart around me, what else should I have done?"

"Nothing, nothing at all. This is good, very good," she said, and smiled. "You know, even if everyone else is mad at you, I get it."

"You do?"

"Yes, I do. But you have to promise to control that temper of yours. We don't need any of that nonsense toward us. We'll love you if you let us. Plus you're going to need all the help you can get—even if you do have all this—it won't matter if you're alone. Now behave, and you'll have friends for life," she finished, giving him a small smile.

"Thank you," I heard Dominic whisper. "I promise."

"But also promise me when we get back you'll eat something and sleep. You look like shit."

And there she was. Right when you think she's sweet, she runs her mouth. She's notorious for saying what she thinks—no matter what it is.

"This is impressive. How do you imagine we're going to get all this crap back in one trip?" I asked. "No one should be out at night."

"I'm assuming you're commenting on what happened last night?" he asked me.

The hairs on the back of my neck stood up.

"Don't worry. They were ruffians that had ideas of their own. They pretty much killed each other," Dominic stated without emotion. "The area should be clear unless something *else* joins us."

Mabel and I caught each other's eyes. We'd forgotten, if only for a moment, he was cold-hearted.

"You were there?"

Dominic shrugged. "I watched. I didn't need to do much because they were fighting each other. It didn't take long for mistakes to be made and well ... They were all shot in a few minutes."

"Glad you weren't hurt or anything," Mabel politely added, eyeing me from across the room. We shared a silent nod.

"I protect what's mine. Don't forget that."

"I wasn't saying—"

"I know what you are getting at," he countered, offended. "I heard the rules your father laid out. I won't do anything to your precious Shielder, but I will protect the lot of you. We got off on the wrong foot, but I'll do my duty. I live by my word. And I did make a promise to you, Miss Mabel."

The three of us looked at each other, letting his words hang in the air.

"Thank you for saying that, Mr. Fuller. It means a lot to us," Mabel said. Her eyes were cold but compassion hid behind the thinly veiled wall she created to protect her emotional state. Her shoulders were squared off as if to dare him to question her resolve.

"Please call me Dom or Dominic."

"Thank you, Dom," she whispered. The corner of her mouth turned upward, barely visible. If I hadn't known her so well, I would've missed it.

"Now, Melissa, you asked me how we're getting all of this from point A to point B? Well, no one told you that part of the reason I ambushed your father was because he had spotted my truck, a Dodge Ram."

"You have a truck?" my sister and I questioned in unison, gaping at him, mouths hanging open.

"Oh, yes! I forgot Dad mentioned that!" Mabel squealed.

For the first time, Dominic smiled. Instantly, he looked younger and a lot more approachable.

"Sure do! Filled with gas and enough canisters to last until I can find more. Ladies, it looks like we're going to be friends *indeed*."

"Would you like my first-born?" Mabel joked. The wheels in her mind began to turn, and the veil lifted to allow him in.

Oh, boy, this guy better be careful, or he won't know what hit him. I laughed, amused, just like Mabel had been amused by me. I hoped Dom knew what he was getting himself into.

Even during hard times, Humans didn't stop. They want what they want and move mountains to get it. Mabel didn't date much for a woman in her early twenties because she knew what she wanted and looked for it; she didn't waste time she felt she didn't have. Now, with very little time left, she'd lowered her standards and set her sights on the only available man for miles. Dominic was in for a surprise if he stayed around long enough. Though Dominic seemed like the type of man who had a hard time connecting with people, she could fix that. I doubted he'd mind her attention while we were together.

Dominic laughed as he gestured for us to follow him. "Let me think on it and I'll get back to you," he chuckled. "Ladies, let's start packing."

When we pulled up a few hours later in the truck, which was as full as it could get, the family cheered with surprise. Dad and Mom thanked Dominic while Grandfather beamed. Clairfic was noticeably absent.

As Mabel talked to our parents about Dominic and all his wonderful abilities—it wasn't lost on me why she was doing it— Grandfather pulled me aside.

"If you're looking for him, he's not here."

"What? He left?" I asked, taken aback.

"I'm sure he's somewhere close by, but he didn't take being left behind very well. I tried to talk to him after you left, but he wouldn't communicate in English."

"Oh, he's just being pigheaded. Look at what we have! He should be grateful! Hell, it was his idea to bring Dominic along."

"I think you called him a sexist pig, Melissa," Grandfather stated.

I winced.

My grandfather smiled at me as his eyes radiated the deep love he felt. "From what I gather of him, he's very sensitive."

"So? You heard what he said! It was sexist—he was being a jerk!" I shouted, my voice shrill, though I didn't mean it to be.

"Sometimes, we say things that sound a certain way and the meaning gets lost. The meaning behind what he said was that he cares about you both and didn't want to see either of you get hurt. Mainly, he didn't want to see *you* get into trouble. He didn't speak up when Mabel said she'd go, only when you did."

I wanted a witty retort, but the only thing I could muster was a bleak, "That's not true."

"Believe me or don't, but you need to apologize. He's going to be on edge with Dominic around, and he'll need to be able to rely on you for support."

"Why does everyone keep pinning me with him? I'm *not* the Shielder whisperer!"

"You're not? Darn, we may need to rethink our selection, then," he teased with a twinkle in his eye.

"Honestly, Grandpa." I rolled my eyes.

"Will you just trust an old man?"

"I always trust you," I told him, leaning into a hug. After letting go, I added, "I'll go and find him."

"I'd head to the roof if I were you … "

"I thought you said you didn't know where he went?"

"I'm an old man, I forget what I said. Now, off with you!"

Annoyed I'd been bamboozled by my own flesh and blood, I headed up the emergency staircase in search of access to the roof.

I struggled up the stairs, avoiding the immense crack over the broken pieces of the apartment. Once I passed the third floor—the memories threatening to haunt me—I was in the clear. I found the passage to the roof easily enough; Clair had left the door ajar.

I found him looking out into the unknown—something I believed he enjoyed, when emotions ran high. His head hung low and his shoulders were heavy. Clairfic's body faced away from the door, but I knew he'd heard me make my way up the stairs.

"Don't pretend you didn't hear me, Clair," I said to him. "You can hear better than any of us."

"I was hoping you would tire eventually," he mocked.

I sighed. *This is going to take a whole lot of ass-kissing, and I didn't even do anything wrong!*

As I approached him, he made no sign he wanted me to leave. I stood next to him looking out into the countryside. It would've been beautiful if things hadn't been destroyed. Trees cut in two, debris everywhere, and buildings in ruins; bits of it all still smoking from the fires of the previous fight.

"What do you see?" I asked.

"The same as you," he replied.

"You know that's not true. You can see further than I can."

"I see nothing. I haven't seen movement all day."

"You've been up here all day?"

"What else would you want me to do? You left, and I was not in the mood to fraternize with your grandfather. Why spread my piggish attitude toward your family?"

"Well, there's lots to do, of course. You could've looked for supplies or, I don't know, could've helped my parents?"

He snorted. "They have everything under control, and that man has everything I would have looked for. My place was up here keeping a lookout."

I closed my eyes, trying to keep my face from giving away my true feelings. "I'm sorry I called you a sexist pig, Clair. It's just not fair—"

"It wasn't that. Words are words. It was more—more than that."

"Well, then tell me. I said I was sorry for calling you a name— and I am, I'm sorry. It was rude and unnecessary." I turned to face him, but he looked away, moving his body farther from me. "Look at me." I pushed him to face me. "Please don't bottle your emotions around me. Tell me what's bothering you so much that you hid up here all day?"

He twisted to face me.

His size made me feel small and insignificant, but I pressed on. "I'm sorry I called you a sexist pig, but you can't go around saying I can't do something because I'm a woman. You should know I can handle myself regardless of my gender."

"It has nothing to do with your gender, Melissa."

"Oh, doesn't it? It's what you said ... "

"I did say that, and I, too, am sorry, but it was more than that, more than I suppose you realize. It was not safe. What you and Mabel did was extremely dangerous. You could have gotten hurt or in serious trouble with no one to help you!"

"You're being sexist! We didn't need anyone's help. We judged the situation and felt it was something we could do—that we *could* handle it. Just like you and Dad went out to find a car. Did anyone stop you even though it was dangerous? *No*. Were you successful? *No*. Did anyone blame your sex? *No*. I do recall you and my Dad needing help, did you not?"

Clairfic's eyes bugged out as color reached his cheeks. He looked like he was going to explode, but stopped, grumbling a *"yes. "*

"I think Mabel and I made a great team and stopped everything from getting worse. We might not get so lucky next time, but this time we were able to defuse the situation in a sensible way. You have to admit we were able to move the situation along and now look! We have more weapons and rations than we know what to do with."

He let out a long, exhausted sigh. "Did he have what he said he had?" Clair asked.

"You can use his name, you know. His name is Dominic. You don't need to like him, and he probably won't like you, but we need each other. It was your idea to bring him along. But yes, he had more than we could ever hope for—he even has a truck! A working truck with gas!"

"He has weapons and skills. I was only thinking about the future. We will need everything we can to build some type of defense for when they come."

"Right and good looking out." I reached out to pat his arm. "That must've been difficult for you to extend a peace offering."

"We needed more supplies and an able body—male or not. I was just trying to plan ahead."

"You did well, Clair. It means so much to us that you *do* plan ahead. I don't know where we would be without you."

We stood awkwardly in silence.

"Now, this may or may not work, but I have a surprise for you," I told him.

"I do not like surprises."

"Oh, you might like this one!" I said cheerfully.

"Doubtful. In all my years, I have never liked surprises. Why would I change for you?"

I smirked. "Fine, then you'll never know what I brought back just for you." I turned to leave, hoping he would take the bait.

I'd almost reached the door to the staircase when I felt his hand gently land on my right shoulder. "Where are you going?"

I spun around. Clairfic's eyes looked despondent, as though he didn't like how I'd suddenly ended our conversation.

"Back downstairs," I told him, painfully aware he was still touching me. "It'll be time to get ready for dinner, and they'll need help finding a place to hide the truck."

"We were not done talking ... "

"Well, for now we are, Clair. I fail to see an ending where we both agree."

"Why is it so easy for you to walk away?"

"It's not," I stammered, taken aback by his quick assessment. "I just don't like to fight. I especially don't like to fight with people I care about. I don't think we'll agree on what happened, but that's fine. I hurt you by doing what I thought was right. You hurt me, too, by your sexist remark. I'm sorry you took it so personally, but it's over. It happened and now there's new work to be done."

Clair shifted his weight from side to side but did not try to defend himself.

I continued, "I also tried to tell you something, but you weren't interested in my surprise, so I decided to give you some more time to yourself, which seems to be what you need right now."

"I do not want any more time to myself," he murmured.

Our big, tough, Shielder was sensitive, and maybe Mabel and Grandfather were right—Clair felt something for me. Those two ideas didn't necessarily have to align, but either way, he seemed to be extremely worried.

"I appreciate your concern, I really do. But I can take care of myself," I reassured him and tapped his hand, which was still resting on my shoulder. I was touched, but I didn't want him to feel like he needed to save me every chance he got.

"I understand that now." He looked a little better, the color lifting from his face. "Can you promise me something?" He squeezed my shoulder and then let me go, twisting his hands nervously together.

"I can try."

"Can you promise to not do that again?"

I sighed. "No, Clairfic, I cannot promise you that. I'm going to do what I think is right, even if you don't agree with it, and even if it happens to be dangerous. I'm going to do what I need to do for my family."

Clair's shoulders slumped, but he nodded in agreement.

"Like it or not, you're now a part of this family, and you're going to have to deal with being saved from time to time. You can't be the boss *all the time*." I smirked, the corners of my mouth bouncing up and down, concealing the beam of light I held in the deep recesses of my heart.

Clairfic smiled back, the stress from the day melting from his features.

"We're going to need your eyes to find a decent place to hide a large truck with no damage, if that's okay with you?"

"Lead the way, boss," he purred, gesturing for me to go before him. I rolled my eyes.

We went down the staircase in silence. Clair passed me, trying to help me down. I accepted his help. Feminist or not, I wasn't going to fall to my death. I might be independent, but I'm far from stupid.

"What was this surprise you mentioned earlier?" he asked, holding out a hand to hold while I awkwardly made my way over a large opening in the stairs.

"I completely forgot! Wait! Oh, *now* you're interested?"

"I was interested earlier," Clairfic said, moving a beam out of my way.

"*In all my years, I have never liked surprises,* you said. *I won't change for you!*"

"Maybe I lied."

I stopped walking. "Are you telling me the great and powerful Clairfic *does* indeed like surprises?"

"Do not abuse this knowledge."

We laughed together.

Stopping on the steps, not wasting my chance to be the same height, I took him by the shoulders, looking in his eyes. "Clairfic, your dreams have finally come true! You don't need to like Dominic, but we hit the jackpot with him. Mabel and I found not one, but two different radios for you to try! Not to mention a radio in the truck!" I happily told him. "Isn't it gr—?"

Without a word, he hoisted me up, flipped me over his shoulder, and ran down the stairs.

23

"This has got to be the place—look, we can move those boxes or something," Mabel suggested, pointing to a pile of boxes crushed from fallen debris. "At the very least, we could use the smashed boxes to cover the windshield?"

"Hey, works for me," Dom agreed with a shrug.

Moving the truck into a deserted garage proved to be a long and daunting task. We were paranoid someone would try to take it in the night—probably just overly cautious. To a passerby, the truck would look like a pile of crap unless they looked at it very closely. Dad, Mabel, Dom, and I did what we could with its hiding place, throwing broken wood and beams over it with a dirty tarp to hide the larger items we didn't need for the night. In the end it was a fine pile of shit.

Dominic wasn't too pleased, but he managed. "Maybe I should take the battery with me," he suggested before we headed back to the apartment. "That way it's another deterrent to theft if by chance someone did get curious."

"Good idea," Dad agreed. "Doesn't take too long to put it back in, right? Might as well do it."

"Nice," I cheered. "Do you think anyone would notice it's a nice-looking truck under some shit?"

"Language, please," Dad pleaded.

I rolled my eyes.

"It would take someone who was looking for it to notice, I think," Dom said, rubbing the back of his head. "Let's not waste any more time on it, the sun's setting, and we don't need a replay of last night. Are your windows sealed?"

"Yes, Mabel did that yesterday—should be fine," I told him, eyeing his muscular form as we headed back.

"Good."

"Plus we're only using candles, so the light should be dim enough," Mabel reminded us. "We'll be fine."

"Excellent. Looks like you ladies have it all covered. I'm very impressed," Dom congratulated, tipping his head to us.

I hated to admit it, but he was growing on me. He might be an ass, but he knew his stuff, and he would keep my family safe. I could try to like the man, not just for Mabel, but because I needed him. I needed his stores of food and ammo. I needed his skill. I needed another body to defend my family.

We entered the apartment with a clatter. Mom had already started dinner with Grandfather, while Clair sat on the floor working.

"It's like watching a kid on Christmas morning," Mabel observed as Clairfic worked with one of Dom's radios we'd brought into the apartment. He'd been working for several hours, completely missing the truck adventure, and still hadn't made contact.

The airwaves were dead.

Clair focused on his task, his eyes holding a peaceful intensity. We left him to his work as he tinkered with various parts of the radio set, placing bits and pieces together like it was some puzzle only he understood.

I chuckled to myself, agreeing with Mabel: Clairfic was excited. He wasn't Christmas excited, as Mabel had said, but he was in his element. He was a communication specialist in his former life, so this was exactly what Clair was trained to do. I hoped he was successful, for his sake. How would he handle being let down by his people again?

"Have you found anything?" Dom asked him.

"No, but I am confident I can within the hour," Clair answered, not looking up from the radio.

"Well, let me know if you need anything," Dom offered, sitting on the edge of the couch.

Mom and I locked eyes. My parents were not fans of this renegade either. They watched him from afar with their sideways glances and constant silent observations. Grandfather didn't show his feelings one way or another.

"That was nice of you," Mabel told Dom as she sat next to him on the other side of the couch. "Looks like you might be friends after all."

"Hey, don't push it. I can admit when I've made a mistake—and I have—but we have a long way to go."

"Mabel, why don't you come help me with dinner?" Mom interrupted. She tensed every time Dom got too close to Mabel and seemed to be trying to disrupt their growing friendship.

"What can I do?" I asked.

"Set the table, please. Viktor, you can help as well," she ordered.

Once finished, I focused on the Shielder, who spent too much time in my thoughts, watching him work in silence while I mulled over my feelings. So much had changed in a small amount of time I could barely understand how I felt. I'd proven to myself I could handle almost anything, but I couldn't handle disappointing Clairfic. It was confusing and jumbled in my mind. I pushed it aside.

I can't think about that now, I thought, *I'll think about it tomorrow.*

"What's the other radio doing?" I asked.

"It's searching the airwaves itself," Dominic answered, "I've used it for days—the battery life is good."

Clair reached over to turn it up to drown us out.

"Did he just—"

"He did ... "

Dom and I exchanged looks.

"Um, no, that's gotta go." I got up and turned it down enough so we could eat in peace.

Clair continued to tamper with the other one, only looking up to glare at me.

"We had a plan," he told us over the static, "if something like this happened, my people would send an encoded message through Human radio airwaves. There has to be something. There has to be ... "

Hours passed, causing Clair to miss dinner, yet nothing jumped out to him.

The rest of us gave up. We wanted a signal as badly as our Shielder friend, but disappointment set in, moving the conversation to preparations. Dad, Grandfather, and Dominic sat looking over various maps, while I listened from the other side of the room—half listening to them and half trying to hear something from the static. Mom restocked her medical stores with supplies from Dominic, and Mabel counted the flashlights and candles we added to our pile. Luckily, Dom had brought a lifetime supply of matches.

It was dark outside by the time we lost all hope. I was ready for bed, exhausted by the day's events. A pronounced yawn was the only thing I could do to try to stay awake.

"You know those emergency notices they have playing on stations?" Dominic asked out of the blue.

"The, *this is a message from your emergency* blah blah blah people?" Mabel clarified.

"Yes, but of course it was different than the old ones. Do you remember those?"

"Yep! Never really heard the old ones in the last few months, but the new ones always said to go to the nearest Shelter or get into a safe house."

"Thank you both for telling us what we already know," Mother interrupted. "What's your point, Dominic?"

"Sorry, ma'am. My point is that it played nonstop since things got hairy—but two days ago, it stopped."

"What does that mean?" I asked.

"I am not sure," Clairfic answered, causing us to jump from the sound of his voice. "It cannot be good by any means, but it should not matter. We should care about Shielder signals."

"Why is that?" Mabel asked, as she began to light various candles around the room.

"Because they're a superior race," Dominic sassed, his eyelids turning to tight slits.

"Oh, God, don't start that again!" Mabel rolled her eyes, turning to face him. "You know, it gets old after a while, repeating the same nonsense over and over again. Grow up."

I flinched. Mabel taunting Dominic wouldn't help, especially in these moods. They might have a special relationship, but Mabel was good at pushing anyone's buttons, no matter who was on the receiving end.

Ignoring her, Dominic shook his head

"Now, Clair, tell us what you mean," she continued sweetly.

"If my theory is correct, the Temorshians know many of the same Human languages we do. In that case, no matter what you tried, they would decode a message and discover the plans. Or even create their own to trap whoever heard it. How would that help save anyone?"

"It wouldn't," I answered, "but it doesn't explain why Shielder codes are better. They'd know La'Mursian, right?"

"Of course they would, but they wouldn't know our codes."

"How can you be so sure?" my father asked.

"Our language is old and complex. We work with the brightest minds on Selucia to come up with codes we embed into our signals. They would need to have someone well versed in our language, culture, and history in order to break the codes." Clair looked up from his work and smiled, "Besides, not everyone is trained to understand the message."

"So how does that help if only *so* many people know how to understand them?" Mabel asked.

"It'd mean only a select group of Shielders would have enough information to decipher the message," I answered. "If only so many people know—let's say a hundred—the chances of the codes falling into the wrong hands decrease, right?"

"Yes, or so our theory goes," Clair confirmed. "Chances of being captured alive by any of our enemies are slim already. Having only a few soldiers with that kind of information is helpful."

"Let me guess," Dominic said in a somewhat captivated tone, "you're one of a few that can decipher the message?"

"There is always one specialized coder on each La'Mursian ship. Everyone understands the basics and could understand a few pieces of the puzzle, but for safety there is only one crewmate that understands it well enough to decipher the whole stream of codes. If something happens and we need to get information out, the coder solves the message and lets the rest of the crew know. Then destroys the information left. To answer your question, Dominic, yes, I can decipher any code."

"That's fancy," added Mabel, who finished lighting the candles and plopped down on the couch near me.

"Why would there only be one person on the ship?" Dominic asked.

I smirked, locking eyes with my mother, who showed the same amusement.

Clairfic went back to work, continuing to be civil, "It takes years to be proficient, many hours of schooling and training. Most do not make it that far, so only a few soldiers are selected. Then each individual gets assigned to a ship."

"And if something happens to the ship or the coder?"

I tensed, part of me worried for Clair. He was still dealing with the survivor's guilt that plagued him. Dom didn't know that, of course. No one knew that except for Mabel and me. I doubt she would've said anything.

"The crew does their best to protect the coder. It is the way of things," Clair deflected.

"It's late," I piped in, ending the questioning. "We should go to sleep."

"I was just going to suggest that," Dad declared, standing to stretch. "We'll make our way up north bright and early tomorrow."

"Where's everyone sleeping?" Mom blurted with pink cheeks.

"Same places as last night?" Dad countered.

Mom quickly glanced at Dominic. A little slow, it clicked for my father.

I smiled to myself. "Dominic, we have space in the next apartment over. You'll be comfortable with Clair and me."

"Great. Thank you. Goodnight, everyone," Dominic declared, getting out of his chair. "Again, I'm sorry about earlier. Thank you for allowing me—"

"There'll be no need for that, son," my grandfather drawled, getting up to give his family a hug. "Just get some rest. Goodnight."

"Goodnight, Grandpa," I uttered, giving him a squeeze.

I looked over to my parents. They nodded their pleasantries as Mom passed me a few burning candles to take with me. "Goodnight, darling."

"'Night, Mom."

I passed one to Dom.

"Are you going to join us, Clairfic?" I stood in front of him, watching his quick but delicate hand movements.

"When I am finished," he said, putting his various items in a pile, barely looking up. "I will take what I need with me and work in the hall. The rest of you can get some rest." Clair stood up, nodding to my father, mother, and grandfather. "Goodnight, everyone, and sleep well."

He waited until I made my move out of the apartment.

If I knew him as well as I thought I did, he wouldn't be getting any sleep until he heard a signal. I sighed. I waved to the rest of my family and headed out the door, Dom and Clair following behind me.

As the door closed behind us, I stopped, making Clair run into me. Thankfully, Dom was there to catch me before I fell on my butt.

"Sorry, Melissa. Are you all right?" Clair asked.

"Should have been watching where you are going!" Dominic sneered at the Shielder.

"No, no, it was my fault," I told them, hoping I didn't start another argument. "How are the radios?"

"They are fine. Now, if you do not mind, I would like to get back to work."

"Fine by me. Let's go, Melissa," Dom turned toward the apartment.

"Yeah, I'm coming. You get the couch!" I yelled after him.

He snorted, heading down the hall.

Clairfic settled himself on the ground and began to tinker. Rolling my eyes, I waited, studying him.

"Make sure to keep the static down. Won't want to invite crazies in here at night," I told him.

"I will keep it down."

"You need to sleep too."

"I will."

"No, for real. You deserve rest, and you've been playing with that thing for hours. You'll find a signal, but you're going to drive yourself crazy working like this."

"I am not playing, I am building. I am so close—I can feel it."

"Why don't you just leave it for a few hours? Get some sleep and then go back to work?"

"No."

Stubborn oaf, I thought.

"Have it your way. Goodnight. You know where to find your sleeping arrangements."

I left him in the dark with one small candle. He would have to deal with lack of sleep himself. I was too tired to worry any more about him.

I wished he'd chosen to go with me. He'd been so worried about Dominic during the day, but now, not even a hint of concern.

I rolled my eyes. *Men. No, that's not right, he's not a man. He's a Shielder.* I snorted. *Shielders and their values; go figure.*

"Melissa, are you awake?" Clairfic probed gently.

I groaned.

"Melissa?"

"What do you want, Clair?" I turned over to face the direction of his voice. I opened one eye. The candle I'd given him was almost out.

"I have news."

"It's the middle of the night, couldn't it wait?"

"No."

I sat up, pushing the covers away from me. I fumbled around for a match to light my own candle. "Just give me a second .... Here we go. Okay, now I am up. What do you want? What's the matter?" The candle burned brightly, giving Clairfic a menacing look.

"I found a signal," he said flatly.

"I knew you would!" I exclaimed, clapping my hands together. "Wait ... why aren't you more excited about this?"

"It is not what I thought it would be. It is weak and some of it is old news."

"So?" I asked in disbelief. "This is what you'd been working toward for hours. How are you not pleased?"

"I cannot be certain what to make of it. I was able to find where it is being transmitted from, but it is very weak."

"Where is it coming from?"

"The northern point of Michigan."

"By the Mackinac Bridge or in the Upper Peninsula?"

"Near the Bridge, but there is more."

"And what would that be?"

"It moves."

I looked at him, confused. "How does a signal move?"

"My only theory is that it is from a ship. That the ship is en route, causing the signal to relocate itself every so often."

"Where was it before?"

"Over Canada. It was moving fairly fast, but in the last hour is slowed down to almost a crawl."

"So it's not Human. Especially if it's moving so quickly."

"No, it is definitely not Human. It is from my people, but a part of me does not trust it."

"You think it could be Temorshian?" A shiver ran down my spine. "I thought you said—"

"I know what I said. I meant it; there are only a few La'Mursian soldiers that know how to code. That does not mean that something could not have happened. That the Temorshians could have gotten a ship and unknowingly or not be broadcasting a signal."

"Well ... worst-case scenario, it's a trap, right? Best case is that we found some of your people," I suggested, trying to think logically.

"Either situation could be dangerous for your family."

"Clair, I'm not sure if you noticed, but simply being Human is dangerous for my family."

He sighed.

"Besides, it's better than nothing. Someone is out there. Now, we have a good chance of connecting with beings other than the seven of us. I'd say we should take our chances."

"We are not prepared to fight Temorshians," Clairfic stated as he sat on the edge of the bed, his weight crushing the mattress.

"You taught us enough. We can handle the weapons you showed us and, now, we have Dominic. I'm sure he'd love to show us a thing or two," I gently reminded him. "We'll be fine."

Clairfic leaned his weight on his knees, hunching over, deep in thought. "I do not want to head into a situation we are not prepared for. It could be a trap." He rubbed his temples with one hand.

I flung myself backward onto the pillows. "Clairfic, you worry too much."

He sat up straight, facing me, his teeth catching the light. "I have to worry! None of you take the invasion of the Temorshians seriously!"

"Look, I'm tired. You're exhausted, too. Why don't we sleep on it and talk it over with everyone in the morning?"

He grumbled in La'Mursian.

"Don't do that, Clair. All I'm saying is that you and I are not going to solve this issue in the middle of the night. Remember Dad's rules? We work together as a team. We're missing several key players right now.

"Another thing: we are taking the threat of the Temorshians seriously. We're not like you. We don't have your training, so you'll have to deal with how we cope. It'll never look the way you want, but we trust you enough to listen and do whatever you say."

"I am sorry. You are right. I need to wait and think about things clearly. I just ... I had to tell someone."

"It's fine. I'm glad you shared your news with me, but I'm tired. Please, let's go to bed."

Gracefully Clair stood up and blew out his now pathetic excuse for a candle. He made his way over to his little nest and sat down. I knew he would lie down, but I doubted he would actually close his eyes and rest.

"Get some sleep, buddy," I told him gently. "We'll work things out in the morning, promise." I blew out my own candle, cloaking the two of us in darkness.

I woke up trying to remember a dream that had plagued me during the night. I remembered Grandmother being in some room that was not familiar to me with the rest of my family, but the fragments faded the harder I tried to recall the details. I waited in bed as I tried to grasp the strange memories the dream left me.

Startled out of my thoughts by Clair getting up and moving around, I opened my eyes, trying to avoid his detection. I watched as be packed his nest, recalling the events of the early morning.

"Did you even bother trying to sleep?" I asked him.

He jumped, muttering in La'Mursian.

I laughed. "I'm getting better at surprising you."

"Yes, you are, and I am not sure if I like it." He eyed me.

I got up and started to pack my own items.

"I did sleep, though it was not as good as the night before."

"I'm sorry to hear that. Were you worried about the signal?"

"Of course." He finished, watching as I packed my last bit, his eyes following me throughout the room.

"Don't worry. We can talk over breakfast and sort it out. I can imagine Dad is wide awake and ready to go, so I'd better hurry."

"I will leave you to it. I am sure Dominic will need help moving and repacking the truck."

"Good plan. I'll see you."

He nodded and left the room, leaving me alone to get ready for the day ahead.

I entered the other apartment thirty minutes later, ready to eat and hit the road.

"Give me the candles you took with you last night." Mabel reached out her hand. I did as she asked. She wasn't a morning person, and it was early for her. "We lost one, I see. Probably from that idiot Shielder; no more for him!"

"Do you need help with breakfast?" I asked, looking around the kitchen and ignoring my sister.

"Yes, I do," Grandpa said as I watched him crack an egg into a frying pan. "If you could cut the avocado and tomatoes, that would be helpful."

I did, impressed yet again by our amazing spread.

"Where did you find these?"

"On our hunt yesterday. Might as well eat them now before they go bad."

"Your father, Dominic, and Clair left for the truck a while ago," Mom told me as she started moving items outside. "I hope they won't take too much longer. We should hurry. In the meantime, Mabel and I will take the gear out and come back to eat."

"Did Clair mention anything about fixing that radio?" Mabel asked, snagging a bit of avocado from me.

"He sure did." I placed the rest of the food away from her reach. "He woke me up in the middle of the night saying he'd found a weak signal."

"That's really impressive," Grandpa approved.

"A weak signal? Does he know where it's from?" Mom asked, stopping before she left the room, arms full of bags filled with food.

"He'll have to explain his theory, but he's certain it's Shielder—he's just not sure if it's real or not."

"Real? After all that one coder nonsense he went on about last night? It better be real if we're going to travel to find it," Mabel said.

"Mabel, grab a bag or two and come with me. Stop bothering your sister. We'll discuss it when we eat," Mom ordered. "Now, help me get the last of all this."

The two women set off to help the boys pack the truck. It left Grandfather and me to work together on breakfast.

We worked for some time, impressed with our feast and ourselves. We didn't want to get comfortable eating the way we'd been because of the uncertain future, but with our eggs, bacon, sausage, tomatoes, some avocados, and cheese—it was a fine treat. I was going to enjoy and cherish the meal with my family—whole, happy, and safe.

As I finished setting the table, I heard the rest of them enter.

"I'm sure it's fine. We should still try it," my father said.

"I am not so sure," Clairfic responded.

"I can't believe I am going to say this," Dominic began, as he and the rest of the crew entered the apartment, "but I think I agree with Clairfic."

"*Stop it!*" Mabel yelled in glee. "You don't really agree with him, do you?"

Dom sighed. "Yes, I do. We don't know what we could run into, and if we're not ready, it could mean disaster. I'm not interested in dying today or any other day, for that matter."

"I hate to break it to you, but one day we're all going to die ... "

"Now you lot, stop talking, and sit down," Grandfather said. "Look at what we made! We're going to need our strength for the trip, so you better eat every bit of it. Now, eat," he said with a wink to me.

The seven of us sat down. It was beautiful, watching everyone sit around the table. I wondered if Grandmother was smiling down at us.

I looked at the food, realizing I was starving. No one waited for grace; we dug in and filled our plates with what we could.

"Tell an old man, Clairfic. What have you found on the airways?" asked Grandfather after the initial feasting.

Clairfic explained everything he'd told me the night before. Clair waited for the information to sink in before he continued. "We need more time to prepare. I think we could all do with some more shooting practice."

"I have to agree—it wouldn't hurt to know what we're doing with all different kinds of weapons and such," Dominic added.

"But what if you're wrong? What if it's others trying to find survivors?" Mom asked.

"Either way it's a gamble," Dad added.

"So? We could still try," I offered. "What is the point of leaving the city to just stay here? Look around you! This place couldn't stand another attack. Who knows when that'll be? The Temorshians will be on the ground—if they aren't already—and this place could not handle that."

"She has a point," Mabel said. The corners of her mouth drooped, her fingers spinning the fork in her hand.

"Like you said, Melissa, what if the Temorshians are already here? Even if we do stay, they'll find us," Grandfather cautioned. "They'll find us and kill us."

"What are you saying, Dad? You want to go after this signal?" Mom asked him, shocked by his statement.

"Yes, I think we should," he agreed. He turned to Clair and Dom, "We know enough to protect ourselves. We're a smart bunch. Do we need more practice, of course, but that doesn't mean we go to the signal ill prepared."

"You don't know how to fight," my father interrupted. "None of us really do."

"Look, we can leave this place today, but not go close enough to the signal until we are ready. We can practice for a few hours and move on. What's the harm in that?"

"You're saying get as close as possible, but not close enough that we'll be detected?" Dom asked. "Waste ammo and the like, hoping nothing big and bad hears us while we're at it?"

"Yes, I am," Grandpa responded. "It doesn't matter where we stop, but we don't need to go straight to the signal, especially if they're not your people, Clairfic. If you're worried about the noise then we practice hand-to-hand combat or something." He paused to take another bite of egg and tomato. "I'm only suggesting this as an option. It's possible to travel and not go straight to the source of the signal."

"Where's the signal now?" I questioned.

"Near Lake Michigan—the northern section," Clair told us.

"That's only a few hours away from here by car," Dad mentioned quietly.

"How far away would we need to be in order for them to not spot us?" Mom asked.

"Since the signal is weak, I am assuming the ship is running low on fuel and power. If that is the case, then it will not be on much longer, and they will lose the ability to track anything in the area," Clair explained. "We should be safe, or at least as safe as can be if we decide to go. We can be within a safe distance and not be detected."

"If that's the case then, how are we going to find it when they lose power?" Dom asked.

"I can follow it long enough to catch its last burst of a signal to find its resting place. That will not be a problem."

"Has the signal moved at all since we've been up this morning?" I probed.

"Not that I can tell."

"Then it's a good chance they're almost out of power."

He nodded.

"What'd happen if they lost power and we snuck up on them?" Dominic interjected. "Would your people be hostile?"

"No, of course not!" answered Clair. "You do not even know if it's La'Mursian. It could be someone else. That is the chance we are all taking—that's the problem."

"You miss my meaning. If they can't see what's around them what would happen?" Dom asked.

Mom and I locked eyes again, both impressed Dom was keeping his cool. Maybe they could eventually work out their differences.

"They would have stopped where they are, then checked the surrounding area for threats and supplies. Once it has been deemed safe, they would start making a perimeter," Clair responded with flushed cheeks. "They would be on guard, but we are not trained to be trigger happy, as you mentioned earlier."

Dominic only nodded. He seemed to be thinking about something else entirely.

"What's on your mind?" Mabel asked him, noting his concentration as well. "Tell us."

"The more we've talked about this, the more I don't think it's a Temorshian ploy," he finally said.

"Why's that?" Grandpa asked, finishing the last of the tomatoes.

"From that Clair's said—can I call you that?" Dom asked, as Clair nodded his approval. "He said that the Temorshians were prepared during the initial attack. They were ready for a fight—they left nothing to chance. They destroyed everything they could, down to our last leader. Does letting a signal loose sound like them? You think they'd be foolish enough to leave a loose end like that out in the open?"

"In theory, no, it doesn't, but they're tricky," I reasoned. "We don't know their strategy at all."

"You have a point, Dominic," Clairfic stated. "If what you are saying is true, they would have to be on planet and begin to try to control much of the essential resources. That way they would be able to capture the remaining Humans easier than going around trying to find survivors in different places all over the world. It is a tactic we have seen them use in the past."

"They've done this in the past?" Mom choked, her face turning a pale green.

"Not to this magnitude. They are a rough group and fight within their ranks," Clair explained regretfully. "We never thought they would be capable of something like this … "

"You mean they never tried to take over an entire planet before … " I added.

We mulled over Clair's words until Mabel interrupted the silence.

"Is anyone thinking what I'm thinking?" she asked with wild eyes.

I shrugged and my parents looked at her, waiting for her to finish her thought.

"Tell us, dear," Grandpa said patting her arm.

Mabel's face was white as a ghost. "When they come, they'll want resources … They'll want to control what is important to us—to Humans. What's one resource Humans need to survive?"

"Water," whispered Clairfic.

"Exactly. We're sitting ducks staying here—we're surrounded by fresh water!"

24

After Mabel's revelation, it didn't take long for us to decide we needed to leave. We'd take our chances with the signal and hope for the best. We couldn't stay in the half-destroyed, poorly defendable piece of junk that was our apartment. We might be able to leave the state if the signal proved to be false, but chances were high that we were already surrounded.

I felt confident in my abilities, in those of Clairfic, Dominic, and the rest of my family. We could face anything if we worked together. We were a team of individuals with skills that worked well together.

"Are we all set?" my father asked the group.

Everyone looked around, eyeing each other for second thoughts.

"Where's Clair?" Grandfather asked.

"He went to the roof for a moment to see if anything had changed or if there is movement on the road," Dominic said, throwing the keys up, catching them in his hand. He seemed eager to get going—a far cry from the man who'd wanted to stay an hour ago.

"I hope he hurries," Mabel whispered, on edge and extremely worried. It had finally hit home that she wasn't safe just because she'd survived the initial attack. It wasn't wasted on the rest of us that she was struggling.

"Are you all right?" I asked, once the two of us stood alone, waiting.

"I'm fine, I just don't like it here. I want to leave," she insisted.

Dominic noticed his new friend's concern as he rounded the front of the truck. "You want to ride shotgun?" he offered.

"No, that's okay," she answered him. "I don't want the responsibility."

"I understand." Dom looked a bit disappointed. "Viktor, are you interested?"

"Sure thing," Dad responded. "I suppose now is a good time to hand out some guns." He reached into a bag of various handguns and knives. "There isn't much room for us to hold the big stuff, but we'll be prepared if something happens."

Mabel refused to hold anything but a knife. She sat in the back in between my mother and Grandfather, who already had a handgun and assault rifle each. Dad carried several weapons with him in the front seat to support Dominic while he drove. Because Clair and I were the best at using Shielder technology, we were stuck in the back with all the junk, to give support when needed.

"Melissa, you good?" Dad asked me.

"Yeah, I'm fine. Just ready to get out of here." He handed me some pellets—a type of bullet for the weapon I was using.

"It's going to work out, mark my words. Everything will be fine, and we'll finally hook up with others," he said to me quietly.

"I just hope these *others* are civil," I cringed, remembering the fight a few nights ago. "I hope whoever we find doesn't try to attack."

"It'll be fine," he said again.

"I think we are ready to go," Clairfic stated, coming out of nowhere, making us all jump.

"God, what were you thinking? We have loaded guns and could've accidentally shot you," I sputtered.

"And here I was thinking it was a game between us," he smirked. "Now we are matched."

"You're right. Looks like the score is even."

We laughed.

Mabel rolled her eyes. "You two are ridiculous. Let's go!"

We piled into the truck, ignoring Mabel completely.

It was a tight fit, trying to get in the back end. We'd taken what we needed from Dominic's bunker, which was enough to almost fill the space, leaving just enough space for the Shielder and me to sit.

I paused. "Are you sure we're going to fit?"

Clair got in first, the truck sinking low, and ignored me.

Dominic waited for us to get in the back. He noticed the movement as well. "You're a big guy. It's going to do that with such a load."

"I am sorry," Clair said, looking back at him.

"Obviously, he's big," I mused.

"The amount we're holding, the truck is going to struggle to carry it all," Dom speculated.

I shook my head and shrugged, "Whatever, it's fine. The truck can pull the weight, right?"

"I think so," Dom said. "Get comfortable, man. She's going to come up, too. Make room."

Clairfic moved around, trying to find space for me. He muttered to himself, trying to get comfortable, unsure where to sit. He sat down and moved his legs close to his chest, his long legs poking out like sticks.

"You won't be comfortable like that for long," I reminded him.

"I will be all right. I hope there is enough room for you."

Dominic held my weapon while I climbed up, and the truck sank lower. "This thing is going to hold, right?" I asked again.

"Yes, of course," Dom chuckled. "It's made for this type of work. You're not that heavy, it'll hold."

"Not what I'm worried about," I breathed. I was standing up in the bed of the truck, uncertain if I could trust it.

Clairfic reached his hand out. I looked down at him, avoiding his gesture. He tried to make himself as small as possible, but he looked awkward with his body contorted into a tight ball.

"Really, Clair, this is stupid. Don't sit like that," I huffed.

"How would you like me to sit?" One eyebrow rose in confusion. "There is not a lot of room."

"Well, first of all, if you just let your legs go straight—as straight as you can—I could sit opposite you, between your legs, and we'd both be comfortable. Second, how could you operate a weapon in that position?"

He sighed, but did as I suggested.

"Does that feel better?"

"Yes, I have better use of my arms, I guess. Will you be comfortable?" The reluctance in his voice was palpable.

I sat down between his legs, trying to calm my beating heart. "I'm comfortable," I lied. To touch him intimately was something I was not interested in doing now or ever. I pushed my nerves deep within me.

Dominic handed back my weapon, grinning. "Not a word," I said to him.

He laughed. "Enjoy the ride, you two." He closed the gate of the truck. "Give a yell if you need anything. We'll have the window open, in case there's any *funny* business." He winked.

"He enjoys this too much, I think," Clair whispered.

"I think he just enjoys making you uncomfortable."

Clairfic snorted. "I do not understand why."

"Well, it's funny to watch you squirm."

"I do not squirm—La'Mursian soldiers do not squirm. It is trained out of us at an early age."

"Whatever you say, bud." I smiled. "If you don't feel weird about this, why are your cheeks purple?"

He was silent for a minute. "It is hot."

I laughed, trying to muffle the sound, tears threatening to spill over.

Clair's cheeks grew a darker shade of purple, making me laugh harder. "I guess they don't teach you how to stop blushing in the military, either?"

He responded in La'Mursian, sending me into another round of giggles.

After my fit of laughter settled down, we watched the scenery go from bad to slightly better. Things weren't as destroyed the farther north we headed. Untouched trees still stood, homes hadn't seen the war that had raged only a few short days ago, and farmlands, with rows of pine trees, were still beautiful.

The weight I'd been carrying on my shoulders lightened with every mile. Things looked a lot better than I could've ever imagined, but where were the people?

I shivered.

We'd been traveling for an hour without saying a word until Clairfic noticed my concern.

"What are you thinking about?" he asked.

My brow furrowed. "Nothing much," I lied.

"That's not what your expression says."

I sighed. "I'm worried. You said yourself we didn't take this attack seriously enough, and now being out here—away from what felt a little safer—I feel exposed."

"We are doing the right thing," Clair said, looking out over the horizon, his hair blowing around his face.

"What? You can't possibly mean that."

"No, I do. If we work as a team, we can survive anything."

"So that's what changed your mind? *Teamwork?*"

"Somewhat, but mostly because you were right. That structure was not fit to defend anyone. It was supposed to last us a night, and then we needed to move on. Though it did feel safe, it wasn't good for the long term. I can admit it felt like ... it felt like—"

"A home."

"Something like that," he said, looking down at his hands. He rubbed them together, almost as if to bring warmth back into them, though it wasn't cold outside.

"It felt safe—especially after the attack. It was a welcome safe space." I watched his hands.

He looked up at me, blushing, his cheeks growing a dark mauve I'd come to appreciate. He immediately stopped moving his hands and pushed them deep within his pockets, his weapon waiting at his side.

"That is true." He looked past me, avoiding my face.

"I'm sure we'll have that again," I reassured him. "You'll see. If we created it once, we can do it again. Will you do me a favor?"

"Are you not comfortable? I can move."

I laughed. "No, not at all. I'm very comfortable." *And I was.* "Please, for the love of God, stop worrying."

He snorted.

"I know it's hard, but it doesn't help, does it?"

"It gives me something to do," he teased.

"Oh, yeah, so much to do." I rolled my eyes. "We should be proactive and make up a plan or something. That way we can both be busy doing something useful."

"Yet again, another great idea."

"What can I say? I'm full of them ... "

"Oh, it could work," I yelled over the noise of the wind.

"If that actually happens," Clairfic gently reminded me. "There are so many scenarios and elements we have not taken into account."

"It doesn't matter. We're as ready as we're going to be."

"I do not doubt anyone's ability to survive, but there are risks involved fighting the Temorshians head-on. Especially when we do not know their numbers."

"Hey, guys?" Mabel said flatly, yelling over the wind just enough to be heard. "We've been driving for hours and, while hearing bits of what you two are talking about is riveting, it's driving me nuts. Enough! I *need* to pee!"

"Where's the signal now?" Dominic bellowed, looking in the rearview mirror. He was a quick study; he understood how to keep my family, namely Mabel, calm and how to avoid drama as much as possible.

Clairfic and Dad had mapped out where the signal stopped just before we left and felt strongly that it wouldn't move again. Clair reassured us several times that the vessel carrying the signal had stopped and stayed where it was for more hours than he imagined possible since if it was one of theirs it would try to look for survivors.

"I doubt it has moved," Clair yelled to him and the others. "It is a good sign."

"Regardless, we should check," Dom shouted. "Where are we, Viktor?"

"By the looks of things and the map, I'd say somewhere outside Cadillac. Not much farther until we're on top of the signal, I think," my Dad told us. I could barely hear him, but I trusted his judgment.

"Can we please stop?" Mabel whined loudly so that no one missed her sentiments. "I really need to use the bathroom!"

As if reading my mind, Mom asked, "Is it safe to stop?"

"We planned on stopping anyway," Grandfather opined from the backseat, just over the noise. "Seems we're far enough away to rest for an hour or two and then keep going."

"Some rest would do some good, but how do we know if it's safe?" Mom pushed again. "We don't know this area well enough to defend ourselves."

Though I didn't say anything, I had to use the bathroom, too, and frankly, I wanted to get up and stretch. Trying to avoid physical contact with Clair caused cramps to tickle my legs.

"It is safe enough," Clair chimed in. "We can set up a perimeter before we take turns to head off and um ... "

"Take care of business," I offered, smiling, trying to keep down my amusement. I loved watching Clair squirm, mauve cheeks and all.

"Fine by me," Dad said. "What do you say, Dominic? This is a good enough place as any!"

"It'll do," he expressed over the roar of the wind. "I think I see an exit up ahead. We can get off and find a secluded place to rest—but just resting!"

"You think we are going to throw a party, Dom?" I asked, raising an eyebrow.

"No," he yelled back, "just don't want to see us getting stuck or worse."

"He has a point," Mom stated, barely audible. "We shouldn't stay long—we need to be careful. Who knows what's out there? I don't want to find out."

"We're not staying here—we know we're going to leave anyway," Mabel yelled. "Just hurry, Dom!"

We reached an appropriate exit. Dom crawled off the highway—deserted just like the miles before. It looked a lot more peaceful with the trees swaying in the breeze, but the air was still.

I strained to hear wildlife. "That's odd," I whispered to Clairfic.

"What is?" he asked, looking at me seriously.

"Where are all the birds or animals? I don't hear a thing."

He listened.

"I don't hear any wildlife, odd for this time of year."

"I cannot explain it, either. Should we mention anything to the others?" he asked.

"No, not with Mabel the way she is, and if you haven't noticed, Mom is starting to ride the crazy train, too."

His brow furrowed, as the metaphor was apparently lost. "Everyone will start to worry and be on edge. This is not the time to panic."

"The lack of noise is enough to cause panic, Clair. It's unnerving."

"Just keep them focused on something else. If you are worried, tell me. If they see you panic, it could set them off." He paused, letting his message sink in. "It looks like we are going to stop here for the time being. Help me make sure no one walks too far away."

25

Dominic found a small path leading to a secluded area off the main road. He parked the truck a mile or so down it to avoid detection. The trail held a wide-open field on one side and a deep, wooded area with pine trees on the other. The land, untouched from the initial attack, was beautiful and peaceful, with a winter wheat field swaying in the breeze.

I inhaled the glorious pine scent, tilting my head back just enough to catch the sun on my face. More of the weight cloaking my shoulders lifted, causing me to almost forget the tragedy of Earth.

"Come on," Clair ordered, interrupting my bliss. "Do you want to help me? We need to create a perimeter."

I crashed back to reality, sighing and pushing myself up. "Why not? Tell me where to go."

Clair hopped out in one quick motion, gracefully getting out of the truck. Startled by the subtle movement of his large body, I fell backward onto the pile of supplies, limbs flying everywhere.

"Sorry about that," he smiled, biting his lower lip in a sad attempt to stop himself from laughing.

"God, you're a mess," Mabel announced as she rounded the back end. "Can I go first? I have to *fucking* go!"

"Please wait until I make sure the area is clear," Clairfic begged her, turning the safety off on his weapon. He looked unmoved by Mabel's inability to pull it together.

Mabel pouted.

"We can always look away while you, um, you know, if you want?" Grandfather offered, walking up to us.

"What happened to you?" Dom asked me, ignoring the rest of the party's drama.

"Shut up," I mumbled to him. "Give me a hand and take this so I can get out of this thing." I tossed my gun to Dominic; he caught it and beamed up at me, his lips on the verge of forming a sassy remark. "*Not* another word," I warned.

"No way! I would be mortified!" I heard Mabel yell, her cries echoing off the trees. "You have two minutes, Clairfic Munal. If you're not back by then, I will walk off!" Mabel yelled after him, but he was already at the tree line. "Did you hear me?"

"Mabel, quiet down," Dad said. "I'll help you, Clair, to make it go faster. Dom, what do you say?"

Barely making it out of the truck, Dom pushed the gun back into my hands, "Yep, I'll head the other way."

The three headed out to scout.

"Really, Mabel, I'm ashamed of you," my Mother huffed. "You have better manners than that, and *no*, I don't care how badly you have to go—that's no excuse!"

"Clairfic is trying to make sure we're safe, young lady," Grandfather chimed in. "You can go right here. What is wrong with that?"

Mabel was quiet for a moment, but then slipped in, "I don't want to go in front of everyone—it's gross!"

"We all have to go, Mabel. It's not *that* big of a deal," I said.

"Shut up!" Mabel spat. "I'm going to pee my pants just thinking about this mess!"

"Can you at least help me get lunch out if you need to focus on something else?" Mom asked in a lighter tone.

Mabel grunted and walked with her to the front of the truck. They got out the cooler with our lunches and another sack full of extra bits to keep us full for the rest of the day.

"Maybe we should keep a lookout, too," Grandfather added, watching his kin. "Wouldn't hurt while the rest of the camp is out and about."

"That's a good idea. You think anything's out there?"

"I'd like to think we're alone, but who knows. As long as we don't run into another one like Dominic. That's all we need."

I chuckled. "I hope we don't, but you have to admit, he's helpful."

"For sure," he agreed, grabbing his assault rifle from the truck. He looked around the clearing. "Can you believe our luck? First a Shielder and now him? We're very fortunate."

"Don't jinx us, Gramps!" I gasped.

"Nonsense, we'll be fine."

Grandfather and I parted ways. He headed down the trail to stand guard as I went the other way.

It was still quiet except for the muffled voices of Mom and Mabel. The four of us waited for the rest to return. Mabel hadn't brought up her need again, which was a relief, but my own began to bother me.

Leaves and twigs broke to my left. I turned, pointing my weapon. Dad and Dom emerged looking relieved; Clairfic was not very far behind them.

"Well?" I asked, dropping my guard.

"Looks good!" Dad reassured me. "Mabel, you're up!"

"Thank God!" she yelled, practically running toward the trees.

"Wait!"

She stopped, turning toward the Shielder. She looked like she could've killed him with her bare hands if he kept her any longer.

"What now?" she asked, through clenched teeth.

"Take the path we just came out of. You will see a fallen tree in the cleared area. Do not go farther than that," he instructed her. "Please, Mabel, do not go farther."

She rolled her eyes, giving him the middle finger. "Go fuck yourself, Clairfic."

Clair seemed to be struggling with the idea of whether or not to follow her or to admit defeat. Danger or not, he knew enough about her to leave her to her own musings.

"Just let it go," I called to him. "She'll be fine. Did you see anything out there?"

"No," Dom responded, heading over to Mom for water. "Thank you, ma'am. It seems quiet. Nice bit of land, though."

"It's nice. I wonder who owned this place," Dad piped in.

As my family passed out lunch and gossiped about the owners, I found Clairfic on edge, looking around in a huff.

I walked up to him, causing him to jump. "You have to stop doing that," he grumbled.

"It's a game, remember?" I teased. "Looks like I'm winning now. Your move, Shielder."

He gave a weak smile but kept looking out over the field. "It is still quiet."

"I've noticed. Do you sense something?"

"Yes, something is not right. We should not stay long."

"Do you want me to move my family along? We don't need to eat here. We can keep moving."

"No, not yet," he whispered. "They deserve to rest and eat in peace."

"Well, if something's the matter, we can move. You know we'd rather be safe than ... "

"Just keep watch with me. I will try to clue in Dominic as well. I hope he can sense something, too."

"I think Grandfather does. He wanted me to keep watch while the three of you were out."

"This makes my job a lot easier," he smiled.

Finally, Mabel made her grand return. Clair's face brightened a little. The rest of us were happy to have her back to her more pleasant self. She waltzed up to the group and dug into a sandwich.

"Well, if there isn't anyone else with pressing needs, I'll take my turn," Grandfather told us.

We nodded in agreement.

"I will take over his spot," Clairfic whispered to me.

"Okay, grab a sandwich on your way."

I turned around to watch the area as the rest of my family relaxed. I couldn't stop worrying. My whole body hummed with anxiety. The familiar cold sweat pooled at the nape of my neck as the hair on the back of my arms stood on end.

I scanned my surroundings one more time. The silence was distracting; I could hear my family chatting about lunch and the ride so far, but I pushed past that. I listened for something but heard nothing. Perhaps we were all going a little crazy. I swallowed my nerves with one gulp.

Grandfather came back sooner than Mabel. He grabbed lunch for himself and brought me some as well. We stood watch and ate as quickly as we could.

As we munched, Dom took the time to chat with Clair and take his own moment out in the woods. After he came back, Mom and Dad went together, much to Mabel's chagrin.

"You two are gross!" Mabel yelled after them. "Gross, I tell you!"

"I'm not going in there alone!" Mom shrieked.

"When did Mabel get so uptight?" my Grandfather asked in a hushed voice.

"No idea," I lied.

I knew exactly why Mabel was acting out. She always got bent out of shape when things became too stressful. If she couldn't handle something, she'd look outward to forget her feelings on the inside. Mom and Dad leaving together proved to be a perfect distraction for our trip, just like her theories about Clair and me a few days ago. If she could avoid her feelings, she felt in control.

"Let's leave her alone for now, Grandpa," I told him after a few moments of silence.

"I'll try to talk to her later," he murmured. "She needs to be reassured that we'll keep her safe."

"We can't promise her that."

He sighed. "No, we can't, but we can help her by allowing her to come to terms with this reality and reassure her we'll stay by her side—no matter what."

"I'll leave it to you then, Grandfather. Looks like Mom and Dad are back. Who still needs to go?" I asked the camp, knowing full well it was me.

"I do not need to go, Melissa," Clairfic said from his post. "Go for it, but remember, no further than the fallen tree."

"Got it! I'll only be a moment!" I patted Grandfather's arm as I headed toward the path, taking my weapon along.

The woods were quiet as I entered. The stillness wrapped around me, almost suffocating me. I pushed the feeling aside as I looked for any sign of movement or wildlife. Nothing moved. The sound of my unsteady breathing met my ears, giving the wooded area an eerie feel.

The pine off the trail was quality timber with picturesque brush underneath. Beautiful property to say the least, but the lack of wildlife mixed with danger in the air made it wicked. Spring had definitely not shown up in this part of the state. The branches were still bare due to the random Michigan weather. The leaves and sticks on the ground hardened by winter with sharp pine needles. A shiver escaped, crawling down my spine with such force I paused, taking a deep breath. Through the clearing, I could see the fallen tree not even a half a mile down the path.

As I trucked through the underbrush to the log, movement caught my eye in the distance. I knew I was on edge—susceptible to seeing anything if I wasn't careful, but I stopped. I held my breath, waiting for it to show itself again.

I shook off my apparent illusion and hopped over the fallen tree. I placed my weapon on the other side of the log. I hurried as I relieved myself, my eyes never leaving the horizon; I scanned and strained to keep watch.

Another motion caught my eye, stopping my concentration. I tried to follow it, but it disappeared again all too quickly.

I might've hopped on the crazy train along with my mom and sister.

I shook it off, avoiding the growing concern. After all, the movement had vanished yet again before I could catch a glimpse.

Finishing my business and slowly standing up, I grabbed my gun and turned to head back, but I again saw something out of the corner of my eye.

I froze.

There was no way that I was seeing things: there was something out there.

Against my better judgment, I slowly turned, deciding to head toward the movement. I walked gradually toward the area, stooping low. I tried to be as quiet as a mouse, moving slowly through the brush, avoiding sticks and branches in my way. As a crunch escaped under my foot, I halted, allowing the sound to travel through the trees.

You should get Clair and Dom. They would want to be here with you. Clairfic is going to be mad.

I kept walking until I came alongside a small stream. The water was shallow and not very wide but deep enough for a cool drink. I watched the stream, surveying the distant bank, searching for movement—for anything to prove that I wasn't going crazy. The stream below me gurgled against the tiny rocks stuck in its way. The woods were empty.

I'm going nuts.

I sighed, looking down at my feet, noticing my boot had come undone during my escapade. I bent to tie it, leisurely working the laces. I stayed down, examining my still swollen ankle, though it felt much better. Rubbing my tired eyes, I let my body weight fall back enough on my heels to rest, closing my eyes to relax.

You're fine. You've been on edge since the attack. It'll work out, you'll see. Everything will be okay. Just get closer to the signal and find more Shielders. Just one more Shielder... You'll make it through this ... Just one more ...

Opening my eyes slowly, fear paralyzed my whole body.

A few feet away stood beings I'd never seen before.

Temorshians, my brain screamed.

They were dressed in black; their large bodies carried their armor well, adding more height to their already impressive stature. Not as big as a Shielder, but larger than a Human, their skin was brown, reflecting a deep blue color in the sunlight. A flat nose lay against their large heads, which had sunken eye sockets. As one turned to face me, I was captivated by the eyes: the menacing, vacant eyes. The round spheres looked like endless pools of black—black holes of death.

I stayed perfectly still as I choked on my breath, unable to get air to my lungs. With small, silent, gasping breaths, air raced to meet my lungs while I tried not to move, horrified at what stood before me.

The Temorshians made no noise or indication they knew they were being watched. They spoke with hushed tones and moved through the brush. They were elegant, but ferocious. Pleasing to the eye, but ugly and mean. I saw this in the way they pushed each other, trying to avoid the stream, as if one touch would burn their skin. There was no kindness in the actions—no love nor friendship. Their selfishness radiated off them. I could feel the waves flow toward me.

My body ached to run, but the trembling of my legs forced me to stay. I struggled to regain control.

You cannot let them find your family. Whatever happens, they can't find out about the rest of them!

A large white hand covered my nose and mouth, causing me to jump with fright. My survivor's spirit fought to be released. As I squirmed, another long arm hugged me across both arms, pinning me down beneath the weight. I could no longer move.

"Stop moving," Clairfic hissed in my ear, pulling me closer, sinking us both to the ground.

I froze at his command, allowing him to move my body.

Immobilized by fear, we stopped, limbs tangled together, letting the moment pass. We watched to see if any of the Temorshians noticed. Thankfully, they made no indication we'd been found out.

Not paying attention to their surroundings, none of them concerned themselves with what could be watching them from the shrubbery. The pushing and yelling became more violent; they were yelling in a language that sounded more like howls than words. Fighting began between several of the members of the group.

My trembling grew in Clair's arms, causing the leaves around us to shake. Clair pulled me closer, trying to make the movement less noticeable. His smell reached my nostrils, keeping me present.

"Stay with me, Melissa. I need you to focus and *stay* with me," Clair whispered in my ear. "I am going to uncover your mouth now. Please, for both our sakes, do not make a sound." He waited until I nodded—barely moving.

He let go, placing the free arm around my shoulders, lowering the other to my waist to try to help me avoid further shaking. Pinned to the rest of his body, my violent shuddering continued. I tried to relax into his broad chest, but it was no use.

As Clairfic held me, all I could do was watch. There were about ten Temorshians and only two of us. He was a good soldier, but my shooting skills needed work. We'd be dead in seconds if we tried to attack.

"They are arguing about something," he murmured, his breath tickling my face. "My Temorshian is not as good as it should be, but if they keep at it, they might fight and move on."

Two of the smaller ones began screeching at each other, shoving back and forth. Soon more and more joined the shouting match, causing more aggravation. Their leader pushed through the crowd as a hush fell over the group, making each member freeze and listen to its howls.

"That's their Captain. He's getting after them for being stupid. They are supposed to be scouting the area or something along those lines."

I gave him a distrustful look. "You suck as a translator," I muttered, resting my head against his exposed neck.

He glared at me. "We would not be here if you had done what I said."

"Really? You want to do this *here?*"

Still cradled in Clair's arms, my shaking ceased as a bit of the shock wore off.

"Shhh, look!" he nodded toward the group. "They are leaving."

The group moved out of the area, leaving in the opposite direction of my family.

"Oh, thank God," I breathed.

One turned and looked in our direction at my words. I could feel its eyes stare toward our hiding spot, then it took a step forward. It crept closer. Its leader called, stopping the movement abruptly, but the soldier eyed our location with intensity, then wheezed, turning to make its way back to the others.

Clair held me in his arms, squeezing tightly, while I pushed myself into his body. If I'd been able to climb into his rib cage, I would have. We didn't separate until the group was out of sight.

He let me go and stood up, throwing me about like a rag doll. I landed on all fours in the mud—dirt and grime splashing my face. He took my gun and headed back to the path in a huff, leaving me alone.

Clair stopped, and without turning he said, "Come."

Still in shock, I sank further into the mud. Trying to stand, I brushed the mud from my hands and legs. My limbs were numb, but I made them follow the Shielder.

"Wait for me," I whispered.

Clair stormed away, never slowing his stride, refusing to wait any longer than he had to. I was all but running after him.

"Clair, slow down," I called after him, refusing to be ashamed. "I'm sorry! Please stop and wait!"

He stopped, turning to face me, rage clearly coloring his features. "Stop yelling! They might hear you!"

"I didn't yell," I said. "I'm sorry, I shouldn't have run off like that but I ... I don't know what came over me. I saw something and I had to check it out. I'm glad I did! Now we know—"

"You could have been captured! *Killed!* We would never have known what happened to you. You put us all in danger by following their group. Those things are not like my kind."

"I know ... "

"They are not like us, Melissa. They would not hesitate to kill you."

"As I have been told many times over, Clairfic."

"What would you have done?" he asked, his eyes filled with fury.

"I was thinking of a plan! I would've gotten myself out of the mess, like when I saved you from Dominic! I'm stronger than you think. I would've been *fine*."

He snorted, nostrils flaring.

"What did you do? *Nothing*. We sat there, waiting and hoping those Temorshians would leave. I might not be like you, but I was doing just fine before you showed up."

"That is what you call being just fine?" he asked through gritted teeth. Before I could respond, he scolded me in La'Mursian. His eyes fell upon me again, full of concern. "I thought ... I thought when you didn't come back ... "

"I'm here—I'm right here. Everything is fine!" I grabbed his hands, pulling him closer. "It worked out. I shouldn't have left, but now we know. We know that they're here, and we can use that information. It wasn't how we wanted to find out, but whatever. It happened. It's done. I'm sorry."

"It would have been useless if you were dead," he breathed. "What would your family have thought? What would I—*they*—do?"

I'd never seen him look so lost. His eyes were merely slits in his head, his cheeks the darkest purple, and his mouth tight as if he struggled to get the words out.

I felt a surge of shame along with the pulsing of indifference for my actions, yet embarrassment mixed it all together, making me lose my resolve. "But I'm not dead. I'm standing right here, in front of you. Look at me."

He lowered his head to gaze in my eyes. He looked disheartened and tired. "This is the problem with Humans. They are selfish and only think of themselves. You could have been taken. I cannot always be there to save you. Teammates do not go off on their own to face untold dangers *alone*."

"I'm sorr—"

"You are a difficult woman."

I grinned. "Did you expect anything less?"

We stared at each other, neither letting go of the other's hands.

"No," he said, pulling his hands away. He walked toward the clearing where my family waited.

"They could've been the ones that had the signal?"

He stopped. "They are not. They are underlings—*nothings*."

"Then there's still hope we're going to run into more Shielders!"

He snorted.

"I'm sorry, Clairfic."

He simply continued to walk away.

I looked over my shoulder one last time, letting out a long sigh, angry at my careless stupidity.

I'd hurt Clairfic. When he noticed the Temorshians, he thought I was dead—the cruelest pain of all. He took his responsibility to my family seriously. At the end of it all, I had messed up. I needed to earn Clairfic's trust all over again.

I felt an awful pain in the pit of my stomach; the light inside flickered, burning itself out.

26

"Oh, my God!" I heard Mabel yell as Clair entered the clearing. "Did you find her? What *the fuck?*"

My family rushed toward him as he walked past them, ignoring their questions, jumping into the truck without a word to anyone.

"I'm fine," I told them as I made my way out of the shrubs a few paces behind Clair. My family looked shocked by Clair's actions but looked back to me with relief. "I got a little lost, that's all."

Calmed by the fact I'd been found in one piece; my family's shifting eyes screamed they were confused by Clair's foul attitude. No one said a word, but they eyed me suspiciously.

Mabel hugged me tightly. "We didn't know what to think when you took so long! You never take *that* long!"

"Oh, you know ... I really had to go," I lied, my checks turning pink.

"Tell them the truth," Clair huffed from the truck.

My family, silenced by his outburst, looked from him to me, waiting for an explanation.

"*What* ... what happened?" Dom asked, breaking the staring

contest forming between Clair and me. Dominic's body tensed because of the sudden change in our demeanor.

"Maybe we should gather up our things while I talk?" I suggested. "It'll all make sense in a minute. Let's hurry and get our stuff ... "

Thankfully, Dad agreed. Though he seemed confused by the whole thing, he was able to get everyone to repack the truck. Clair sat in silence, staring me down the entire time. I ignored him and helped where I could.

I tried to act natural, to downplay our fight, but with a large Shielder pouting in the truck and my red cheeks, it was pretty obvious we'd had a lovers' quarrel.

"Tell us what happened!" Mabel demanded as she repacked the cooler. "You look all right, so it can't be that bad. You two just fighting about who loves who more?"

I ignored her, while the awkward glances from the rest of my clan made me sweat. "I thought I saw something when I was out there. I saw something move in the trees and ... "

"What did you think you saw?" Dominic asked, fingering the gun at his hip.

"Well, I wasn't sure at first," I confessed, "but I followed some movement to a stream." I quickly glanced over to Clair, whose eyes were narrowed on me.

"K, so what happened at the stream?" Mabel asked, placing both hands on her hips.

"Unfortunately, the Temorshians are here," I said all at once.

My family collectively gasped at the news.

"I ran into them, by accident. They're not too far. We should leave as soon as possible."

"Clair, did you fight them?" Dad asked.

"Did you hear anything, Viktor?" Dom asked hotly. "We didn't hear guns—not a sound. What happened? How are you both still here?"

"No, nothing happened like that. They fought each other and left in the opposite direction when they finished," I reassured them. "We're lucky. We came back as quickly as we could."

Clair snorted.

"We really should be going," I said again, ignoring the brooding Shielder.

They moved quickly to leave, throwing things in the back.

"You know, young lady," Dad told me, once everyone else was out of earshot, "I remember Clair giving you orders before you left."

Clair whipped his head in Dad's direction, a smirk forming on the corners of his mouth.

"Yes, Dad, and I should've listened," I admitted. "But aren't you glad I trusted my instincts? Now we know they're here."

"It doesn't matter. You could've gotten hurt or worse, Melissa Ann. We don't have time to talk about it here, but we will—mark my words. He might be mad at you, but your Mother and I are very disappointed. We expect this sort of behavior from Mabel, but not you." He left us in silence.

I watched him climb into his seat in the truck as another pain shot through me. I let out a breath I didn't realize I'd been holding. I wanted to sink into a black hole and escape the feeling of shame enveloping my heart; instead, I made my way into the truck.

I plopped heavily down between Clair's legs, avoiding his glare. He made no attempt to give me space. Our legs touched, but it seemed that neither of us cared anymore about the other's comfort. The electricity sizzled into my legs.

"Any suggestions on how I should drive up to the signal?" Dom asked.

"Get as close as you can—within a mile if it's possible—and I will go up ahead *alone*."

His words stung. The damage I'd caused was now obvious; our friendship was slowly dissolving in front of my eyes.

"All right, sounds good, but do me a favor," Dom asked.

"What do you need?"

"Allow *me* to go with you."

Clair nodded to the man that used to be his enemy.

"I could help, too," I offered quietly.

Dom smirked, "I'll leave you two to hash out the details." He walked off, shaking his head.

I turned my attention to the Shielder as the truck started.

"No," he said.

"Why not? I can be useful."

"You have done *enough* today."

"I said I was sorry. I made a mistake, but we know they're here. We're heading toward the signal with that knowledge, what more do you want?"

He acted as though I wasn't even in his presence.

I dropped my voice, "What do you want from *me*?"

"You do not understand, do you? You think I am mad that you did not listen to me. That I could be mad at you for doing whatever you want. Do you think I am stupid? I know you—I might not know you like your family, but I know enough about you to know that you will always do what you think is right." His eyes blazed with anger.

I rolled my eyes, trying to turn away from him, but he placed both hands on my shoulders, forcing me to look at him. His left thumb caressed my right cheek. Entranced by his touch, I let my body weight sink into his hands. The light inside grew larger, but I kept it hidden, dousing it with regret.

"*No.* I am angry because you put yourself—*willingly*—into harm's way. You did not think of anyone else when you went off on your own. What would we have done if you were taken?" He looked as though he'd swallowed his tongue; his eyes lost their sparkle. He lowered his head and whispered, "Or worse ... *killed?*"

Clairfic looked pained, but he pushed through it. "Do you think any of us could have lived with that knowledge? That you had been killed without any of us there to save you?"

"I didn't think—"

"Exactly!" he said. "You did not use that brilliant brain of yours! You cannot be so selfish as to think you would not have been missed?"

I tried to pull away from him, but he was too strong. "Let go of me!" I demanded. "Of course I don't think that—don't be ridiculous."

He kept his hands where they were, dropping his thumb to rest with the others. "Why am I *here*?"

"W-what?" I asked, shocked by the change of subject.

"Why did you ask me to come with you?"

I thought back to only a few days ago. "Did I ask? I ... I don't remember asking you," I admitted sheepishly.

The corners of the Shielder's mouth dropped.

"I'm sorry, Clairfic, but I don't think any of us asked for your help."

His eyes darkened. "I know none of you asked." He leaned in close so I could feel his breath on my skin. His scent was intoxicating, making it hard for me to focus. "No one had to ask for my help because I freely gave it."

"I don't understand. What are you trying to say?"

"I saw *you*. I saw your fear, your struggle, and your determination to live. I knew if I were to get back to my people, I would need to follow you. I trusted what I saw of you. In the moments I watched, I knew I could not let any harm come to you and that I would make sure you lived through this war. I could not think of myself, I could only think of your wellbeing."

Air escaped my lungs, as my stomach dropped. Clairfic was trying to tell me how much he cared about me and how much I meant to him, but I could not return the sentiment. My shame dampened any feelings I had toward the sensitive Shielder.

"You let us all down," he whispered.

"No," I corrected him, "I let you down. I can handle my parents, but you—you're different. I'm sorry, I really am, but I did what I had to do—what I felt was right, like you said. I can't change the past, and if I had to do it all over again, I would." I paused trying to collect my thoughts. "You can't possibly tell me you wouldn't have gone after them if our roles had been reversed?"

Clair closed his eyes in silent protest. "I would have gone, yes, but no one would have gone with me."

"That's a lie and you know it."

His eyes flew open. "I would not have allowed it."

"I call bullshit. You know Dom would have wanted to help. I would have followed you. You wouldn't have been alone."

"I do not need your help. I would have been able to easily destroy that horde of Temorshians."

I attempted to pull away from Clair again. I wanted to be alone and lick my wounds in private. I didn't want to be so close to him, because he was making me feel something other than fear for the first time in forever. He fought me, slightly lifting me, forcing our bodies closer together—my hands awkwardly resting on his thighs. A jolt of pleasure rippled through me.

"Oh, really?" I asked, fighting the beam of light in my heart. "Why didn't you, then?"

"You were there." Mere inches separated us. "I did not want to show them a Human was only a few feet away."

"Bullshit," I said into his face, squeezing the top of his legs.

He snorted. "Why do you not believe me?"

"Because if you'd killed them, we wouldn't be in this mess, would we? You wouldn't be so angry with me."

"I still would have been angry with you."

"So?" I asked. "That's not the point. There is another reason why you came to me and did not fight. You say you know me; well, I know you too. You would've loved to kill a few Temorshians—pay back for the loss of your crew and the destruction of the planet you love so much."

"You do pay attention."

"So why didn't you fight?"

Clair was quiet for a moment, looking deep into my eyes as he thought over his next few words.

I tried to look anywhere but his lavender eyes. Being so close to him, I could feel my own anger slipping, my resolve changing into something I was unfamiliar with. I was hurt that he was angry and, of course, I understood why. But my feelings were bigger than that. I was ashamed that I'd hurt someone I cared about, and if I was to continue to be honest with myself, I felt a strong connection to him, too.

Finally, he spoke, "After you didn't come back right away, we got worried. They said it was not like you to take your time. So I grabbed my gun and ran after you. When you were not by the fallen tree, I panicked. I found your trail and tracked you deeper into the woods. I heard the Temorshians before I saw you and was afraid you had been ..."

"You thought I was dead?" I asked quietly, instinctively squeezing his inner thighs with my small hands, this time with more care.

"Yes," he breathed, looking down at his lap, slowly raising his gaze. "I thought that they had killed you. The pain I felt was nothing compared to the anger that rose up inside me. I thought I had felt loss before, when I lost my crew, but this was different. I was prepared to kill them all."

"I'm so sorry, Clairfic." Tears begin to form in my eyes, as a ball of self-pity grew in my throat.

"I prepared myself to fight until the death. I needed them to pay. I made my way to the bank and then, with such powerful relief, I saw you hiding in the bushes."

My tears fell; I was unable to find words to express my feelings.

"That is why I did not fight. I was so happy to have you in my arms. You were alive and that was enough."

My head hurt from the rush of adrenaline, while my heart ached for a clearer idea of what was happening between us.

With all of my strength, I pushed the Shielder off of me. I curled up into a ball, trying to make myself invisible. I felt his body shift as Clair withdrew his right leg to give me more space. The two of us retreated to our own private corners to lick our wounds.

I replayed the scene over and over again, trying to come to terms with my failure and my feelings while we spent the rest of the ride in silence, tears falling down my raw cheeks.

"Okay, folks, this is our stop," my father called from the front. "Everyone ready to see what we can find?"

No one answered him.

The first part of our journey had been easy compared to the dramatic mess we faced after lunch. The rest of the family had sat in silence after Clairfic and I spoke.

"Are you sure we have to connect with the signal?" Mabel asked, sounding defeated.

"We have to at least check it out," Dom answered her. "We owe it to ourselves to at least see if there are other survivors."

Grandfather interjected, "Just knowing we aren't alone would be nice."

"We already know we aren't alone, Grandpa," Mabel said. "Melissa found the Temorshians ... We're *so* screwed."

"Not necessarily," Mom mused. "We have Clairfic, right? And Dominic?" She smiled at him as he looked down, embarrassed to be praised for the first time. "Not to mention we've learned a lot in the last few days—we can defend ourselves too. We will be just fine."

"And if not?" Mabel asked.

"We've made it this far," Mom stated. "It's more than we thought possible a few days ago. We've come a long way already. I think ... I think we can make it through anything."

"Except another attack," Clair interrupted, dissipating any positive feelings Mom had tried to create. He'd left the back of the truck without a word or glance in my direction.

I slowly prepared myself to join the rest of the family, hoping they hadn't heard our dramatic discussion.

As I grabbed my weapon, I made a mental promise to myself: *You will not allow him to take you away from your goal. You will make sure your family lives through this. You don't need his help—you never did.*

He would go on to connect with his kind and be too busy to help a small Human family. We had to learn to be on our own sans Shielder involvement.

"Here we go ... " Mabel said to Clair. "Okay, wet blanket, what doom and gloom do you want us to worry about now?"

"We could not stand another Temorshian attack," he plainly stated.

"He's right." Dom fingered his gun on his hip as he spoke, "We left any security we had back there. Hell, we could've stayed in my bunker and been just fine."

"But for how long?" Grandfather asked skeptically.

"Who knows, but the point is we left security—a place that would work out and that already had proved itself in the initial attack."

"We could make that again, right?" my Dad asked.

"Maybe, maybe not. All I know now is that we need to set some priorities," Dom stated. "We need a game plan."

"Like what?" Mabel asked. "Find the signal, find shelter, and build a bunker?"

"Something like that," Clair said. "We—Dominic and I—will go on ahead and scout the area. We will follow the signal and see what we find."

"What do you want us to do in the meantime?" Mom asked, looking ready to help in any way she could.

"We can find a place to stay," offered Mabel.

"That sounds good," Dom said. "We aren't going that far away and could be back within a few hours. We shouldn't lose the sunlight just yet."

"Don't go too far from this truck. We cannot get separated," Clair reminded us.

"I should say not. We'll stay close. Especially with those Temorshians about," Grandpa reassured him. "Don't you worry about us while you're out there—we can handle things on our end. You just do what you need to do."

Clairfic nodded. I could tell he was relieved Grandfather had recovered from his shock at losing his wife and was ready to get down to business.

Clair turned his attention to Dominic, and the two of them got ready to head out. They loaded themselves with various weapons and ammo. Mom brought them two sacks of food—enough to last a day or two—just in case.

Mabel stood next to me, searching my eyes. Her frown increased when she saw my tear-stained checks. She rubbed my left shoulder tenderly.

The pit of my stomach sank. "What if ... " I stammered. "What if you don't come back?"

Everyone stopped whatever they were doing.

"What do we do if neither of you come back?"

"That won't happen," Dominic tried to assure us, avoiding all eye contact. "We'll be fine. We're just going to take a look around—you'll see."

Clair went on with his ammo check, ignoring me completely, counting his guns as he prepared to leave. He gave no indication he believed he'd return with Dominic.

Mabel left my side and headed over to Dom for a quick goodbye and a few threats about making sure he came back in one piece. The two laughed and hugged.

I said to no one in particular, though it was obvious whom I meant, "You better come back. You're still a part of this family."

Clairfic threw his gun over his shoulder, grabbing another. "Are you ready, Dominic?"

Dom nodded, looking back at me. He sent me a quick smile. "We'll be back."

We watched as the two headed off the road and into the tree line.

I might not be able to return Clair's feelings the way he wanted, but I still cared about him—he was family now.

27

My family and I tried to stay busy while Dominic and Clairfic tracked the signal. Doing odd jobs around the truck to help pass the time and fend off worry didn't really help. Instead, Mabel and I went to find shelter. Both of us were too afraid to head out very far, so we were unsuccessful. We turned our attention to finding kindling for fire, trying to make it look as if we were trying.

"We might camp out if we need to," I told Mabel. "The weather is decent and the area's heavily guarded by shrubbery. It would be a fine to stay for a night."

"What was that?" my sister asked, panicked, dropping all of her sticks. "Stop and listen!" She raced over to me, grabbing my arm to pull me closer.

"You need to stop doing that," I whispered, trying to break free. She'd been jumpy since we'd left the others. This was the fourth time she'd asked if I'd heard anything. "You're going to drive yourself crazy acting like that."

"Shut up," she responded. "You can stand being taken by

surprise, but I couldn't. I don't even know how you handled running into those things! What did they look like?"

"Ugly. Smaller than a Shielder but mean—you could just tell they were a bunch of assholes. Brown but when they moved in the light they had a weird blue color to them. Oh! And their eyes—big black holes of nothing."

She shivered. "Sounds awful. How did you manage?"

"I lied to you all," I admitted, holding the random sticks I'd collected close to my body.

She turned, not looking surprised. "I figured. What did you do?"

"I love that you think I did something, Mabel."

"You're always getting yourself into trouble, why would this be different?"

I felt myself get angry but shrugged it off, pushing the sensation away. This wasn't the time for another sisterly fight. Instead, I told her the truth.

She stood listening, trying to be empathetic to my predicament. Her face was calm, but her eyes roamed over my face, trying to put the pieces of the puzzle together.

"Then out of nowhere, Clair showed up," I finished.

"And?" she asked. "What did you two do then?"

"Well," I thought back to how we'd sat together frozen by fear. How would she take *that*? Could she understand the fear we felt and his relief at finding me alive? She already thought there was something between us, so telling her the whole story would make things uncomfortable. "Honestly, we just hid in the bushes. It was the only thing we could do."

"I'm glad you're all right. Even if you did run off, we needed to know about them and now we do. I don't care how mad everyone is at you, I think it was important we know," she said, then paused, picking up another twig. "Especially with those two out there following some random signal."

"I don't think it's a trap, if that is what you're getting at."

"It could be anything, Melly. I'm tired of speculating. Come on, we better head back. These woods give me the creeps."

"Things are only as scary as you make them. At least we can hear the birds in this area."

She didn't comment.

We made our way back to the truck in silence.

"Oh, girls, we're glad you're back," Mom said. "Find anything?"

"No," Mabel told her. "Just some sticks for a fire."

We placed them near the rear tire.

I looked around. "Where are Dad and Grandpa?"

"They went off in the other direction. I don't think we're anywhere near civilization, so I'm not sure what they expect to find. I just hope they didn't wander off. You know how your father is, always getting lost."

"Yeah, and Grandpa is no better," Mabel added. "Should we go after them?"

"No, not yet," Mom answered her. "I don't want to start making a camp just yet, but I don't want to lose the daylight either."

"I think we can wait another hour," I told them.

We waited—the three of us pretending to stay busy while we watched the daylight fade.

"It's unfair the women are left behind, while the men go out and do things. Aren't we helpful?" Mabel complained. "We can do *things*."

"Weren't you afraid to ride shotgun a few hours ago?" I asked pointedly.

"Yeah, so? I didn't want that responsibility, but I could do other things ... "

"Like what?"

"I'm good at finding sticks!"

We laughed, taking the edge off.

"Then go find more sticks," my Mom suggested.

"You know what, I will do just that."

"Don't go too far," I called.

"No, *Clair*, I'm not going into the woods," she sassed. "I'll just be around here."

As we watched Mabel hunt for sticks, Mom asked me, "How are you holding up?"

"I'm fine," I muttered. "Dad said you were disappointed. I'm really sorry for wandering off."

"You know better than anyone not to do that, Melissa Ann, but after the initial shock, it's for the best. I mean, it was irresponsible and stupid, but I get it."

"You do?"

"Yes. I've noticed since those things came to Earth that you've been on edge. You've been doing everything in your power to stay ahead of the game. You've done your best to keep us safe," she admitted, "but, honey, it's not just your responsibility. We're your parents—your family—we're just as capable of protecting you and your sister. Your grandfather would do anything for you girls, as well. We can keep each other safe."

"I know that—I really do. I just feel such a desire to be proactive!"

"It's only natural, but promise me, you'll let go. Give us your burden. Let us help you. We're all in this together, you know. You don't have to do this alone."

I felt tears sting my eyes. Mom noticed and came to sit next to me.

"Just let it go, baby. Just let yourself go," she whispered, placing her arms around me and enveloping me in a big hug.

Mabel returned and placed herself on the other side of our mother. The three of us held each other, making peace with our new reality.

I felt a huge weight leave my shoulders as I became lighter and less inhibited by my fickle emotions. I didn't lose the desire to stay alive, but I finally realized I wasn't alone.

After some mother-daughter bonding time, the rest of our family returned. Dad mentioned they'd found a barn that could work for a place to stay for the night, though no one was thrilled at the idea.

"We really are in the middle of nowhere," Grandfather told us, taking a seat next to Mabel.

"We wanted to go north," she said. "This is as far away as we can get from the city."

"It's perfect," I reminded everyone. "We needed to get as far away as we could from civilization."

"Yeah, but for what?" Mabel asked. "We still ran into Temorshians up here—here of all places!"

"We knew it was going to be a possibility. We have to accept that we aren't alone anymore. We could run into anything, at any point, *anywhere!*"

"Ugh, don't remind me." She looked pained, the corners of her mouth landing in an exaggerated pout. "I hope the boys come back with good news."

"I'm sure they will," Grandfather added.

"I just worry that it won't be enough for Clairfic," Mom said.

"What do you mean?" I asked her.

"He just seems so alone. He lost his people and now he's stuck with us. I know he'd like to know what's going on up there." She pointed to the sky. "He deserves to connect with his own kind again. He doesn't need to babysit us."

"Is that what you think he's doing?" Mabel questioned her.

"I don't think he feels that way at all," I added.

"I wouldn't be so sure, Melly," Mom continued. She rubbed her hands together in her usual nervous way. "I got the feeling he felt obligated to help us. He's done so much already. Yes, he's done things in record time based on his size and knowledge, but we could've still done everything ourselves."

"No one doubts our ability, Sandra," Dad interjected.

"I don't know."

"I can kind of see that, Mom," Mabel added after a few moments of silence. "He helped us with Grandma, then helped Grandpa when he was tired from walking, plus he scouts every single new area we visit ... Maybe he sees us as less than a Shielder?"

"I wouldn't say it's just him," Grandfather voiced, picking his words carefully. "They all seem that way—all of his kind act like that. I noticed it when they first showed up on Earth. They're an old bunch and, sure, they have more knowledge then we do, but they acted somewhat superior."

The rest of my family nodded in agreement.

"I'm glad you said it, Dad," my father told him. "I felt that way too, but who am I to say otherwise? They seemed to know a great deal more than we ever could."

"They really did fuck us over," Mabel added. "Maybe the Temorshians wouldn't have found us if the Shielders hadn't come."

I listened to my family in horror. Of course, I'd blamed the Shielders for bringing the Temorshians, too, but Clairfic wasn't one of them, not really.

"How could you say such things? You can't possibly mean that about Clairfic," I said. "After everything he's done, you don't see him as a part of us? Whether it's internalized guilt or duty, Clair strives to do his best in the name of peace—for us. We just happened to cross paths."

"We're forever grateful for him, Melly," Mom said. "But he isn't one of us and he never will be."

"He's a Shielder," Dad added. "They don't think like we do. They aren't driven by the need to love. He left his kind to join us. He didn't think about them when he left."

"They're all dead, Dad!" I shrieked. "They're gone and he went out to find more!"

"That's what he said, honey, but we don't know."

"You're kidding me. Do you believe that he would make something like that up?" I stood up, the pain running through my veins. "You don't know him. You don't know what he went through to live! He gave up a lot to fight for us—for the planet. You can't judge him.

The rest of them messed up and brought trouble, but they tried to help and protect us—they *did* something. What did our government do? All they ever did was lie to us!"

"Melissa, please calm down. Your father didn't mean it that way," Mom tried to reason. "No one knows him like you do, dear."

"You're right! None of you took the time to talk to him. You pushed me at him and now what? You talk poorly about Clair while he's out there risking his life for you!"

"He's doing what he was told to do, Melissa Ann. He received orders and he's following them," Dad replied, equally as angry. "He doesn't care about you or me or anyone here. He received orders to save Humans. So what did he do? He saved the first lot of Humans he could find. If it wasn't us, it would be some other group."

I stared at my own flesh and blood, unable to believe my father really believed what he was saying, until it all made sense.

"That's why you had him come with us."

"Of course," he confessed. "I'm not stupid. We needed help and what better way to stay safe than to take a Shielder with us? He wasn't doing anything. We needed him. You honestly think he would've had the idea to help us on his own? No, of course not. He needed some pushing. Before he would help anyone else, I made sure he came with us. There's no way I was going to head north without some kind of security."

We looked at him in disbelief.

"You made sure he couldn't help anyone trapped in the shelter!" I cried.

"Casualties," he said. "Sometimes you have to think of yourself over anyone else. I did it to protect my family."

"But we didn't need his help, Dad," Mabel added. "We're capable of protecting ourselves."

"Darling, I love you and I think the world of you, but you're a little girl. Did you think my little women would be able to defend themselves?"

"Viktor!" gasped my mother.

"You really mean that?" Mabel asked.

His cheeks flushed as he avoided her gaze. My mother stood up to move away from her idiotic husband.

"You're wrong. You didn't raise us to be weak," I spat back in his face. "The three of us are strong and capable—whether you believe in us or not. As for the Shielders," I added, rage radiating off my body, "I don't care about the rest of them. I care about Clairfic because he's a good, kind soul. He does care about us. We aren't just orders to him—we matter."

"You're smarter than this, Melissa. Use your brain. He could never care about you the way you do for him—that is just a fact. I don't care what he says."

"He's my friend!" I shouted. "He deserves our respect. He's part of this group—our family!" I turned to leave, walking away in a flurry of emotions.

"Melly, don't go!" Mabel pleaded, but I kept walking.

I stormed past the truck and out into the line of trees. I needed to be as far away from my father as I could get.

"Didn't this get you into trouble in the first place?" a voice asked.

I froze, nearly jumping out of my skin. I flinched so far backward I almost fell over as a hand reached out to help steady my balance.

"Where do you think you're going?" Dominic asked with a smile. "You'll miss the fun if you leave."

My heart was pounding, but I was relieved. "God, you scared me!"

"I should say so, but it was funny on my end," he laughed. "Where are you going?"

"Out."

"Uh huh."

"I need to get some air."

"You're outside, dear. There's air all around you."

"Can you just mind your own business? What did you find?" I asked, annoyed, looking around for Clair.

"He's not here."

"Why? Where did—*what* happened!" My stomach sank.

"Nothing. We found them." Dominic stepped around me, walking back to my family.

"Wait, what? Wait for me!" I ran after him like a mad woman.

"Good to see you," Grandfather said, patting Dom's back.

"How did it go?" asked Mom.

"It was just fine—better than fine, actually," he told us.

"Where's Clairfic?" I asked again. I locked eyes with Mabel. She didn't need to say anything, but I knew she was concerned by his disappearance, too.

"He's fine," Dom told me. "He's with his kind now."

"What!" Mabel shouted. "You mean he did it? He found *more?*"

"Oh, yeah," Dom smiled, and continued, "and then some! We found survivors and Shielders. We're all going to be just fine!"

Cheers rang out through the trees.

Finally, I thought, *more Shielders.*

Mabel hugged me and then turned to jump on Dom, who wasn't sure what to do. He ultimately hugged her back, looking pleased with himself, a smile escaping his tight lips. Mom and Dad kissed while Grandpa made his way over to me for a celebratory hug.

"You did it, kid," he said. "You got us out of the city and now we're going to be protected. How do you feel?"

"Relieved," I breathed. "Nervous, too, but at least for now, I feel better than I did."

"We should get back in the truck and head over," Dom suggested.

The four of us scrambled into the truck while Dom made sure we hadn't forgotten anything. I made Mabel make room for me by allowing me to sit on her lap. I wasn't going to sit in the back alone and miss the story.

"Is this place safe?" Dad asked once Dom was inside.

"It's pretty secure. They were able to build a camp around a house and use various ships as a type of blockade. I mean, it's primitive compared to what we're used to, but it's something. It can only get better."

He went on to explain that people were living in makeshift shelters and tents, but it was comfortable. There were less than a hundred humans and fifty or so Shielders living in the camp. They'd worked together to create a fortress.

"Every day new people come and join. It's good, they say, because we need to rebuild a task force. We got whipped in this last round," Dominic explained as he drove us to the mecca. "They're worried, of course, that another attack is on the way. They're training anyone willing to fight."

"I'm in," I told him.

"Me, too," said Grandfather.

"Really, Dad, is that a good idea?" Mom asked.

"They need soldiers, Sandra. I have to at least try," he told her, and I realized where I got my stubbornness.

"Well, I can't have my old man show me up!" Dad added. "Looks like you'll have me too."

"Um, there are other things to do, right? I could help in another area?" Mabel asked.

"Yes, of course!" Dom exclaimed. "There's a lot to do. Mrs. Pebbles, there is a doctor at camp, you could help him."

"I'd love to," Mom answered, looking pleased. Instead of ringing her hands together, she wiped them against her pants. "I'll help with whatever I can."

As we got closer we realized the mecca we'd envisioned was not what we'd be getting. Pulling up to the camp, there were several sentries posted, making a solid perimeter. Seeing them made the knot in my stomach shrink. Dom had not been lying when he said the camp was, well, crappy looking.

Not only had they set up Shielder ships to block the way, but they'd used Human buses and cars—anything they could find to create a wall, making a solid defense. The house was difficult to see from the truck and the makeshift wall, making it feel safe—safer than staying out in the woods. It was a far cry from the bases they'd made only a few short months ago.

"Okay, let's go meet our hosts!" Dom said, turning off the truck.

"This is it?" Mabel asked.

"This is not what I was expecting," Mom confessed.

"Is there more somewhere else?" Dad questioned. "There's a military base not too far from this area, I thought ... well, I thought we'd be going *there*."

"It's gone," Dom told us, stepping out of the car. "Come on, guys. I'll have them explain everything. A lot has changed in the last few days."

"Why do they need Human cars?" Mabel asked quietly.

Dom frowned. "Well ... they ran out of their own fuel."

"Are things that bad?" I asked.

"They aren't good. They say ... well, we aren't out of the worst of it."

I gulped. Mabel and I caught each other's eyes again.

"It's not over?" Mabel asked quietly.

Dominic stopped to look at his new companion. I caught his sad eyes as he watched her. He tried to say something, but he was at a loss for words. He knew, just like the rest of us, that Mabel was fragile.

"It'll be okay," I interrupted, reaching for her hand. "I'm here, Mom and Dad are here, and I'm sure Dominic will be here for you as well. We'll keep you safe."

She sighed, her face showing tears beginning to form.

Dom stepped closer to her. I watched as he brushed a piece of hair behind her ear. "I'll always be here for you. Remember you owe me your first born?"

She snorted. "That's right—I really am safe."

They laughed as they turned to join the rest of my family, her hand slipping from my grasp.

The pain of Clairfic's disappearance hit me hard. My heart was already heavy from the loss of my grandmother, but this was my new burden. I'd hurt him in ways I couldn't understand. Perhaps I'd hurt myself by denying my growing feelings.

We walked toward a small opening in the vehicles to enter the disheveled fortress. Shielders let us in, while Humans eyed us cautiously as we approached. There wasn't a lot of noise or life in the camp.

I scanned the crowd looking for Clairfic, but I only found others who looked similar to him.

I sighed.

"Welcome," a large female Shielder waved as we approached the house. "My name is Beenishia, and I am in charge here. We know your story, and we are glad you made the long journey. I trust your friend here, Dominic, filled you in on the necessary information," she said, and gazed at Dom, who nodded. "Clairfic has been pulled aside to fulfill his own duties. He will be joining my ranks from now on, so please respect that he will be working."

Mabel reached for my hand and squeezed, holding it tightly as the Shielder continued.

"Since it is my responsibility to ensure your safety during our time together, please field any questions to my Human counterpart, Henry. He will be able to assist you with anything you need outside of basic defense.

"We all have jobs here, and we expect everyone to put in their fair share of work. Henry can also help you find an assignment and get you situated. We have several options for work and anyone that is interested in fighting will be given special training. I suggest you submit at least two people for this type of work," she said, and turned her cold eyes to Mabel, my mother, and me.

"You don't need to worry about that," I told her. "I'm volunteering and so will my father and grandfather. My mother is a healer and my sister will help where she can. We're willing to work, ma'am."

Beenishia eyed me intently. She gave a curt nod and continued, "I know it is tempting to help us, but please do not unless specifically asked to do so. We will let you know if anything changes. Thank you again and welcome." She looked to Dom and turned.

"Come on, I'll take you to Henry," Dominic announced. "He's a good guy, she's ... well, she's a piece of work."

"What's up her butt?" Mabel whispered to Dom once we were out of earshot.

"She's the general or *Mezda*. You need to respect her, Mabel. She's in charge and knows her stuff. You should've seen how pleased Clair was when he realized she was here. He told me she's good at what she does and it's an honor to be in her presence. I suggest you stay out of her way and just deal with this Henry fellow."

"Who is the guy?" I asked.

"I don't know, some young man who Beenishia trusts. I didn't recognize him from TV so I'm assuming he's some guy she found and liked. He's a nice guy—smart. He did something to earn her respect, so he's all right in my book."

"Interesting, she didn't seem like the type to like Humans," Mabel stated.

"Who knows?" Dom shrugged. "Come on, I see him over there."

We made our way to an open tent with several different people waiting in line. They parted seeing us approach. Several greetings reached us as we made our way up to a man wearing Shielder garb. Tall for a Human male, with light brown hair; he looked fit and ready for anything.

With his back to us, Dominic coughed, "We're back. I'd like to introduce you to the Pebbles family."

He turned slowly, still looking down at a map in his hands, completely ignoring our presence.

My breath caught in my throat once I saw his face.

"*Henry!* Henry Rickner?" I choked in shock.

He looked up, surprised, "Do I know—*Melissa Pebbles?* Is that really you?"

"What are you doing *here*?" we inquired together.

"Are you with Kayin?" we asked each other.

"No!" in unison.

"*What?*"

I gasped. "God, Henry, fucking stop repeating me!"

"Where is she?" he asked, his eyes wild with anticipation.

"Last I heard she was going home. How the hell did you get to Michigan and how are you in charge?"

"She didn't make it home, Melissa," a woman interrupted.

I turned toward the voice, my stomach dropping. "Layla Aves? What the fuck?" I ran to her, enveloping her into a bear hug. "What the fuck are you doing here?"

"I should ask you the same thing!" she laughed, and then became serious again. "You're not with Kayin, are you?"

"When's the last time you saw her or spoke to her?" Henry interjected.

"Excuse me, sorry to interrupt this reunion," Dominic said. "But can one of you explain what's going on and how the fuck you guys know each other? And who's this *Kay-In?*"

28

"Life sure is weird," I said, sitting back in my chair.

After brief introductions and an overview of camp life, my family, Layla, and Henry made our way to the giant kitchen in the house. We ate and talked about our three unique experiences during the attack.

"Who would've thought we'd ever see each other again?" Layla asked, looking down at her dangling feet as she sat on the countertop.

I could tell her mind was on her sister, but I was too afraid to bring up such an emotional topic. It was hard for me to imagine what had happened to my best friend.

"Everything happens for a reason," Henry said, "or so they say."

"Or so they say," she whispered.

"All right, now that we know each other and have some idea of our new life here, now what?" Mabel interrupted, changing the subject.

"You'll help where there's work—watching the kids or cleaning, stuff like that. Your mother will help Harrison, our physician. Mrs. Pebbles, I forgot to ask earlier, would you be willing to learn how to operate on a Shielder?"

Mom blushed, "Henry, you know I'm not really a doctor."

"Oh, come on, Mom, you know you're good with that stuff," Mabel told her proudly.

"It really doesn't matter, Mrs. Pebbles," Henry continued. "We need all the help we can get and if you're as good as I hear—which I don't doubt is true—you'll be a great help to Dr. Rhodes. It's him and one Shielder doctor, so I'm sure they'd love your help."

"Oh, okay. I'll start whenever they're ready." Mom's cheeks glowed red. Dad reached over and squeezed her hand. She blushed harder.

"Thank you! As for the rest of you, training starts bright and early tomorrow."

"We'll be ready," I told him.

"Dominic, I might have a special job for you if you're up for it," he asked.

"What do you have in mind, sir?" Dom responded, coming to attention.

"I knew you'd be the man. Clair said you have considerable skill, and I want to use it to rescue survivors further south."

Dom smiled. "I can be ready to move out within the hour, sir."

They finished their conversation elsewhere as Henry escorted Dom out of the house. It was obvious Dom was in his glory, but I noticed the rest of my family looked tired. Their energy deflated, they were running on fumes.

"Layla ... "

"Yes?"

"Where are you and your family staying?"

"There are pods for us—like little tents. The Shielders use them when they're on campaigns and such. Though there aren't many, we use what we can. Now that I think about it, there's an open bedroom here in the house and about three more pods, but some just use what they have—tents and such. We get by. We don't have a choice."

"How many in a pod?" Mabel asked.

"Some can fit up to five Human adults—only two Shielders to a pod. The bigger ones we usually save for families with small children."

"You going to try to make it up to Clair by sharing his pod, Melly?" Mabel teased.

Layla's eyes widened. "You don't have a Shielder boyfriend, do you?"

"No," I snarled through gritted teeth, giving Mabel the eye of death.

"Too bad."

"What?" Mabel and I asked.

"It might've meant you got rid of Joel and hopped into someone's bed that's actually worth a damn."

Mabel laughed. "Layla, I can see we're going to be best friends. I'll share a pod with you any day."

The two shared a knowing smile.

"Ha *ha*, so funny. Joel is out of the picture, Layla. Clairfic is just a friend."

"A *special* friend," added Mabel, clasping her hands together in glee.

"No."

"Girl," Mabel said to Layla. "They totally shared a room—who knows what went on in there, but I swear to God he came out the next morning happy as a clam."

"Stop it! Really? Melissa, you're holding out! I saw him when he came in—he's pretty damn cute, too. Tell us what happened!"

I sighed, storming out of the kitchen, straight through the impressive dining room. I slipped through the sliding door.

I didn't want to be reminded of my odd choices over the last few days. He was a friend, right? Nothing more—there should never be anything more. My body thundered with deep exhaustion, mixed with a rage I couldn't explain.

I looked around, trying to find a quiet spot to clear my head. Everywhere I looked a sharp-toothed alien greeted me. They watched as I turned this way and that, trying to see anything but them with their long hair, pale skin, and dark lavender eyes.

I finally fell to my knees and screamed.

When the air in my lungs released, I gathered myself up and ran into the clearing on the other side of the house. Not too far away stood a beautiful row of pine trees, not blocked off by junk.

I ran as fast as I could toward the tree line, letting my hair flip out of its ponytail into the wind. The breeze on my skin calmed my nerves, and the sweet scent of pine washed away my worries. The sun was beginning to set, causing the pines to glow in the amber light.

When I made it to the woods I was out of breath, but happier than I'd been in days; I listened to the wildlife around me, relieved to be in undisturbed nature.

I took several deep breaths, trying to center myself and forget my reality.

"I am certain I have told you not to run off by yourself," a voice rang out.

I pulled the *katlan* from my side and spun around, holding the blade to use its power.

"God damn it, Clairfic Munal, why do you have to do that!"

"It is our game, remember?"

I sighed, unable to still my beating heart.

He continued, "I am impressed."

"Fuck you."

"So many new words you are throwing at me this evening. *Fuck me?*"

"Your Earth classes didn't teach you to swear?" I asked hotly.

"No," he smirked, walking further into the tree line.

"You're just fucking with me now."

"Am I?" he laughed.

I followed him deeper into the trees while my emotions tangled themselves into knots, twisting together, molding one into the other.

"What are you doing here? I thought ... I just thought ... "

"That I was busy?"

"Kind of, but more you were so pissed at me the last time we spoke." I paused, trying to gather my courage to be honest with him. "I was afraid you'd never want to talk to me again."

He stopped walking to sit under a tree that didn't have any lower branches to hit him in the head. I watched as he stretched out his legs, patting the ground next to him.

"No, thank you, I'll stand." I put the *katlan* away in one motion. "Why are you here? I thought you wouldn't want to see me ever again."

He looked up at me, the corners of his mouth threatening to turn into a smile. His eyes sparkled. "I would never want that. I followed you to make sure you were all right. I know all of this has been very difficult ... "

My insides loosened, relieved to know my burning cheeks were more from running than from the embarrassment growing within me.

"I am not mad," he continued. "I was angry with you, but now I have found my kind and my anger has been replaced with something else—"

"Gratitude?"

"Hope."

"Well, that's good. I'm glad you're happy. I'm glad you're back with your people and that we can all rest a little easier."

"Are you happy?"

I didn't answer. I couldn't explain my feelings to myself, let alone another, so I avoided his question and sat down near an opposite tree.

"I start training tomorrow, will you be there?" I asked.

"Yes, it is mandatory for every able-bodied occupant here."

"Will it be hard?"

"It will not be anything you cannot handle. Look at you today— you were ready to kill me."

"Probably should have," I teased.

"But then how would we finish our game?"

"I think that would mean I won ... "

"How?"

"Well, if you're dead, I'm pretty sure that would mean you automatically lose. I get all your points, and I keep the *katlan* and anything else of value."

"The *katlan* is yours already," he gently reminded me. His lavender eyes were bright, and the corners of his mouth threatened to expose the smile he was fighting desperately to hide. The stress from his eyes had vanished and been replaced with something else—something I hadn't noticed before. His hair had been brushed out and placed intricately upon his head. Layla was right. He was good-looking, especially when he was happy.

"I know but ... it's a family heirloom, and I want to give it back to you after all this. It's only right."

"But I gave it to you." He rubbed his legs with his hands, a nervous tick I'd come to love about him.

"You gave it me when I was afraid and unarmed. Now I'm about to learn how to fight. I feel a lot safer already. Besides, it wouldn't be right to keep something that's so personal to you and your family."

He shrugged, both corners of his mouth evaporating any threat of a smile. Clair still rubbed his legs but looked off into the distance.

We watched the sunset together in silence until the sun was almost gone. Near the house, people started to light small fires, but the last few rays of sun still lit the way.

"We should return. It will be extremely dark soon." He lifted his large body and stretched his limbs.

"How do you know?" I asked, getting up and brushing the pine needles off my legs.

"It seems it will be a starless night."

I looked up to examine the night sky that was coming to life in the east. "You're right—no stars tonight. Have you noticed any new ships in the atmosphere?"

"No, but they have powerful technology that can disguise their crafts. I would doubt—" Clairfic clutched his weapon at his side, whipping his head in the direction of the house.

"Do you hear that?" he asked.

I strained to listen but no sound met my ears. "And I thought I was paranoid. Maybe we need to come out here more often and get you to relax."

Clair froze, slowly turning away from the house to the trees behind us. His lavender eyes searched the horizon. They moved back and forth while he reached for the weapon at his side—a long knife. I followed his move, pulling out the *katlan*.

"Stay here," he whispered.

"No way," I said. "I'm going with you—you're not leaving me here in the dark alone. What do you see?"

He didn't bother to respond as he moved behind a tree, tugging me with him. His right hand covered my mouth before I could protest. With my heart beating out of my chest, I allowed him to hold me, the *katlan* firm in my grasp.

"We are not alone," he breathed into my left ear. "Do you trust me?"

I nodded.

"Do you see that clearing over there?" he asked, tilting his head in its direction.

My eyes followed his stare. It wasn't far, maybe a handful of yards away. I nodded again.

"When I release you, run as fast as you can to the clearing. As you get closer, you'll see a thicket. Jump in and do not leave until I say. Understood? I mean it, Melissa, am I clear?"

Rolling my eyes to land on his smug face, I glared at him.

"I will not let go and we will both die. Do you want that?"

Through his tense fingers I snorted, nodding my head. He released my mouth.

"I want to hear a *yes*," he whispered. His eyes had lost their sparkle, and the lines of his face had reappeared.

"Yes," I murmured.

He turned away from me to scan the area again. He sucked in his breath, lifting his arm off my shoulders, freeing my body.

"Go!" he whispered.

Without another thought, I raised my legs, sprinting into a run. Piercing cries filled the silence as three large bodies chased after me. The hums from their weapons, indicating they were about to fire, propelled me faster as I bolted between the trees toward the clearing. Every fiber of my being pushed me to run faster. Two rounds flew by me in a whirl of blue light. A third grazed my left arm, causing me to falter but not stop.

I could feel their breath on my neck as a large oak entered my path. I darted out of its way as the trunk snapped in two, destroyed by two more rounds of blue flame. The splinters pelted my back, the smoke making it harder to see. When it subsided enough, I realized I'd gone too far off course—to the right of the clearing, the thicket too far on my left.

Another shot flew over my head. Ducking instinctively to avoid the heat, I screamed, but it was too late. I'd been hit in the arm.

A black, scaly hand grabbed my injured arm, pulling me down. With the *katlan* safely in my right hand, I hurled it around, making contact. The knife slid into the flesh, penetrating deeper into the chest cavity. Warm, thick goo gushed over my hand. The creature shrieked, trying to get away, but the *katlan* was stuck and I refused to let go. Pushing it farther into the wound, I silenced the beast.

The body, now limp, fell upon me. We tumbled to the ground with a clatter. The thick blood spreading across my upper torso smelled of filth and decay. Using all of my strength, I tried to push the Temorshian off me.

"Melissa!" Clairfic cried.

"Over here," I yelled, still pushing. "Help me!"

He rushed over and with little effort pulled the vile thing off me. "Are you all right? Are you hurt? Did he—"

"I'm fine, just covered in this mess."

"You're bleeding!"

"It'll be fine. I don't feel anything. Mom can clean it up later."

"Here, let me help you." He sat me up, brushing my hair out of my face. He rested his palm on my upper arm. His eyes were bugging out of his head with worry. "Are you—"

"Clair, I told you I'm fine. Just give me a minute to process this ... "

He knelt down next to me, still not letting me go. Wrapping his arm around my shoulders he pulled me close to him, just as he had done at the stream. This time he clasped my open dirty hand in his.

"Did I worry you again?" I asked, squeezing his hand. "I didn't mean to get so far off course."

Clair turned his head, looking down at my blood-covered body. "No, you did very well. I am proud." Without hesitation, he bent down and kissed the top of my head.

The light I'd been trying to hide spilled over.

Forgetting myself completely, I tilted my head up, locking eyes with him, moving my body closer. In seconds, his mouth was on mine. I parted my lips and let him in, tasting him for the first time. He let my hand go to encircle me in his arms. I turned to position myself to move onto his lap.

I reached for him, trying to get closer, but failing. The same feeling of wanting to be within his ribcage overpowered me as I tried to bring his large body even closer to mine, pulling on his clothes and armor. He held me tighter, the same urgency apparent from his kiss.

Though I knew he had sharp teeth, my tongue didn't feel a thing. It traveled safely in his mouth as his carefully searched mine.

We pulled away from each other just enough to take a few breaths, but then we were at it again. This time I dropped the fabric I'd been trying to rip off of him and wrapped my arms around his neck. He pulled me further onto his lap, tangling his hand within my matted hair as the other clutched my waist.

"Melissa," he murmured between kisses. "We have to stop. It is not safe here."

I let him go, but didn't slide off his lap. My eyes searched his face, trying to see if I'd made him uncomfortable.

"You are so beautiful," he said, brushing a piece of hair out of my face and tucking it behind my ear. "I could never have imagined finding someone like you—in such a mess as this."

I blushed. "I'm sorry for—"

"Do not apologize. I thought I made my feelings clear earlier."

My checks burned but I didn't look away from the smile that crept across his face. "You did and I'm afraid I didn't. Clairfic, this doesn't change anything."

His mouth fell open, color draining from his face.

"No! I don't mean ... I like you, Clairfic Munal. You're just going to have to give me time to figure out how much." I paused. "We might not make it through this war, but I need you to know that I want you by my side no matter what happens."

He pulled me into a tight hug, gently kissing my lips.

I kissed him back and after our lips parted, I stood up, brushing the flakes of dried alien blood off my pants.

"I will be by your side no matter what happens," Clair said, getting up, his eyes never leaving my own.

When he finally looked away, he turned his attention to the body. "You killed him with one blow," Clair said. With one short tug, he pulled the *katlan* out. He wiped it off against his pants. "I believe this is yours." He turned the knife so the handle faced me.

"Thanks, but first let me get this goo off. Are the others, um, *dead?*" I asked, bending down to run my hands over the grass, trying to get the junk off, the blood already sticky.

"Yes. You helped create a diversion, so I was lucky enough to sneak up behind them."

"Well, that's good, I guess." Standing up beside him, I took the knife and looked down at the mangled body. "What do we do now? We'll have to tell the others. They were too close. Do you think there are more? We aren't ready. God, I'm *not* ready! I barely got away. But I did all right, didn't I? I mean this was close, but we did it."

Clair walked off toward our meeting place.

"Wait for me!" I yelled after him. "We're going to have to move camp, aren't we?"

I followed him through the trees to the edge of the woods. My words hung in the air, floating away in the breeze that was steadily picking up speed. He didn't turn to wait for me nor did he look back to make sure I was following him.

"Clairfic, you have to slow down. You know I can't walk as fast as you—and if you make me run, I promise I'll never kiss you again," I threatened, a smile spreading across my face. I was already hungry for another round with him and I couldn't wait to get back to camp to try to do it again.

Just as he was about to step out into the clearing, he stopped, freezing in place.

"What's wrong," I asked, standing beside him.

"Stop talking," he said, pushing a button on his armored suit.

He'd stopped breathing, and even with the little sunlight left, I could tell he'd gone even paler. His eyes moved from me, to his suit, back to the sky three times before I decided I needed to know what he was listening to on whatever airwaves only he could hear.

"Clairfic, what's going on?" I asked, the taste of him forgotten on my tongue as it was replaced by bile. "What is wrong with your suit?"

"Please be quiet, Melissa. I'm listening to a transmission."

"A transmission from who?"

"Melissa, please, stop talking."

"From who, damn it!"

"I think we should go back to camp," Clair said, grabbing my hand before I could protest.

THE END

ACKNOWLEDGMENTS

Some say the writer's life is a lonely place because it's just you and a computer as you spill out your heart and soul. Yet, I've found that it's not the case. *Dawn Among the Stars* wouldn't be in your hands, dear reader, without the love, support, and dedication of a few of my favorite people.

I would like to thank my husband, Michael, for telling me he wouldn't read my work until it was a "real book." Without your constant loving pushes to be my best self, none of this would be possible. Your love keeps me shooting for the stars.

To my dream team of beta readers turned friends, Hannah Bauman, Kayla Cox, Leah C. Davis, and Katelyn Uhrich: Without your dedication to excellence, *Dawn*, wouldn't be where it is today or have the character's readers will fall in love with. You inspire me to keep learning our craft and becoming the author I've always dreamed of being.

To Chris, Jessica, Danielle, JT, Jalon, Kysoo, and Mike: I'm so sorry you had to read the countless versions of this story. With your thoughts, suggestions, and love, you kept me going through the good times and bad. Thank you for honoring me with your friendship.

To my family: who never stopped believing in my ability to make my dreams come true. Thank you for making me the woman I am and allowing me to follow my heart no matter where the road took me.

Most importantly, to all the educators who helped turn me into the writer I am today: Without your love and patience, none of this would be possible. I've overcome my disability because of you and your hard work. Thank you for teaching me that no matter what, anything is possible.

Thank you to everyone at Trifecta Publishing House for helping me share my stories with the world.

Lastly, thank you, dear reader, for taking a chance on this author. Let's keep reaching for the stars together!

ABOUT THE AUTHOR

Samantha Heuwagen works as a Marriage and Family Therapist that specializes in Sex Therapy in Atlanta, GA. She is a graduate of Mercer University School of Medicine where she earned her second Master's degree in Marriage and Family Therapy. Her first Master's degree is in Women's and Gender Studies from the University of South Florida where she first realized her passion for sex education and the power of the written word. When she isn't working with clients, she writes about faraway places and tries to change the world through fiction bridging mental health awareness and social justice together.

CPSIA information can be obtained
at www.ICGtesting.com
Printed in the USA
BVHW03s0028180618
519275BV00001BA/83/P